Tales From
she is people
next two or
pubs and restaurants which she bears

Tales From a
Hen Weekend

Olivia Ryan

PIATKUS

Copyright © 2007 by Olivia Ryan

First published in Great Britain in 2007 by
Piatkus Books Ltd of
5 Windmill Street, London W1T 2JA
email: info@piatkus.co.uk

The moral right of the author has been asserted

A catalogue record for this book is available from the British Library

ISBN 978 0 7499 3806 2

Typeset by Phoenix Photosetting, Chatham, Kent
www.phoenixphotosetting.co.uk

Printed and bound in Great Britain by
Mackays of Chatham, Chatham, Kent

Acknowledgements

Thanks, girls, for sharing your hen party memories – and Neil for the guided tour of likely Dublin haunts. Best Guinness in the world! I'll probably never recover!

Dedication

For Charlie

ABOUT KATIE

'I can't believe it. I just can't believe you're finally getting married,' says Mum through a mouthful of pins.

'Watch you don't swallow one of those. And anyway – thanks a bundle! What do you mean, finally? Anyone would think I was a seventy-year-old confirmed spinster!'

I'm only thirty-one, for God's sake. Katie's my name – Katie Halliday – and I'm getting married in a couple of months to Matt Davenport. My mum, Margie, is in a terrible state already, fussing about dresses and flowers and menus. I'm beginning to think I'll be glad when it's all over.

'We didn't want all this fuss,' I say wearily, for the thousandth time; not that anyone's listening. 'We wanted a quiet wedding. Simple. Just close family and friends.'

'I know, I know, but you've got to have a *wedding dress*, dear, whatever you say.'

I'm wearing the wedding dress right now. I'm standing on a stool in the middle of my sister's living room, with the unfinished hem trailing over the carpet and the three of them, my mum, my sister Lisa and my Auntie Joyce, walking around me as if I was an exhibit in a museum, shaking their heads, tugging at seams here and darts there, sticking pins in random places and sighing about my waistline.

'If you could *just* lose a couple more pounds before the day,' says Lisa with a sigh, 'it would hang so much better over your hips.'

'Sorry to disappoint you, but this is me. What you see is what you get. If you can't make a dress that fits me as I am, Lise, then don't bother about it – I'll get married in my jeans and—'

1

'Hey, hey, come on, calm down! No need for that' Mum reprimands me. Honestly, standing here on this stool with my arms up, being prodded and poked and measured, I feel like I'm about six years old again, being kitted out for the new school year. 'Lisa's being very good to you, making you this lovely dress – you're lucky you've got such a clever sister!'

Tell me about it. Lisa's only two years older than me but there's such a huge gulf between her life and mine, she might as well be from a different generation and a different family. She's been married to Richard for six years, they have a perfect marriage and two perfect children, Molly and Charlie; she cooks like Jamie Oliver *every day*, works out at the gym twice a week while the kids are at their Yoga for Tots class, and is a professional wedding dress designer. Hence the dress. I suppose it was a bit unrealistic of me to expect to be allowed to get married in my jeans.

'I know. I'm sorry. But I can't think about dieting right now. I've got enough to worry about. Just make it hang however it wants – OK, Lise?'

Lisa sighs again and shakes her head as if she's a doctor with an uncooperative patient.

'I won't sue you if I look rough in the wedding photos,' I say, in an attempt at a joke.

She looks aghast.

'You're *not* going to look rough! You're going to look *beautiful*!'

Blimey. Didn't think we could stretch to plastic surgery.

'At least you haven't got to fork out for a proper wedding dress,' says Matt at home later.

I might have joked about wearing my jeans, but I'm not thrilled by his choice of words. *Proper?!*

'Lisa designs wedding dresses for a *living*! I couldn't get much more *proper* ...'

'You know what I mean. Steve at work – his girlfriend wouldn't settle for anything less than this bloody great frothy meringue thing from some posh shop in the West End, cost a fortune.'

'*Most* girls spend a fortune on their wedding dress – or

2

hire one. I'm just lucky that Lisa's my sister,' I point out, realising I'm sounding exactly like my mum.

'Yeah, well: we haven't *got* a fortune to spend, have we, babe. So I guess I'm lucky I'm marrying someone who doesn't care about all that stuff!'

'Just don't you forget it,' I tell him lightly, trying to sound like someone who *doesn't care about all that stuff*. To be honest – and I know I'm being contrary here – it rankles slightly to be cast in the role of some kind of latter-day Cinderella who's happy to go to the ball in her rags.

'And I'm sure the dress will look lovely,' adds Matt, watching me carefully; as usual, he seems to guess what I'm thinking.

'Lisa thinks it'll hang better if I lose some weight.'

'I'll bin the last chocolate biscuit then, shall I?'

'No! Matt, give me that ... I can't *believe* you've eaten the whole packet! You pig!'

Look at him. The bastard, he's holding the packet above his head, laughing at me jumping up and down trying to reach it.

'Go, girl! That's it! Work up a sweat! Work off those pounds!'

'*Not* funny. So *you* think I need to lose weight too?'

He sighs and drops the biscuit packet into my hand. It's not the last one: there are three left.

'It was a joke, Kate.'

But I don't want the frigging biscuits any more. I put them down on the worktop, crossly, and start rummaging in the fridge for something to cook for dinner.

'A *joke*, Kate, for fuck's sake!'

'All right, all right! Enough! Chicken or fish?'

'Whatever. Pasta or rice?' He gets a saucepan out of the cupboard and fills it with water.

'Whatever.'

And we're preparing the dinner in silence. Very mature! Does planning a wedding do this to everybody?

'I'm sure it's normal,' says Emily in the pub later. 'I'm sure Sean and I would be the same. It's just the tension, with all the preparations and everyone getting on your case, telling

3

you what you should be doing, what you should wear, who you should invite ...'

She's right, of course. Everyone says how stressful it is, don't they. You only have to read the problem pages of *Wedding* magazine to see how true that is. Brides have nervous breakdowns. Mums and daughters fall out over the guest list. Whole families split up and never speak to each other again. Marriages break up before they've even happened. Why do we bother?

'Why are we bothering, Em? We've been perfectly happy living together ...'

'Don't be silly. You *are* perfectly happy. You and Matt are fantastic together. You can laugh off a bit of stressy bickering. It's going to be a lovely wedding. You'll both have a great day.'

'So why aren't *you* bothering? Eh? If it's such a great idea what's stopping you and Sean doing it?'

They've been together nearly as long as Matt and me. Emily and I were at university together so we've known each other nearly half our lives, and we see each other at least once a week. If I didn't have Em to talk to, I'd explode – all the worries and mess inside my head wouldn't have anywhere to go. You can't talk to men about half the stuff that goes on in your head – it would scare the shit out of them.

'Maybe we will, one day,' she says casually. 'Maybe. We'll see how you two get on, first!'

'You can have my dress when I've finished with it. It'll hang better on you,' I say gloomily.

'I bet it looks gorgeous. Come on, finish your drink. The boys are getting another round in.'

The boys are laughing together at the bar, punching each other the way men do when they're being friendly. It's hard to imagine what they laugh about together when we're not listening. Em thinks it's something sexual and disgusting, but my money's on football. Some obscure joke about a rubbish goal, or a bit of teasing about the rubbish team one or the other of them supports. Matt's an Arsenal supporter and Sean's West Ham. To hear them insulting each other at times, you wouldn't guess they're actually good mates.

'Yeah, right – and what about that goal kick in the second half?' Sean plonks my glass down on the table in front of me without noticing it slopping over the side. 'The referee was a *total* fucking idiot. That decision was fucking criminal!'

'Bollocks!' says Matt. See? I was right. Bloody football. Anyone would think it was important. 'Face it, we were the better team. We played a fantastic game.' *We*? Since when did Matt play for the Arsenal?

'I didn't realise you were playing,' I say without looking up.

'What?'

They're both staring at me as if I've spoken in tongues. Emily giggles.

'Lighten up, you two,' she says. 'Can't you talk about anything other than football?'

Look at their faces! They're completely stumped now. They blink at each other over the tops of their beer glasses. *Other than football?* Jesus! What else is there?

'Um ... so how's work then, Matt?' says Sean.

Em raises her eyebrows at me.

'Let them get on with it. Bless them, they've got simple needs. Work, sport, beer, sex ...'

'And who cares about work, sport or beer?' I laugh.

Emily's right. I know that really. Matt and I are great together. We like the same things (apart from football): Italian food, forests, mountains, rock music, cheese and pickle sandwiches, cats, autumn, hot chocolate. We like the same sexual positions. Well, sorry, I know that's too much information, but it's important in a relationship. I've heard of couples breaking up because one loves doing it standing up and the other one would rather never have sex at all if it means getting out of bed for it. We're compatible. We pass all those psychological tests with flying colours – you know, the ones in women's magazines that give you situations and ask you to tick *Sometimes, Never, Always* or *Don't know,* and then you add up your scores and they tell you whether you should stay together forever or call it a day immediately. We always do brilliantly on those, and I try not to cheat. We know each other really well. We share everything; we're not like those couples who have separate bank accounts and charge interest if they borrow money from each other. We've been together for nearly four years, lived together for three and a half, and we do everything together. Tell me one good reason why we shouldn't get married?

Exactly. There isn't one, is there?

So just remind me, if I keep panicking about these little bickering sessions we've started having: it's just the stress of this build-up to the wedding, that's all.

I did plan to keep it simple. I was only having two bridesmaids. Well – one bridesmaid, and one matron-of-honour, if you want to use the proper old-fashioned correct terms – Emily, and my sister. It was stressful enough getting my own dress made, without all that old malarkey about bridesmaids, until I remembered The Pledge.

The Pledge took place in the summer of 1989, on the back seat of the bus home from St Peter's Comprehensive School in Romford. Jude and I were fifteen at the time, and we'd been best friends since we started infants' school ten years earlier. We went everywhere together; people called us the Terrible Twins, but actually we were like negative images of each other. She was blonde, I was dark; she was tiny, I was big; she was quiet, I was noisy; she was sweet-natured, I was your typical stroppy teenager. I should perhaps warn you at this point that neither of us has changed one bit since we've grown up.

Jude's family were about to move to Ireland, and we were considering a suicide pact. We'd been considering it ever since Jude broke the news about her dad's new job in Cork, but we couldn't agree on the means to our ends. Jude wanted to get the train to Southend, go to the end of the pier and jump off, holding hands – but I was terrified of water so I didn't fancy it. I was all for putting our heads in the oven, but Jude's house was all-electric and I wasn't sure my mum's oven was big enough for both our heads at the same time. We spent so much time debating the methods, we never actually got round to it, and here we were on our last day together. Jude was off to Ireland the next morning, and we were both still alive. Tragic!

'Let's run away,' she said.

'Where to?'

'I don't know. Somewhere in Ireland. It's a big place. They'd never find us.'

'Why Ireland? That's not fair. Just because your family are going ...'

'All right, then. Where?'

'London. Everyone goes to London to run away.'

'Bor*ing*. Twenty minutes on the train. That's not running away, it's commuting.'

'But we can disappear there. And eat in the soup kitchens.'

'What type of soup? I can't eat tomato, it brings up my mouth ulcers.'

'Jude, we're talking life or death here, and all you can worry about is your mouth ulcers.'

'I don't want to disappear in London. I want us to stay together, but ...'

'But what? How can we? I've begged and *begged* my mum to let me come and live with you in Ireland, but she's just completely cruel.'

'Mine too. How do you think *I* feel, being taken away from St Peter's, and everyone? At least you'll still have all the *others*.'

We brooded in silence, staring out of the windows, both probably thinking the same thoughts about who would want to be my friend after Jude had gone. And who would be *her* friend in some strange school in her new, strange country.

'I suppose we'd better not, then,' I said at length, with a sigh. 'If we run away, they'll just get the police after us.'

'My mum and dad say you can come and stay as soon as we're settled.'

'Yeah. Mum says you can come back and stay with me whenever you want, too.'

I can't remember whether we hugged each other at that point, or whether we cried. Probably not. A load of the other fifteen-year olds from St Peter's were on the same bus and we wouldn't have wanted to look uncool. But I remember The Pledge as clearly as if it was yesterday.

'When I get married,' said Jude, still staring out of the window as the bus trundled along the suburban roads back to our estate, 'you can come over to Ireland to be my bridesmaid.'

'What if I get married first?' I pointed out.

'Then I'll be *your* bridesmaid, of course!' She turned and flashed me a grin. 'You'll probably be first, anyway. Loads of boys always fancy you. They never look at me.'

'Don't be stupid—'

'Anyway ...' she cut me short. 'Let's make it a pledge. We'll be each other's bridesmaids, yeah? No matter what? Even if you get a new best friend?'

'Definitely! And I won't! *You're* my best friend,' I said stoutly. 'And you always will be.'

So you see – Jude has to be a bridesmaid too. There's no way I can renege on The Pledge. Without me even trying, this wedding looks like it could go from a small, quiet, private do, to being the social event of the century.

The three lilac bridesmaid dresses have been finished for months and hanging up in Lisa's wardrobe. Jude sent over her measurements, and when the dress was at the tacked-together stage, she came over for a weekend and had a fitting. Since then Lisa's been on at me about fifteen times a week:

'Tell Jude she'd better not put on any weight. Not even an *ounce*, tell her! When she comes over for the wedding there won't be time to let out any seams.'

'Jude's as skinny as a twig,' I tell her wearily. 'She's not like me. She doesn't have to go on a diet every time she nibbles a biscuit.'

'Yes, well, she'd better stay skinny, otherwise it's going to be a *complete* disaster.'

'She'll have to wear her jeans,' I say, grinning. Lisa's just too easy to wind up.

She closes her eyes and shakes her head.

'Don't even *joke* about it, Kate. I can't bear it.'

See what I mean about weddings? They make people lose all sense of proportion. Someone getting too fat for their bridesmaid's dress is *not* an international incident. At the minute I think it might actually lighten things up a little.

'You're not putting on any weight, are you?' I ask Jude on the phone. Again.

'Jesus, God, can you ever give it a rest about me putting on weight?' Over the years, along with the Irish accent, Jude's developed this weird habit of blasphemy that sometimes even extends to the theatrical *Jesus, Mary and Joseph*! To my English ears it sounds so fake, I'm never quite sure whether she's kind of taking the piss out of herself. 'I'd be thrilled with meself if I even put on so much as an ounce, but it just never happens, no matter what I eat.'

'Well, *don't*. Not even an ounce. Lisa's doing my head in about letting out seams at the eleventh hour.'

'Not a chance, Kate. Tell your sister she can sleep easy in her bed. She's no need to worry on that score – I'm as bony as ever. I wish I *could* put on a little weight in some areas. Like me boobs for instance. It'd be nice to be recognised as a woman from one angle at least.'

'After the wedding you can have a boob job. Just don't go sprouting any till after the twenty-first of May.'

'Katie, I've gone all through puberty, my teens and twenties without sprouting any, as you put it, so why in the name of God you think I'm suddenly going to become Madonna herself just to ruin your wedding ...'

'It's not me. It's Lisa, going on and on about the dress ...'

'And I *don't* want a boob job, thank you very much for the thought, even if I could ever afford one in a million years!'

'So think yourself lucky, then, you skinny thing!' I'm a size 14 on a good day (don't ask me about the bad days) and when I talk to people like Jude I become so conscious of my size I can practically feel my bum, stomach and legs flopping and flabbing about like giant jellies. 'And big boobs are overrated. They get in the way. I can't buy nice pretty little bras with delicate shoestring straps, you know. I have to go for industrial harnesses.'

'Overrated? Not to men, they're not!'

'Come on, Jude – we're not going out with fifteen-year-old schoolboys now! Men do grow out of the breast-fixation stage. Fergus loves you the way you are, doesn't he.'

'Yeah. I suppose.'

There's a silence I can't quite work out. Is she upset? Have I offended her? It's so hard not seeing someone's face. It's hard being best friends, oldest friends, but only getting together a couple of times a year.

'I can't wait to see you, Judy.'

'Me too. Only a couple of weeks now!'

'Yeah. God, I'm looking forward to the hen weekend so much! I think I'm looking forward to it more than the bloody wedding at the moment.'

She laughs.

'I don't think Matt would be too flattered to hear that.'

'No.' Suddenly this topic isn't funny any more. 'No, he wouldn't.'

'But he'd know you were only joking, Katie, so he would.'

Maybe. But I'm not so sure.

The hen weekend is a bit of a sore point, actually. Rather, the stag weekend is. Or to be more accurate, the stag *week and a half.* You know I told you about how compatible we are? Well, the hen and the stag are the first things we've really disagreed about. I'm trying to keep off the subject, to be quite honest. But how do you keep off the subject of something that's going to happen in only two weeks' time?

ABOUT MATT

Yes, let me tell you a little bit about Matt.

I met him in the corniest way you can imagine. We were both with other people, having lunch in a pub. I was with a guy called James who I'd only been out with twice (and never did again), and Matt was with Sara – his soon-to-be ex. He walked past our table on the way to the bar and accidentally nudged my arm so that I dropped a sausage I'd been about to cut into. It hit the floor rolling and he trod on it. He stopped, looked at the squashed mess under his shoe, looked at me, and we both burst out laughing. I fancied him instantly. He scraped up the remains of the sausage and offered to buy me another one, which just made me laugh all the more. James was looking less than thrilled. I'd already decided he was boring and I wasn't going to see him again, so the sausage episode brightened up the day. After Matt went back to his table (and to Sara) I sneaked a couple of glances at him and caught him looking at me. But he was with Sara, so I didn't think about it too much afterwards.

A few weeks later I was in the same pub one evening with Emily and some other girlfriends, and there was Matt, with another guy, leaning up at the bar. It was one of those heart-jerk moments; I fancied him even more.

'That's him!' I whispered to Emily. 'The sausage guy!'

'Ooh – he's *nice*. Where's his girlfriend?'

'Don't know. At home, maybe.'

'He's coming over,' said Emily, nudging me. 'Introduce us, Kate. I quite fancy his friend!'

'Hi!' he said, with a smile that made my toes tingle. 'Can I buy you a drink? Make up for the sausage?'

11

'No need!' I laughed. 'It probably saved me about two hundred calories. Sausage and chips is a ridiculous thing to have for lunch when you're trying to lose weight.'

'You don't need to lose weight,' he responded instantly, looking me up and down and returning his gaze to my eyes.

He's flirting with me, I thought, with a shiver.

'Hello!' said Emily loudly, nudging me again. 'Are you going to introduce me, or is this a private party?'

'Sorry – this is my friend Emily,' I said.

'Nice to meet you, Emily. I'm Matt. Are you going to introduce me to *your* friend?'

'Oh! Sorry – I'm Katie!' I giggled before she could open her mouth.

'So now I know your name, what you like for lunch, and what you drink,' he said, nodding at the glass in my hand. 'But what I really need to know is – are you having a night off from your boyfriend or is he going to walk in any minute and beat the hell out of me for chatting you up?'

Chatting me up? I shivered again. He fancied me. I could see it in his eyes.

'He wasn't my boyfriend. Just a date. A one-off,' I lied only slightly.

'Never to be repeated? Then it's OK if I say he looked like a boring prat?'

'Absolutely OK. He was. He talked about politics all through lunch.'

'God. No wonder you threw your sausage on the floor.'

'You nudged me!' I laughed. A delicious thought came to me. Did he do it on purpose? 'And anyway ...' I added, hardly daring to ask, 'what about your girlfriend? She not with you tonight?'

'No. And she's not my girlfriend any more.'

He told me later that they'd have broken up anyway – they were arguing all the time, it hadn't been good for ages – but that meeting me had been the pivotal point for him.

'I was suddenly forced to accept something I'd been trying to ignore,' he said.

'Which was what? You were clumsy in pubs? You enjoyed stamping on sausages?'

'Apart from that! I didn't fancy Sara any more. And I'd seen someone I did.'

Do you know one of those girls – I think everyone does – who doesn't seem to be able to settle down, even though she's edging into her thirties and all her friends are either married or sorted out with a serious relationship? The girl who has plenty of boyfriends, but never seems to find one she wants to stay with? Who's got her own flat, her own life, and her own space, and nobody to share them with because she's still *waiting for Mr Right*? Yep – I was that girl. But I'd finally met my Mr Right.

We fell in love frighteningly quickly. Almost overnight, we became one of those couples who used to irritate the shit out of me before I met Matt: phoning each other constantly, e-mailing each other several times a day from work, going everywhere together, neglecting the rest of the world. He moved in with me after only two months. Mum said it was much too soon and that we were still in the honeymoon period.

'Isn't that exactly the right time to want to live together?' I said.

The truth was that I was absolutely mad about him and nothing else would do – we had to wake up together and spend every possible moment in each other's company.

We've settled down a bit by now, of course. We've got a bit less ... intense. Emily says she thinks it's healthier.

'To be honest,' she says, 'you two were an embarrassment to be around, the first year you were together. Everyone was frightened you were going to rip each other's clothes off any minute.'

'Oh, please! We were *not* like that!'

'Katie, the way you looked at each other, the way your *passion* was so obvious to everyone – sorry, but it unnerved people. You want to know the truth? I think when other people see couples so *aggressively* in love, it makes them feel inadequate. They measure their own relationships against yours, and think theirs are a weak and watered down version of the real thing.'

'But surely everyone's like that at the beginning, aren't they?'

'Sean and I weren't. It was much more of a gradual thing. We were friends first, we liked each other, we got on well together, then we started to fancy each other. We'd been together for about six months before it kind of dawned on us that we were in love with each other. It was a *gentle* experience for us. Yours was headlong – violent – I watched it happening and it scared the shit out of me.'

'Me too,' I admit sadly. I'm sad, because that stage is over now. I don't care what anyone says: you can't recreate it. No amount of wearing black lingerie, having candlelit dinners or sex in unusual places is going to catapult you back into those fiery first few months of insatiable desire. 'But we're still in love!' I add quickly, to reassure myself almost as much as Emily.

'I know you are, you daft thing.'

We're at my flat, in the bedroom. Matt's in the lounge watching TV. Em's come round in response to an emergency phone call. Well, when you're getting married in a couple of months and your boyfriend calls you a moaning miserable cow, you kind of need your best friend. Badly.

'What was the row about?' says Emily.

'Same thing again. Prague.'

OK: this is what it's all about. For my hen party, I'm having a long weekend in Dublin with Jude, Emily, my mum and sister and a couple of other friends. I think that's quite reasonable, don't you? And Matt, for his stag, is having *ten days* in Prague, with about twenty of his mates. When he first told me about it, I flipped – and I've been annoyed about it ever since.

'How the hell are you getting so much time off work?' I asked him. 'You *have* booked the two weeks off for the honeymoon, haven't you?'

It'd be just like a man to forget.

'Of course I have! I'm taking some extra leave, unpaid.'

Unpaid!

Last time I'd checked, we weren't Lottery winners. We hadn't suddenly come into serious money or robbed a bank.

'What are you *thinking* about? It's just *so* irresponsible! How much will this cost, with all the alcohol you're going to consume out there? We can't afford it! Not with what we're spending on the honeymoon!'

'It's really cheap flights, Kate, and a dead cheap hotel. They had a special offer: book a week and get three extra days free. Sean's organised it all, and it was such a good deal, I wasn't about to scotch his plans.'

'You didn't think it was worth discussing it with me, then?'

'Sorry? No, I didn't, to be honest! I didn't think it was anything to do with you.'

Well, how nice is that? For nearly four years, we've shared every moment of our lives. We've hardly farted or hiccuped without the other one knowing about it. And suddenly, just before we commit ourselves to loving each other forever, he's doing something that's *nothing to do with me*.

'I didn't expect you to consult me about your hen weekend!' he added.

'You *knew* we were going to Dublin! I always promised Jude we'd have the hen weekend in Ireland!'

'So you're doing what you want, and I'm doing what *I* want! What's the problem?'

'The problem is,' I said, spitting the words out through my teeth, 'that you're spending a jolly ten days not earning anything, while *I'm* at work bloody paying for it!'

And the problem is that I'm still furious about it. I'm so furious, it's eating away at me, and whenever he talks about Prague I feel like chucking something at him.

Really auspicious start to a lifetime of happiness, eh?

I know, I know – we shouldn't really have spent so much money on the honeymoon. We let the travel agent talk us into it. We went into the shop with the idea of a week in Spain or the Canaries, and came out with a booking for two weeks in the Caribbean. Well, it was the pictures of the white sand, the palm trees, the clear blue sea ... it looked *perfect*. At the time, we were much more entranced with the idea of jetting off together as husband and wife on our perfect honeymoon than we were about the wedding itself. We'd had this naïve idea that perhaps we could just book our local church on a quiet day when the vicar could fit us in, turn up with our immediate family and half a dozen friends, do the business, retire to the pub for a bar meal and a few rounds of drinks, and it'd be a done deal.

And now look at us: not much more than a handful of loose change and two steadily growing credit card bills between us, a two-week luxury honeymoon booked in the Dominican Republic, a ten-day stag holiday in Prague for the bridegroom which probably won't be worth the money because all those going will be pissed every night and hung-over every morning, and a long weekend in Dublin for the bride, which I might be too miserable to enjoy.

'To be honest,' says Emily, 'the break from each other will probably do you both good.'

'Do you think so? Matt and I have never thought in terms of having a break from each other. We've always thought it was bad enough being apart every day when we're at work.'

'Yuk!' laughs Emily. '*Your* problem, Katie Halliday, is you're just too bloody romantic by half!'

Well, I'm sorry, but it's my job, you see.

I haven't told you about my job, have I? I read, and sell, romantic novels for a living. Nice one, eh?

I've got a pretty good idea what a relationship is *supposed* to be like. It's supposed to be all about long, lingering looks, and kissing in the moonlight, and making love on rugs in front of crackling log fires. We've done a bit of all those. We *like* romance. But nowhere, in these books I read every day, is there any mention of the guy booking a ten-day piss-up in Prague and telling the girl it's none of her business. There's never anything about the girl calling him a selfish inconsiderate pig, or the bloke saying she's getting more like his mother every day.

I just wanted it to be like it is in the books. That's not so very terrible, is it?

ABOUT MARGIE

I'm at Mum's today, and she's driving me round the bend. My mum married my dad in 1972 and divorced him in 1980. Considering how few years it lasted, it's strange how she's now holding her marriage up as a shining example of how things ought to be done.

'People didn't used to live together before they got married,' she announces as she hands me a mug of tea. 'Our parents would never have allowed it.'

'That's not strictly true, Marge,' pipes up Auntie Joyce, who's been sitting quietly in the corner reading the paper. 'I moved in with Ron before the wedding.'

I've got a lot of time for Auntie Joyce. She often does this – very quietly, without any fuss, puts Mum right and knocks her off her high horse.

'Yes, well,' huffs Mum, 'it was all very well for *you*.'

This, too, is a well-worn theme. Joyce is twelve years younger than Mum, and inevitably, I think, my grandparents held the reins a lot more loosely in her upbringing.

'Society had probably moved on a bit by the time you and Uncle Ron were going out together,' I say, trying to keep the peace.

'Moving on isn't always for the better,' mutters Mum. 'In *my* day, weddings were for a purpose. They marked the beginning of your life together, as a couple.'

'So you don't see the point of all this? You don't know why we're bothering?'

'I didn't say that!' She shakes her head impatiently. 'Of course I'm glad you're getting married. Happiest day of a mother's life, isn't it!'

'Happier than the day I was born?'

'Don't be facetious.' But she's laughing now. 'All I'm saying is that it seemed more of a ... significant *event* ... when the bride was moving out of her parents' house into her new home with her husband.'

'Not sure about that.' Lisa looks slowly from Mum to me with her head on one side as if she's considering the differences between us. 'In some ways, it's *more* significant nowadays, if a couple have been living together, been through all the ups and downs of getting used to each other, and then make a public commitment to each other. There's no social pressure on them to do it, but they still want to.'

'Yes. It's more romantic ...' I begin, but as I should have expected, everyone else laughs me down.

'What are you reading at the moment? *Love and Marriage*? *Happiest Bride in the World*?' teases Lisa.

'Actually it's called *Betrayal* and it's a really powerful story about a polio victim whose fiancé gets killed in the First World War and then she falls in love with an alcoholic ...'

'Sounds like a jolly read!' says Mum dismissively.

Not all romantic fiction is light and fluffy. Some of the books I read make me cry. If true love always ran smooth, in fiction or I guess in real life, there'd be no story to tell.

I'm used to my family teasing me about my work.

'You sound like Greg,' I tell them with a shrug. 'He thinks a good story is the life history of a man who discovered a scientific formula, or a mathematical equation. He doesn't like reading fiction.'

Which, of course, is how I got my job, so I'm not complaining.

'I'm surprised you two don't end up throwing your books at each other,' says Lisa. 'How do you stand it? I can't think of anything worse than sitting in that man's office all day, working on his computer, listening to him going on and on about his boring old books ...'

'I like my job,' I say, defensively. I get to spend half my days at home, catching up on my reading. 'And Greg's not that bad.'

Lisa's only met him once, although to be fair it wasn't a very good first impression. I invited her to a very boring literary event, introduced her to my boss and left them to chat while I went to talk to a couple of authors. When I came back over half an hour later, her glass was empty and her eyes had glazed over, and Greg was subjecting her to an animated but incomprehensible monologue about the book he was reading: *The Technology of Tunnels*.

'He's boring!' insists Lisa.

I can't argue with that. But if you really want to know boring, try working as an admin assistant in the editorial offices of a major publishing house for four years – opening the post, doing the photocopying, sending out the standard rejection letters – waiting for your promotion, your big break that never comes despite your first-class English degree, because everyone else in the office is overqualified too and no one ever leaves. Try giving up on that and working as a temp for another two years – drifting from job to mind-numbing job and never even staying long enough to make friends or get a desk of your own. And then imagine seeing an advert that could change your life. A guy who'd set up his own on-line bookshop and review service, bookshelf.co.uk, who'd been running it on his own for eighteen months and now needed help because he was snowed under and wanted someone to help him develop the website and review the fiction. With his background as a commissioning editor for a scientific publishing company, it wasn't really his forte. Within another year, he'd become so successful he needed a second fiction specialist – allowing *me* to concentrate on the romantic fiction. As I say, I love my job. I'm not about to complain if Greg occasionally bores the knickers off me.

Today's the Saturday morning, the week before my hen weekend. Matt leaves for Prague this evening. He's gone into town to buy himself a couple of new T-shirts. Why do men leave everything to the last minute? I've had all my clothes sorted out for the hen weekend, the wedding reception and the honeymoon for about two or three months. I've come round to Mum's to get away from the flat for a couple of hours, because all I can see while I'm there is Matt's half-packed suitcase, and it's making me crosser and crosser the more I look at it. I didn't expect the whole gang to be round here: Auntie Joyce, Lisa and the kids. My brother-in-law Richard's here too, but he's outside doing something to Mum's car.

'He's a good lad,' says Mum, although the 'lad' is thirty-eight if he's a day. 'I'm sure there's something wrong with the handbrake, but I'm afraid to take it to the garage. It's so difficult when you're a woman on your own.'

This is another common theme of Mum's. How she's stayed alive for the twenty-five years since the divorce must be a miracle. To listen to her, you'd think there was a dangerous wild beast lurking on every corner of every street, with its talons drawn ready to attack any lone woman venturing out of the safety of her home without a man on her arm.

'Matt doesn't know anything about cars,' I say with a shrug. 'I have to sort mine out myself.'

'Richard would always help, if you have a problem,' says Lisa, glowing in the reflected glory of her *good lad*.

'It's OK. I did that car maintenance course, didn't I.'

'Funny, isn't it, Joyce,' says Mum. 'Funny how the kids do these things nowadays – girls doing car maintenance, boys cooking the dinners.'

'We're not exactly kids ...'

'And anyway,' says Joyce, 'it's a positive thing, Marge. You don't want your girls to be tied to the kitchen. What would be the point of giving them such a good education?'

Auntie Joyce and Uncle Ron have never had any children – I've never liked to ask the reason – but this is why she's always taken such a lot of interest in Lisa and me growing up. She was only nine when Lisa was born, so she's actually closer in age to us than she is to Mum. When I was a stroppy teenager, there were a lot of times I stormed out of the house after a row with Mum, and went to stay the night at Joyce's house. She never took my side against Mum – just made me hot chocolate and listened to me.

'We had a good education too,' Mum points out. 'But I didn't expect to have a career and a family.'

'Who's talking about having a family?'

'Well,' Lisa looks at me pointedly. 'Isn't that why you're getting married?'

'What? No, it isn't!'

I stare around the room. No one looks convinced. They're all kind-of smirking to themselves as if they know perfectly well that I'm secretly planning a baby at this very minute, working out my fertile period so that I can go home and get one started as soon as possible.

'That's why we got married,' says Lisa smugly. 'We were ready to have children, and we didn't want them to have different surnames and be called ...'

'Hang on, hang on! For a start I'm *not* ready to have kids! And for another thing it's not like that these days, Lisa. Nobody bothers about—'

'Well, *I* do,' she says, protectively putting her arms round Charlie and Molly, who've both just trotted in, to the accompaniment of the closing music of a kids' cartoon show on the TV in the other room.

Charlie and Molly are lovely kids. If I wanted kids, I'd want them to be clones of these two. Lisa's a great mum. Like she's great at everything.

'But I don't want kids,' I mutter, half to myself. Not yet? Or not ever?

'You're thirty-one,' Mum reminds me with great solemnity.

'Thanks. I know.'

'In my day, you would have been considered an elderly primigravida.'

'Great. Thanks. I'm actually not *any* sort of gravida, elderly or otherwise. Matt and I haven't even *thought* about having kids, OK?'

At this there's a silence, broken only by Charlie asking for a drink and Molly going 'Daddy gone? 's Daddy gone? 's Daddy gone?' over and over.

'I don't mean we haven't *discussed* it,' I backtrack quickly. 'Just that it hasn't been high on the agenda ... it hasn't been an issue ... it hasn't been ...'

Actually, we've barely spoken about it.

Any more than his bloody stag party.

'So he's off tonight, then, Katie?' says Lisa as if I've spoken aloud.

'Yes,' I say, a bit curtly.

'Ten days, eh? Blimey, you're really letting him off the leash, aren't you!' she laughs.

There's a trace of admiration in her voice. Am I a good girlfriend, then, for allowing my bloke to go off and bankrupt us just before the wedding? Like I had any choice in it?

'In my day,' says Mum predictably, 'the bridegroom just had a night out at his local pub. There wasn't any money for jetting off on these separate holidays.'

Don't worry about it. There isn't now, either.

'What about the bride?' says Lisa. 'Didn't you have a hen night, Mum?'

'Of course I did!' She shrugs to herself and I wonder what exactly she's remembering. How it felt to be happy, and in love with my dad, before it all started to go wrong?

'We went down to Southend on the train,' she says wistfully. 'Four of us. We all worked together at the hospital. We got drunk and went on the Big Dipper. I was sick on the train home.'

'Sounds lovely,' I say.

'It was,' she retorts quite fiercely. 'It was – because we didn't expect too much.'

'Fair enough.'

'That's the trouble, you see,' she adds darkly as she picks up our mugs and takes them out to the kitchen. 'That's the trouble, nowadays.'

Lisa and I look at each other and smile.

But I don't want to ask her what she thinks the trouble is. I don't really want to dwell on trouble, this close to my wedding, thank you very much.

ABOUT HELEN

The flight takes off on time. I'm sitting in the middle seat of three, between Lisa and my friend Helen, and as we lift off the Stansted Airport tarmac a cheer goes up from the row behind us, where Emily's sitting with our two other friends from uni – Karen and Suze.

'YEAH!! DUBLIN HERE WE COME!' shouts Emily.

'Watch out you Irish lads!' adds Karen, and everyone starts laughing and cheering, even people further down the plane who don't know us.

They might not know us, but they certainly know why we're going to Dublin. Emily's made sure of that. We're all wearing bright pink T-shirts, with *Katie's Hen Party* printed on the back. Mine also states in bold print (in case anyone had any doubt): *BRIDE*. Emily's says *CHIEF BRIDES-MAID*, Lisa's says *BRIDE'S SISTER* and Mum's says *MOTHER OF THE BRIDE*. Mum, sitting across the aisle from me with Auntie Joyce, has put her cardigan on over the top of her T-shirt so nobody can read it. Anyone would think she was ashamed of me!

'You're quiet,' Helen says to me as the *fasten seat belt* signs are turned off and everyone bustles about, putting their seats back, their trays down, getting their magazines or books out and settling down for an hour before we start to descend again. 'You OK?'

'I'm fine.' I flash her a grin. 'Relaxing. Saving myself for tonight.'

'Relax while you can, then,' she says with a grimace. 'Sounds like your mates have got a full programme of intoxication lined up for you.'

Helen's a bit strange.

23

She's the other fiction reviewer from Bookshelf. We split the fiction between us, right down the middle, the middle being a kind of cultural line. She takes the literary fiction, I take the chick lit. She deals with the crime, I deal with the romance. She reads serious, I read humorous. It works well. We don't conflict with each other's interests. And surprisingly we get on well, together, too. Helen's not like me at all. She's forty, single, and determined to stay that way. She's not gay, but she doesn't like men either.

'I don't understand,' she tells me sometimes, in tones of great exasperation, 'why intelligent young women with university degrees, good careers and the world at their feet, should want to chuck everything out with the garbage as soon as some arrogant twat gets inside their knickers. It's such a waste!'

'But we can have both, can't we? A career, a life of our own, *and* a man?'

'Huh!' she sniffs. The sniff speaks volumes. 'Trust me, Kate, it just doesn't happen. It doesn't work out like that. You start living by your hormones, you sacrifice your own identity. Every time you fall in love, a few more brain cells die. Look at the heroines in the books you read. Do they strike you as being in full command of their senses?'

I laugh at her. She's so intense, she's funny.

'Have you *been* in love?' I ask her quietly as we speed across the Irish Sea. I can't imagine her willingly shedding any of her own formidable brain cells. 'Has there ever been anyone ... special?'

'Don't be ridiculous,' she snorts dismissively. 'I haven't got the time, or the inclination. Men bring you down, Kate. Sooner or later – whatever you think, however perfect they seem at the beginning – they bring you down to their own level. "Would a lark tie itself to a snake?"'

It's a quotation from a book she read last week. She told me at the time how impressed she was with it.

'Not all men are snakes, surely.' I smile.

'"They slither in the dust," she continues. "They'd drag the poor lark along with them, breaking her wings. She'd never fly again."'

'Shit. Glad I'm not a lark,' I say lightly, but she just shakes her head at me sadly. A lost cause.

Lisa's looking out of the window, watching the clouds, listening to her MP3 player. She's smiling to herself. I wonder if it's her music making her smile, or her own thoughts. What's she thinking about? Richard? Mr Wonderful? I have this private nickname for him – don't laugh – I'd never tell her, of course – *Rick the Perfect Prick*. I can't help it: he's such a goody-goody, he irritates the shit out of me. She talks about him as if he was the last angel in heaven, delivered to her personally as a gift from the gods. They never argue. He washes up every evening, gets up to the children if they're sick in the night, brings Lisa flowers for no reason at all, tells her he loves her even after six years of marriage. She says they're ecstatically happy. *Ecstatically!* Says their sex life is fantastic, says she can't wait for the kids to be in bed every night so they can get down to it. I should be pleased for her. Correction – I *am* pleased for her, of course – but I'm sorry; I just can't see Perfect Prick in that light. It makes me cringe, to be honest. He might be very useful in terms of motor vehicle repairs, but I wouldn't want him tinkering with *my* big end, not if he was the last man in the universe. Just as well we don't all have the same taste in men, I suppose, or the human race would have died out almost overnight if Mrs Noah held fast to her underwear and said 'Not tonight, Noah, and not ever again either, even if you *are* the only man on board.'

Helen's reading a hardback called *Solitaire*. The cover's black, with a single white rose in the very centre, beneath the title – the significance of which nobody could even begin to guess at, probably not even after they've read the entire book. Always presuming they could struggle through all of its six hundred and odd pages. Just looking at it makes me feel tired.

'Good plot?' I ask her, nevertheless. My own current paperback, the latest Ginny Ashcroft romp, is at the bottom of my suitcase. I don't really know why I brought it. *Get a life!* said Lisa when she saw me sliding it into the case under my knickers and bras. *This is your hen weekend! You are so NOT going to get time to read your bloody book!*

'The narrative is superb,' says Helen, smiling, tearing her eyes away from it, closing the book with a brass paperclip-type bookmarker placed carefully over the edge of the page. 'Durant manages to capture the *taste* of Paris café culture in the eighteen-sixties, the very *essence* of the move towards symbolism in literature as well as in art ...'

Sometimes I think Helen and Greg would be perfectly suited, if only Helen didn't hate all men. They could both put a slow reader off making the effort with literacy, for life, without even trying, despite the fact that they're both passionate about books themselves. I can never quite work out how Helen manages to read a work of fiction as if it was a well-crafted instruction manual. Give her *Bridget Jones's Diary* to read (not that she would, from choice), and she'd start taking it apart and talking about its social message and the author's use of cliché and colloquialism and before you knew it, she'd have ruined the story for you. Sorry, but I had enough of the dissection of literature when I was in uni. Now, I read books. I either like them or I don't; I recommend them or I don't. The Bookshelf customers know where they are with me. They read my reviews to help them decide which books to buy – and help them is what I do: I don't bamboozle them with jargon.

'A good yarn, then, yeah?' I interrupt her, digging her in the ribs as she's in full flow.

She's used to this. She takes it in good part. It's my little joke at both our expense – my admission of my intellectual inferiority; her admission of her tendency towards being anally retentive. She puts the book in the seat-back pocket and closes her eyes. I wonder if she's taking a nap, but, with her eyes still closed, she says:

'So this is it, then, Katie Halliday: your rite of passage.'

'I guess so.'

'Half a century ago we'd have been regaling you with old wives' tales about your forthcoming nuptials. What to expect, how to bear it, what to think about while he's claiming his marital rights.'

'Yes. Jesus, must have been pretty scary for those virgin brides. If they really *were* ...'

26

'Good point. A lot of dishonesty's gone out of the window, along with the mystique. May be a good thing after all.'

I look at her and wonder. For some reason I've never fathomed, I seem to be one of those girls other people tell all their problems to. I've often thought that if I was out of work I could get a job as an agony aunt. But not Helen – she's never confided in me. She's a closed book. Has she *really* never loved anyone? Never lived with anyone? Never had a relationship?

As if she can hear these questions going on inside my head, she opens her eyes and tells me as if it's a topic of general interest like the weather in Dublin:

'I've had quite a lot of sex, you know. Just not often with the same person too many times.'

There's not a lot that can usefully be said in response to this, is there?

'Oh. Right,' seems to just about cover it.

The *fasten seat belt* sign has come on and I can feel the beginning of the descent from the pressure in my ears.

'We're there!' calls Emily from behind me. 'We're coming into Dublin, girls!'

'Yeah!' chorus Karen and Suze, who sound like they've been hitting the white wine already.

'Yeah, cool!'

'Hubblin', bubblin' Dublin!'

'Bloody hell,' says Lisa, packing her MP3 away in her bag and giving me a quick grin. 'I feel excited already, and I'm not even the bride!'

'Bringing back memories?' I suggest. We went to Edinburgh for her hen weekend. To be honest I don't remember much about it except for Lisa getting rat-arsed and going on, and on, and on, about how lucky she was to have found Perfect Prick, and how wonderful he was, and how much in love she was, and how wonderful their sex life was, and eventually throwing up at just about the same point that we all felt like it.

'Your turn now, little sister!' she says with an unusual gentleness.

My turn to see how pissed I can get in the shortest possible time?

My turn to throw up in the toilets in a city nightclub, stagger home in the early hours wearing a torn, tatty veil, an 'L' plate and no shoes, and lie in bed the next day with the worst hangover of my life?

My turn to hang round the necks of my best mates, slop my drink down their clothes, cry and tell them I'll always love them more than any man?

OK, then: bring it on.

'Are you ready for this?' Helen asks me quietly just before the wheels hit the tarmac of Dublin airport with a jolt that makes my backbone shudder.

'Ouch!' I wince afterwards. 'No, I wasn't!'

But we both know she wasn't talking about landings.

ABOUT JUDE

We're booked into a three-star hotel in Temple Bar. We arrive in two taxis, waving and calling out of the windows at any interested or interesting specimens of Irish manhood as we pass.

I've called Jude on her mobile, and she's waiting for us in reception. She looks up as we swing in through the door, alerted by the shrieks and laughter. Immediately we're both legging it across the foyer, grabbing hold of each other by the shoulders, hugging as if we haven't met for years. It's only been a few weeks, actually, since she came over for the fitting of the lilac dress.

'When did you get here? Did you have a good journey?'

'I did, thanks. How was your flight? Kate, you're looking well! Are you OK?'

'I'm fine,' I assure her. 'I've been looking forward to seeing you.'

'Me too. God, it's desperate, I can't believe you're all really here!'

'Christ, Jude – have you been on the booze already? Of course we're all here!' I'm laughing as I'm hugging her.

'But I can't *tell* you how pleased I am to see you, Katie – I've been looking forward to this for ever, and here we are already ...'

'Get a grip, Jude!' laughs Lisa, coming to join us. She dumps her suitcase, narrowly missing Jude's feet, and gives her a hug too. 'How're you doing, girl?' She holds her out at arm's length and studies her. 'Not putting on any weight, I hope? There's *no* room to let out in those seams, I keep telling Katie ...'

'Sure, Lisa, and there's more fat on a stick of celery than

there is on meself, you should be knowing that. Leave off with your nagging, for the love of God, or we'll all be scared to touch a drop all weekend, so we will.'

'I hardly think that's likely,' I mutter, watching Karen and Suze weaving their way towards us, arms linked, giggling. 'Those two got started on the plane!'

They don't seem to have changed since our university days. Still the good-time party girls – show them a bottle of wine and they'll have it opened and poured out quicker than you can blink.

'Good job it's a once in a lifetime experience, eh?' says Lisa, smiling at them with the condescension of the big sister who's had a lifetime of tolerating the immature ways of the younger generation. Despite her superior ways, Lisa's always liked my friends and she's particularly fond of Emily and Jude, having got used to them both practically living at our place over the years.

'One hopes so, anyway,' chimes in Mum. '*Far* too expensive, these days, to go through it all more than once – how *do* people manage it two or three times?'

'Not really an appropriate thought at the moment, Mum ...' points out Lisa.

'No, well – in *my* day marriage was considered to be for life,' she begins, but there's a silence at this point and she stops, looking embarrassed, evidently realising it's not clever to advocate eternal fidelity when your own marriage only lasted eight years. 'So, Jude, dear. How are you?' she continues blithely. 'Are your parents well?'

'They're grand altogether, thank you, Margie – and how're you yourself?'

'Bearing up, dear, under the strain, you understand. Not every day your youngest child gets married, you know. Want to do her proud, of course.'

She gives me a sad smile as if this is going to be an almighty effort.

'And you're looking well, so y'are, Margie. You're going to have a blinder of a time here in Dublin with us girls, are you not?'

'Quite probably, Jude. Quite probably,' says Mum, nodding thoughtfully.

'All checked in, then, girls!' calls Emily, who's been sorting out the paperwork with the reception desk. 'Come on – rooms are on the second floor.'

I'm sharing with Jude. She arrived by train from Cork an hour ago, so she's already unpacked and hung all her stuff in the wardrobe. The dressing table's covered with her pots of cream and bottles of make-up.

'Whoops, sorry!' she says, sweeping them all over to one side. 'There's plenty of space, Katie, I'm just making a mess as usual. Can't go anywhere without me war paint, you know how I am!'

Jude's a funny mixture.

She takes enormous care of herself. I mean, you'd never catch her going out for a walk in the rain, or the wind, for instance, in case she got her hair mussed up. She can't be seen in public without at least one layer of make-up and a full set of false nails. She doesn't possess slobbing-out clothes. I've never seen her in her dressing gown in daylight hours. We've spent dozens of holidays together – all through our teens I used to come over to Ireland for two or three weeks every summer – and I don't think I ever saw her in pyjamas that hadn't been ironed. Sometimes I wonder what she does when she goes to bed with a guy. Sorry – I don't mean that to sound gross. I just wonder if she finally gets to be spontaneous, 'cos she sure as hell never is when *I've* shared a room with her. Her bedtime can take so long, I've been to sleep, had my first dream, woken up and wondered whether it's the next day, before she even gets her clothes off.

The finished result, Jude Barnard robed, coiffured, and made up to the nines, is a sight for sore eyes. She's petite and slim, with perfect blonde hair, big blue eyes and little delicate features like a china doll. And on top of that, she's the sweetest natured girl you could ever meet. Never says a bad word about anyone. She makes me feel like Attila the Hun as soon as I open my mouth to utter the slightest, mildest criticism, because no one is ever too bad for Jude to see their hidden good points. She'd probably tell you that Hitler was just a bit misguided and Judas Iscariot was having a bad day.

But the sad thing is, guys don't tend to notice Jude. When she's around people she doesn't know, she's as timid as a mouse. She always takes the corner seat, keeps quiet and doesn't meet people's eyes. She's got no confidence. She was the same at school, but I thought she would have grown out of it by now.

That's why I was so pleased when she told me about Fergus. They've been together about five or six months now and apparently he's Mr Wonderful personified. And good luck to her.

'How's Fergus?' I ask her now, throwing myself on my bed and leaning on one elbow, watching her tidying the dressing table.

'He's grand,' she says, smiling shyly at me in the mirror.

'It's about time I met this guy. You can't hide him from me for ever, you know!'

'Aw, come on, Katie, you know well how much I'm looking forward to you meeting him!'

'Well, me too. I hope he's being good to you?'

She laughs.

'Sure, and why would he not be? Give over with your fussing, for the love of God!'

I roll over onto my back and stretch out on the bed, arms above my head. I could fall asleep quite easily. I'm knackered from the stress of all the wedding preparation, and this is the first chance I've had in weeks to relax.

'Aren't you going to unpack?' says Jude.

'Nah, I don't think I am. I haven't got the energy.'

'Would you like for me to do it for you?'

I open one eye and manage a lopsided grin at her.

'You're the best friend I ever had. I don't know how I live without you.'

'Be off with you. You and your nonsense!' She pauses. 'Katie. Are you sure you're OK?'

'Of course I am. I'm here to party. Let's get on with it ...'

But I'm asleep before she's even unzipped my case.

We've arranged to meet up in the bar at seven o'clock. I'm expecting Emily, Karen and Suze to be first there, already getting stuck into the booze, but surprisingly, Mum and

Auntie Joyce are the only ones already ensconced at a table. They've both got gin-and-tonics in front of them and they're deep in conversation, hugging their handbags on their laps.

'We didn't have a honeymoon,' Mum's saying as Jude and I bring our drinks over from the bar to join them. 'There wasn't any money for things like that. We spent everything we had on the deposit for our first house.'

We're back in 1972 again, by the sound of it.

'I know, Marge,' says Joyce, 'but you've got to hand it to the youngsters. They don't rush into marriage. They work hard and save up ... bloody good luck to them, I say. Ron and I went to Guernsey for a week. But if we could have afforded a honeymoon in the Caribbean, we'd have gone for it. We *all* would have done, wouldn't we?'

'We didn't expect luxuries,' insists Mum, taking another sip of her drink. 'We *expected* to be hard up. That's the difference.'

'It's not so very different, Mum. We're still hard up, trust me,' I tell her.

'God, everyone's hard up these days, aren't they, so?' says Jude.

'Who's hard up?' asks Emily, joining us at the table. 'Is someone trying to get out of buying a drink?' She laughs. ''Cos before you all start arguing about it, I think we should have a whip.'

'Good idea,' says Lisa, and between the two of them they're getting organised, getting the right amount of euros from everyone and keeping it in a separate purse.

'Hope one of you two is going to stay sober!' I tell them.

'Yes, Emily, dear – that's a lot of money. Be very careful,' says Mum, giving her a stern look. 'We don't want you getting mugged.'

'Well, that's nice to know, Marge! I'll do my best *not* to be.'

'I know you will, dear, and it's very good of you to take care of everything for us. Katie's very lucky to have such good friends,' she adds. The look she gives me implies that it's far more than I deserve.

'Here's to good friends, then!' I suggest, raising my glass. Everyone's turned up in the bar now and got themselves a drink.

'Cheers!' they all respond.

'And here's to the *hen*!' laughs Emily. She raises her glass again, takes a big gulp of her vodka and lemonade, and gives me a hug. 'Have a wonderful weekend, Katie! Just relax and have fun!'

'It'll be the last chance you get!' says Helen darkly.

Everyone laughs. But knowing Helen, I don't actually think she's joking.

'Time to get the gear, on, Emily, isn't it?' says Lisa when everyone's got a second drink in front of them.

'Gear?' I suddenly remember all the other hen parties I've ever been to, and experience a moment of pure panic. Am I mad, putting my fate in the hands of this lot? For a start, Lisa's going to want to get her own back on me for the huge inflatable willy I made her wear, along with the veil and L plates, at her own hen party. For the first time I notice the plastic carrier bag Emily's stowed under the table. Well, at least there can't be too much in that, can there? No room for an inflatable willy ...

'Come on, Katie, on your feet!' commands Emily, delving into the carrier bag and pulling out a pink feather boa.

Well, that's pretty harmless, anyway. She drapes it round my shoulders and then sticks a sparkly pink tiara on my head.

'Thanks!' I say, hugely relieved. This is almost a pleasure to wear, considering what some of the alternatives could have been. Emily's a good friend. I reckon she's insisted on keeping the fun clean and the embarrassment minimal.

'And now here's something for everyone else,' she adds with a giggle, getting a handful of big badges out of the bag and passing them around. Probably 'Katie's Hen Party' badges, I suppose. Nice idea. I feel a warm glow of gratitude towards Em, and in fact I'm just about to give her a hug when I notice that everyone else is almost bursting with suppressed laughter.

'What?'

I lean over to take a look at Jude's badge. She grins at me and holds it up for me to see. Sure enough, it has my name on it. And what it also has on it is a picture of me at the age of about twelve, with braces on my teeth, my hair in pigtails and wearing a hideous pair of pink striped trousers my mother should never have allowed me to go out in.

'Where did you get hold of *that*?' I demand of Emily.

'Nothing to do with me!' she says, laughing.

'Mum! Did *you* supply this horrible picture?'

'No, dear,' she says, smiling innocently at me. 'I think Jude found it herself. But I did supply *this* one!'

On her own badge is a picture of me as a baby, sitting in a high chair, with chocolate dessert all over my mouth. Lovely.

'And I supplied this one!' says Auntie Joyce excitedly. It's me as a toddler of about three, red in the face, mouth wide open in full screaming temper tantrum. 'You haven't changed, dear!' she teases.

Lisa's got me at about six or seven, in a school nativity play, dressed as an angel, with my halo hanging off. Emily, Karen and Suze have all managed to find pictures of me in various states of drunkenness at the student bar. In Emily's picture I'm holding onto someone whose name I can't even remember, and I look as though I'm just about to vomit.

'I didn't have any photos of you, unfortunately,' says Helen seriously. Thank God for that! 'So I had to use my phone to take this one, specially,' she adds, turning her badge round to show me.

I'm sitting at my desk at work, the computer on, a book open in front of me – sound asleep.

Everyone falls about laughing. They obviously think this is the funniest one of all.

'When did you take this?' I ask indignantly. 'I do *not* go to sleep at work. I must have just dozed off for a minute!'

'Must have been a really exciting book!' says Lisa sarcastically.

'It was the night after Emily's birthday party!' laughs Helen. 'You were slightly hungover, if you remember . . .'

'Shit, that is *so* mean of you!'

But I'm joining in the laughter. As jokes go, it could have been a hell of a lot worse.

'Congratulations, love!' calls a middle-aged woman at another table across the room.

'Rather you than me!' says her friend.

'Sure, does she know what she's letting herself in for, do you think?'

'Be away with you now, the first twenty-five years are the worst, so they are!'

At this, the two women lean back in their chairs and laugh so hard, one of them goes into a horrendous coughing fit and her friend has to go to the bar to get her another drink.

'And one for me little bride over there,' she says to the barman, giving me a wave. 'It might be the last pleasure she ever has on this earth, bless her heart.'

'Thanks!' I say. 'Blimey, Jude – it's really bloody encouraging, isn't it!'

'Aw, pay no attention at all, Katie,' she says, giving me a hug. 'Sure, you'll be grand.'

'Yeah – you and Matt are going to live happily ever after!' joins in Emily. 'I just know it!'

The third drink goes down a treat.

ABOUT LISA

We move on to a pub, just along the street from our hotel, where they serve food. It's still early so it's not packed yet, and with a bit of a squash and a couple of extra stools pulled up, we all fit round a big table by the window. We order pies, burgers, fish and chips – alcohol-soaking-up food – and luckily it's served quickly as we're all hungry and raring to go. We've got a lot of catching-up to do with Jude, and everyone needs to do a bit of ice-breaking with Helen, who doesn't know anyone else very well, so we're talking nineteen to the dozen all through the meal, as well as knocking back the white wine.

'OK,' begins Emily afterwards, as we settle down with a fresh round of drinks. 'The forfeits are in my handbag ...'

'Forfeits?' say Mum and Auntie Joyce in unison, looking horrified.

'Don't worry,' Lisa reassures them. 'You won't have to take any clothes off.'

'Well, I should hope not, Lisa!' says Mum.

'It's a bit too cold altogether for that sort of thing, isn't it, Marge?' laughs Jude.

'The rules for tonight are like this,' Emily goes on. 'One – no talking about our boyfriends, husbands, partners, whatever. Not even a mention of their names. We're here to get away from them! Agreed?'

There's a chorus of cheers.

'Two – no talking about work. Anyone who mentions anything about their job has to do a forfeit. Three – anyone who can't, or won't, answer a Truth question properly has to do a Dare. That includes anyone who we don't believe is being truthful.'

'Who makes up the dares?' says Karen.

'They're the same as the forfeits. Give me a break. I sat up all night writing these!' laughs Emily.

Everyone's gone quiet now, sipping their drinks, contemplating the table, probably too scared to talk in case they stray onto forbidden subjects.

'This is all very strange to me,' says Mum suddenly. 'We never did anything like this on our hen nights, did we, Joyce?'

'No, Marge. But they were much more tame affairs, after all. Do you know, girls – I just had a few drinks at my local pub with Marge and our mum, and my best friend. I was scared to drink too much in case I overslept and missed the wedding!'

'You actually had the hen party the night before the wedding?' squeals Emily.

'Of course – everyone did. That was the whole point of it!' retorts Mum. 'It's all very strange, this business of having it weeks before the wedding. I can't get used to it at all.'

'One of our mates from uni had a hen party in Tenerife the *year* before she got married,' says Karen.

'And I know someone who went out to Australia for hers, and liked it so much, she and her husband went back out there to live, after the wedding,' joins in Lisa.

'Tenerife, Australia – honestly!' says Mum, emptying her glass and beginning to sound a bit slurred. 'What's wrong with a trip to Southend, like I had, that's what I want to know!'

Everyone groans. Not again. I wish she'd be quiet about bloody Southend.

'You may laugh!' she says, although we're not. 'But we had a brilliant evening in Southend. We knew how to have fun in those days without spending a lot of money – that was the difference, you see.'

'Let's start on the Truth or Dares game,' suggests Emily, to change the subject. She pulls a little plastic bag out of her handbag, shakes it up and offers it to me. 'Bride-to-be goes first!'

'Oh, God!' I groan, dipping into the bag obediently and taking out a folded piece of paper. 'I don't think I'm drunk enough yet!'

'Go and get her another drink, someone,' commands Emily. 'And I'll have another vodka while you're at it.'

I unfold the paper.

'*"Tell the truth: Have you ever slept with your boss?"*'

'Oh, well, that's an easy one!' I laugh with relief. 'No! Not fucking likely!'

'What's the matter with him, then?' giggles Jude.

'Greg? Oh, I've *told* you how boring he is! He'd probably be as boring in bed as he is in the office ...'

'You don't actually know that,' points out Helen, surprisingly. 'You can't tell what someone's like in bed, unless you've slept with them.'

I raise my eyebrows at her. A couple of the girls go '*Oooh!*' in a silly giggly way.

'I'm just interested in factual accuracy, that's all,' she says with a smile and a shrug. 'If Katie hasn't slept with him, she can't actually say whether he's boring ...'

'I *haven't* slept with him! And I don't want to!'

'Nor any other boss? Ever?' persists Emily, taking the slip of paper back from me and holding it up, inviting comment. 'Do we believe her, girls?'

'Yeah, I've had to listen to her whingeing about all her bosses ever since she started her first Saturday job,' says Lisa. 'She's never had one she fancied.'

'Never had one I even *remotely* fancied,' I agree.

Emily drops the dare back into the bag.

'Come on, then, Lisa – your turn,' she says.

Lisa takes a piece of paper out of the bag and I watch her expression change as she reads it. Then I watch her composing her face and looking around the group. I know straight away that she's going to lie.

'What's the question?'

'It's a stupid one,' she says dismissively. '*"Have you ever begged for sex and been turned down?"*'

'Well!' says Mum. 'Honestly!'

Auntie Joyce nudges her.

'It's only a bit of fun, Margie.'

'Lisa?' prompts Emily. 'Have you?'

Everyone else is laughing. I'm still watching Lisa's face.

'No,' she says, with a false laugh. 'As if!'

'You're lying,' I say, straight away. 'Give her a dare to do!'

'What d'you mean, I'm lying?' she says indignantly, but she's flushed red.

'You *are*, aren't you!' squawks Emily. 'Who was it, Lise? Were you pissed?'

'Oh, just someone, years ago,' she says, shaking her head, flustered. 'It doesn't matter ...'

'We'll get it out of her later,' Emily whispers to me. 'Take a dare, Lisa. I can't believe you'd lie to your friends!'

'Piss off,' says Lisa, mildly, recovering herself and dipping into the other bag for another piece of paper. '*"Hop on one leg for thirty seconds"*. Well, that's easy, anyway!'

'She's too sober!' says Jude disappointedly as Lisa jumps to her feet and performs this easily, grinning with relief.

'Give it time,' says Emily with a nasty grin. 'They'll get harder.'

'*"Have you ever had sex on a train?"*' reads out Jude. 'Well, that's a desperate idea. I haven't, and that's the truth, so it is. But I wouldn't mind a try!'

Everyone laughs, except Mum, who says 'Honestly!' again and downs another drink. She's swaying a bit in her seat. 'I hope *we* don't have to take part in this silly game, Joyce?'

'We'll let you off, Margie, if you don't want to play,' says Emily kindly. 'We wouldn't want you revealing all your deep dark secrets in front of your two daughters, would we, now?'

'And we wouldn't want to hear them, either,' I mutter, but Mum's got into her stride again about her hen night in Southend.

'We didn't need to play silly games like this, you see, because we *talked* to each other.'

'I thought you said you got drunk and threw up on the Big Dipper?' I remind her.

'Not *on* the Big Dipper,' she corrects me quite crossly. 'It was the Big Dipper that made me *feel* sick.'

'Not the booze you had before you got on it?'

'Don't be facesh ... faceshi ...'

'Facetious?'

40

'Of course we had a *drink*,' she continues. 'But we *talked* in the pub. About ... you know. The wedding night.'

'Oooh!' exclaims Karen. 'Get your mum another drink, Katie, while she's talking about the wedding night!'

'I think she's had enough already ...'

'Don't be mean! Come on, get another round in!'

I don't like the way Mum's eyes are going funny. But what can I say? It's a party, after all.

'*"Do you seriously fancy anyone in here?"*' Emily reads out, as we're getting into the next drink, and we insist on her taking a turn at her own game. 'Well,' she lowers her voice and takes a quick look over her shoulder, 'I wouldn't say no to him at the bar, with the green top.'

We all spin round, instantly, and there's a chorus of appreciative comments that predictably results in the guy in question turning and grinning back at us.

'*Would* you?' I whisper back to her. 'If you got the chance?'

'That's not fair, Katie! It's not one of the questions,' says Jude.

'So? *Would* you?' I persist, watching Emily as she's still sneaking glances at the guy at the bar.

'Of course not,' she laughs quietly. 'I might like to, though, if I wasn't seeing Sean.'

'*FORFEIT*!' shouts Lisa. 'You mentioned Sean!'

'Oh, fuck! That was Katie's fault ...'

'Get on with it!'

'OK, OK.' She dips into the bag. '*"Approach a stranger and pretend you know each other."*'

'Good one!' I laugh. 'Why not try *him*!'

The guy in the green top's still looking at us with interest. Emily pushes back her chair with determination, gets up and takes a couple of steps towards the bar. 'Hello!' she calls out as she approaches her target. 'What a surprise to see you! What are you doing in Dublin?'

He picks up his pint of Guinness and takes a long drink, watching her over the top of the glass, before putting it slowly back down on the bar and saying, 'I live here,' and turning his back on her.

'Shit!' she says, loudly, as she sits back down at the table, her face burning. We're all falling about laughing, of course.

'Shit, I don't fancy him at all, now. Miserable git. I wouldn't shag him if he was the last man in Ireland!'

'Yer man next to him is all right, though,' says Jude thoughtfully.

'Honestly!' says Mum again. 'You girls, you've all got boyfriends, partners, whatever, but to hear you talk ...'

'No harm in looking, Mum! Just a bit of window shopping,' I tell her.

'Just a bit of fun, Marge,' says Joyce again, giving her another nudge and almost sending her drink flying.

'It's where it all starts, though, isn't it,' says Lisa, who's beginning to sound almost as drunk as Mum. 'Seriously. I know this is just ... you know ... a bit of fun, but if you're not careful, playing around, before you know it ...'

'Oh, leave off, Lise! What, you think him in the green shirt is going to jump on Emily and she's going to go out the back of the pub with him and be unfaithful to ... to that person at home that she's not allowed to mention?'

'No. But it just shows. Doesn't it.' The drink is making her talk in short, staccato sentences. She sways a bit between each one. 'It just shows. If you fancy other blokes. There must be something. Not quite right. Don't you think?'

'Bollocks,' says Emily.

'Yeah. Your trouble is,' I start, and then I forget what I was going to say her trouble was, so I have to stop and have a bit more of my drink until I remember. 'Your trouble is, your marriage is *perfect*.'

'Perfect,' echoes Emily, who seems to be unable to say more than one word at a time.

'Your marriage is so *bloody* perfect!' I tell Lisa. For some reason it seems like a good idea to put my arm round her and kiss her. 'You're so *bloody* lucky to have such a *perfect* marriage to Perfect Prick!'

There's a horrified silence.

'I mean Perfect *Rick*!' I correct myself, sobered up slightly by the shock of what I've said and at the look on Lisa's face. 'Rick, perfect Rick!'

'Yes,' she says stonily, shrugging my arm off her shoulders.

I put it back round her again.

42

'Sorry. Don't be like that. Didn't mean it! Rick's Mr Perfect, isn't he, you're always saying how great he is ... how you have all this wonderful sex ... every bloody night ... even now you've got two kids ...'

'Not *every* night. But yes, he's certainly ...'

'No talking about partners!' Suze reminds us sharply, just as everyone's looking like they're about to throw up. 'Forfeit, forfeit!'

'Fuck the forfeits! Let's get another drink!' I say slurrily.

'Not for me, thank you,' says Mum before anyone even asks her. 'I think I've had ...' She pauses, frowning. 'I've had ...'

'Too much!' says Joyce, firmly.

'I think I feel a bit ...' She looks up at me, puzzled.

'Drunk!' supplies Joyce.

'I just feel a bit tired,' Mum finishes lamely.

Not really surprised. She started drinking before the rest of us and she's been putting them away like there's no tomorrow.

'Come on!' Joyce pulls Mum to her feet. 'Let's get you back ...'

'Home?' says Mum, looking around the pub as if she's wondering where her bedroom is.

'Home's a long way away, dear. Over the sea. Over the Irish Sea!'

'Over the Irish Sea?' echoes Mum, staggering after Joyce, knocking her chair over in the process. '"Oh Danny Boy, the pipes, the pipes are calling ..."'

'Oh, bloody hell!' says Lisa, covering her ears.

'Will she be all right?' I ask Auntie Joyce, grabbing her arm as she passes. 'Should we come ... ?'

'Don't be daft! I'll take her back to the hotel and put her to bed. It won't be the first time.'

'Really?' I'm intrigued by this. 'Well, OK then, if you're sure you'll both be all right?'

'I'm fine, love. I've only had a couple, and the hotel's almost next door, isn't it. See you all in the morning, girls! Be good ... ' She winks at us. 'Or maybe I should say be careful?'

At least we've heard the last of bloody Southend for tonight.

We manage a few more turns of Truth or Dare before everyone gets too drunk to be bothered. It's interesting stuff. Karen refuses to answer a question about whether she's ever snogged someone else's boyfriend, so she has to stand up and sing 'Like A Virgin'. She can't remember the words and her singing is so awful we let her off after the first three lines. And then Helen, of all people, admits to having gone to work once wearing no knickers, but she won't tell me whether it was before she worked for Greg, or since, which only serves to convince me it must have been recently.

'Because you forgot to put them on? Or on *purpose*?'

'That's not part of the question.'

'But I want to *know*!'

'Sorry!' She smiles calmly. 'Not telling.'

Well, it couldn't have been for Greg's benefit so she must have been meeting some guy after work. Or in her lunch-break. Unbelievable! I look at her with a new respect. I know she doesn't *like* men but she doesn't seem to have a problem with having sex with them.

'Fair play to you!' mutters Jude, with her face in her wine glass.

'Go, girl!' agrees Suze, who sounds too tired to say it with very much enthusiasm.

The tiredness is catching. Before we know it, we're all yawning.

'I hope no one's expecting me to get up early in the morning!' says Lisa with a groan. 'I'm looking forward to a good lie-in. I never get the chance at home, what with Richard being so fucking *righteous* about getting up early, every fucking day, even at weekends.'

I look at her in total shock. She's slagging off Perfect Rick? This is unheard-of! I realise she's drunk, but let's not go for complete personality changes here – that's just too freaky.

'You mentioned your husband,' says Emily sleepily. 'Forfeit . . .'

'Can't be arsed,' says Lisa. 'It's too late. Game's over.'

'Anyway . . .' I can't let this go, or I won't be able to sleep tonight. 'Anyway, Lise – it's great, isn't it, Richard getting up early, bringing you tea in bed, doing the kids' breakfast, all that stuff ... you're so lucky, aren't you! You know you are!'

'Am I?' she retorts. 'Huh. That's all you know, 'cos that's all I tell everyone. You want the truth? You want the fucking truth, now you're getting married, little sister? Now I'm pissed enough to tell you? Do you?'

I've got a horrible feeling I'm going to hear it, whether I want to or not.

LISA'S STORY

I know what everyone thinks. They're all looking at me now with those kind of smiles people give you when you're very drunk and talking rubbish, but they're going to pretend to go along with you rather than let you get upset, flip out of control and spoil the party. It's true I'm a bit drunk – but only a bit. I'm not used to it any more, that's the thing; not like Katie and her friends, still going out to pubs and clubs at the weekend. I'm married with two kids, don't forget. How could I ever possibly forget?

My marriage, actually, is shit.

There. You weren't expecting that, were you?

Katie thinks I've got a wonderful, perfect marriage, and to be honest I don't bother to disillusion her. It's all part of the pretence. I'm a good actress. I don't admit the truth to anyone – not to Mum, not to my sister or any of my friends.

It started off good. I suppose it always does – otherwise why would we bother? All the time I was a teenager, I wanted to get married and have kids. It isn't fashionable these days to admit to that. We're supposed to have fabulous careers or at the very least go and travel the world, if not both, and to not even consider settling down until the tick of our biological clocks becomes so deafening we can't hear ourselves think. I was actually twenty-seven before I got married, but it wasn't for the lack of trying. I'd had serious relationships with two other guys before I met Richard, and I was considering marrying both of them. One of them turned out to be already married so that was a bit of a non-starter, and the other one cooled off when I started buying *Brides* magazine and window-shopping in Mothercare. In fact he emigrated to New Zealand. I considered following him but perhaps it would have been taking desperation one step too far.

I was attracted to Richard for a lot of reasons. One: he was older than me, so probably more likely to be ready to settle down than the men of my own age who I'd been seeing. Two: he was sensible. He had a savings account. He owned more than one suit. He knew how to hang wallpaper, lay crazy paving, buy shares. Three: he earned enough to make it *possible* to buy shares. You can see why I fell in love with him.

I don't think I ever had a romantic dream, like Katie does. I didn't long for a tall dark broodingly handsome stranger to sweep me off my feet, flying me off to fantastic destinations, strolling hand-in-hand in the sunset on white coral beaches, etcetera, etcetera, etcetera. She gets all that from reading too much romantic fiction, and in my opinion it doesn't do her any good at all. My dream was far more prosaic. I wanted to live happily-ever-after in a semi-detached house on a nice estate, with a husband in a good job, two well-behaved children and a tidy garden.

A good sex life was kind of taken as a given.

Well, I got the house, the job, the kids and even the garden. Can't have it all, I suppose.

We lived together for a year before we got married. We rented a flat in the area where we wanted to live, and every Saturday we went out house-hunting. Richard took house-hunting very seriously. He dressed up for it. I think I could trace the very first time I felt irritated with him back to the day I asked him why he was bothering to wear a shirt and tie to go and view someone's house, and he looked me straight in the eye and said: *If something's important to me, why would I want to look as if I don't care?* I can remember having the same urge to tell him to go and fuck himself that I used to get when my French teacher closed her eyes, shook her head and told me to try to make my accent sound as though I *actually thought my thoughts and dreamed my dreams* in French. Of course, I didn't say anything to Richard, any more than I did to the French teacher. I pretended to be impressed. Perhaps that was the very beginning of the acting career that I've made of my life.

We found our perfect house, we got our mortgage, bought our furniture, planned our wedding, and all the time I kept thinking that maybe the sex would get better in due course. I wasn't sure whether I was expecting too much. After all, if Richard was happy with a quick bonk once a week regularly on a Saturday night, it seemed a bit unreasonable to want more. I wasn't even sure exactly what I wanted more of, though certainly not the same predictable, unsatisfying and rather unfriendly encounters he saved himself for all week. I'd experienced better sex with my previous boyfriends, but how could I admit that, even to myself, when Richard was supposed to be the love of my life? It was all very confusing.

To take my mind off it, I got pregnant. We were both over the moon when Charlie was born, and Richard turned out to be a great dad. He was there at the birth, talking me through the whole thing with a textbook open on his lap, and took his responsibilities very seriously, as with everything else he did. He'd read all the childcare manuals. He knew about stuff like when Charlie should be started on solid food and potty training and learning the alphabet – whereas I would probably have just muddled through and made lots of mistakes along the way, if he hadn't been so involved. If I sometimes found myself wishing he'd *let* me muddle through and make a few mistakes, I told myself I was being very ungrateful and unfair.

I don't know why I lied about my marriage. I think it kind of frightened me to admit the truth. Look, all anyone talks about these days is sex – and it's always good sex, perfect sex, amazing sex. Nobody ever admits to rubbish sex; and certainly not to hardly any sex at all, which is what we were having by the time Charlie was born. Maybe if I'd had the guts to be honest about it from the start it wouldn't have been so bad. I can't for the life of me remember how Molly was conceived because it sure as hell must have been a one-off, and it obviously wasn't memorable. Soon I had my two lovely kids, I had my nice house and my nice life, and a good husband who worked hard for us all. And I was living this huge lie, telling Katie, and anyone else who would listen to me, how passionately in love we were and how great everything was. It wasn't. It was so bloody awful that when we were on our own together, we were hardly even talking, never mind anything else.

I've sat for hours looking at myself in the mirror, wondering why Richard didn't fancy me, wondering what was wrong with me. It could drive you mad; in the end you give up caring.

Well, there's this guy at the gym. Andy. He started chatting to me when we were on the rowing machines next to each other. It's kind of hard having a conversation when you're puffing and panting like that, and after a few weeks he asked me to have a coffee with him afterwards, to carry on the conversation. We were having fun. He's divorced, no kids, teaches at the local sixth-form college so he's at the gym a lot during the daytime in the holidays. I started going there more often when I knew he'd be there. We got into the habit of having coffee afterwards every time. It wasn't hurting anyone, was it? I felt so much better, looking forward to seeing Andy, having a chat and a laugh with him, feeling like someone was *interested* in me. Then one day he asked me to go out for a drink with him in the evening.

I knew this was a turning point. If I crossed that invisible line, I was making myself available for an affair. And I wanted to – desperately.

That evening, when Richard got home from work, I'd put the kids to bed early. I put soft music on, turned down the lights, lit all the candles and cooked his favourite dinner. I served it wearing a black negligee with nothing on underneath.

He ate his dinner slowly, watching me carefully, without saying a word. When he'd finished I poured him some more wine and pulled him over to the sofa. I undid the negligee and sat astride his lap, put my arms round him, undid his collar and tie, started kissing his neck and his chest ... still he didn't say a word. I pushed him onto his back and dangled my boobs in his face. *Hold them. Suck them*, I was saying. *Take me. For Christ's sake, Richard, fuck me!* I grabbed his hand, pressed it against me, tried to take hold of *him*, but he wasn't even hard. *Please, Richard! Please!* I begged, starting to cry.

'What's the matter?' he asked tonelessly, as if he wasn't even remotely interested.

What's the matter? I need you! I need you to want me! I don't even care if you can't do it – if there's something wrong with you, if you can't do it any more, it doesn't matter, but I need you to at least WANT to!

He looked away from me and shrugged. That shrug made me so angry, I nearly hit him. I wanted to tell him: *This was your last chance. If you wanted me, I wouldn't go to some-one else.* Instead, I got up, got dressed, blew out the candles, put on the lights.

'I'm going out,' I told him, and went to meet Andy.

He turned on the TV as I walked out of the door.

We've never discussed it since. Does he know I'm seeing someone else? He surely must have guessed. In a way, I've got even less respect for him because of this – although it does at least mean I don't have to lie to him, as he never asks any questions.

Perhaps I should leave him. Andy wants me to, but I've got the kids to think about. They adore Richard and, as I say, he's a great dad, and a good husband too in lots of ways.

So now you know. To be honest it's a relief to talk about it.

Perfect Rick? The perfect Prick? Ha! You must be bloody joking.

ABOUT DUBLIN

'D'you think he's a closet gay?' says Emily. 'You hear about these things, don't you. They get married because they want a family and respectability, but they don't really want a woman.'

'Or perhaps he just doesn't like sex very much at all,' says Jude. 'Poor Lisa. Who'd ever have thought it?'

Emily yawns and looks at the clock. It's half past two. Apparently Lisa went to sleep as soon as she fell into bed – tired herself out with talking – so Emily came round to our room and we've been sitting here talking about it ever since. We've used up all the little sachets of tea, coffee and milk in the room and have all completely sobered up.

I still can't believe my sister's having an affair.

'She's always been such a kind of *shining example*. I thought she was better than me at everything.'

'Maybe she is!' laughs Emily. 'Sounds like she just didn't get a lot of opportunity to prove it, with Richard.'

'It's not funny!'

'No. But it gives a whole new meaning to that Truth or Dare game, doesn't it?'

'Poor Lisa,' repeats Jude sadly. 'Of all the unlucky questions for her to be asked – that one about begging for sex.'

'How humiliating for her. I could strangle bloody Perfect Prick. How dare he treat her with such ... such coldness? Such bloody *contempt*? He could at least have *pretended* ...'

'Would you *want* a man to pretend to fuck you, though?' points out Emily, and somehow this is so funny we all fall backwards on the beds laughing and yawning simultaneously.

'Wake me up when it's time for breakfast,' I mutter, closing my eyes.

'Jesus, God, are you not going to undress yourself and take your make-up off, Katie?' asks Jude in disbelief. She should know me better by now.

'No, I'm fucking not.'

'Well, I'd best be going back to my own room,' says Emily. 'Night night.'

'See you tomorrow,' I start – but I'm asleep before I even finish the *tomorrow*, and, fortunately, long before Jude's finished in the bathroom and put out the light.

Some of us are quiet at breakfast in the morning, and several of us have difficulty looking a fried egg in the face.

First in the queue for black coffee is Mum, who looks like she can hardly bear the sunlight coming in through the dining-room windows.

'How's your head?' I ask her gently, sitting down next to her with two slices of toast and marmalade.

'Not good, dear, I'm afraid. Oh, move that food away from under my nose, please, if you don't mind. The smell's making me feel a bit faint.'

'Sure you'll be fine when you've got a bit of fresh Dublin air in your lungs, Margie,' says Jude cheerfully, joining us and plonking her plate of sausages and fried potatoes down on the table. Mum winces and turns away, covering her mouth delicately with her serviette. 'It's a lovely day outside, so it is. I've been up since seven o'clock watching the world warm up.'

'She's a raving nutcase, Mum. She hasn't been watching the world, she's been doing her bloody hair and make-up!'

Mum tries to laugh but it obviously hurts her head. She groans and has a mouthful of coffee.

'I hope I wasn't embarrassing last night,' she says somewhat stiffly, 'while I was feeling under the weather?'

'Not a bit of it, Marge,' says Jude stoutly, 'You were grand altogether. Sure and we were all fluthered, were we not?'

'*Fluthered?*'

'Hammered, so we were – but didn't we have a great time and all? Is it beating the shit out of your own hen night at Southend, do you think, Margie?'

'Southend ... did I mention Southend last night, for God's sake?'

'Of course you did, Mum! You never left off going on about bloody Southend!' I laugh. 'It must have been fan-bloody-tastic, I'll give you that, the amount you keep going on about it!'

'It wasn't,' she says, dropping her coffee cup into the saucer with a crash. 'It wasn't good at all.' She looks stricken, like she's going to cry. 'I don't know what I was blabbing on about last night, but I've never told anyone the truth. It was a terrible day. It was the worst day of my entire life!'

'I feel awful leaving Mum and Auntie Joyce behind,' says Lisa as we leave the hotel a little later. 'Are you *sure* they didn't want to come?'

'I think Mum still feels a bit hungover. And Joyce looks knackered. I reckon she didn't get a lot of sleep – she says Mum was groaning and carrying on in her sleep all night. They'll both be fine if they stay here and rest, this morning.'

I haven't said anything to Lisa about Mum and the Southend Hen-Night Outburst. I feel pretty sure she's just feeling tired and overemotional, like we all do when we're recovering from a piss-up, and probably didn't mean it. Anyway, I'm hardly going to bother Lisa about it when she's spent half of last night spilling the beans about her own personal disaster.

'Are you feeling OK this morning?' I ask her quietly as we walk down the street together.

'Course I am!' she says sharply. 'Why wouldn't I be?'

Christ, has she forgotten it all already? Sobbing in our arms about the night her husband wouldn't look her in the eyes, or under her negligee? Confessing to an affair with a younger guy who wears black Lycra shorts and a sweat-band? It was such riveting stuff, you could have heard a pin drop in that bar last night.

'I'm absolutely fine,' she goes on, giving me a sideways look and a sly grin. 'I feel better than I have for months. I should have told you about it ages ago.'

Something about confession being good for the soul? Blimey. Maybe we should play Truth or Dare more often.

Today Jude's in charge. Emily asked her to organise some sightseeing, as she knows Dublin a lot better than any of us. We're all wearing the pink 'Hen Party' T-shirts and getting a few smiles as we walk through Temple Bar arm-in-arm. And a few comments.

'Is "Rather You Than Me, Love" the mainstay of Irish conversation about weddings?' I ask Jude a bit tersely after the fifth of these remarks from passers-by (all women).

'Can you blame them, when you look at what they're married to? Sure yer average Irish husband is a complete eejit, out on the piss every night of the week and about as much use to his wife as a babby.'

'That's a bit harsh!' laughs Emily. 'Maybe you should look for a nice English guy for yourself, then, Jude – or is Fergus the exception to the rule?'

She flushes and smiles.

'Well, to be fair to Fergus he does *not* go out on the booze every night, so I've no complaints in that department, now.'

'And what about the other department, eh, Jude?' Karen calls out, with a suggestive gesture that nearly stops a group of lads in their tracks as they're passing us in the street.

'Be off with you, you and your dirty mind!' But she's laughing and blushing and I think to myself – *I hope this Fergus realises just how sweet and lovely she is.*

'He'd better bloody treat you right,' I tell her fiercely, 'or I'll be over here to sort him out.'

'I'll let him know that, so I will, Katie! Now then, are y'all paying attention to your tour guide? As you know, we're in the Temple Bar area here, where most of the bars, live music and nightclubs are, so ...'

'So we'll just stay here then, shall we?' says Karen.

'No, we shall *not* be staying here, there's a city to explore and sure you'd not want to go home without visiting the famous Guinness Storehouse, would you?'

'Now you're talking,' says Helen appreciatively. Helen's a beer drinker and she spent most of last night on the Guinness, informing us with every single pint that it was the best she'd ever drunk. By the time she got to the last one I was surprised she could even remember the others, but there you go.

'Lead on, then, MacDuff, or should I say O'Duff?' quips Lisa in a lousy imitation of Jude's accent that makes us all laugh.

'Well, I thought we'd get ourselves a trip on the city bus tour. You can see some of the sights from the bus, and we'll get off at the Guinness building. Is that OK for you all?'

'Abso-bloody-lutely, Judy baby!' says Lisa, flinging an arm round her extravagantly. 'A bus would be great. I'm not up for walking too far on these bloody cobbles.'

'Jesus, God, will you listen to her giving out! Sure it's only in Temple Bar you'll see the cobbles, Lisa, and it won't kill you for a few minutes to walk on them either!'

'Yeah, Lisa, stop whingeing and keep up with the rest of us!' I tease her. 'How far to the bloody bus stop, Jude?'

We sit on the top deck of the bus, half listening to the commentary as we pass close to Dublin Castle and St Patrick's Cathedral. Suze, who's been frighteningly quiet this morning and didn't manage any breakfast, has fallen asleep by the time the bus arrives at the Guinness Storehouse, and we enjoy shouting in her ear to wake her up.

'Come on! Lovely Guinness!' says Emily cruelly, and we all laugh as she turns a bit green and clutches her stomach, promising never to drink again as long as she lives.

'Yeah, right,' mutters Karen. 'I'll give it a couple of hours at the most . . . '

Not everyone likes Guinness, but Jude tells us it's definitely impolite to refuse the complimentary pint in the bar at the top of the Storehouse, the highest bar in Dublin. After traipsing around the building looking at how it's made, I think the least we can do is enjoy a pint of it, and I'm gasping with thirst anyway, so it goes down a treat. Helen, however, is sipping hers reverently, with her eyes closed, like it's a religious experience. It's supposed to be the best Guinness you'll ever taste in your life. I nudge her, making her swear furiously when the beer splashes onto her jeans.

'Better than sex, is it?' I tease her.

She takes another sip, closing her eyes again, obviously considering this carefully.

'It's a close thing,' she says eventually. 'And it certainly lasts longer.'

The other girls fall about laughing at this all-too-obvious crack, but I smile back at Helen, because I know her, and she doesn't joke about things like this. I think she actually does prefer the Guinness. Maybe she's got a point.

We get back on the bus afterwards and finish the rest of the tour. Jude's doing her best to encourage us to listen to the commentary but by the time we end up back at Temple Bar again, Suze isn't the only one who's fallen asleep.

'Will you look at the lot of you – what a shower of bloody eejits!' she says in disgust. 'And there was I thinking you'd be up for a spot of lunch in one of these fine hostelries, with a little live music, but of course if you'd rather be back in your rooms asleep on your beds . . . '

We all seem to have woken up miraculously at the mention of lunch and hostelries.

Lisa takes it upon herself, despite complaints about the cobbles, to go back to the hotel to bring Mum and Auntie Joyce out to join us for lunch. We find a table in one of the biggest bars, where the live music consists of a lone singer, accompanying himself on the guitar.

'He could do with cheering up a bit,' I whisper to Jude. 'Music to slit your wrists by, or what?'

'Oh, he'll liven up in a while,' says Jude with surprising confidence. 'Come on, let's get something to eat, for God's sake – it's been hours since breakfast and me stomach feels like me throat's been cut.'

That's another strange thing about Jude. For someone so slim and petite, she's got the appetite of a horse. Where does she put it all? Why doesn't she ever get an ounce of fat on her bones? And why am I already feeling like I'm two dress sizes bigger than yesterday, after just one night of booze and junk food? Why is life so full of unfairness and contradiction? Why am I sitting here feeling sorry for myself in the middle of a gang of riotous crazy friends whose only mission in life is to get me pissed?

'Get that down you,' says Emily, plonking a glass of white wine in front of me.

Seems churlish to refuse, really.

Within ten minutes we're all back on the booze, even those who pledged only a few hours ago to give it up forever. We've ordered sandwiches and we're getting stuck into packets of crisps and nuts as if we've never eaten before. It must be the fresh air.

Mum's sitting next to me, sipping delicately at her glass of wine, giving it the occasional suspicious look as if something's going to leap out of it and bite her.

'Just take it easier today and you'll be fine,' I tell her quietly.

I feel a bit sorry for her, and guilty for letting her get drunk last night. Lisa and I should have kept more of an eye on her. She's not really used to the amount of drink we were putting away.

'I know. I'm not daft,' she says tetchily. 'You don't have to treat me as if I'm five years old.'

'I'm not! Sorry! I just thought ... you're not used to it ...'

She gives a little laugh that isn't really a laugh, and mutters something into her wine glass just at the same moment that the singer suddenly leaps to his feet, grabs a violin from under the table, and is joined by another guy who'd been sitting, apparently half asleep, at a neighbouring table, who produces a tin whistle out of his pocket. Without seeming to pause for breath they immediately launch into a frenetic Irish jig, swaying together dangerously, fingers moving like sparks of electricity on the whistle and the fiddle, tapping their feet and nodding their heads in time to the music but never passing a smile or even a blink towards each other. The explosion of this music into the bar is so dramatic and unexpected that we're all sitting up, staring, open-mouthed, for a good two or three minutes, before a couple of people at the back of the room start clapping in time and, amazingly, someone else produces a mouth organ and begins, still sitting at his own table, to join in with the tune.

'This is bloody great!' exclaims Emily. 'I can't believe it!'

'You'd never get this down the White Hart at home on a Friday night,' I agree.

It's probably about another five minutes before I think to look back at Mum again. And by then she's finished the glass of wine and started on the next one.

'Hey! I thought you said you were going to take it a bit easier today,' I laugh.

'No, Katie, I didn't. *You* said I was going to,' she says, taking another mouthful.

'Well, OK – come on, I didn't mean anything … I just didn't think you were quite used to it … so be careful. You'll get drunk again really quickly 'cos you're topping up from last night …'

The look she gives me is something I'm going to remember for the rest of my life.

'I have had a bit too much to drink once or twice before in my life, thank you very much,' she says very calmly.

Hearing this, Auntie Joyce stops swaying and tapping on the table and leans across to touch Mum on the arm and whisper to her:

'All right, Margie. That's enough, isn't it. No need to—'

'No need? What, I'm not allowed to talk to my own daughter, now? When she's getting married in a few weeks' time?'

'Let's just eat our sandwiches, Mum!' I laugh, feeling embarrassed. 'Sorry I said anything about the wine. OK?'

'I *like* a drop of wine,' she says a bit huffily by way of agreement, taking another long swig.

I watch her warily. Whatever she says, this is taking social drinking a little too fast. Joyce, obviously thinking the same, leans across again and asks her quietly:

'Are you all right, love?'

'Of course I'm all right!' she retorts. Her glass is empty. This is bothering me. 'Who wants another drink?'

A sea of surprised faces turns towards her. We're all still holding full glasses.

'Margie,' says Joyce firmly, laying a hand on her arm, 'Don't do this, love. Not today. Don't spoil the day for Katie.'

For a horrible moment, I think there's going to be a row. Mum shakes Joyce's arm off, picks up her glass and starts to get up. She's going to the bar to buy another drink.

No, she's not.

She slumps back in her seat, hangs her head for a moment, and when she looks up she's wearing a very false, very bright smile.

'Thank you, Joyce,' she says. 'You're quite right. Of course I don't want to spoil things for Katie. My little Katie.' She turns to give me a lopsided smile. 'My baby girl – all grown up and getting married! *Married!*'

'All right! No need to cry about it,' I say. It's a feeble attempt at a joke. Mum looks as if she *is* going to cry.

'Cry? You'd cry all right, girl, if you were marrying someone like I did.'

This isn't really what I want to hear. 'Come off it, Mum. You and Dad were happy enough at the beginning, weren't you. Fair enough, it didn't last, but . . .'

'Happy!' She shakes her head, snorting with mirthless laughter. 'If only you knew, dear. If only you knew!'

'Margie,' warns Joyce again. 'Let's not get started on all that, just now.'

'Why not? Don't you want to hear all about it, Katie? Hm? Your mother's hen night? It's quite a story. '

'I think we've already heard it, Mum.' Bloody hell, not Southend again, surely!

'I don't really think this is the time, do you?' repeats Joyce, gripping Mum's arm and looking at her very pointedly.

'No time like the present,' she responds heartily, looking with disappointment at her empty wine glass. 'Why shouldn't I tell my daughter about my wedding, eh, Joyce? Kind of fitting, don't you think – make her realise how lucky she is not to be marrying a *pig* like her father?'

Oh, God.

The only thing I'm grateful for is that no one else can hear. They're all too busy singing along with 'Whisky in the Jar.'

MARGIE'S STORY

It's the hen party, you see. It's brought back all these memories.

I was only twenty when I got married. Even so, I wasn't the first of my group of friends to *tie the knot*, as we used to call it in those days. It was fairly normal to marry young, because, as I tried to explain to Katie, it still wasn't quite the done thing to live together before you were married. Not in our part of suburbia, anyway, whatever might have been going on up in Swinging London.

Terry was twenty-five, and a fireman. He was drop-dead gorgeous. I couldn't believe my luck when he asked me out – never mind when he asked me to marry him. One of my friends said afterwards that I couldn't get him up the aisle fast enough; I suppose she had a point. I reckoned if I hung on too long he might get fed up and find someone else.

As it was, I was always worried about him going off with other girls. *Birds*, he called them. Men don't use that term nowadays – it's considered insulting, isn't it.

'Margie,' he used to say; 'Margie, why would I be thinking of running off with some other bird, eh, when I've got my little princess?'

But there was no getting away from the fact that he used to eye up all the other *birds*, even if he wasn't thinking of running off with them. You couldn't really blame him. He was so good-looking, the girls would turn their heads in the street to look at him, even when I was with him. They'd giggle and toss their hair and wiggle their bums, and he'd just smile and pretend he wasn't interested, but what man wouldn't be? I was anxious to get that wedding ring on his finger pretty smartly, I can tell you.

I wasn't supposed to be seeing Terry on the night of my hen party. It was meant to be unlucky for the couple to see each other the day before the wedding. He was having his stag do at his local pub in Brentwood, and he phoned me before he went out.

'You be careful tonight,' he told me. 'Don't go drinking too much and getting yourself into trouble!'

I didn't normally drink much more than a couple of Bacardi-and-Cokes. That was everybody's favourite drink in those days.

'Don't be silly!' I said. 'Shirley's looking after me. And anyway, *I* don't drink too much. It's *you* that has to be careful!'

'Don't you worry about me, darlin'. I can handle it! See you in church tomorrow, eh?'

Less than twenty-four hours till I'd be Mrs Terry Halliday. I thought I was the happiest girl in the world.

My friends were the other student nurses I worked with at the hospital: Angela, Linda and Shirley. Shirley was my best mate; she was two years older than me, already married and very sensible, so I wasn't worried. She'd make sure I got home all right even if I did have a few drinks. It was Shirley's idea to go to Southend.

'It'll be much more fun than sitting in the local pub,' she said. 'We can have a drink, get a Chinese, maybe go bowling on the pier.'

See what I mean? We didn't expect so much, in those days. Just a nice evening out with our friends. None of this dressing up they go in for nowadays, and certainly none of these naughty games with dares and forfeits and things. Girls used to be a lot more *civilised*, if you know what I mean. We used to leave the excessive behaviour to the blokes. That was considered normal; we didn't expect any better of them.

Well, anyway, we went to Southend on the train and had a couple of drinks in a pub on the seafront. I'm not saying we didn't get a bit silly and giggly, but that was just excitement. I remember Angela – a nice, quiet girl, younger than me, who'd only left home a few months before – admitting she was still a virgin and the rest of us all teasing her and suggesting how she should go about finding somebody to change that for her. We might have got a bit rude, I suppose, but we weren't *loud* with it. We didn't get complaints from other people in the pub. We were just enjoying ourselves.

We went on to the Chinese restaurant. It was a bit of a treat in those days, not like now, with people having a takeaway any time they don't feel like cooking. We used to have proper old-fashioned dinners every night of the week – steak and kidney pudding, shepherd's pie, toad in the hole. Our mums taught us to cook; there weren't any of these ready-made microwave meals in the shops then, you know. So none of us were very good at choosing what to have from the menu in the Chinese, and we ended up ordering a bit of almost everything, and sharing it around. For some reason we found sweet and sour pork balls absolutely hilarious and kept passing them from plate to plate, getting more and more hysterical the more glasses of white wine we had. But I still maintain it was all perfectly innocent fun, nothing rowdy, nothing spilt on the tablecloth – you understand?

By the time we came out of the restaurant we couldn't be bothered to go tenpin bowling. We were probably a little bit too tipsy for it, or at least, I certainly was. Not that I was incapable of walking straight, or anything like that. It was June – a lovely summer evening – and we strolled along the seafront arm in arm, just chatting and laughing, and ended up at the Kursaal.

You wouldn't know about the Kursaal as it was then: it was an amusement park – probably the biggest and best in the country, in its day. Our parents used to take us there when we were kids, as a big treat on a day out at the seaside. You youngsters don't know you're born, what with your foreign holidays and day trips to France at the drop of a hat, just to go shopping for wine and cheese. We thought we were in heaven when we had a day out at Southend. We used to go swimming in the sea, too – never mind that it was mud right up to our knees, never mind all the warnings nowadays about dirty beaches, turning everyone into namby-pambies if you ask me. A candyfloss and a few pennies to spend on the rides in the Kursaal kept us kids more than happy back in the 1950s, even if we *were* wearing hand-me-down clothes and our school plimsolls.

Anyway, as I was saying – the Kursaal, by this time, 1972 – was past its best and in fact it closed down, I think, a year or so later. But we had a ball, there, that night. We only left, in the end, because we'd run out of money. We went on all the rides, had a go at all the hooplas, shooting galleries, coconut shies, you name it; and we laughed until we cried – not about anything in particular, just out of the sheer fun and excitement of being out together, the four of us, the night before my wedding.

We saved the Big Dipper till last. You must have heard of the Big Dipper. It was the biggest thrill in the park: the original roller coaster ride. Oh, I suppose it would be tame by today's standards – nowadays something's only a thrill if it's so dangerous you have to have a medical before you go on it – but it made us scream ourselves hoarse, I can tell you. Going up that first long steep climb to the top of the ride, my heart was in my mouth, and as we lurched over the top and sped full-pelt down the other side, dipped at the bottom and shot back up again, I could feel my chop suey and sweet and sour pork balls shooting back up too.

I seemed to be the only one who felt sick afterwards. It was getting late so we walked back to the station anyway. The others were teasing me.

'You've gone white!'

'No, green! You've gone green! Your face matches your cardigan!'

I couldn't talk. I was too busy concentrating on putting one foot in front of the other and not throwing up on the pavement.

'Will you be all right on the train?' Shirley asked me anxiously as we waited on the platform.

I nodded yes, but moving my head made everything spin. I held onto her arm and allowed myself to be helped up into the carriage of the last train back to Romford.

I managed to hold on till we were almost at Brentwood – only a few stops from home – and then I suddenly knew I was going to be sick.

'Get the window open!' yelled Linda. 'Get her some fresh air!'

'No!' I mumbled, my hand over my mouth, trying to stop myself from vomiting. 'No! Got to get off! Going to be s . . . '

Fortunately for me, and for everyone else in the carriage, the train pulled into the station just at that moment. I wrenched the door open, stumbled out, ran to the fence at the back of the platform and threw up over the bushes. Hanging onto the fence, panting and trying to wipe my mouth with my hankie, I heard Shirley behind me saying:

'Well, I expect you'll feel better now. But I think we'll have to get a taxi home.'

I looked round just in time to see the train disappearing down the track. The last train. Apparently, at Shirley's insistence, Linda and Angela had stayed on the train but she'd jumped off to look after me.

'No point all four of us being stranded,' she said briskly.

'Thank you,' I said feebly. 'Sorry. You should have gone on, too.'

'Don't be ridiculous. I wouldn't dream of leaving you on your own. Come on, let's get outside and see what a taxi will cost.'

'But I haven't got any money left!'

We didn't have credit or debit cards in those days. No cash machines on every corner. You either had cash, and spent it, or you didn't, and you had to go without.

'Nor have I. I'll have to wake Graham up when we get back, and get him to pay the taxi. If he's got enough money at home.'

'Or I could phone my dad to come and pick us up,' I said doubtfully, knowing how annoyed he'd be to be woken up so late, the night before the wedding that he and Mum had worked so hard to organise.

'No, that wouldn't be fair. He'd be cross.'

We joined the queue for taxis outside the station.

'It's going to be a long wait,' I said gloomily. 'And it's going to be very expensive ... and it's all my fault.' I stopped, suddenly laughing out loud. 'Hang on a minute. How bloody stupid of me! We don't need to get a taxi, or a lift back to Romford tonight. We can wait till the morning!'

'What the bloody hell are you talking about, Marge? Are you still drunk? What, you want to sleep on the pavement here? You want to miss your wedding or something?'

'No! For God's sake! It's obvious, isn't it. We can stay at Terry's place.'

Terry rented a room in a house with two other blokes, only a five-minute walk from Brentwood station. It was his last night there, of course – we were moving into our own place straight after the wedding. It was easier, then, you see – getting a mortgage – and we'd just managed to get in before the huge leap in house prices that happened about that time.

'Don't be silly, we can't go there,' said Shirley, grabbing my arm to pull me back into the queue. 'You mustn't see him tonight. It's bad luck!'

'Oh, that's rubbish! I'm not superstitious. Come on, he won't mind. We can get the first train in the morning and I'll still have time to get ready for the wedding.'

'I'll have to phone Graham ...' said Shirley, doubtfully, looking around for a phone-box. 'I'm not really sure we should ...'

'Yes, we should.' I pulled her along the street by the arm. 'Come on, you can phone Graham from Terry's place.'

She gave in, then – I suppose because it did seem the best option – but she was still looking worried as we walked up to the door of the old terraced house the boys shared, and I rang the doorbell.

'They're probably all in bed,' she said anxiously.

The house was certainly in darkness. For the first time, it occurred to me that the boys might not even be in. They'd been out on Terry's stag night, after all, and even though the pubs were shut by now, they could well have gone on somewhere else.

'I suppose we could sit on the doorstep and wait,' I said, looking up and down the street in the vague hope of seeing them coming home.

But just then a light went on upstairs.

'Yeah!' I laughed with relief. 'Good old Terry. Home early and asleep in bed – good for him!'

Well, as it happened, he'd certainly come home early and gone to bed – that much was true, anyway.

I can still see the look on his face when he opened the front door and saw us standing on the step.

'Margie! Christ almighty! What the hell ...!'

'Hello!' I said, giggling.

I started to lift my face to his for a kiss, but thought better of it when I remembered that my breath would be vomit-laced. But he showed no sign of wanting to kiss me anyway. Instead he looked behind him, nervously.

'Sorry – did I wake you up? Only we've missed the last train, and—'

'I thought you were supposed to be in Southend!' he said. I was taken aback by the tone of his voice.

'We were. But I didn't feel well, so ... look, can we come in, and I'll explain?'

'I thought it was the other blokes coming home, ringing the bell,' he went on, ignoring me. Once again, he looked over his shoulder, and then dropped his voice to a whisper. 'I don't think you ought to come in, Marge. It's the night before the wedding, isn't it. We're not supposed to see each other.'

'Come on, Marge,' said Shirley. 'Let's go back and get a taxi. Terry's right. We shouldn't have come.'

'That's *rubbish*!' I exclaimed, getting annoyed. 'It's just stupid superstition, and anyway, I need to go to the toilet. I'll wet myself if I have to walk back to the station now! Come on, Terry, let us in, for God's sake. We'll sleep in the lounge if you're worried about stupid old wives' tales. We can pretend we didn't see each other! Only we can't afford a taxi and—'

'Who's that, Tel?'

The girl was very tall – taller than him, I remember noticing – with long, long, straight black hair that fell over her shoulders and down to her waist. She was wearing his dressing gown. It was navy blue with his initials on the pocket. I'd bought it for him for Christmas. It would always smell of her now. She reached out to put her arms round him and the dressing gown gaped open. She was naked underneath.

'What's going on, Tel?' she asked, stroking his arm as she stared at us.

I was struck dumb.

'It's all right, Barb,' he said. His voice was shaking. His eyes looked wildly from me to her. It wasn't all right at all, and he knew it.

'Terry ...' began Shirley. 'Terry, what the *fucking hell* are you playing at?'

'Oi, bitch!' said the girl, pushing past Terry to square up to Shirley on the doorstep. 'Who you talking to? Watch yer fucking mouth! Who do you two think you are anyway, turning up 'ere in the middle of the fucking night?'

'I'm Margie,' I said, faintly, finding my voice at last. 'I'm Margie, *Barb*, that's who I am. I'm supposed to be marrying *Tel* in the morning. And I paid for that *fucking* dressing gown. So you can get out of it before I rip it off you, and then you can sling your bloody hook.'

It should have been satisfying to watch her turn on Terry and slap him round the face, shrieking at him that he should have told her he was engaged. It should have been even more satisfying to see the red welt come up on his white cheek as she stormed upstairs, stomped back down with her clothes on and tottered off down the street in her four-inch high stilettos.

But it wasn't. I cried all the way home in the taxi. Some bloody hen night! Some bloody husband.

And that was the start of my married life. Now can you see where I'm coming from? Can you understand why I get a little bit depressed thinking about weddings and hen parties?

I'm sorry, Katie darling. But is it any wonder I like a little bit of a drink now and again?

ABOUT A LITTLE DRINK ... NOW AND AGAIN

'Why on earth did you still marry him?'

I look round, startled. It's Helen, her voice surprisingly gentle, reaching across the pub table to touch Mum on the hand. I didn't realise she'd been listening.

'You don't know what it's like,' says Mum, staring into her empty glass. She's sobered up completely. Understandably. 'It's harder than you think, cancelling everything, and all at the last minute like that. Can you imagine it? The embarrassment – all the family getting upset.'

'But surely ...' I shake my head, unable to take this in. I mean – look – you *wouldn't,* would you! You find another woman in his house, in his fucking *dressing gown*, and you still go ahead and walk down the aisle with him the next day? I think *not*! 'Did you not even *want* to call it off?' I suppose I could understand it if the wedding was the next year, or even the next month – time to think about it, talk it over, kick him in the bollocks a few times, whatever, but – the *next day*? 'Mum? Just because of the family being embarrassed? It was your *life*!'

'I know, I know!' she says fiercely. 'Of course I wanted to call it off. I was shaking with rage by the time I got home that night – I'd done all my crying in the taxi, on poor Shirley's shoulders. I poured myself a whisky from the bottle my dad kept in the sideboard for special occasions. On top of the booze I'd had during the evening, it went straight to my head, but I drank a second one straight down. I sat in

68

the lounge, trying to decide what to do. To be honest, the thought of telling everyone – my parents, all my friends – the vicar! – was almost as bad as the thought of going ahead and marrying him. When Terry phoned, he was crying. Nice touch. Apparently he'd already tried earlier, before I got in, and woke up my dad, who thought he was drunk and wasn't very amused. "He's going to be a lot less amused,' I said, "When I tell him why I'm calling off the wedding." He sobbed, begged me to give him another chance ...'

'Huh! He'd never have got another chance with *me*,' says Helen through gritted teeth. 'He'd have been lucky if he ever walked again.'

'Yes, I'm sure!' retorts Mum. 'But you're a strong, confident woman, Helen. I was stupid, and young, and naïve. And I believed everything he said.'

'What *did* he say?' I ask her quietly.

I feel light-headed with the shock of all this. I can't believe Mum's kept it to herself all these years. Why hasn't she told Lisa or me about it? If my dad was still around I think I'd kill him. Kind of difficult as we haven't seen or heard of him for about fifteen years. The bastard.

'Oh, you can imagine. That it was a one-off. She came on to him, he was drunk, he didn't know what he was doing. It didn't mean anything; he was sorry, ashamed, disgusted with himself. It'd never happen again, he'd make it up to me, he'd never look at another woman as long as he lived ...'

'Yeah, right,' says Helen angrily. 'Typical.'

'And did he?' I ask. My voice comes out a bit croaky. I'm not sure I really want to hear the answer. 'Did he ever do it again?'

'Of course he did it again,' she says without looking at us. 'All the bloody time. Every year a different girl. Every time a different excuse. Always the same old song – please forgive me, never again, blah de blah de blah. It took me eight years to realise I was being made a bloody fool of. He was still crying and protesting that he loved me and he'd never do it again when the divorce came through.'

'You always told us you got divorced because you just argued too much.'

'What did you expect me to do?' she demanded. 'How could I tell two little girls that their daddy was a lying, heartless, adulterous pig?'

This is a lovely thing to find out about on your hen party.

I feel sorry for Mum, of course I do, but at the same time I can't believe she's chosen now, of all times, to tell me about this shit. How the bloody hell is *this* supposed to cheer me and encourage me on my way to wedded bliss? *Your father was a lying pig who cheated on me the whole time we were together. Can't wait to see you married, darling.*

'Sorry, love,' she says, a bit shakily, blinking at me as if there are a million tears in her eyes, never to be shed. 'Me and my big mouth. Take no notice. Forget I spoke.'

'Oh – just like that? That's great, that is . . .'

'What's the matter, Katie?' calls Lisa, hearing me raising my voice.

I hesitate. I think this'd be one home truth too many for Lisa at the moment, after all her own outpourings last night. We'll have to talk about it another time. I catch Mum's eye and shake my head.

'Nothing!' I tell Lisa, trying to sound cheery. 'Just having a laugh about something down this end of the table.' Yeah, a laugh a minute, we are.

'And what's all this about you liking a drink?' I ask Mum a bit crossly when everyone else is chatting again. 'Should I be worried about this, Mum? What are you trying to tell me?'

'Nothing. Don't be silly; of course you shouldn't be worried, dear. For goodness' sake! Anyone would think I was an alcoholic!' She gives a silly peal of laughter. Lisa looks up again and frowns at me.

I don't want to start anything while we're all intent on tipping as much alcohol as possible down our throats this weekend. It's hardly appropriate.

'As long as you're all right, Mum,' I tell her quietly. 'Only – for God's sake! You've worried the life out of me now, with all this. Are you depressed? Do you think you should be seeing someone?'

'No, Katie, I'm not depressed. This all happened a long time ago. I'm over it. All I'm saying is that I like a little drink occasionally when I get fed up with myself. Nothing wrong with that, is there?'

'I suppose not. I just wish you hadn't chosen today to tell me this stuff.'

'It's your hen party!' she says, looking at me with alarm as if she's only just realised. 'I've ruined it.'

'No. You haven't. But can we *please* talk about something else now? Something more cheerful?'

'Your wedding?' She smiles.

'No. Not that, at the minute. Let's talk about Dublin. Or music. Or books. Or the political situation in the Middle East.'

Anything but marriage, at the moment! Anything!

It's late in the afternoon by the time we get back to the hotel.

'If I never have meself another comfort in this life,' says Jude as we go up to our room, 'Sure I swear to God I won't complain, if I can just have a nice cup of tea and a hot bath.'

'Me too. And an hour's kip under the duvet. Jesus, I can't believe I actually brought *Love in the Afternoon* with me, and expected to read any of it. I'm too tired to even focus my eyes properly.'

'*Love in the Afternoon*? Would you look at the lot of us? We look more like Death in the Afternoon.'

We're giggling together as we stumble into the room, fighting over running the bath and making a cup of tea.

Thank God for friends, I think to myself, watching Jude padding about the room getting her oils and potions ready for her bath. Within less than twenty-four hours I've found out my sister's having an affair and my father was a cheating bastard who ruined my mum's life. Times like this, friends seem like a very good option indeed.

An hour or so later, I feel a lot better. It's amazing what a bath, a couple of cups of tea and a nap can do; and I've even managed to read the first page of *Love in the Afternoon*, although so far (and experience has taught me it isn't fair to

71

judge a book on its first page any more than its cover), I have to say that it doesn't seem to have much to do with either love, or afternoons, but presumably that's all to come. The reason I haven't got any further than the first page is that every time I try to concentrate, I find my mind drifting and I start remembering things.

Lisa's wedding, for instance. She had a lovely wedding to Rick the Prick – by all accounts the only really nice day they've had together. I recall thinking at the time how nice Mum looked in her sea-green mother-of-the-bride suit, matching hat and shoes, and fixed smile. Now I come to think about it in more detail, was her smile just a little *too* fixed? Certainly she put away a lot of champagne while she was waxing lyrical to everyone about her lovely new son-in-law. She was completely drunk by the end of the reception. She tripped, and almost fell, on her way out to the car when it was time to go home, and blamed it on the new shoes. But then again – come on! Every mother gets a little bit tipsy at their own daughter's wedding. We were all pretty drunk that day, as far as I can remember.

And look what happened when Charlie was born. Her first grandchild! She was ecstatic when Rick phoned from the hospital with the news. She got out the wine glasses and said we should all drink a toast to the new baby. It seemed like a good idea. That's what people do: wet the baby's head. Except in her case, she nearly bloody drowned it. We all laughed about it at the time – Joyce and Ron and I, and even Rick when he called in later on his way home from the maternity ward, to find the new grandma virtually passed out in the chair. We'd all stopped at one drink, but she'd just gone on ... and on. ... Fair enough, we thought – it's not every day someone becomes a grandmother. Let her enjoy her little drink.

She did the same thing when Matt and I got engaged. It was low-key. We didn't want a party or anything like that – bad enough with all the fuss of the wedding. But we called round to show Mum the ring and her instant response was: 'Let's get the bottle out! This calls for a celebration!' And of course by the time we left, she'd celebrated so hard we couldn't even wake her up to say goodbye.

I'm not worried about any of this. After all, everyone has a few drinks on these occasions, don't they – I'm hardly one to talk. I was drunk on and off pretty well the whole way through university. I suppose I just assumed that Mum got drunk quickly because she wasn't used to it.

But now I'm thinking about it – doesn't she seem to have a glass of wine to hand most of the time when I call round to see her? Doesn't she always have 'a little pre-dinner drink' while she's cooking the evening meal? As well as the frequent top-ups during and after dinner?

But I'm not at all concerned about that. As she admitted today, she might like a couple of little drinks to cheer her up – doesn't everyone? But she's obviously only drinking in moderation, because I can't remember ever seeing her drunk before, apart from those special family occasions. Everyone gets drunk at those. I've never even thought about it before.

So I'm not going to start now.

For God's sake! As if there wasn't enough to worry about! This is *not* a problem. OK? Just keep reminding me, if I seem to be reading too much into it. I've got enough problems of my own without taking on those of the whole family right now.

Or maybe that's the point. Maybe worrying about everyone else's problems is stopping me thinking too much about Matt.

ABOUT HARRY

As arranged, we meet up again at half past seven in the hotel bar, and the first thing I notice when I walk in is that Emily's got another big carrier bag under the table. Surprisingly, and I know this makes me sound slightly dim, only the *second* thing I notice is that everyone is in school uniform.

'Oh, no,' I say weakly. 'What the bloody hell ...?'

Everyone – even Mum and Auntie Joyce. They've got fishnet tights on, white shirts and school ties, and Joyce has even managed to plait her hair into pigtails which must have taken some doing as it isn't very long.

'But Jude hasn't ...' I begin, and then I realise why Jude told me to go on ahead as she hadn't finished getting dressed. 'The crafty minx!'

'Come on, let's go back to your room and see how Jude's getting on,' says Emily with a wicked gleam in her eyes, picking up the carrier bag.

'I know what's in that bag.'

'It could be worse,' she says, laughing, pushing me ahead of her. 'We considered Naughty Nurses or Mischievous Maids, but we thought Sexy Schoolgirls would be less embarrassing for you.'

'Nice of you, I'm sure. Why?'

'Wait till you get the outfit on. You'll thank me for it.'

It's a micro-gymslip, barely covering my bum. Fortunately it comes with matching navy-blue knickers, but I'm tugging it down as I walk and terrified to bend even an inch from the waist. To go with this trendy and sophisticated garment are: a pair of knee-high white socks, black plimsolls, a regulation blue school shirt, striped tie and a school hat. I look at myself

74

in the mirror and see a reflection of the most unpopular prefect at my school looking back at me.

'Brilliant!' says Jude, who's already got herself kitted out in a blazer and skirt.

'Terrific!' agrees Emily, holding me at arm's length and surveying me. 'Now we just need the badge.'

She pins a big badge on my tie that says NAUGHTY SCHOOL-GIRL BRIDE.

'There you go. Now, can you be trusted to behave yourself tonight?'

'No!'

'Good! Let's go, girls!'

I thought we were going out straight away, but Emily's got other ideas in mind.

'It's too early for dinner,' she says. 'We need to work up an appetite.'

'Doing what?' I ask warily. 'I am *not* going to the gym on my hen weekend ...'

'They wouldn't let us in, dressed like this,' points out Helen. 'Over eighteens only.'

'We're going to have a treasure hunt,' announces Emily, ushering us all back to our tables in the bar and handing out sheets of paper. 'Winner gets to choose where we go for dinner.'

Everyone goes quiet as we study the papers.

'So what's the idea?' we're all saying at once – but Auntie Joyce, surprisingly, is one step ahead of us.

'I know. I've been on car rallies like this, with my ladies' group. You have to run around and find the things on the list. The first one back to base with all the items is the winner.'

'Bloody hell,' I say. Most of the others are stunned into silence. 'Are you *sure*, Emily?'

'You've got half an hour,' she says cheerfully. 'Get as many of the things as you can, but you must be back here at eight fifteen. OK?'

'Hang on, hang on,' says Mum, looking worried. Who can blame her?

'Do you not want to play, Margie?' asks Jude sympathetically. 'Sure you could just sit here with Emily and be one of the judges, could she not, Emily?'

'Don't be silly, Jude – of course I want to play!' she retorts indignantly. 'I just think – the way we're dressed – don't you think we'd be safer, Emily dear, in a strange city like this with so many drunken savages on the streets, if we go out in twos?'

'You've got a point, actually, Marge. Good idea. But don't go straying too far from the hotel, anyway. You should be able to find most of these things without leaving the building.'

Speak for yourself. There are things on this list I wouldn't know where to look for even if I had the whole world at my disposal!

Lisa pairs up with Mum for the game, and I find myself with Auntie Joyce.

'Come along, dear,' she says gamely, grabbing the list from me and pulling me out of the door. 'Let's show them what we're made of!'

'But where the hell are we going to find a red thong, for a start?'

She looks at me in surprise.

'Well, that's probably the easiest one on the list, Katie. I've got one in my room. Come along!'

I should have learnt by now. However well you know somebody, you can *always* be surprised by their underwear.

We've got the red thong, a chocolate condom, and we're on our way to the kitchens to ask for a phallic-shaped vegetable when Joyce suddenly takes hold of my arm and says:

'I'm only going to say this once, dear.'

Oh boy. I don't like the sound of this.

'Don't be too hard on your mum.'

'I presume you knew all about this? This stuff about my dad?'

'I've known for a good few years. Don't forget I was only a little girl when she got married.'

'To be honest, Auntie Joyce, I can't even begin to get my head round it at the minute.'

'Of course not. It was bad timing, telling you this weekend. She's absolutely beside herself with guilt for upsetting you just before your wedding ...'

76

'It's OK. I'm not upset. At the minute I'm just numb. I'll have to deal with it when I get home, I suppose.'

'You're not angry with her?'

It's nice of Joyce to be concerned; she's probably worried that there's going to be a major family bust-up and no one's going to be speaking to each other on the wedding day.

'Don't worry about it,' I tell her calmly. 'I'm not going to freak out. I'm here to have a good time, and that's what I intend to do.'

'Good girl,' she says, squeezing my hand.

I'm just ignoring the wobble in her voice.

Everyone gets a bit emotional on hen weekends, don't they.

It's a laugh and a half when we make it back to the bar just before eight fifteen. We're the last-but-one pair back ... the only ones still missing are Helen and Jude.

'You haven't got Number Six – Most Gorgeous Bloke You Could Find,' says Emily accusingly.

'Sorry. Ran out of time. Who's that sitting next to Mum?' I ask, dropping my voice.

'The most gorgeous bloke she and Lisa could find, obviously.'

'Christ. I don't think much of their taste!'

But then again, what could you expect, considering Rick the Prick?

We're comparing notes with the others while we wait for Helen and Jude. Everyone seems to have raided the kitchen for carrots, cucumbers and bananas, and we all seem to have managed to get our photos taken with someone young enough to be a real naughty schoolgirl; but it looks as though the only ones to have brought back a sex toy are Karen and Suze. I really *don't* want to ask whose it is ... they're sharing a room, for God's sake!

'It's not *mine*!' says Karen indignantly in response to the look I'm giving her.

'I only brought it along,' says Suze, trying her best to look prim and proper about it, 'because I've been to these things before and there's *always* a game where someone needs a vibrator.'

I raise my eyebrows at her.

'And I won it in the raffle at an Ann Summers party,' she adds, raising her eyebrows back. 'Before you ask!'

'What about the phone number?' says Emily, ignoring us all. 'Did anyone manage that one? I thought that'd be the hardest.'

'Phone number of a guy who speaks Irish? Yep! Got one!' I say triumphantly. 'Bet no one else has …'

'Yes we have,' retorts Mum. 'It was easy. Nowadays they all seem to be learning it at school over here.'

'We'll check those in a minute,' says Emily. 'And: Gorgeous Man – you seem to have cornered the market there, Marge and Lisa. Well done.'

Their Gorgeous Man (who so *isn't*) gives them a smarmy grin, showing no sign of wanting to leave. Obviously got nothing better to do on a Saturday night.

'And where are those other two?' says Mum, looking a bit anxious. 'They're very late …'

Right on cue, in come Jude and Helen, huffing and puffing as if they've run all the way back, dragging behind them a tall blond guy who makes everyone in the room (even Mum's Gorgeous Man, I'm afraid to say), sit up very straight and do all the smoothing of hair, blinking of eyes, crossing of legs and stuff that goes on when you see somebody really, *really* sexy.

'Bloody hell,' whispers Emily in my ear. 'They've won. No contest!'

'But they're late!'

'Who cares?'

'And what about all the other items?'

'They don't count!'

'Huh!' I mutter, but to be honest, right at that moment, looking at Mr Totally Sexy, who's walking across the bar towards me, I have to admit I agree with her.

'Hi!' Jesus, his voice is as sexy as he looks. Shouldn't be allowed! 'I take it you're the bride-to-be?'

'Y..y..yes!' Haven't blushed and stuttered like this since I was about thirteen. 'I'm Katie.'

That's about all I can manage to say. I *so* wish I wasn't wearing a gymslip and holding Joyce's red thong on my lap. I stuff it down the side of my chair but I think, from the smile in his eyes (*gorgeous*) and the crinkle of his mouth (*breathtaking*), he's already noticed.

'Katie,' he says, as if it's the name of an exotic foreign holiday destination or a really expensive perfume. 'Katie, it's great to meet you. *Love* the uniform!' He looks me up and down. I give the mini-gymslip a futile tug in the direction of the knee socks. 'I'm Harry, by the way. Hope you're having a good weekend?'

'Yes! Thank you! Great, really great!' I gabble, unable to take my eyes off him. I can hardly wait to ask Jude and Helen where the hell they found him. 'Are you ... um ... on holiday in Dublin yourself, or do you, like, um, live here?' Shit, if I can't manage to utter a proper sentence in a minute I'll die of embarrassment. 'Only you don't sound very ... er ...'

'Irish?' he says, with another smile. 'No, I'm not; I'm over here for my friend Rob's stag do. They're all going wild down at O'Grady's, just round the corner. I'd probably better be getting back there or they'll think you lot have kidnapped me!'

'We have, actually,' smirks Helen, coming up behind me. 'And I do believe you've won us the treasure hunt.'

'That is *so* unfair,' says Lisa, who's still hanging on to her own trophy male as if he was anything to be proud of. 'We've got Ernest ...'

Ernest?

'... *And* we've got Number Three, *a pair of men's underwear, preferably warm.*'

'Which no one else seems to have managed,' joins in Mum.

I'm just thinking *please don't let them be Ernest's* when Harry, without saying a word, strolls into the centre of the group and, quick as a ... well, quick as a *flash* is quite appropriate, really ... unbuckles his belt, unzips his jeans, drops them to the floor and does a twirl on the spot, exhibiting a snug-fitting pair of black shorts that don't leave a lot to the imagination. Laughing out loud at the shocked silence and sea of stunned expressions, he whips his jeans straight back up again, zips and buckles and saunters off.

'*Nice*,' says Karen breathlessly in my ear.

'*Very* nice,' I agree.

'Catch you later, girls!' he calls back over his shoulder. 'Have a great evening!'

'Jude and Helen win,' announces Emily. Her voice is slightly hoarse. '*Absolutely* no contest!'

Hardly surprisingly, nobody argues.

ABOUT O'GRADY'S

'Up to you two to decide where we go for dinner, then,' Emily reminds Helen and Jude as we make our way out of the hotel.

'Oh! Well, now, that's a difficult one, isn't it, Jude?' says Helen, standing still and putting her finger to her chin as if she's pondering the situation.

'Difficult in me arse!' snorts Jude, marching out of the door without looking to see if any of us are following. 'Sure I'm heading over to O'Grady's for the craic, and it's got nothing to do with yer one that just walked out the door, there, if you're thinking, so!'

'Yeah, right!' says Emily, nudging me, and imitating Jude. 'In yer arse is it not, so!'

'So, to be sure, will we go?' I say in the same lousy accent, and we follow Jude out of the door, giggling together.

''What's all this about *crack*?' says Mum complainingly, tagging along behind.

'Don't worry, Marge,' says Joyce, linking arms with her. 'We'll come home if there's any drugs going on.'

'I'm not altogether sure about getting involved in *drugs*,' calls out a worried voice from the back of the group.

Shit. Ernest is still with us.

'This is a hen party, Ernest,' Emily tries to tell him kindly as we find a table for dinner. 'It means girls only.'

'But I was invited!' he says, genuinely taken aback.

'Only for the bloody treasure hunt,' mutters Mum, who's apparently washed her hands of him now the game's over, and who can blame her?

He stands, stricken, at the end of the table, looking around at us all uncertainly. We're being a lot of bitches, really, I suppose. He was probably looking forward to a nice meal. But it's no good – it just won't do. I can't spend the Saturday night of my hen weekend with a bloody *Ernest* in tow.

'Sorry, Ernest,' I tell him, trying to sound as if I mean it. 'But – you're not dressed appropriately. This is a school reunion.'

'Ah!' he says, looking relieved. 'I see! No problem!'

'I'm not sure about that,' says Emily thoughtfully as she watches him toddle off out of the door. 'I've got a horrible feeling he might be going back to his hotel to get changed ...'

The conversation, over dinner, is pretty predictable. We don't only talk about Harry, you understand. We're not *that* sad. There's a clash of opinion amongst us about whether he's too full of himself, a show-off, probably a bastard, someone best avoided at any time and certainly on a hen weekend – or whether he's as gorgeous as he looks, has a terrific sense of humour, is up for a laugh and would be great to get to know better ... if only we weren't on a hen weekend. I'm inclined to think the latter. He seemed like a nice guy. Nothing to do with how he looked.

'So where *is* he?' is the constant theme.

'Sure, he'll be upstairs with all the lads,' Jude keeps reassuring us.

Upstairs is the nightclub, and we'll be heading up there just as soon as we get this last mouthful down. Indigestion is a small price to pay, trust me.

'I hope you're not displaying a bit too much interest in some other guy, so close to your wedding, little sister?' says Lisa teasingly, after Mum and Auntie Joyce have decided to call it a day and head back to the hotel, and the rest of us finally make for the entrance of the club.

'Course not!' I smile back at her. 'Just joshing.'

I might have said more, but the music hits us as we walk through the doors, and I think that's it for the night, unless we shout through a megaphone.

*

82

We're attracting quite a lot of attention. Not that we're the only hen party in here; there's another group dressed as Red Indians and some girls wearing green tops with bunnies' ears on their heads, which I can't quite fathom. But the men are really going for the schoolgirl outfits. Funny how it never seemed to cause such a stir when I was legitimately dressing like this every day. Well, maybe not quite like this. I'm conscious of showing the navy blue knickers almost every time I move.

'Does yer mammy know you're out, love?' breathes a nasty beery slimeball, trying to touch my arse as I weave my way back to our table from the bar. 'Will I take ya home, an' we can do our homework together in me room?'

'Feck off,' I growl, making all his mates roar with laughter. Easily amused!

We're several drinks into the evening, and quite a few numbers onto the dance floor, when we finally spot our stag party. They're not exactly in fancy dress but it's easy to pick out the prospective bridegroom, who's got condoms hanging all the way round his belt, his pockets and even the back of his collar. He's also got a very glazed look in his eyes and is having trouble coordinating his limited dance movements. In fact he might very well fall over pretty soon, and it's not even eleven o'clock yet.

'This is my mate Rob!' shouts a familiar voice close to my ear.

'I guessed!' I shout back.

'This is Katie!' he bellows at Rob. 'She's getting married too!'

'What?' slurs Rob, holding onto Harry's shoulders and squinting at me. 'Getting married? *I'm* getting married.'

'We know you are, mate. So's Katie!'

'No! Not Katie!' Rob looks at me anxiously. 'No – it's Anna. I'm getting married to *Anna*. She's ... where is she?' He tries to turn round to survey the dance floor but ends up almost falling into Harry's arms.

'Anna's at home, Rob. Katie's marrying someone else. She's ... oh, fuck it, never mind,' he finishes as Rob staggers off, possibly in search of Anna, possibly in search of another drink. 'How you doing?' he adds, leaning closer to me to make himself heard above the bass beat.

We're both trying to dance at the same time as we're talking. You know what it's like. Not easy. I'm trying to reply, to tell him that I'm doing fine, thank you very much – but he can't really hear me. That's the only reason he takes hold of my arm and pulls me closer to him. Obviously. For a couple of minutes we dance like that – close together, but holding each other only very lightly. It's just so we can finish the conversation, you understand. But I'm tingling all over like I've had an electric shock and I feel kind of weak and shaky by the time the music finishes and we step apart from each other. I'm wondering if I'm going down with a dose of flu. That'd be bloody typical, wouldn't it.

The girls are all on the dance floor with me and I'm getting a few looks – particularly from Helen. I know what she's thinking.

'It's OK, don't worry!' I shout. 'I'm only *talking* to him!'

'Yes,' she says.

I don't like the tone of that *yes*.

The music hots up from about midnight. We're getting a lot of numbers played for us – new favourite girlie ones by The Scissor Sisters, Beyonce and Destiny's Child as well as all the old traditional ones: 'Ladies' Night', 'A Night to Remember', 'Girls Just Wanna Have Fun!' I can't count how many times I've been clubbing, over the years, and joined in the dancing and singing along to these hen night favourites – but this time, it's all about *me*.

'It feels really strange!' I shout to Emily. 'All this is about *me*!'

'Of course it is, you daft cow,' she laughs. 'You're the one getting married!'

By now my school hat is lying somewhere, probably trampled, on the dance floor, my tie has come off, my socks are round my ankles and I seem to have stopped caring about the length of my gymslip. I'm only a little bit drunk – it's the music, the atmosphere, the party mood that's really got me going – but the alcohol, as always, has given me the mistaken impression that I'm a great dancer. I'm out in the middle of the dance floor and my mates have formed a ring round me, clapping and cheering me on as, in a state of heightened excitement I'm performing a one-woman show of elaborate and tricky movements that probably bear more resemblance to a chicken laying its eggs than a disco queen going through her routine. Nobody seems to care, though, and when the DJ announces that he's going to play 'School's Out' by Alice Cooper for *all the naughty schoolgirls on the dance floor* we go wild, screaming and whooping as we grab hold of each other and form a kind of rugby scrum, arms round each other's waists, swaying and jigging to the music, singing along with the chorus which is all that we can manage between the lot of us.

'Need another drink!' I gasp as the music ends.

I push my way through the crowds to the bar, presuming the other girls, or at least some of them, are following me.

'Shit,' I mutter to myself when I get there and realise I'm on my own.

Emily's got the money for the evening in her purse and where the bloody hell is she?

'What's up?'

Wouldn't you just know it. Right now, as I'm leaning on the bar, probably looking at my least attractive *ever*, with my school shirtsleeves rolled up, collar askew, dripping sweat from everywhere it's humanly possible to drip it from, is not the time I would choose to be spotted by the most sexy man in Dublin.

'Dying of thirst,' I tell him, not wanting to meet his eyes in case he's looking disgusted at the state of me.

'Can I get you a drink, then?'

'No! No, you see, Emily's got the money. The euros. You know, the drinking money. Emily's in charge, but I … I think I've lost Emily.'

I'm only just about sober enough to make sense. Or am I?

'Well, not to worry. Let me buy you a drink, 'cos I don't want you to die of thirst. Not before your wedding!'

'Wedding. Yes.' That rings a bell. 'OK, yes please. I'll have …' I'm too thirsty for vodka. 'I'll have a Becks, please.'

Harry orders this, and a Guinness for himself.

'Got to drink it while we're over here,' he tells me, taking a great slurp from his glass. 'It's beautiful.'

I notice he has trouble with the word *beautiful*. So he's not quite as sober as he seems.

'Have you been drinking that all night?'

'Yep. 'S beautiful,' he repeats. 'Rob ought to have stuck with the Guinness. Then he might not have been sick.'

'Poor guy. What happened to him?' I ask, looking around.

'Had to go back to the hotel. Being sick all over the ...'

'Ugh. What a shame. On his stag weekend!'

'Been drinking all day. He won't remember in the morning.' He gives me a sudden look. 'What about your boyfriend, then? Is he away on his stag do?'

'Yeah.'

'Where's he gone, then?'

'Prague. But I don't want to talk about it.'

'Fair enough. I like Prague, though. Been there twice. Two different stag weekends.'

'Good for you.'

'Sorry,' he says, looking at me a bit more closely. 'Sorry, you didn't want to talk about it. I won't talk about it, OK?'

'OK.'

He takes another gulp of his Guinness.

'I didn't mean to upset you. I'll change the subject, all right?'

'All right.'

'I mean, if you're upset about something, the last thing you want is someone going on and on and on about it, isn't it ...'

'Yes, it is.'

'You're not *really* upset, are you? Only, you know, you're getting married soon, and you're supposed to be enjoying yourself, so don't be upset. I won't say any more about Prague, OK?'

'OK! For fuck's sake! Shut the fuck up about fucking *Prague*!'

It's suddenly gone very quiet at the bar and I realise I was shouting at the top of my voice.

'Thanks for the drink,' I say in a whisper, plonking the empty bottle back on the bar and turning to slink away, my face burning red.

'Hey!' He's following me, trying to catch hold of my elbow. I keep going through the crowd. I need to find the other girls. It's getting late and the club will be closing soon. They'll be looking for me. And I think I need to get away from this guy. Quickly.

'Hey, Katie! Don't be like that! I didn't mean ...'

He's got me firmly by both arms. I could shake him off, push him away, carry on looking for my friends, but I suddenly feel too drunk to try. At least, I think it's the drink.

'I'm sorry, Katie. I'm drunk, and I'm a prat. And I've upset you on your hen weekend. If you don't say you forgive me, I'll spend the rest of my life feeling guilty that I might have ruined your wedding.'

'No you won't.'

I'm smiling now. Can't help it really.

'Then we're friends, yeah?'

Friends? We're virtually complete strangers. All I know about him is his first name, the fact that he likes Guinness and that he's been to Prague twice.

'Yeah,' I say, nevertheless. 'OK.'

He only kisses me because of that. You see? Because we're friends, apparently. That's fair enough, isn't it?

But I can understand how it looks when my friends find me a few minutes later ... still kissing.

On the way back to the hotel I'm being talked about as if I'm not here.

'Look, it's her hen weekend. It's what people *do* on their hen weekends. Get pissed, kiss a bloke or two ...'

'Not *that* sort of kissing!'

'Not that any of us would breathe a word to Matt, don't get me wrong, but ...'

'Of course we wouldn't! What sort of friends do you take us for?'

'But even so! How would she feel if *he* was snogging other girls over in Prague?'

'Who's to say that he isn't?'

'It's our fault – we should have been looking after her. We shouldn't have let her go off on her own ...'

'For the love of Jesus! Will you ever give her a break, the

lot of you? Katie's fine, so she is, and if she can't have a little bit of fun on her hen weekend without you eejits all giving out like a shower of holy nuns, sure she might as well be dead and buried instead of going to her wedding!'

'Thanks, Jude.'

I've sobered up alarmingly since the frosty reception I got from a couple of the girls when I surfaced from kissing Harry.

'You're welcome, Katie. Fair play to you, girl, he was too gorgeous not to be kissed. I'd have done the same meself, if I could only work up the courage, and I don't think I'm the only one here who's a tad jealous of you, if the truth be known.'

There's a silence at this, which speaks volumes. I glance at Jude. She's actually pink and cross with indignation on my behalf. Bless her.

'Well said, Jude,' agrees Emily.

'She's right, I'm as jealous as hell,' laughs Lisa. 'I could give him one as soon as look at him!'

We're all laughing together about my naughtiness as we totter back into the hotel. All except Helen. Helen's not saying a word, but I can see from her expression that she's not amused. I don't know why it bothers me, but it does.

It's very late when we get to bed, but I can't sleep. I'm lying here with my eyes shut, listening to Jude trying to tiptoe around the room, doing her cleansing and toning and whatever the hell else she has to do before she undresses, folds her clothes immaculately and finally gets into bed. About another hour goes by. I stare into the darkness, wide awake, thinking my own thoughts, wondering what's the matter with me – how I can feel the need to snog another bloke if I'm supposed to be totally in love with Matt, how upset he'd be if he knew what I'd done, and how I almost managed to cause World War III on my own hen weekend by doing it. And how I'm ever going to get up in the morning if I don't go off to sleep soon.

I'm thirsty now. Shit, I'll have to get up and get a glass of water. I sit in the chair and drink it, wondering about Helen and why she seemed so pissed off. What did it matter to her whether I kissed someone or not? Come to that, why does it matter to me if she's in a mood with me?

But it does. I'm on my special weekend away with all my favourite girls. I don't want it spoilt by any bad feeling. I wish I could have it out with Helen, but she's bound to be asleep by now. Maybe I'll send her a text. Yes, that's an idea. I fumble in my bag for my phone. A text won't wake her up – she can read it in the morning and talk to me when she's ready. Maybe she's just drunk and crotchety, but I don't want to leave anything festering.

Hi. Have I upset u? Please tell me. Luv K xx

That's enough. Hopefully she'll laugh about it in the morning and we can both just . . . Oh! I nearly drop the phone with surprise as it bleeps with a return message. Jude stirs and turns over in bed but doesn't wake up, and by the light of the phone's screen I read:

Sorry. Feeling a bit down. Come and talk.

She's still awake! I blink at the message. Well, *I'm* wide awake anyway, so I might as well . . .

I slip a cardigan on over my pyjamas and, grabbing the room key, let myself out quietly and tiptoe down the corridor to number 142.

Helen's the only one with a single room. There's an odd number of us; we wanted it to be ten, but my friend Donna couldn't make it and there wasn't really anyone else I wanted to come, just to make up the number. I was worried at first about the odd one – but without even knowing the problem, Helen asked if she could have a single room. I think it's partly because she didn't really know anyone else. Or maybe she just doesn't like sharing.

I tap on the door and she opens it immediately. She's got the main light on, which makes me blink after the darkness of my own room and the low lighting in the corridor.

'I've got the kettle on,' she says, indicating the tea-making equipment.

'Lovely. Any biscuits?'

She opens the regulation packet of custard creams and puts them on the tray.

'Sit down, Katie. You have the bed. I'll take the chair.'

I don't bother arguing.

'You couldn't sleep, either, then?'

'No. Couldn't stop thinking about ...' She stops, sighs, takes a sip of her tea.

'About what? Are you mad at me? Look, I ...'

'No. It doesn't matter. I know Jude was right. Why the hell shouldn't you have a bit of fun? It just makes me ... sorry; I know you think I'm weird, but it just makes me *so depressed.*'

I stare at her through the steam from my tea. I can't make her out. She's been quite open about the fact that she doesn't think it's a good idea to get married. She says she doesn't believe in committing yourself to one man, giving up your freedom, all that crap. So what's this about?

'*What* makes you depressed?' I ask her, trying to hide the irritation in my voice. 'You've been on my case all this time about getting married, and now ... well, it seems to me like I can't win!'

She's silent for a minute, looking down at her cup, dunking her biscuit, watching it drip. Then she looks back up at me, and to my surprise, she looks like she's going to cry.

'You're so wrong, there, Katie,' she says quietly. 'You *always* win. And you don't even know it.'

What is it about everyone? Are they all determined to tell me their sob stories? I know I'm the bloody agony aunt, but why *this weekend*? And why Helen, who's hardly ever spoken to me about anything more personal than her taste in breakfast cereals and music before?

'So tell me,' I say, leaning back against the pillows with a sigh. Best get it over with. 'What is it I don't know about?'

I'll probably be sorry I asked.

HELEN'S STORY

I'm jealous of Katie, obviously.

Who wouldn't be? Look at her. She's lovely, and she doesn't even seem to realise it. She's not little and delicate and perfect like her friend Jude; but she doesn't even have to try. Jude spends hours making herself beautiful, but men don't look at her – any more than they look at me. It's girls like Katie who get noticed. She's a natural. She smiles all the time. She laughs, and sparkles. She knows the right things to say; she knows how to make people like her, *instinctively*.

I used to spend hours, when I was younger, worrying about stuff like this. What I was doing wrong, why I didn't appeal to people. Why I didn't make friends. Why nobody ever fell in love with me.

It's easy enough to pretend you don't care. Trust me – I do it all the time, now. I've got used to my own company. Not many people like the same things as me, anyway: the books I read are too serious, the music I listen to is too old-fashioned, the plays and films I see and places I visit aren't most people's idea of fun. So I'm better off on my own, enjoying my own kind of things, not having to pretend to like the Kaiser Chiefs, or Harry Potter. Not having to compromise just to fit in, just to suit some guy that I've got nothing in common with.

Don't misunderstand me. I like men.

Katie thinks I despise them, but she's wrong. I've had my share of boyfriends, if you can call them that. They never last long. Usually I get bored with them at about the same time that they give up trying to puzzle me out. I'm sorry they find me difficult. I don't do it on purpose – I'm just not very good at the things they normally like. Coyness, silliness, giggling, flirting, being cute and fluffy and *girly*. Some girls just seem to be like that; others do it on purpose. It annoys me when they're strong, intelligent women but they seem to feel the need to play-act all this crap just to get a man. But then again, what do I know? Who's the one sitting on her own every night with a cat and a microwave dinner?

Before I started working at Bookshelf, I never had any real friendships with my colleagues. It wasn't their fault; most of them were nice enough to me, but when they wanted to talk about pop music, or they spent hours – literally hours! – discussing *Big Brother* or whatever peculiar, inane programmes they wasted their time watching on TV, I couldn't contribute anything. I didn't know how to join in. I just don't *do* that type of meaningless social chitchat; I don't understand how to. I'm not criticising them – you see? I know it's my problem, but I can't change the way I am.

Katie's not the same as all the others. She recognises our differences but she doesn't seem to find it a problem. She doesn't stare at me as if I've come from Mars, if I admit I haven't heard of a pop group that's been top of the charts since Christmas without me knowing about it, or a so-called celebrity who's apparently in the news because their boobs *accidentally* popped out of their bra on TV. She treats my lack of interest in these things as inconsequential, just as she does her own lack of enthusiasm for architecture, for opera, for poetry and all the things that matter to me. She laughs at her own inadequacies, and makes me laugh at myself. We tease each other. It's refreshing, and delightful. I enjoy her company so much and, however much I know I can never be like her and doubt whether I'd *want* to be ... I envy her.

I envy her because she's popular, and easy to be with. Because she's charming and natural and she doesn't have to agonise over how to talk to people. Because men like her, and fall in love with her, and I've never cared to admit it, but I want that too. If only it was the right man.

The right man?

Oh, I'd given up on that idea! After the first few short-lived and disappointing relationships, I'd built this kind of protective shell around myself, so that I could have boyfriends, sexual encounters, without becoming emotionally involved. Without giving up anything of *myself*. Who wants to go through all that crap and end up getting hurt?

But when I started work at Bookshelf, Katie wasn't the only person who turned things around for me.

How can you live for forty years, travel the world, study cultures and histories of every continent, meet people from all walks of life, without ever meeting someone who could come remotely close to being your soul mate – and then, on taking up a post with a tiny, quiet, backstreet enterprise in your own home town, suddenly find him staring you in the face?

Greg.

He's perfect.

He's intelligent and serious, gentle, and wise. He speaks softly and precisely about things that matter. If there's nothing interesting to say, he doesn't bother to say anything. It's so restful being with him. I don't have to think. I don't, for once in my life, have to *try*.

I don't hold with the soppy romantic rubbish that Katie reads. People falling in love because someone smiles at them in a certain way. Falling in love because of something to do with stars, or sunsets, or even because of the way someone looks, or how good they are in bed. I'm sorry. It's misleading a whole generation of women into believing that's how they find love.

Katie thinks that means I don't believe in love.

But I do.

I'm totally, utterly, and helplessly in love with Greg Armstrong.

It's hard to explain what this has got to do with last night.

That guy – Harry? It was a bit of a joke to begin with. Just part of the game. I'm not good at this sort of thing, but I'm determined, this weekend, for Katie's sake, to do my best to join in and enjoy myself. She'd do the same for me, you see; if I invited her, as my friend, on a trip to Vienna, say, to go to a concert, or a weekend in Florence, to visit museums and art galleries, I know she'd put a smile on her face and make an effort, to please me, and that's what I'm doing this weekend for her.

Jude and I were never favourites to win the treasure hunt thing. She's as shy as I'm awkward – what a pair to put together, to go out in the street accosting people and asking for underwear and vibrators. We'd used up nearly the whole of the allotted half-hour without getting any of the items on the list. We just kept running round in circles asking each other what to do. And then, at the eleventh hour, so to speak, along came this group of guys, spread out across the pavement, laughing and jostling each other, the way they do when they're young and good-looking and being macho together on a good night out.

A couple of them nudged us as they passed. It was deliberate, but not malicious. A kind of teasing, probably because we were too intent on studying our list and panicking about being so useless at the game to take any notice of them.

'What's the matter, girls?' laughed one of them. 'Don't look so worried!'

I don't know what possessed me. Maybe it was because I'd already had a couple of drinks in the bar. Or perhaps I was showing off slightly, because I was aware that Jude was even worse than me at engaging in conversation with strangers.

'We need all the things on this list,' I told them, quite curtly. 'And we need them in less than five minutes!'

They passed the list round the group, laughing and scratching their heads and saying *fucking hell!* until finally, just as I was about to snatch it back and get on our way, one of them – Harry – stepped forward, smiling that amazing smile, and said:

'You won't get all that lot in five minutes, love. But if you want a volunteer for the *bloke* – there's no gorgeous ones around here, that I know of! – I'll come back with you, to save you getting *nul points*!'

Obviously he knew he *was* gorgeous. We probably wouldn't have cared, at that stage, if he wasn't – but looking at him, we were beside ourselves with excitement. I'm not much of a game-player, but I do have a slightly competitive nature when I'm challenged, and I knew the other girls would go wild when they saw what we were taking back as our Number Six. He was so gorgeous, we might even be declared the winners, despite our lack of sex toys and vegetables – but at least we wouldn't have the indignity of coming back with nothing at all.

I had to try to hide my impatience at the time he spent taking leave of his mates. I'd have thought it was enough to arrange a time and place to meet up again, but a good five minutes were spent discussing the merits of O'Grady's versus several other Dublin bars, following which there was at least another ten minutes of loud and obscene speculation about exactly what Harry was coming back to our hotel with us for, whether he was equipped for it, whether we were (as hypothetical schoolgirls) actually old enough for it to be legal, and how long it was likely to take him supposing he could manage it.

Once we eventually got him away from his mob and walked him back to our hotel, though, he dropped the big macho act and was utterly charming. I was feeling amazed at myself for achieving something so completely out of character for me, and couldn't wait to see the reaction of the other girls – especially Katie. I wasn't disappointed. They were all totally bowled over by Harry, hardly surprisingly, and as for his finale with the striptease – well! I couldn't have dreamt it up.

He was the star of the evening; and through him, Jude and I got our five minutes of fame. Can you see what I'm getting at? How can I explain it? It wasn't so much that I fancied Harry myself, although of course he was very attractive. To be honest I don't like men like that. Too sure of themselves, too overtly masculine; I actually find them quite offensive at some personal level. It was more that he was *my* piece of work. *My* achievement. Well – mine and Jude's, at least.

Not Katie's. Not this time.

That sounds ridiculously childish, and I know it. I'm ashamed of thinking it. Why do you think I'm so upset?

When I saw her kissing him at the nightclub, all I could think was: *even him*. She's got her own boyfriend. She's got all these other men, everywhere she goes, falling under her spell, and she isn't even aware of it. Now even this one, the one *I* picked up, is making a play for her!

And if you think I'm a pathetic, sad, jealous old bitch for having such uncharitable thoughts about my friend on her own hen weekend, then you're right. But you also ought to understand one last thing.

You see, when I say she's got all these other men falling for her, I know what I'm talking about. I don't care about any of the others. I only care about Greg.

But he doesn't even notice me.

Like everyone else, he's only got eyes for Katie.

ABOUT FRESH AIR AND EXERCISE

I'll be honest with you: I'm slightly irritated by all this.

Don't get me wrong – I really like Helen. I've sat here listening to her, without interrupting, without arguing, and it's gone four thirty in the morning now and I'd like nothing better, at this point, than to crawl back to bed; but I'm trying to be nice, trying to be a good listener and a good friend, you know? As usual, as always. But what the fuck is all this about?

This is the trouble, if you ask me, with people like Helen – self-confessed introspectives. They're always teetering on the brink of self-obsession. Isn't that what this whole thing sounds like? One long complaint, one long tragic story about Helen, written by Helen, starring Helen, with Helen in every supporting role.

I don't even believe half of it.

Since when was she in love with Greg? Since when did she even want to *be* in love with anybody? And since when did Greg, of all people, even look at *me*?

'Greg's never even looked at me,' I tell her, leaning back on her bed, watching her get up to put the kettle on again. Fucking hell, I really don't want another cup of tea. 'That's completely ridiculous.'

'You see? You're not aware of it. I know you're not. It's not your fault.'

'My *fault*? But there's nothing ...'

'I'm afraid you're wrong. He's told me, you see.'

Well, this at least makes me sit up and wake up.

'Told you what? When?'

'After you go home. Before you get in.' This, naturally, is a thinly veiled reference to the fact that Helen and Greg both work from dawn to dusk and beyond, while I do a normal nine-to-five with an hour for lunch. 'He spends at least an hour a day pouring out his heart to me ...'

'*Greg* pours out his *heart*?!'

It's a revelation to me that he's actually got one.

'Yes, he seems to have cast me in the role of some kind of counsellor. Some kind of Mother Confessor.'

The thought of Helen as anyone's Mother Confessor would probably be hysterical if it wasn't for the subject in hand.

'And ... what? You're saying he talks about *me*?'

'Of course he does. What have I been telling you? He's completely infatuated with you. He never talks about anything *else* but you.'

'Helen, stop it. This is giving me the creeps.'

'Do you think *I* like it? I've always hoped ... I suppose I was just being silly ... but I actually hoped that when he realised you were definitely getting married he'd have to turn to someone else ...'

'You ...'

'Well. It was all I had. That faint hope.'

I get up, put my arms round her. This is a strange new side of Helen, one I'd never imagined existing. A soft side, a romantic side. It's almost unbelievable.

'I had no idea – honestly.'

'I know you didn't. Maybe I should have told you. Or encouraged him to tell you himself.'

'Jesus! For God's sake, it would have freaked me out! He knew I was with Matt ...'

'And *I* knew he was in love with *you*, Katie – but knowing these things doesn't stop us feeling the way we do.'

I can't think of a thing to say to this. I'm just standing here, shaking my head, staring at her. Unbelievable.

'I'm sorry,' she says at length. 'I shouldn't have kept you all this time – making you listen to my problems, when you should be getting your beauty sleep.'

'It's OK. I just – I think I need a bit of time to take it in. I'm gobsmacked, to be honest.'

She smiles sadly.

'You didn't have me down as pathetic and lovelorn, did you?'

'I still don't. Funnily enough I've always thought you and Greg were really well suited. I just didn't think *you* would be interested.'

What do I know? Seems like I don't notice what's going on right under my nose.

'You don't want another cup of tea?' she asks, toying forlornly with the teabags.

'No. No thanks. Try to get some sleep, Helen. See you at breakfast.'

Greg Armstrong. Bloody hell. Bloody, fucking hell!

I'm very late for breakfast. Everyone else has finished when I make it to the dining room. Even Helen.

'I tried to wake you,' says Jude, who's sitting at a table with Lisa and Mum, having a cup of tea. 'But you told me to fu—' She glances at Mum and grins. 'You were very rude and told me to go away.'

'Did I? Sorry. Didn't get much sleep.' I glance across the room at Helen, who's chatting to Emily and seems to be avoiding meeting my eyes.

I order myself sausage, bacon, and eggs. I don't care if it's greasy, high in cholesterol and is going to make me fat while it clogs up my arteries. I need fuel. I need to eat my way out of my hangover, or tiredness, or whatever's causing the stupor I'm in this morning, to clear my head and try to make sense of everything. What's happening here? Everyone I thought I knew really well has suddenly decided to turn themselves inside-out for me. First my family, now my work colleagues. Helen – of all people! In love with Greg? Greg in love with *me*? It's ridiculous. It can't be true. I'm not having it.

I'll have to leave.

This thought comes to me, like a white-hot stab of clarity, as I take my first mouthful of fried egg. How can I carry on working with the pair of them now? I cut a rasher of bacon into pieces, fiercely, crossly. This isn't fair. I like my job, and now I've got to leave. This situation isn't of my making.

I wish Helen hadn't told me. I glare at the back of her head as I chew the bacon, thinking about how selfish she is. I thought she was my friend! Why couldn't she keep her stupid loved-up nonsense to herself?

But then again, how much worse if I'd found out from Greg! How embarrassing would that have been? I'd have died on the spot. I'd have had to walk out without even giving my notice. I'd have been traumatised for life.

'What on earth's eating you this morning?' says Lisa mildly. 'The sausage is already dead. You didn't need to murder it.'

I look up with a guilty start from stabbing the sausage with my fork.

'Sorry.' Mum and Jude have gone, and I feel the need to say something to somebody. 'Spent half the night talking to Helen. About ...' Ah, shit, it's no good. I can't tell her. 'About work.'

'Work? For God's sake!' She glances over at Helen. 'What the hell's the matter with her? Talking to you about *work* on your hen weekend!'

'Oh, just about ... a few issues. Things that were worrying her.'

'Well, she should have damn well worried about them on her own. Can't she ever switch off? I knew it was a mistake to invite her ...'

'It's OK,' I say wearily. 'It doesn't matter.' I stuff a piece of sausage into my mouth and add, through the chewing of it, 'You know what it's like, Lisa – when you've had a couple of drinks. All sorts of things come out, that you might not have chosen to discuss this particular weekend.'

She's silent for a minute. Then:

'OK, yes. Point taken. I'm sorry I blabbed the other night.'

'Well, I wish you'd told me before, to be quite honest. It'd be nice to think you could have confided in me.'

'I thought you'd disapprove. In fact, I thought you'd have been disgusted.'

'Why? Am I such a prude, or what?'

'No, of course not. But you're such a *romantic*. I didn't think you'd be able to accept the idea of me having an affair. Falling out of love with my husband.'

'Love?' I splutter, scraping the last of the fried egg off my plate and throwing down the knife and fork. 'Beginning to wonder about it all, Lise. Really beginning to wonder.'

'That's not what I'd expect to hear you say, so close to your wedding,' she says, reaching out to touch my hand.

The touch nearly does for me. I'm so close opening up to my sister at this point, to telling her a load of stuff I'd only regret mentioning later on, that I have to sit up straight, take a swig of coffee and turn my head away.

'Katie?' she says quietly.

'OK!' I say brightly, turning back to give her a smile. 'Come on, that's enough of all this deep and serious stuff. It's a hen party, so let's bloody well *party*! Where are all the others?'

'We're meeting them in half an hour in reception,' she says. 'Are you sure you're all right?'

But I've already got up from the table and I'm walking ahead of her out of the dining room, pretending I can't hear.

'Have y'all got your flat shoes on and your cameras packed?' says Tour Leader Jude Barnard half an hour later.

We have. We've already had our instructions.

'I've got a rare treat for you all this morning, girls, so let's get going, before the sun goes in. We're getting some fresh air and exercise, so we are!'

'I thought you said it was a treat?' whinges Karen half-heartedly.

'Yeah, can't we just exercise ourselves as far as the pub?' laughs Emily.

'Would you listen to the pair of you? Sure you'd be going home from Ireland tomorrow without seeing a single corner of it outside of Temple Bar if I didn't put me foot down with you. Dublin's a beautiful city, so it is, with the mountains behind it and the sea in front of it – it'd be a crime altogether to miss seeing some of that.'

'OK. Very lyrical, Jude. Mountains and sea – fair enough,' says Karen.

'Actually, it's a lovely day outside. Jude's right, some fresh air would be good, and I quite fancy seeing the sea,' I agree.

'Well I'm glad that's settled, then,' says Jude, leading us out of the hotel. 'We'll be getting the DART along the coast as far as Killiney, and—'

'What's the DART? It sounds painful.'

'It's just a train, for the love of God ... and we'll have a walk on the beach ...'

'Yay!'

'Yeah – the beach!'

'Cool!'

'You see, now?' Jude smiles back at us all smugly. 'I knew the lot of you would come around to my way of thinking ...'

'Beach is *good*, Jude. Beach is *holidays*.'

'And we'll walk back along to Dalkey, where there's a grand little pub.'

Ah! Now you're talking!

The DART, it turns out, is a railway that runs the entire length of Dublin Bay. We get on the train at Tara Street station and after a few stops we're following the coast. We're all looking out of the window and getting excited as if we're little kids who haven't been to the seaside for a year. I'm only hoping it doesn't start Mum off about Southend again, but I think that's unlikely now.

Our loud English cackling is getting us a few looks from people on the train.

'Don't trouble yerselves about this shower of savages,' Jude says cheerfully to a couple of elderly ladies sitting near us. They were probably looking forward to a nice peaceful Sunday morning ride. 'They're not as frightening as they look.'

'We're not frightening in the least!' exclaims Emily. 'This one here's getting married soon, that's all.'

'God bless yer heart, me darlin'. Rather you than me!'

We're in good spirits when we finally get off the train at Killiney. The DART station's right on the coast and we run down to the beach, whooping and shouting with excitement as if we've never seen the sea before in our lives.

It's midday by now and the sun is, unexpectedly, quite warm – for Ireland in April – and it's not long before we've all got our shoes and socks off and the legs of our jeans rolled up and we're skipping over the sand and shingle beach to have a paddle. All of us except Jude, who's standing back on the beach watching us with a smile like an exasperated parent whose children are being very silly. I wish she'd lighten up. I suppose she doesn't want to get the bottoms of her jeans wet, or her hair splashed, God forbid. Even Mum and Auntie Joyce have got their shoes off. How much harm can a little paddle in the sea do ...

'Oh! Oh, fucking hell! Oh, Jesus, Jesus Christ – it's *cold*!'

I'm screaming it at exactly the same moment as everyone else. I look around and they're all doing the same as me – running back out of the sea full pelt, looking over their shoulders to make sure the freezing waves aren't following them.

Jude walks down the beach to meet us, laughing out loud.

'Did you think it was the Mediterranean, you mad eejits? And were you thinking of walking to Dalkey with your feet freezing the arses off you and squelching sea water in yer shoes, were you now?'

We all stand, shivering from the shock of the cold sea, hanging our heads like the silly children we seem to have become, shrugging to each other and waiting for Jude to announce that the walk's now off and we'll have to go, barefoot, to the nearest pub instead to warm up. Shame.

'Sure and isn't it a good job *one* of us has come prepared?' she adds smugly, pulling a towel out of her rucksack. 'I just brought the one. You'll have to share!'

Once we've passed the towel around and dried off, we're all laughing and chasing each other along the beach to warm up again. Jude, whose neat little pink girly rucksack seems more like a Boy Scout's expedition kitbag every minute, has, amazingly, produced a Frisbee out of it now and we're skimming it to each other, making each other run, narrowly missing the sea several times, shrieking and insulting each other and generally acting like a day trip for disturbed teenagers. If we notice that Jude's strolling along with Mum and Auntie Joyce and not joining in our nonsense, we're not going to mention it. Not after the freezing sea episode!

'Up here,' calls Jude after a while, leading us up off the beach.

Probably a good job. I was getting a bit knackered there and didn't want to be the first to admit it.

'Through here!' calls our Leader, still striding ahead as we follow her through a tunnel under the railway line and up some steps.

And up.

And up.

We were laughing and chatting when we left the beach. By the time we're a quarter of the way up the steps we've all stopped talking. Halfway up, all I can hear is the sound of my own heavy breathing. By the time we reach the road at the top, I'm being deafened by the sound of everyone else's breathing.

'Sure that was a good bit of exercise, wasn't it?' gasps Jude.

No one's up to answering.

Mum and Auntie Joyce haven't even appeared yet.

'I'll nip back and give them a hand,' says Lisa.

With all her working out at the gym, to say nothing of the other kind of exercise I now know she's getting *after* the gym sessions, she's by far the fittest of us and hasn't even worked up a sweat yet.

'No, I will ...' protests Jude, darting ahead of Lisa.

I don't think she's showing off. Not exactly. You see, Jude's normally the quiet one, the one who stays at the back of the group and doesn't have a lot to say. But this weekend in Ireland, she's automatically become the unofficial leader of the pack. She's the one with the maps, the guidebooks, the local knowledge. She speaks the dialect. She understands the natives.

She's planned our day out, and she's enjoying herself showing us the way. So if she's forgotten, for a moment, that two of our group are middle-aged and not quite up to speed with climbing great steep flights of steps, then in her mind she probably feels responsible.

'Hold on, ladies!' she shouts down to Mum and Joyce, who've stopped for a breather halfway up. 'I'm coming back down for you ...'

But in her haste to get ahead of Lisa, she treads awkwardly on the first step down. I feel myself flinch as I see her ankle turn over. Seconds later, she's sunk onto the top step, out cold, and it's only Lisa's quick grabbing of her arm that stops her tumbling the whole way down.

ABOUT JUDE'S ANKLE

'Oh Jesus! Fucking hell! God, it *fucking* hurts!'

To be honest I'm just glad she's finally spoken.

She didn't come round from her faint till we'd carried her onto a bench beside the road and sat her with her head down. Then when she did regain consciousness, she took one look at all of us staring at her and fainted again. I don't think it was anything we said.

'You poor thing! You've sprained it. I know how much it hurts – I did that when I came off the treadmill too quickly a few months ago,' says Lisa sympathetically when she opens her eyes again.

Probably too busy looking at someone in Lycra shorts on the next treadmill.

'I feel sick,' groans Jude. She looks terribly pale.

'It's the shock. And the pain,' says Lisa knowledge-ably.

'It's probably going to swell up. She needs ice on it. And painkillers. Has anyone got any aspirins? Paracetamol? Anything?' says Emily.

We're all shaking our heads pathetically.

'I've got two diarrhoea tablets,' says Suze, rummaging in her bag, 'and an old Elastoplast.'

'Very helpful,' sniffs Helen, who isn't offering anything any better.

'We need to strap it up,' I decide, trying to remember my first aid. 'With something cold, I suppose.'

'I know!' says Lisa. 'Where's that towel? I'll run back down to the beach and soak it in sea water.'

The very idea of *running back down,* with its concomitant thoughts of *running back up again*, is enough to make the rest of us shudder. Significantly, Mum and Auntie Joyce still haven't even joined us at the top.

'Not the towel – it's too big and thick. What we need is ...'

I'm looking round the group, and my eyes fall on Helen's scarf. It's one of those nice silky knit ones, blue and lilac stripes with a thread of silver running through it. She takes it off without saying a word, which is nice of her as it looks expensive.

'I've got a bottle of water in my bag,' says Jude, sitting up a bit and wincing as she moves her ankle slightly. We all wince with her. 'Wet it with that. No point going back down to the sea.'

What *hasn't* the girl got in her bag? I peek inside. Sure enough – a bottle of water, still nice and cold. I pull it out and underneath I can see a rolled-up plastic raincoat, gloves and spare pair of socks, a bar of chocolate and packet of nuts and raisins. Was she planning a nice little stroll to the next village, or a trek into the mountains? I'm surprised there's no torch or compass. And she never even *was* a Girl Guide!

'Why the spare socks?' I can't help asking, 'if you weren't even going to paddle?'

'In case it rains,' she mutters, looking at me as if I'm daft.

We've soaked the scarf in the cold water and bandaged Jude's ankle fairly tightly by the time Mum and Joyce finally appear, gasping and holding their sides, at the top of the steps.

'What on earth ...?' cries Mum, standing stock-still on the other side of the road and staring at us.

'Jude twisted her ankle, Mum. It's probably sprained.'

'She's in agony,' joins in Emily, who likes a drama. 'She fainted twice.'

'Well for God's sake!' pants Mum, coming over to join us. 'She needs a doctor! Phone the poor girl an ambulance – don't just stand there!'

'I do *not* need the doctor, Marge,' says Jude, trying gingerly to stand up on just her good foot. 'Sure I'll be fine altogether if I can just get on me feet and get to a chemist's for some aspirin or ... oh! Oh, God!'

At the first attempt to put any weight on her bad foot, she collapses back down onto the bench, as white as a sheet again.

'I don't think you're going anywhere, Jude,' points out Emily. 'Not walking, anyway.'

'Well, now, do you see any sign of a wheelchair around here?' she retorts, between her teeth.

'No. We'll have to carry you,' says Lisa.

Good old Lisa with her strong back and her toned muscles! That gym membership must be worth every penny.

'You're only little,' agrees Helen. 'It won't kill us.'

'Yes, come on, dear,' says Mum, still panting from the climb up the steps. 'Let me help you up.'

'*You're* not carrying anyone! And anyway, where are we carrying her to? It doesn't exactly look like there's a shopping centre just round the corner.'

'Sure there'll be a chemist in Dalkey,' says Jude. 'But it's a walk and a half from here. We'd not even *begun* the walk.'

Now she tells us.

'It's a nice walk, too,' she adds, looking miserable. 'Sure and I've spoilt everyone's day with me stupid ankle, haven't I, so.'

'Course you haven't,' we all chorus.

'Can we not just carry you back to the Tube station, dear?' suggests Mum.

'DART station,' Lisa corrects her. 'But it's a good idea. It can't be far, can it, Jude?'

'No, if you look down the railway line there, sure you can see the station just round the bend there, see? 'Tis only a little way, but 'twould mean missing the lovely walk and all ...'

'Bugger the lovely walk,' says Mum with surprising spirit. 'We need to get you back to the hotel, Jude, dear, and get you resting with that foot up.'

'Poor Jude,' says Emily sadly.

'And Dalkey would have been such a grand place for you to visit, too, with the castle and the fine pub and all ...' Jude's still wailing.

'Well, you can sit with your foot up in a fine pub just as well as you can back at the hotel, can't you?' points out Helen. 'What's stopping us from getting off the DART at Dalkey and having lunch there anyway?'

*

108

Once the notion of the fine pub has resurfaced, it's surprising how efficiently we get ourselves organised. It's quickly decided that Jude won't actually have to be *carried*; with someone on each side of her to take her weight she can get along on her good foot as if she's using crutches. The only trouble is that she's shorter than everyone else so she has to lean on their elbows rather than their shoulders.

'No problem,' says Lisa airily, supporting Jude under her armpit so that she practically lifts her off the ground.

'You don't all need to come on the DART,' says Jude pitifully. 'Why don't some of you do the walk, and we'll meet you in Dalkey?'

'Yes, go on, dears – off you go and enjoy yourselves!' says Mum briskly to nobody in particular. 'We'll get Jude to this Dorky place and I'll sit with her while Lisa goes and finds a chemist for some tablets. Then we can all have lunch in the pub.'

'I'll come with you, then,' says Helen. 'You don't want to be taking her weight, if you don't mind me saying so, Marge. You look done in already.'

'I hope they'll be all right,' says Emily anxiously as we set off down the road in the direction Jude showed us. 'I feel a bit guilty leaving them to it.'

'No, it wasn't far to the station. And Jude was worried about spoiling the day for us all,' smiles Joyce, who's recovered from climbing the steps now and is striding along quite energetically, swinging her arms and breathing in the sea air. 'She was pleased some of us are doing the walk.'

'Bless her. It *is* lovely, walking along and looking down at the sea, isn't it,' says Karen.

'It's certainly done away with our hangovers!' I laugh.

The sunshine, the fresh air, the run on the beach and even the shock of the cold sea have all helped to clear my head, sharpen my senses and cheer me up, despite the calamity with poor Jude.

'And look at the houses along this road. Aren't they beautiful! What a fantastic outlook they've got.'

'Yeah – I read somewhere that Bono lives round here,'

says Suze excitedly. 'I wonder which one is his house? Wouldn't it be great if we bumped into him!'

We all laugh, but the thought of bumping into Bono suddenly round the next bend keeps us walking with a spring in our step for quite a while.

'Jude says there are quite a few celebrities living in this area, actually,' I tell them as we pass a particularly impressive house with views straight over the bay. 'You can see why, can't you.'

'Yeah,' jokes Emily. 'It's downhill all the way to the *fine pub*!'

We're absolutely starving by the time we arrive in Dalkey.

'Where are we meeting the others?' asks Joyce. 'At the pub?'

'I suppose so. They didn't actually say, did they? Oh, bugger – that's a point.' I laugh. 'We don't know the name of the pub.'

'Well, there can't be many, in a little place like this,' says Emily reasonably.

'This is Ireland, remember – almost as many pubs as there are houses,' I point out.

'So what do we do? Try them all?' Suze asks hopefully, peering through the window of the first pub we come to.

'No. Don't want to waste time – I'm too bloody hungry.'

I get out my phone and send a quick text message to Jude: *OK, no use hiding from us! Which pub are you in?*

We look through the windows of the pub again while we're waiting for her to reply. It looks nice in here, but there's no sign of Jude and the others.

'Maybe we should walk on to the next one – oh, hang on!' My phone's ringing. 'Hello? Jude? Oh – who's that?'

'Who's this? Well, *you* sent a text to *me*!' laughs a very attractive male voice with an English accent. 'We're in the Halfpenny Inn in Dublin if you want to join us – we're certainly not hiding from you. Who are you, by the way?'

'Oh! Oh my God, I'm sorry – how the hell did I get the wrong number?' I stammer, embarrassed. 'I mean, this is

Jude's number – it's in my phone – I couldn't have made a mistake ...'

Auntie Joyce has walked on down the road a bit, looking for another pub, but needless to say the others are standing around me, giggling.

'No problem! Nice talking to you ...'

'Wait!' I shout, so loudly that Emily next to me, taking photos of the village, nearly drops her camera.

I know this voice.

'It's Harry.' I don't know whether to laugh or cry. This is ridiculous. 'It's *Harry*, isn't it?'

'Yes!' he sounds a bit startled. There's a pause. I can hear his mates, behind him, laughing and shouting about another pint of Guinness. 'Who's this? Is it *Katie*?' He says my name softly, like a prayer. 'Katie from last night?'

'Yes! God – how embarrassing. How the hell ...?' A ridiculous thought occurs to me. 'You didn't put your number in my phone, did you?'

I'm embarrassed, now, that I've even asked it. Even thought it. Emily and the others are staring at me. Their expressions range from surprise to outright dismay.

'I didn't,' says Harry almost apologetically. 'But I'd have liked to.'

This just adds to my discomfiture.

'Yes, well, look – I don't know what happened here,' I say in a rush. 'I'm really sorry. I'll let you ... get on with your beer ...'

'Nice to talk to you again, Katie,' he says.

I can hear the smile in his voice. I bet he thinks I've got hold of his number somehow. How humiliating!

'Enjoy the rest of your weekend.'

'You too,' I mutter, hanging up.

'What the bloody *hell* ...?' starts Karen, almost accusingly.

'You had his *number*?' says Emily, looking at me as if I've suddenly sprouted horns and a tail.

'No! No, I didn't! I don't understand ... someone must have put it in my phone as a *joke*!'

I scroll back through my Contacts, feeling hot and upset under the suspicious gazes of my friends. Could I have hit the wrong number? Jude's is an Irish number. I know it's correct. I've only got two other J's: Joyce, and a Jenny who I used to work with.

'It doesn't make sense!'

'Try looking under H,' Karen advises me caustically.

'No! Look, it's not in here – see.' I show her the phone. 'Not under H, not anywhere.'

'What's that?' points out Emily, looking over our shoulders. '*Irish*? Who's *Irish*?'

'Oh!' I raise my eyes to the blue, blue sky and burst out laughing. 'Oh my God! I get it now! Oh, how weird is that! How absolutely *weird*!'

'What's weird?' says Joyce, suddenly appearing behind us. 'Come on, girls. I've found the others – they're only in the next pub up the road here. Hurry up! Marge is getting the drinks in.'

At the mention of drinks, everyone turns and practically sprints down the road to the pub. And thankfully it's not till we've taken some of the dust of the road out of our throats with a pint of Dalkey's finest Guinness that I'm called upon to explain myself.

A LIKELY STORY!

It was the treasure hunt, you see. *Phone number of a guy who speaks Irish.*

After getting the red thong, the condom and the cucumber, Auntie Joyce and I were just leaving the hotel to start scouring the streets of Dublin for gorgeous men, schoolgirls and Irish speakers, among other things, when we practically fell into the arms of this guy who was rushing headlong in through the swing doors, looking around the reception area with panic in his eyes.

'Whoops! Sorry!' I said, stepping back to let him past as he was obviously in such a hurry.

'Toilet!' he shouted, staring at us – as well he might, considering the way we were dressed.

'Sorry?'

It was pretty obvious he was either very drunk, very strange, or some kind of pervert, if not all three.

'Toilet!' he repeated urgently. 'Is there one?'

'Over there!' said Auntie Joyce, with a smile, pointing in the appropriate direction. 'Poor thing,' she added as he made a bolt for it. 'I could see he was desperate. He was practically wriggling on the spot, the way you used to when you were a little girl ...'

I didn't particularly want my infantile toilet habits to be the subject of conversation.

'He's got a cheek, hasn't he? If he's not even staying here?'

'Yes, dear, but sometimes, you know, you just can't help it. I remember when your mum was pregnant with you. God almighty! She couldn't go for more than five minutes without needing the loo. We had to ask in the most embarrassing

113

places. Shops, pubs, libraries – we found out where all the toilets in the town were, I can tell you …'

If there was one thing I wanted to discuss even less than how much I peed when I was a little kid, it was how much my mum peed when she was expecting me. However, we'd both been so involved with this line of conversation that we hadn't got any further than just outside the hotel door when our Mr Desperate came hurtling out again.

'Thanks, ladies – or should I say *kids*!' he said, with a grin, sounding (understandably) much calmer now. 'Couple of Guinnesses too many – you know how it is. You all right? You lost your teacher, or something?'

We'd been studying our treasure hunt list and gazing up and down the street, hoping for inspiration.

'No, no, we're not lost,' I said. 'We're just trying to find something.'

'It's a treasure hunt,' explained Joyce. 'We've got a list of things to find.'

'Need any help?'

'We-ell.'

Now, this was both an opportunity, and something of an embarrassment. You see, it obviously crossed my mind straight away that we could ask him, by way of returning a favour, to come back with us as our Most Gorgeous Man. The trouble was, he so patently *wasn't*. (Mind you, if I'd known Lisa was going to appear with Ernest, I'd have thought we were in with a chance.) Don't get me wrong – I'm not completely shallow. I've got nothing against men with strange thin curly hair combed over their bald spots, with tattoos on their necks, and weighed down with heavy gold jewellery. I don't even mind if they've got a bit of a beer gut and wear their trousers too tight and far too short. Everyone has their own look, you know, their own personal style, and some people … well, some people just haven't got it *quite* right.

But I couldn't ask him to be our Most Gorgeous Man. I just couldn't! I knew I wouldn't be able to say it without my face betraying the fact that he was actually the only man available so we'd have to make do. And he surely must have known he wasn't gorgeous, so he might think I was taking the piss.

I looked at Joyce, and wondered if she was thinking the same. I didn't want her to jump in and ask him.

'Well?'

He was certainly keen to help, I'd give him that.

'Do you speak Irish?' I asked, with a sudden spurt of relief, having noticed this one on the list. 'We need the phone number of someone who speaks Irish!'

'No, sorry, not personally. Can't help you there. But ... just a phone number, is it? That's all you need?'

'Yes – do you *know* anyone who speaks Irish?' asked Joyce excitedly.

'Here you are.' He got his phone out of his pocket, scrolled down his Contacts and called out a number.

'Hang on, hang on!'

I didn't have a pen, so I grabbed my own phone out of my bag and entered the number. What to save it as? Well – obviously – *Irish*. I'd only need it till we checked back in with Emily with all our treasure hunt booty.

'Thanks a million!' I told our friend.

'You're welcome. Will you be calling him, then?'

'I expect so. He'll probably have to say a few phrases, you know, to prove it.'

'I reckon he'll be glad to oblige,' he said, with a grin. 'See you, girls!'

'Well, that was a bit of luck!' I said, as he sauntered off.

'Yes, wasn't it,' agreed Joyce. 'Thank goodness we didn't have to ask him to be Mr Gorgeous!'

Of course, when Helen and Jude turned up with Harry, no one else got the chance to show off the rest of their treasures. We were all so completely overcome by him that we just kind of abandoned the game. It was a bit of a shame really, because I don't think they all had a red thong, for a start, and our cucumber was definitely bigger than anyone else's. As for the Irish speaker's phone number, it went completely out of my mind. Till now.

So is this the coincidence of the century, or what?

No wonder the others are all looking at me as if I've concocted the most unlikely fairy story they've ever heard in their lives. This oddball throws himself at Joyce and me because he wants to use the hotel toilets, insists on helping us with the treasure hunt, and gives us the phone number of the very same person who's helping Helen and Jude by being a Gorgeous Man? Like there isn't more than one man available in the whole of Dublin?

'And Harry speaks Irish?' says Lisa, giving me a look that says *Yeah, right, and I'm the Queen of Sheba*.

'He wasn't speaking Irish when we met him,' says Helen accusingly.

'And he wasn't speaking Irish to you later on in the club, was he,' points out Karen.

'He couldn't speak *anything* to her in the club,' snickers Suze. 'She had her tongue too far down his throat ...'

'Get over yourself now, with yer nasty talk!' Jude interrupts as everyone else joins in the giggling. 'Sure and *you've* got a tongue on you yerself, Suzy Smith, that would clip a hedge, so it would!' This just sets everyone off giggling even more, but at least it's taken the heat off me a bit. 'And why would yer man be speaking Irish to us, when we're talking to him in English, and he's English himself, would you ask yerselves that?'

'And anyway,' says Joyce eventually when the laughter's died down, 'It's *true*. I was there. This young man gave Katie the phone number, and she saved it in her phone under *Irish*. She asked me to remember what she'd saved it as.'

'Thank you, Joyce,' I say, with supreme dignity. 'And as I is next to J in my Contacts, I must have hit the wrong one ...'

There's a kind of grudging silence. Jude shifts in her chair, propping her bad foot up a bit higher on the seat opposite. Everyone sips their drinks. Our sandwiches and chips are brought over and we all tuck in with a vengeance.

'Phone him, then,' says Lisa suddenly.

'Yeah! Phone him!' everyone joins in immediately. 'Go on, phone him!'

'I already have! I made *enough* of a fool of myself. OK, it's very strange, and very embarrassing, but let's just forget it. Please?'

116

'No!' insists Helen. 'Come on – phone him again, and ask him to speak some Irish.'

'Yes, come on. Just for the hell of it!' laughs Emily. 'We can all have a listen. Jude will know whether it's real Irish or not.'

I'm not actually finding this very funny. They're teasing, I know, and they think it's a laugh, but they're also still not one hundred per cent sure if I'm telling the truth. They can smell a bit of gossip and their noses are quivering for it. The trouble is, if I make too much of it, if I take it too seriously, get all petulant and refuse to join in the fun, I might as well stand up and announce that I'm up to no good.

'I'll do it,' says Joyce suddenly.

'You will?'

'Yes. Come on. I'm not embarrassed.' She holds her hand out for the phone. 'What's the worst that can happen?'

'He'll swear at you in Irish?' suggests Mum.

'Big deal. I won't even understand. Come on, Katie, dial the number, or whatever you have to do.'

You could hear a pin drop in our corner of the pub. We're all watching Joyce, open-mouthed, as she waits for Harry to answer. Lisa has actually got a chip in her mouth waiting to be chewed – not a pretty sight.

'Hello? Harry? It's ... um ... Joyce here. I'm with Katie – you know? The hen party? Yes, that's right – the bride. What? No, no – she's fine. No, there's nothing wrong with her – I've just borrowed her phone. Harry, look – I hope you don't mind me asking. Do you speak any Irish?'

We can hear him laughing. Even from the other end of the table I'm sure they can hear him.

'Why? Well, you see, I know it sounds strange. Yes, I realise you're English. But we were given your number last night. That's why – yes! That's why Katie had it in her phone. Someone who knew you gave us your number, for the treasure hunt – you know? We needed someone who spoke Irish, and this *friend* of yours ...'

The laughter from the other end of the phone is even louder now. It sounds like there's a whole room of them guffawing there.

'What? He's no friend of yours? Well, quite. Yes, that's him. Tattoos, yes, gold chains. Chris, you say? Well, tell Chris from us he's *very funny*.' Joyce raises her eyebrows at the rest of us. 'Katie? Yes, she's here, next to me. Hold on – I'll pass you over.'

It's not exactly a private conversation. I'm being closely listened to by eight pairs of ears. But it's nice to hear his voice again. Even if he is still laughing.

'I don't speak a word of Irish,' he says. 'Sorry about that. Bloody fool Chris. His idea of a joke ...'

'Is he with the stag party? We didn't see him at the club.'

'He was there all right, but doesn't get up off his arse to dance or anything like that. He lurks in dark corners – best place for him,' he says, still laughing.

'Sorry for bothering you, then. I'll let you get back to your mates.'

'It's no bother. It's given me another chance to talk to you, Katie. And now I've got your number, too.'

I feel myself blushing. Eight pairs of eyes are watching me.

'Yes, well. OK, then. Enjoy the rest of your weekend. Don't get too drunk!'

'Actually today's my last drinking day. When this mob fly back tomorrow morning, I'm picking up a hire car and driving down to County Cork to spend a few days with my cousin.'

'Cork? My friend lives in ...' I begin, glancing at Jude, and then stop, feeling silly. County Cork's a big place. So what if his cousin lives in the same county as Jude? It's not exactly a riveting coincidence. 'Well, have a good time with your cousin, then,' I finish lamely.

'Thanks. He speaks Irish, incidentally,' he says with a laugh. 'I guess that's why Chris picked on me. Well, I might not have been any good for the Irish speaking, but you've got my number if you need anything else ...'

'OK, yes, thank you. Goodbye!' I say hurriedly, feeling myself grow hot again.

'Another striptease, or anything, you know ...' he says softly.

I hang up, put the phone down and take a bite of my sandwich. I can't meet those eight pairs of eyes until my pulse has returned to normal.

'There you are!' says Joyce triumphantly. 'How about that, then. Just a joke, and a coincidence. Now – get on with your lunch, everyone, for goodness' sake.'

But when everyone else has gone back to their own conversations and they all seem finally to have forgotten about it, I look up and catch Joyce's eye. And she gives me a wink.

I hope she can't read my mind.

ABOUT BOXTY

The plan, this evening, is for a traditional Irish meal at a place that Jude's booked for us in Temple Bar, followed by (naturally) a few drinks, as it's our last night. I can't believe how quickly this weekend is going. I'm actually quite surprised that I'm having such a good time, considering that everything in my life seems to be going pear-shaped. I'm wondering whether the constant topping-up of alcohol is keeping me from grasping anything with any real clarity. I'm drinking, and smiling, and laughing, and drinking, and all the time there are these dark clouds forming somewhere on the edges of my consciousness. Like an unexpectedly bright sunny day in the middle of a bad winter, the alcohol and the laughter are giving me a false air of cheerfulness. Underneath, I'm not sure what cold depths of reality are lurking.

So far Helen hasn't tried to talk to me any more about Greg. I think she may be embarrassed. I'm sure if she hadn't had a few drinks last night, none of this would have come out.

And I'm equally sure that if *I* hadn't had a few drinks this lunchtime, I wouldn't be walking next to her now on the way to the DART station in Dalkey, bringing up the subject again myself.

'I'll have to leave,' I tell her, quite nonchalantly, as if I'm not talking about the job I love.

'What? Leave?'

She's looking at me as if I've spoken in Japanese, although on second thoughts, knowing Helen, she'd probably have understood me if I had.

'I'll have to leave Bookshelf. Obviously.'

'Of course you won't!' She looks stricken. 'Don't be ridiculous! Why should you?'

'I didn't say I *should*. I said I'll *have* to.'

'But ...'

'You must have known that. You must have realised I won't be able to stay, now you've told me all this stuff. How can I? I'd feel like ... well, like a third shoe when there's only two feet. A third glove for a pair of hands. A ...'

'Yes, yes, I get the picture. But you won't! We've worked so well together all this time.'

'Only because I didn't know what was going on in your head, or Greg's. Now I know, it changes the whole dynamic of our little *ménage à trois*. It'll be impossible.'

'If you go, he'll be distraught, and he'll blame me, and then he'll *never* ...'

I look at her almost indifferently.

'He'll never want you? Well, how can I help that? You'll have to work it out between you, Helen. I'm going to start job-hunting when we go back.'

'You've got enough on your plate as it is,' she says quietly, 'with the wedding.'

Yes. That too.

We have a couple of quiet hours in our rooms when we get back to the hotel. We're all tired out from the fresh air, the exercise, and the alcohol. And poor Jude's in a lot of pain with her ankle. It's really badly swollen.

I put some extra pillows on the end of the bed and help her to lie down with her foot up and some cold towels around it.

'Are you sure you shouldn't see a doctor?' I ask her.

'Jesus, no. Sure it'll be grand if I just rest it for a while.'

She swallows a couple more painkillers and closes her eyes.

Oh well – might as well read a chapter or two of *Love In The Afternoon*. I pick up the book and turn a few pages but I can't concentrate. My thoughts keep straying to what sort of job I might have to take if I leave Bookshelf. *When* I leave Bookshelf. I might have known it was too good to be true. Who in this world gets to have their perfect job?

Come to that, I wonder, skimming the words of chapter one and turning another page, who in this world gets to have their perfect man? I lie back and close my eyes for a minute, thinking about Matt. I remember all the good times we've had during our years together. All the fun, and love, and laughter, before we started arguing. I need to focus on that, on the happy times, forget about Prague, and all the cross words and bickering and sulks recently. That's just a blip. It'll pass. Everything's going to work out fine.

Helen thinks her perfect man is Greg, which is the most unbelievable thing I've ever heard in my life – but what good will that do her, if it's not reciprocated? She'll just be even more unhappy than if she'd never met her so-called Mr Right in the first place.

And look at Lisa. She thought Perfect Prick was her perfect man at one time. And now he's turned out to be the booby prize, she thinks this Andy from the gym is Mr Perfect. Until when? Until their first argument? Until he finds someone else, or she does, or she finds out he's just another prick in disguise?

I've always believed in love. I *love* believing in love and I don't want to stop. But look around you: where is it? Where's the evidence for it? Look what happened to Mum, for instance. What was the point of her falling in love with my dad – what good did that do her? It ruined her life! Apart from getting me and Lisa, of course. Is that what it's all about, at the end of the day? Just God's little trick to get you to reproduce, keep the population going? I'm *not* going to believe that. I can't give up on it. It's always been my dream. One woman; one man; one lifetime. It's got to be true. It's got to work! I'm going to read this bloody book if it kills me, and I'm going to believe in *love in the afternoon*, and the evening, and the morning, and all the time, despite every-thing I hear to the contrary.

But I'm not thinking about Matt as I finally immerse myself in the story of the two star-crossed lovers in my book. It's completely silly, and it's probably just because I'm still a bit drunk. And I'm certainly not going to be telling anyone. But the face I keep seeing in my mind's eye is Harry's.

*

'What in God's name is a boxty?' demands Lisa, about one second ahead of the rest of us.

Jude's taking us to a boxty restaurant. She says it's an Irish tradition and we'll love it. Luckily it's only just round the corner from our hotel, and we're taking it in turns to be Jude's 'crutches'.

'It's a kind of potato pancake, with all kinds of different fillings. Sure you've never been to Ireland if you haven't tasted a boxty. You'll be full to the brim, it'll soak up any amount of alcohol, so it will.'

'Sounds like it was invented for us!'

'It's an ancient Irish dish. They say you won't get married if you can't make it. *Boxty on the griddle, boxty in the pan. If you can't make boxty, you'll never get your man!*'

'Blimey,' says Emily, nudging me. 'You'd better get the recipe for one of these boxty thingies off the chef, love, or you might as well call the wedding off tonight!'

'*Not* funny, Emily,' says Lisa, looking at my face. 'Don't upset the bride on the last night of her hen weekend.'

'It's OK, I'm fine,' I say quickly. 'Yes, very funny, Em – get the bloody recipe off the chef, then, good idea.'

Maybe I'll open a boxty restaurant in Romford after I leave Bookshelf.

'Are there any vegetarian boxties?' asks Karen suspiciously.

'There are too. Sure I've had one meself and it's probably the tastiest of the lot. Then there's fish, and chicken, and beef with stout, or of course you should really try the bacon and cabbage – that's the most typically Irish boxty ...'

'Have you got shares in this place?' says Emily. 'You could get a job standing outside the restaurant, getting people in off the streets.'

'That's one thing they don't need!' laughs Jude, as we turn the corner and she points to the queue already snaking out of the restaurant door. 'This place is always busy.'

Good job Jude got us a reservation. We squeeze our way in past the queue and make our way to our table. Everything's old and dark in here, with ancient wooden tables and chairs. You feel like you're in someone's farm-house kitchen.

'Cool!' shouts Suze, settling down with the menu. 'Get the drinks in!'

'I think it's Guinness all round, tonight. No excuses! We should all be used to it after three days here,' says Lisa.

'And I'm having some homemade Irish broth to start,' decides Helen.

'Would you maybe not think of having a starter,' says Jude. 'Or you'll never get the boxty inside of you, to be sure.'

Our waitress is rushed off her feet and we have a bit of a wait for our meal, so by the time it arrives we're all onto the second pint of Guinness and most of us have had enough of it and are more than ready to get stuck into the wine.

'I feel pissed already,' complains Emily.

'Well, get outside of your boxty, that'll take care of you, so it will.'

Jude knocks back a couple more painkillers. She's sitting at the end of the table with her foot up on an extra chair. Her ankle's strapped up now with some proper bandages we got from the chemist's, but you can still see how swollen it is.

'Should you be taking all those pills, with the alcohol?' I ask her.

'Ah, be away with you and yer nagging, Katie. To be sure if the pain doesn't kill me, the drugs and the alcohol will!'

'But seriously ...'

'They're only paracetamol, for the love of God. I'm having a laugh with you. I'll be grand altogether when I've got a couple more glasses of this wine down me neck.'

It's warm in the restaurant. Halfway through my beef boxty, I'm having doubts about Jude's claim that it'll soak up the alcohol. I guess it might if you don't drink as much as we're all putting away.

'Hey, everyone!' calls Emily, trying to stand up but getting pushed back down by Lisa, sitting next to her. 'As it's our last night I think we should all raise a glass to our bride.'

'To the bride!' goes the cry around the table.

'To Katie!'

'To Katie and Matt!'

'May your days be touched by a bit of Irish luck ...' begins Jude, waving her glass in the air.

She stops, rubs her head, frowning, but before she can remember the next line Karen finishes for her:

'And may your nights be warmed by a bit of Irish fuck!'

'Karen!' exclaims Mum, scandalised, as we all screech and squeal and roll around in our chairs with laughter. 'Honestly!'

'Come on, Marge,' laughs Joyce, wiping the tears from her eyes. 'You have to admit, that was very funny!'

'What *are* the correct words to that nice Irish blessing, Jude?' asks Mum sniffily.

'Buggered if I know, Marge,' giggles Jude, spilling half her wine over her plate. 'I prefer Karen's version!'

Look at the state of us, by the time we move on to a bar a little way down the street. There's live music in here so we reckon it'll be a good finale to our last night. At least I think that's what we reckon. We're all so full of boxty, booze and general high spirits we can hardly hold a rational discussion.

The bar's absolutely crammed; we find a spot near a window where there's just about room for us all to stand. The music's lively and the crowd's good-natured, and someone lets Jude have a chair although there's nowhere for her to put her foot up.

'Should have been wearing our schoolgirl outfits again!' shouts Lisa, as she and Karen come back from the bar with the drinks. 'I bet we'd have got served a lot more quickly.'

'Yeah – and attracted a lot more attention!' I laugh.

'Oh, God – I almost forgot!' shrieks Emily, diving into her handbag. 'I brought these for us to wear again tonight!'

The photo badges. Great.

'Do I really need everyone in here to see what I looked like as a baby?' I groan as they all start pinning on their badges.

'Yeah – come on, love, let's see!' laughs a guy at the next table. 'Your hen party, is it?'

Well done.

'Ha! Brings back memories,' says the girl sitting next to him, who looks too young but is evidently his wife. 'Had a brilliant time on mine last year. Went to Prague. Great, it was.'

I freeze at the mention of Prague. Bugger. Just when everything was going so well.

'We went for a week – it was so cheap. Everything! The hotel was cheap, the drink was cheap ... *much* cheaper than Dublin. Dublin's the most expensive place in the world, I reckon. We've been saving up ever since the wedding to come here for our first anniversary.'

This is really, *really* not what I want to hear.

'Yeah, it's very expensive, is Dublin,' chimes in her husband. 'And as for London! I went to London just for three days for my stag, and it cost more than her week in Prague. Unbelievable!'

'Never mind, love. You enjoy yourself while you can! Plenty of time for economy after the wedding, eh!' giggles Mrs Happy First Anniversary.

I feel sick. I don't want to talk to these people about their hen party and their stag party. I walk away from them, push my way through the crowd to the Ladies.

I don't really need to go to the loo; I just need to be on my own for a minute. I lean against the sinks and close my eyes. When I open them, Emily's standing next to me.

'You all right, little hen?' she says, frowning at me through the mists of her own drunkenness.

'No.'

'Whassup?'

'Prague. Anniversary Annie out there went to bloody Prague for her hen party – her hen *week* – and it was cheap. Cheap, cheap, cheap. Cheaper than a weekend in Dublin.'

'OK, Katie,' she says, grasping my point straight away, despite the alcohol. 'So the stag's cheap. So what? That's not really the point.'

'Of course it is. It's the whole point! I made all that fuss, and I was wrong about it.'

'No. No, you *weren't* wrong.' She's got hold of my arm now and is talking right close to my face. 'Matt was wrong, Katie. He was wrong because it mattered to you, and he didn't care how much it mattered. That's the bottom line. That's what I *told* him. . .'

'You what?' I stare at her, totally lost. 'When? When did you tell him?'

She's realised what she's said, the minute the words are out of her mouth. She's covered her mouth with her hand as if to stop herself saying anything else.

'*When*?' I repeat, staring at her. Staring at the flush rising in her cheeks, the shifty look in her eyes, the slight shake of her hand as she takes it from her mouth and scratches her head with it. '*When* were you talking to him? Why were you discussing this with him behind my back?'

'Not now, Katie. Not tonight.'

'*Yes* now, Emily! For Christ's sake! What's going on? You never told me you talked to him ...'

'I was trying to help.'

'So why didn't I get to hear about it? You try to help, but you can't tell me?'

She shakes her head miserably.

'I don't want to talk about this.'

'Well, I *do*.'

We're both leaning on the sinks now, looking into each other's eyes, almost holding our breath. I'm thinking I suppose I could back down. Tell her not to worry. It probably doesn't matter. We'll discuss it another time.

But before I open my mouth to say so, she takes a great, long sigh and starts to talk. And although I'm wishing she hadn't started, it's too late now. We've crossed that line. I have to hear it.

EMILY'S STORY

There's no way I'm going to be able to tell Katie the whole of this story. She'll get an edited version. I've got to live with the rest of it. What else can I do?

You need to understand where I'm coming from. I've known Katie since we were both eighteen and in our first term at Sheffield University. We were a long way from home. In fact I don't think either of us had ever been that far north before in our lives. It was like a foreign country. Nearly all our new friends were from the north and we pretty soon gravitated towards each other because our accents were the same. We were the only two Essex girls in our halls. Karen and Suze both came from Birmingham and even *they* were looked upon as southerners.

Before long, Katie and I were inseparable. We came home together for holidays – sometimes on the train, sometimes with one of our parents picking us both up. My family lived in a little village halfway between Colchester and the coast. There was nothing much to do there but Katie loved it. She used to borrow Lisa's car and drive over during the long summer holidays, and we'd lie in the garden under the apple tree, studying and chatting. Then we'd drive back to Romford for the evening and stay over at Katie's house.

In all the time Katie and I have been friends, we must have had about a hundred boyfriends between us. OK, maybe that's an exaggeration, but you get the picture. We went out with guys we met at Sheffield, and then came home and went out with different guys we met at pubs and clubs in Romford. I went out for a while with a boy I'd known all my life, who lived in my village – but it didn't stop me going out with someone else when I went back to uni for the next term.

It wasn't as bad as it sounds; we weren't pretending to anybody that we were serious about them. We were just having fun.

It wasn't until after we graduated, when I got my first job in London and moved to Romford to share a flat with Katie, that I sensed a change in her. She was getting fed up with the clubbing every Friday and Saturday night, the coupling-up with new guys and the inevitable swift dumping by either party with no particular regrets.

Her first serious boyfriend was a guy called Stuart from the publishing company where she worked. I didn't like him; he was too possessive, too controlling. Thank God, she finished with him after about six months. I still remember what she said, when she phoned me in tears to say it was over.

'I wanted him to be *The One*.'

'But he wasn't,' I said. 'You couldn't make him be.'

After that, I think she spent the next five years hoping that every guy she went out with would be *The One*. Of course, she was disappointed every time. Why? Well, because she was looking for something that didn't exist. Mr Right. Tall, dark, handsome, well dressed, beautifully mannered, intelligent, compassionate, understanding ... you follow my drift? He doesn't exist. *I've* known that since I was about sixteen. By this time, when we were in our mid-twenties, I was happy with a series of boyfriends who were Mr Not-Too-Bad. Average-looking, average income, fairly normal, quite kind. But it wasn't enough for Katie. Every relationship she had started with the same great expectations. She always thought *this* man was going to be *The One*. And every relationship ended in tears when she found out he wasn't perfect.

Matt isn't perfect either.

How could I tell Katie that? You've already heard how they fell for each other. It was like a volcano erupting. Like a tornado. I hardly ever saw her any more because she couldn't tear herself away from him. She cut herself off from everyone, and thought being in love made it acceptable. I met Sean soon afterwards, and eventually, Katie and Matt got a bit more settled and we started seeing each other as a foursome. I knew our friendship was never in danger. I'd just had to bide my time till she calmed down a bit.

But she's never wavered from her conviction that he's her perfect soul mate. That's why, I know, it's affected her so badly now they're having these arguments. Especially this big one about the stag party.

He's an arsehole, isn't he?

I mean, at the end of the day, it didn't matter who was being unreasonable, or whether they both were. It was his refusal to compromise, his insistence that he'd made his mind up and he was going to have his own way, that was the problem. It was unloving. That's what bothered me. If you love someone, even if you disagree with them, you don't go ahead and do something to upset them.

And yes, I told him so.

I was so annoyed, the evening Katie phoned me to come over – the evening we had to hide and whisper in her bedroom because Matt was watching football in the lounge and we mustn't disturb him – I wanted to walk in there and tell him what a selfish pig he was being. Obviously that wasn't going to help matters, so I did the next best thing I could: tried to cheer Katie up, talked about pre-wedding stress and told her not to take it all too seriously.

The next day, I phoned him at work.

'What's the matter?' he asked sharply. 'Is Kate all right?'

'Not really. Haven't you noticed?'

He was silent for a minute. I could hear the voices of the other people in his office. Someone was whistling. Another phone was ringing. I waited.

'Emily,' he said eventually, with a long drawn-out sigh, 'If you weren't one of Kate's closest friends I'd tell you to mind your own fucking business.'

'If I wasn't her friend,' I replied tightly, 'I wouldn't be phoning.'

'I can't talk now. Look – what time are you finishing work tonight?'

'About five.'

His office was half a dozen Tube stations across London from mine.

'I'll meet you at five thirty. Liverpool Street. In the bar. OK?'

I got the impression I was an annoying extra chore he had to fit in, to clear up.

'OK. I'll be there.'

I was at the station early, so I got a drink, found a seat in the corner of the bar and sat reading my paper. He arrived looking irritated and impatient, which put my back up straight away.

'You could at least try to look as if you care,' I snapped as he joined me at the table, 'that I'm concerned enough to need to talk to you.'

'I'll tell you what I care about,' he retorted. 'The fact that you ring me up at work and start ranting ...'

'I did *not* rant!' I gasped. 'I just wanted to know if you understood how upset Katie is.'

He looked at me with annoyance.

'With all due respect, Emily, you don't know everything that goes on between Kate and me. She's upset? Well, *I'm* upset too!'

'Well, then, sort it out, Matt. For God's sake – you're getting married soon! What's more important, ten days with your mates or your lifetime with Katie ...'

'I suppose Kate's been telling you that I'm being unreasonable and extravagant.'

'Well – ten days ... and taking time off without pay ...'

'Emily...' He ran his hands through his hair. I noticed, for the first time, that he looked exhausted. As if he hadn't slept for a week. 'Look, there's more to it than that. It's not just about the stag party.'

'I realise that. I know you've been arguing. I understand that it gets tense just before a wedding, but ...'

'You understand *fuck all*!' he spat back at me.

It was so vicious, it took my breath away. I took a gulp of my drink.

'Right. I think I'd better go.'

I went to pick up my bag, but he rested his hand on mine.

'I'm sorry, Emily,' he said quietly. 'Don't go. I want to talk.'

131

'Talk away, then,' I returned, still rattled. 'If you can do it without swearing at me.'

He spread his hands wide in a gesture of apology.

'You're a good friend to Kate. The best. You're better for her than I am.'

'Girl friends are always good to each other. We're generally nicer than men,' I said with feeling.

'I can't disagree with you there.' He gave me a rueful half-smile, turning his glass round and round on the table without drinking from it. 'But Katie and I ... we had something special.'

'*Had*?'

I felt a shiver run down my spine. What's with the past tense, here?

'I've fucked it all up, Em.'

He looked up at me, and I froze. He had tears in his eyes.

'What is it, Matt? Come on, it can't be that bad. Katie loves you! Can't you just tell her you're sorry – say you realise you could have been more considerate about Prague, but you don't want to cancel now. Compromise. Promise to make it up to her. She's a forgiving person ...'

He gave a mirthless snort.

'I keep telling you, this isn't about Prague. I *need* to go to Prague, Emily. I need those ten days away from Kate. I have to put some distance between us before I go mad. She looks at me with those spaniel eyes, making me feel like shit ...'

'Because you've *hurt* her!'

'And she doesn't even know how much.'

I swallowed the rest of my drink and closed my eyes. I had a really, really bad feeling about this. I was thinking I should just get up and walk away. I was wishing I'd never started it. But it was too late now; I needed to know.

'Tell me,' I said flatly, without looking at him.

In the silence, I was thinking: *It can't be another woman. They're hardly ever apart.*

'Her name's Claire,' he said, almost in a whisper.

Another woman. I'd spoken aloud without realising it. My heart was throbbing like a wound. *No, not this. It isn't fair. Katie doesn't deserve it.*

'It's not an affair,' he said. 'I'm not having an affair.'

'What is it, then?' I had to speak through my clamped teeth because I felt like I was going to be sick. 'A one-night stand? Is that all? A fucking stupid, drunken *shag* with some *slapper* ...'

'*No!*' His voice rose like a wail. 'No, not that.'

I stared back at him. I wasn't going to help him out. I wanted him to suffer while he told me.

'We're just friends,' he said. He leant his head on one hand. 'We work together.'

'And?'

'And we've fallen in love.'

'Oh, *please*!' I smacked the table with the palm of my hand, so hard that both our glasses jumped off the surface. 'You're not fourteen years old! You're a grown man, in a relationship, about to be married ...'

'I know.'

'What the *fuck* has got into you? All this time, you and Katie have been like Siamese twins, like the original perfect happy couple, and now, suddenly, just because you're having a few arguments, you decide you don't love her any more, you love this ... this *Claire*.'

'It isn't like that. It isn't because of the arguments. The arguments are because of the state I'm in. I'm falling apart, Em!'

'I don't give a shit what state you're in! You *deserve* to be in a state. You can't do this, Matt! You can't just switch from loving one person to loving another ...'

'I haven't. I still love Katie. I love them both!'

'Of course you don't, you stupid fucker. Who is this Claire? What's her phone number? Where does she live?' I was ready to go round there and beat the shit out of her. 'How *can* she do this? The cow! How can she have it off with someone else's bloke – just before the wedding!'

'But I've told you: we're not having an affair. We haven't had sex. We haven't even ... Don't shake your head at me like that, Emily. I'm telling you the truth. We haven't even kissed.'

'Well, maybe you should have done!' I retorted illogically. 'Shag her, go on – get it out of your system. That's what it's all about, at the end of the day. That's all it's ever about with you bastards.'

'No. It's not like that. Claire feels the same way. She respects the fact that I'm with Katie. She's waiting for me to make up my mind ...'

'Oh, spare me the bleeding hearts and fucking flowers!'

'Emily, I didn't *ask* for this situation. I didn't *want* to fall in love with someone else!'

'Well, you should have fought it harder. You should have moved offices! Changed jobs! Turned away from her! You *idiot.*'

I searched my pockets for a tissue to blow my nose. I hadn't realised I was crying. I'd run out of steam.

'Why have you told me?' I asked him tonelessly. 'I hate you for telling me.'

'You wanted to know.'

'I wanted to know everything was going to be all right. Not this.'

'I needed you to see why I have to go away. Away from both of them. I need time, and space, on my own ...'

'Yeah, right. With a crowd of drunken friends.'

'No. It's just me and Sean.'

'Sean *knows* about this?'

He hung his head.

'I had to tell him. I had to get him to cancel the stag. I couldn't face it. We're going on our own.'

My head was spinning. Sean knew, and didn't tell me?

'I'll kill him. He should have talked to me.'

'No. I told him to keep it to himself.'

'Well, I hope he's going to talk some sense into your thick, stupid head ...'

'Yes. I hope he is, too. He's just as mad at me as you are.' He suddenly gripped my hands, across the table. 'Emily, I'm *trying* not to hurt Katie!'

'Well, you could have fooled me.'

'I haven't done anything wrong ...'

I shook his hands off mine, looking at him coldly, furiously.

'You haven't got a clue, have you, Matt? You're telling me you're in love with two women, but you don't under-stand the first thing about women – how we think, how we feel. Katie could have forgiven you a one-night stand. Maybe even an affair. Sex doesn't mean anything – it's just bodies, at the end of the day. But she'll never forgive you for *loving* someone else. Not even if you never touch this other woman as long as you live. So take my advice. Go to Prague with Sean, if you must. Cry on his shoulder. Do your male bonding bit. And then come home, marry Katie, change jobs and don't ever, *ever* tell her about Claire. If you do, she will *never* forgive you.'

I got up, shakily, grabbed my bag and started to walk away, turning back only once to add, over my shoulder: 'And neither will I.'

ABOUT A FIGHT

I may be drunk, but I'm not stupid.

Emily's just told me half of a story, and I want to know the other half. The part she's swallowed back and kept to herself. I can see it in her eyes, burning in her brain, hurting inside her because she wants to tell me but she won't.

'So *why* was he feeling so mixed up? *Why* did he need *time and space*? For God's sake, Emily – you're talking in riddles.'

'So was he! I had no idea what was up with him. That's why I didn't say anything to you. I didn't see the point in worrying you ...'

'You're lying.'

'Don't say that to me.'

'I'll say it again: you're lying. You're keeping something from me, something he told you. What is it?'

'Nothing. Just what I said – that he was feeling mixed up, and he knew he'd been upsetting you, and he was sorry ...'

'No he wasn't. If he was sorry, why didn't he say so? How come he can tell you stuff that he can't tell me?'

I can't believe this. Emily, of all people. She's supposed to be my friend. I trusted her more than anyone – and now it turns out she's been sneaking around, behind my back, talking to Matt and not even mentioning it to me.

'Because I asked him, I suppose, Katie,' she says, sounding aggrieved. What's *she* got to be aggrieved about? 'I bothered to ask him what was wrong with him.'

'Oh – and I suppose you think I didn't?'

'No. You were probably too busy being upset about the stupid stag party ...'

'You *agreed* with me! You agreed that he was in the wrong – being inconsiderate – spending too much ...'

'I agreed with you, yes. I just didn't think it was the end of the fucking world.'

She turns away from me and picks up her hairbrush, starting to brush her hair in the mirror with hard, hard brush strokes as if making her hair shine is going to make anything better.

'You cow!' I grab the brush out of her hand and try to hit her with it, but she gets hold of my wrist and swings me away from her.

'Katie! Calm down!'

'Calm down? How can you say that? This is my *hen* weekend, Emily – do you realise that?'

'Of course I do.'

'I've had my sister telling me she's having an affair! I've had my mum telling me my dad cheated on her! I've got to leave my job because Helen's in love with Greg and Greg's in love with me ...'

'*What*?'

'Yes, yes – it's like a fucking love triangle at Bookshelf – and now, *now*, Emily, as if I really need anything else to go wrong ...'

'Nothing's gone wrong, Katie. I'm just telling you I agreed with you about the bloody stag party. I agreed with you – OK? That was why I went to talk to Matt ...'

'You had no *right*!' I swing at her again with the brush, nearly losing my balance.

This time she strikes back, shoving me against the sinks.

'You're drunk,' she says, breathing hard. 'Let's drop it. Let's talk about it tomorrow.'

'No!' I push her away from me. 'Let's talk about it now, Emily. Tell me what else he said!'

'*Nothing* else.'

'*Liar!*' I push her again 'Tell me! What are you hiding from me?'

'Nothing, Katie! Calm down!'

'If you don't tell me, Emily, I'll think the worst.'

I'm crying now. I know I'm being ridiculous, and hysterical, but I've had enough. You see? I've had just about enough, this weekend. I'm supposed to be having a nice time, and all I'm getting is one shock after another. Are they all conspiring to ruin everything for me? As if everything isn't bad enough already. *It's my party and I'll cry if I want to.*

'There's no worst to think,' says Emily quietly, slowly, as if she's talking to a child or an invalid. 'This is all going to seem really, really silly in the morning, Katie.'

It's her, isn't it.

Is that what it's all about? Is that why she's looking so shifty, acting so guilty and secretive?

'I wondered, for a while, if Matt was seeing another woman,' I tell her.

My voice sounds strangely calm to my ears.

'Don't be daft. He loves you. He wouldn't ...'

'Is it you?'

For a minute, she looks totally gobsmacked. For a minute, I think maybe I was wrong. She wouldn't do that. She's my friend, for God's sake.

'You're mad!' she says then, bursting out laughing.

How is this funny? My life's falling apart, and she's *laughing*?

'Bitch!' I shout, slapping her face.

Even as I do it, even as my hand makes contact with her face, I'm shocked at myself. I didn't mean it. I just wanted to stop her laughing.

'Bitch yourself!' she yells, slapping me back.

Ouch. That *fucking* hurt.

I lunge at her, pulling her hair.

She grabs a handful of mine and pulls harder.

I try to trip her up.

She kicks my ankles.

I dig in my nails.

She pinches.

I scratch.

We're both screaming. There's blood on her face. I don't know if it's hers or mine. The door into the toilets is opening – someone's coming in. The red mist in front of my eyes begins to clear a little and I can't believe what we're doing.

'Get *off*!' I shout, giving one last desperate shove. She catapults away from me, overbalancing, skidding on the wet floor. She reaches behind, making a grab for the hand towel dispenser, the tampon machine, anything to stop her falling. Instead, her flailing right arm makes contact with someone's face.

It's so sudden, Jude doesn't see it coming. Balancing on her good foot, holding onto the sinks with one hand, she's just hobbled in through the door when Emily's fist lands squarely on her nose. As her head jerks back, Emily topples over, knocking Jude flying. There's a radiator next to the row of sinks. As Jude's head hits it, it makes a sound like a gong, and then suddenly everything's gone very, very quiet.

'Jesus Christ,' whispers Emily, struggling to her feet as I rush to kneel by Jude's side. 'Have we both gone *mad*?'

I can't answer.

I'm too busy praying.

ABOUT A HOSPITAL EXPERIENCE

There's always a lot of blood from a scalp wound. I didn't know that before, but I do now.

I know a lot of things now:

The amount of blood isn't necessarily as serious as it looks;

You can lose consciousness for just a few seconds and still suffer concussion;

For those few seconds, you can be so frightened you've killed one of your best friends, you can sober up instantly;

And too much alcohol can make you behave like the worst kind of out-of-control teenage thug roaming the streets looking for trouble, when you're actually, despite appearances to the contrary, a respectable thirty-one-year-old woman from a decent law-abiding family.

I'm so ashamed, I'm never going to drink again.

'They all say that, love!' says Patrick, our ambulance man, cheerfully. 'Sure nearly every accident we get called out to at the weekends is because of someone drinking too much. Everyone's always going to stop drinking after someone gets hurt, aren't they, so? If they all stopped when they say they're going to, sure it's strange altogether that we're still being called out at all, at all.'

There's some Irish logic in there somewhere, but I'm too upset to work it out.

'Cheer up, love. Your friend'll be grand,' says his mate.

Emergency medical technicians, they call themselves over here – not paramedics, apparently. I think they're kind of first-aiders anyway but they certainly seem to know what they're doing.

'They'll just want to keep an eye on her for twenty-four hours, so they will. She could have a bit of mild concussion, but she seems to be well orientated so far.'

Jude's lying in the ambulance and I'm sitting on the other side. They're just about to drive us to the hospital.

'I feel a bit strange,' she says, touching the wound on her head delicately. It's been cleaned up now and the bleeding seems to have stopped. 'But could that maybe be the paracetamol?'

'Paracetamol can't hurt you, Jude ...' I start, wondering if the knock on the head *has* made her lose the plot after all. 'You've been taking them all day, haven't you, for your ankle.'

'But that was why I came to find you, in the Ladies, Katie. I can't remember how many I've taken. With the drink, and all, I've ... lost track, if you know what I mean. Have you still got the packet?'

I'd put her packet of tablets in my bag for her, as she was carrying one of those little purses with no room for anything in them. The ambulance guys are suddenly looking at me with a degree of concern. I fumble in my bag.

'No. Can't find them. Are you sure you gave them back to me after the last two you took?'

'No,' says Jude, shaking her head. 'No, I'm not sure, to be honest with you, Katie. In that case, I think ... I think I might have taken the whole packet.'

The driver leaps into his seat and pulls away so fast, the ambulance shakes from side to side and I have to hang on to stop myself sliding off the seat. The lights and sirens are going, and Patrick's firing questions at me about how long, how often, how much paracetamol Jude *might* have taken.

'I think I'm OK, though ...' she says weakly, looking at me anxiously.

'We'll let the doctors decide that, so we will, Judith,' says Patrick very seriously.

'Oh God! Oh, Jude, I'm *so sorry* ...' I start all over again.

We've been through this already, before the ambulance arrived. I did a lot of crying, and a lot of apologising, to

Emily and to Jude. I told them both I didn't deserve to be their friend. That they should never talk to me again. That I loved them both. I think I told Jude I'd kill myself if she died. Like that was going to make her feel better.

'It's not your fault, Katie, if I took too many tablets,' she says, reasonably. 'Sure I was drinking too much myself. We all were. I think maybe we should all give it up after this.'

Patrick doesn't even make a joke about it this time.

That's what worries me.

The A & E Department at the Mater Hospital in Dublin doesn't look a lot different from any of the ones I've been to on the odd occasion at home in Essex. The waiting room's full; people are standing, leaning against walls, because all the chairs are taken. A drunk, sitting on the floor in front of the toilet door, is singing 'It's A Long Way to Tipperary' in a strange, warbling voice, and crying at the same time. Two nurses are trying to prevent another drunk from taking his trousers off. A teenage girl is being held up by her two bleary-eyed friends as she sways and vomits onto the floor.

I'm never, ever, drinking again. I mean it.

I'm running beside Patrick as he wheels Jude straight through all this mayhem to a treatment room where a doctor barges in, seemingly fresh from another patient, as if he was expecting us.

'Judith. Hi. I'm Dr East,' says this rather gorgeous guy with a faint American accent. 'Now, can you tell me . . .'

'She fell!' I gabble before Jude can open her mouth.

I know about these things, you see. I watch *ER* and *Casualty*. One false word to these doctors, and they call the police in. Emily and I will be banged up for assault.

'Because of her ankle! She sprained it, you see, so she was unsteady. She was limping – and she fell, and hit her head . . .'

'Yes, we'll get to her head injury in a minute,' he says calmly, without taking his eyes off Jude. 'First I want to assess the possibility of a paracetamol overdose.'

There are two nurses performing a silent dance around Jude's trolley. One's setting up a drip while one's taking and recording her blood pressure. Then they step back, circle the patient in opposing directions, one takes her temperature and one writes in her notes. Any minute I expect them to curtsy to each other.

'Judith, can you tell me when you started taking the paracetamol?'

'Lunchtime. About one o'clock, I think it was, and then I took some more when we got back to the hotel . . .'

'And you say you've taken a whole packet? Sixteen tablets? Since one o'clock?' He glances back at me. 'Do we have the empty packet, here?'

'No. No, that's the trouble, you see – we can't find the packet, and she's not sure, now, how many she's taken, because . . .'

'How much have you had to drink, Judith?'

Jude looks up at me helplessly.

'Well, let me see now, 'twould be hard to put a number on it, to be sure, being as it's me friend's hen party an' all, but to be honest with you, doctor—'

'We've had loads,' I interrupt. 'Guinness, then wine, then vodka. But I'm giving it up after tonight.'

He ignores this. I suppose, to be fair, he's not really interested in me. He's got enough on his plate with Jude, what with her concussion, and her ankle, and her possible overdose. She's providing him with enough material to pass one of his exams without even moving from the spot.

'It's not serious, is it?' I ask him, unable to take my mind off the stories of people going into kidney failure from taking too many paracetamol.

'That depends,' he says, giving me a weary look, 'on how many she's actually taken. Unfortunately there's a very small margin between a safe dose of paracetamol and an overdose.'

'Jesus, Jude!' I tell her. 'What's the matter with you? Can't you count the bloody tablets?'

I'm only snappy because I'm so frightened.

'The problem with paracetamol,' continues Dr East with a sigh, as if I haven't spoken, 'is that the symptoms of an overdose often don't appear until up to twelve hours later. Judith hasn't got any symptoms right now, but if she *has* overdosed, we need to start treatment within eight hours.

And the blood screening isn't helpful until after four hours.'

'So what are you going to do?' I squawk.

Twelve hours? Eight hours? Four hours? I can't do the maths.

'Assume she's overdosed. There's something we can give her, if the blood test shows a toxic level of paracetamol; but in the meantime, what we'll do is give Judith something to make her sick; and possibly give her a gastric lavage – that's a stomach-washout.' He looks at Jude's stricken face. 'I'll need to discuss that with my consultant,' he adds. 'But first let's just get your charts written up. Have you had a bowel movement today, Judith?'

'SHIT, Jude! Are you all right!'

The serendipity of Emily's greeting as she bursts into our cubicle is lost in the heat of the moment, but even in these dire circumstances some perverse part of my brain is storing it away for future amusement. I promise I'll only laugh about it if Jude comes through all this OK.

'I found these!' shouts Emily, pulling a paracetamol packet out of her pocket. 'Under our table in the pub! I made the taxi driver belt over here like a lunatic!'

I have to hand it to this doctor. Without missing a beat, without a single sarcastic comment or look of disdain at any of us, he takes the packet calmly out of Emily's hand and opens it up. Eight tablets still sitting there, intact in their little plastic bubbles on their little foil strip. They are the most beautiful sight in the world. We all gaze at them for a moment without speaking.

'OK,' says Dr East finally. 'Looks like we can forget the gastric lavage, then. Now, I just need to assess the damage from the head injury ...'

I'm multi-tasking now, so I must be sober. At the same time as I'm firing questions at Emily about how she found the tablets, how she called the taxi, is her face OK now (where I scratched it), can she ever forgive me and are we still friends, I'm answering the questions being fired at *me* by Dr East about Jude's head injury.

Were you with Judith when she hit her head? How long did she lose consciousness for? Was she confused when she came round?

These are all the same questions that Patrick asked us before we got in the ambulance. I'm not so worried any more. I think Jude's going to be OK. Hallelujah. Not only am I giving up the drink, I might also go to church.

'Where are the others?' I ask Emily as soon as Dr East has finished interrogating me.

'Helen came with me. She's outside in the waiting room. The others have all gone back to the hotel. No one felt like having any more to drink.'

Quite.

We leave Jude to the tender mercies of the medical profession for a few minutes and pop outside to tell Helen how she's doing.

'Thank God you brought the paracetamol packet over here so quickly,' I tell them both. 'It was getting really scary in there for a little while.'

'Poor Katie,' says Helen. 'You really shouldn't have had all this trauma, on your hen weekend.'

She gives me a very direct look. She's not just talking about Jude's ambulance dash. I ignore the direct look, though, and what it means, because I'm struck by the fact that in all the worry about Jude, I'd actually forgotten it was my hen weekend anyway.

'It's kind of got things into perspective, to be honest,' I say, sitting down and suddenly realising I'm dead beat. 'I'd been feeling sorry for myself. All the things that've come out this weekend – well, some of them have been pretty upsetting.'

'Katie, I'm so sorry ...' begins Helen.

'So am I,' joins in Emily. 'I can't believe I thought it was a good idea to start telling you that stuff.'

'I think we've all grovelled and apologised enough. It's all down to us drinking too much, isn't it, at the end of the day. I wonder how many friends end up falling out during hen parties?'

'Don't say that!' groans Emily.

I give her a hug.

'But not us. Can we pretend we didn't carry on like drunken street-brawlers, d'you think?'

'Yes, please. I'll die of embarrassment if Sean ever finds out.'

'Jude's going to be OK. That's all that really matters.'

There's an annoying little voice whingeing away at the back of my head about all the things I'll have to deal with as soon as this weekend is over. But I'm in no mood for listening to annoying little voices in the back of my head. I'm telling it to shut the fuck up for once.

Jude's being kept in overnight because of possible concussion. When we go back to say goodnight to her she's got her bad foot propped up really high, and she's been given some kind of anti-inflammatory drug to help with the pain and swelling. She looks a lot more comfortable.

'God alone knows how long I'll be lying here on this trolley – I could be old and grey before they get me into a ward,' she says with a shrug. 'I might as well close me eyes right here and get meself some kip, although they're saying something about waking me up every now and then to ask me name and address. Jesus, if I forget me own name and address they'd better transfer me to the mental institution. I might get a bed there quicker.'

'Well, we'll sit with you till they move you to a ward,' I tell her, looking around in vain for any chairs to sit on.

'No, you won't. You'll get yerselves a taxi now before it gets any later and the streets turn into a zoo. The others will be worried back at the hotel.'

'Are you sure?' I feel mean, but on the other hand I can see she's on the point of falling asleep and, to be quite honest, Helen and I are both having trouble staying awake ourselves. 'We'll be back first thing in the morning ...'

'Not too early you won't, if you don't mind. I'll need a lie-in if these eejits keep waking me up all night long. And your flight isn't till the afternoon, is it, so?'

'Half past six.' I feel suddenly really, really sad at the thought of going home tomorrow. Despite everything. 'I don't want to think about that yet, though.'

'Sure and why would you need to think about it yet, when there's another whole day ahead of you?'

'It's Serious Shopping day tomorrow!' says Emily brightly.

'And time for a little more drinking at lunchtime!' adds Helen.

If I hadn't already committed enough acts of violence this evening, I might have hit her.

ABOUT DREAMS

I'm nearly asleep in the back of the taxi when Helen touches my arm gently.

'Katie. I know you don't want to talk about it; but I just need to tell you one thing.'

My eyes pop open. I've heard too many *one things* this weekend.

'It's just,' she goes on, 'that you're not leaving Bookshelf.'

'I am. But you're right, I don't want to talk about it.'

'You're not leaving, Katie – because *I* am.'

'Don't be ridiculous. How's that going to work? You wouldn't see Greg ...'

'Well, it might be for the best. I'm not happy in this situation. I preferred myself the way I was before.'

'"The snake drags the lark along with it, breaking its wings – it never flies again,"' I quote back to her with a smile. 'You only told me that on the way over here.'

'I know. I'm full of shit, aren't I?'

'No you're not. It's *normal* to fall in love. You seem to think it's a weakness.'

'I do,' she agrees. 'If it made me happy, perhaps I wouldn't.'

'Perhaps he's just not the right man ...'

'Katie, they're *all* the wrong man!' she replies, more vehemently. 'I've just been fooling myself. I'm not *meant* for all this romantic nonsense.'

'Look, I don't think either of us should do anything too hasty. When we get back, we'll talk about it again ...'

'We can talk again as much as you like. But I've made up my mind. I'm going to Australia.'

'*Australia!*'

'Yes. I've told you my brother's a teacher in Melbourne, haven't I? I visit him every three or four years. He's nagged me for a long time to settle out there permanently. So I think I will.'

'But ... come on, Helen – you can't make a decision like that, just on a whim – going off to the other side of the world, just because of some ... some silly feeling, some silly idea ...'

She looks at me sadly.

'Thanks for trivialising my suffering.'

'Fuck; I didn't mean to. I didn't mean that.'

'It's OK.'

Australia. Bloody hell. That's certainly putting some distance between the lark and the snake.

There's a reception committee for us in the hotel foyer. They all jump to their feet as we walk in, running to meet us, anxiety etched into all their faces.

'How's Jude?'

'How is she? Have they kept her in?'

'Did she have to have her stomach pumped?'

'Have they done a brain scan?'

'It's all right, she's OK,' I say quickly, before it turns into an episode of *Holby City*. 'Emily and Helen brought the paracetamol packet in before they started any treatment.'

'They think she might have mild concussion but they don't seem too worried,' adds Emily. 'They're just keeping an eye on her through the night and then they'll let her go.'

'Thank God,' says Suze.

'You look done in,' says Lisa, putting her arm round me. 'This wasn't how your hen weekend was supposed to go, was it, love?'

'I don't care. It's not important. Lise, I thought for a minute back there that we'd killed Jude ...'

'Don't be silly!'

'I'm not. I'm not exaggerating. Emily and I were completely out of control.'

'It was my fault,' says Emily quietly. 'I was drunk, and I was talking out of the top of my head ...'

'And *I* was drunk too, otherwise I'd never have reacted like that.'

How many times are we going to go over this? Now it's all over, now everything seems to be OK, I feel like crying. Shit, I *am* crying. Shit. So is Emily.

'Come on.' Lisa pulls us both down onto one of the deep leather sofas. 'No harm done ...'

'But I'm so disgusted at myself ... I didn't know I had that side to me.'

'Me neither,' sniffs Emily.

'It's the drink,' Lisa reminds us. 'You're *not* really like that.'

'No. And I've given it up, now.'

'Yeah, right,' smiles Lisa.

'I mean it. I *so* have. What's the point of it? It's not even pleasurable, is it? It's just a drug.'

'So you're not having any more Guinness? Nothing to drink tomorrow, on the last day of your hen weekend?'

'No.'

'And you're not having any wine, or any vodka any more, when we get home? When you go out with Matt, or with Emily?'

'No.'

'No champagne at your wedding? Not even for the toasts?'

'No. There's nothing wrong with orange juice.'

'Well, I'll believe it when I see it.'

'Lisa, I mean it. It's a slippery slope. Binge drinking ...'

'On your hen weekend, for God's sake! Everyone does!'

'But it can get a hold of you. I ... haven't said anything to you about this but – I've been thinking a bit about how much Mum drinks. Just for instance.'

Not that I'm worried about it.

'What? She's had a few drinks too many, on her daughter's hen weekend! Like all of us! Give her a break.'

'But ...'

I shrug. I haven't said anything to Lisa yet about what Mum told me, about Dad and their marriage and why she likes the 'occasional little drink'. I do need to tell her, but not now. I'm much too tired and much too emotional.

'I just think sometimes people drink to cover up their unhappiness.'

She gives me a puzzled smile.

'But *you're* not drinking because you're unhappy.'

I sniff and blow my nose.

Maybe not.

It's very late. We all traipse up to the bedrooms together, in a straggly tired group, whispering goodnight to each other. Mum and Auntie Joyce have missed out on all this drama; they'd come back to the hotel before things got really freaky back there at the pub. I'm glad they didn't have to see it.

It's odd being in this room without Jude. I feel strangely lonely, getting into my single bed, lying down and looking at the other empty bed across the room. It's been a long day, and I didn't get much sleep last night either; I'm so tired I feel like my eyes are going to come out of the back of my head. I turn off the light and close my eyes. And it's only now that I start thinking: *So what did Matt really say to Emily?*

Bugger. I so *wasn't* going to think any more about this. I was going to shut it out of my mind till I got home. I've got to trust Emily, haven't I. Now I've sobered up, I realise how ridiculously paranoid my reaction was to her meeting with Matt. She had my best interests at heart – I should never have doubted her. She only met up with him because she knew I was upset. And she kept quiet about the meeting because she didn't want to worry me. That's all. Emily's a good friend. She would never do anything to hurt me. How could I have *thought* that?

So what was all that about him being confused and mixed up?

About what?

Or about whom?

I toss and turn, and turn and toss. I sit up and punch my pillow, shake it and throw it back down. I put the light on, have a drink of water, turn the light off again. Still I can't stop my mind going over and over and over. *Why* did he say he was mixed up? *Why* did Emily look so embarrassed and shifty? *What* is she hiding from me?

151

It must be about five o'clock before I finally drift into a troubled, twitchy sleep. I dream that Matt's working with Greg at Bookshelf. Greg gives me piles and piles of horrible scientific books to read. He piles them so high on my desk that I can't see Matt any more over the top of them. Then he suddenly appears on my side of the barricade, naked, and we start to have sex on the desk. At first I resist, but to my surprise he turns out to be a fantastic lover. I want to enjoy it, but I can't because I'm worried Matt will see us. *Don't worry about him*, says Greg. *He's having it off with Helen. They're going to Australia together in the morning.*

'No! Not Helen! No!' I'm moaning when I wake up.

I look at the clock. Shit, I've only been asleep for twenty minutes. This is ridiculous. I've got to think about something else.

I put the light back on yet again and reach for *Love in the Afternoon*.

Chapter Two

Georgia couldn't wait to see James again. She'd tried her best to fight the attraction – after all, it was completely pointless. James was a rich, powerful man and Georgia knew he'd only ever see her as his secretary – the silly little new girl, who couldn't even do shorthand or spreadsheets like the famous Mary who worked for him before. When he was in her office, standing behind her, watching her clumsily working on the document he was waiting for, she became all fingers and thumbs and felt herself growing hot and bothered under his impatient gaze.

This is crap. Still, I suppose it's going to get to the sex scenes soon; Ginny Ashcroft's novels are always fifty per cent crap, fifty per cent soft porn. I doubt whether this one would even have got as far as a publishing contract if she wasn't already a best-seller. It's hardly worth reading on, because I already know Georgia is going to end up on the desk with her knickers round her ankles and James shafting her from behind while he waits for his important document.

I'm surely not getting bored with romantic fiction, am I?

I'm so shocked by this thought, I actually flip a chapter or two forward and start reading one of the sex scenes, just to liven up my own interest. Yes, this is better. Georgia's sitting astride James on his leather executive chair, unbuttoning her blouse and getting her tits out when I'm sure she really ought to be getting on with that typing. It didn't take her long to stop worrying about it all being completely pointless, then, by the look of it.

She's gasping with pleasure and he's groaning as she arches her back and they give in to the sensations of the moment.

Why am I reading this rubbish? I slam the book shut and throw it back on the bedside table. I'm going to give it a bad review, and I've only read about twenty pages of it. It's not that I'm bored with romance. I *love* romance, but this isn't it. Romance is about walking on the beach in the moonlight with someone you really love; not about shagging someone in the office because he's powerful and filthy rich and he's got a leather executive chair, for God's sake.

I fall asleep again with the light still on, and instantly start to dream that it's *me* sitting astride the boss with my skirt up round my waist, gasping with pleasure and giving in to the sensation. The dream is so erotic I can remember every detail of it when I wake up. I want to dream it again. How bad is that? Because the boss in my dream wasn't some fictional rich and groaning James. And it wasn't Matt, either. It was Harry.

Once again we're a sorry-looking group at breakfast this morning. Mum and Joyce are the only two who look even halfway to being bright-eyed and bushy-tailed, and they soon lose their cheerful smiles when we fill them in on last night's events. I've been a bit economical with the facts actually. I haven't told them about Emily and me fighting. I might be over thirty but I still don't want my mum to hear about anything really bad that I've done, if I can help it. Do we ever grow out of needing our mums to think the best of us?

'Poor little Judy!' gasps Mum. 'Is she going to be all right? Shouldn't someone have stayed at the hospital with her?'

'No, she didn't want that. She was practically asleep when we left her. We're going back as soon as we've had breakfast. They're going to discharge her this morning.'

'*We'll* go back,' says Mum firmly. 'Joyce and I. We can be at the hospital this morning, and let you girls go off and have your fun ...'

'No, don't be silly. I can bring Jude back in a taxi.'

'I'll come with you,' says Emily at once.

'No, Katie, Emily – Margie's right,' says Joyce. 'You girls looked after poor Jude last night; let us go to the hospital this morning and bring her back. We'd like to, wouldn't we, Marge? You can all go off and do whatever you've got planned for your last day.'

'Not without Jude,' I say stubbornly.

'Katie,' points out Lisa, 'I don't think Jude's ankle will be up to her traipsing round the shops, to be quite honest.'

'No. She shouldn't be traipsing round the shops anyway, when she's just come out of hospital,' says Mum, going straight into Nurse Mother mode. 'She needs to come back to the hotel and rest, and be looked after. Joyce and I will take charge!'

'Poor Jude,' I mutter.

'She'd probably prefer a couple of stiff drinks,' suggests Joyce.

She looks completely taken aback when we all start groaning and turning white at the mention of drink. I haven't told her yet that I've given up.

With Jude's rescue from the hospital being taken out of our hands, the rest of us decide the right thing to do is to carry on with the proposed shopping expedition to Grafton Street.

'It's what she'd want us to do,' points out Emily. 'She'll be on our case, otherwise, about going home without any souvenirs of Ireland.'

'I suppose you're right. Maybe we can buy her something to make up for missing out ...'

'That'd be cool. But she's been shopping in Dublin lots of times, hasn't she, so I don't think it'll be too devastating for her.'

154

Fortunately, as none of the rest of us have much of a grasp of geography, Jude's Dublin guidebook is lying neatly on her bedside table, and from its pullout map of the city centre we can see that the main shopping streets are only a short stroll away from where we're staying.

'Let's cross the river,' suggests Lisa, pointing to the map while we all try to peer over her shoulders, 'and walk up O'Connell Street on one side and down on the other. Then we can cross back over and do Grafton Street.'

'If we haven't spent all our money by then,' says Karen.

'Pace yourself, girl!'

'Come on, then! Let's get going.'

'Yeah, my last few euros are burning a hole in my purse!'

'I need a new handbag!'

'I want to look for shoes.'

'A new dress for Katie's wedding!'

We seem to be pretty cheerful again, then, as we set off from the hotel for our major shopping expedition. Not that we've forgotten about poor Jude lying in her hospital bed. But she wouldn't want us all to be moping around, on our last day, would she? She'd want us to be having fun and spending money. Helping the Irish economy. That's the way we're looking at it.

ABOUT SHOPPING

I'm not too good at working out the exchange rate, but I'm getting the impression that everything's more expensive in Dublin than it is at home.

'Yeah, no point buying things from shops like Next or River Island that we've got at home. You'll end up paying more,' says Lisa.

She's found a couple of things for the kids. A book of Irish fairy stories for Molly; an Irish whistle for Charlie. Little green leprechaun hats for both of them.

'I suppose I'd better buy something for Richard,' she says without any enthusiasm.

'What about Andy?' I ask her. I'm intrigued. Do you buy presents for your lover *and* your husband? Just one? Just the other?

'He gets his present when I get home,' she says, winking at me. But there's a catch in her voice as she says it.

'Do you love him?' I ask her very quietly.

'I don't know. I don't know what I feel. I think I'm frightened to ask myself that.'

'But he wants you to leave Richard and live with him.'

'Yes.'

'He loves *you*.'

'Yes. He says he does.'

'Don't you want to be happy, Lise?'

She looks at me sharply.

'Katie, it's just not that simple. Not when you've got children.'

'But nowadays loads of people split up – children adapt ... We should know that better than anybody. It didn't hurt us, did it – growing up without our dad.'

'Look,' she says patiently, laying a hand on my arm. 'Look, perhaps I do love Andy. I know I don't love Richard any more. But more than anything in the world, I love my kids. They come before *everything* else – and *they* love *Richard*. I don't want to do anything that might hurt them. You'll understand, when you have children yourself.'

When I have children myself.

I feel so stricken at the thought of this that I can't even reply.

'You will, one day,' says Lisa, glancing at my face. 'Of course you will.'

'I'm thirty-one. You've heard what Mum says. An elderly primigravida.'

'Thirty-one's nothing these days. People are having babies when they're middle aged. Once you're married, once everything's settled down ...'

'I haven't really thought about it much before. Not till now ...'

'Well, your body's telling you – you see? You're *ready* now.'

I think my body and I are about to have a major falling-out.

Celtic jewellery is what most of us are buying. I've got myself a silver necklace and matching earrings. I've bought a necklace for Jude too.

We stop for coffee and compare all our purchases. Emily's bought so much, I think she's going to need another suitcase.

'Most of these are for Sean,' she says lightly, rummaging through her carrier bags. 'He never goes out and buys stuff for himself.'

'That's sweet,' says Karen, who's only been buying for herself. 'What about you, Katie? What have you bought for Matt?'

There's a heartbeat of silence before Emily answers for me, quick as a flash:

'She's giving him *herself*, isn't she? Christ, isn't that enough of a present for any man?'

But the carrier bags full of clothes and gifts for Sean sit between us on the café floor, taking on the dimensions of a mountain in their significance.

We're just about to pay the bill and move on for the next hour of shopping when my phone bleeps with a message.

Where are you? Can we join you?

'It's Joyce,' I tell the others, puzzled. 'I don't think they ought to be bringing Jude ...'

'Not for *traipsing round the shops*!' says Lisa, imitating our mum.

I quickly text Joyce back:

What about Jude?

Still in the hospital. Got to go back for her later, comes the reply.

It doesn't take long to arrange to wait for Mum and Auntie Joyce here in the café, and we don't need much persuasion to stay for another coffee. But I'm tense with anxiety about Jude.

'What's happened?' I demand as soon as they appear. 'Why hasn't she been discharged?'

'Oh ... they needed her to stay for a bit longer,' says Mum vaguely.

'Just waiting for the doctor to give her the all-clear,' says Joyce, smiling too brightly.

'You're worrying me. Tell me. What's happened? Is there something wrong?'

'Oh, no, no, nothing to worry about ...'

'No, she'll be fine, she's just waiting for the doctors ...'

'OK!' says Lisa, sharply and very loudly. Everyone looks at her in shocked expectation. 'Come on, you've got us all worried now. You'd better tell us. It can't be worse than what we're all imagining.'

Mum and Joyce exchange a look. I don't like that look. I saw it a lot, when I was growing up, and it usually meant a trip to the cinema was off, or my pet gerbil had died, or (most often) my dad had let us down yet again and cancelled another proposed Saturday visiting arrangement.

'Well,' says Mum in very measured tones, looking around at us all, 'We don't want you to worry.'

'But the doctors discovered something after you left her last night,' says Joyce.

Have you ever been so scared, just for the time it takes for somebody to utter a couple of crucial sentences, you actually think you're going to faint? I can't breathe. I can't even find enough strength to tell them: *For Christ's sake spit it out!* I'm trembling. Jude's got something terribly wrong with her. It's so bad, they can't even bring themselves to tell us. The knock on the head has given her brain damage. She's gone into a coma. She'll need twenty-four-hour nursing care for the rest of her life. Or she took too many paracetamol after all. The packet Emily found on the floor was someone else's. And because of us, they didn't give her the antidote. She's gone into liver failure. She's dying ...

'She's broken her ankle,' says Mum solemnly.

'*Fuck!*' I shout, bursting into tears. '*Is that all?*'

I'm sorry I sounded uncaring. In fact, it's awful, isn't it? Poor Jude.

'She's OK,' says Auntie Joyce. 'But she's in plaster.'

'Yes, and she actually says she's in a lot less pain now it's been plastered,' says Mum. 'Poor thing – can you imagine it? She was trying to walk on it.'

'No wonder she was in so much pain,' says Emily. 'No wonder the paracetamol didn't seem to be doing much to help.'

'So are they keeping her in?' I ask.

'Only till this afternoon. Something to do with the orthopaedic consultant signing her off. She was practising walking on her crutches when we left her.'

'*Crutches!*'

'Well, of course.'

I look around the group. Everyone's sipping their coffee, looking pretty subdued.

'How's she going to get home?' I say. 'She came up by train. She can't ... on her own ... on crutches ...'

'Joyce and I were saying that to her, weren't we, Joyce?' says Mum importantly. 'We said to her: *Jude, that boyfriend of yours will just have to drive up from Cork and fetch you home ...*'

'Kinsale. She lives in Kinsale, now.'

'Wherever. Down in the depths of Ireland. He'll have to come for her, won't he.'

'And is he going to? Has she phoned him? Asked him?'

'Well, I don't know, dear, do I? I mean, we've left it to Jude, and she's going to phone us, or send us one of those message-things later on, to let us know what's happening.'

So it looks like I might get to meet the elusive Fergus sooner than I anticipated – and not for the best of reasons.

It's difficult to get excited about shopping again now.

We stroll along Grafton Street in smaller groups, stopping to watch the musicians and street entertainers. I remember my camera, and manage to take a few souvenir photos. It's probably the first time I've been sober enough.

'I'll just have a look for something for the grandchildren,' says Mum, disappearing into a shop with children's books and toys in the window.

Charlie and Molly are coming second only to Sean in the presents stakes, by the look of it.

'Are you buying anything?' I ask Joyce, as we wait for Mum outside the shop.

'No.' She turns away from the toyshop window, and stares at the young guy across the street playing the whistle while two small children dance a jig around his feet. 'No – I don't like to buy for Charlie and Molly every time. Don't like to outdo their mummy and their nan.'

'I know what you mean. I feel like that too, about being an auntie. I love them to bits, you know, but it's not as if they're exactly mine, so …'

What have I said?

Joyce has turned away from me and is walking slowly along the length of the toyshop window, looking down at the ground. I follow her, catch her by the arm and turn her back to me.

'Hey! Sorry – what did I say? Joyce! I'm sorry. Please don't be upset!'

'I'm not!' she retorts quickly, giving me a very false bright smile. 'I'm fine. Don't take any notice of me. Just being a silly, emotional old woman.'

'Old?' I tease her affectionately, slipping my arm through hers. 'You'll never be old!'

'No?' she smiles wistfully. 'Maybe that's because I'll never be Mum, or Nan, to anyone.'

We walk on, arm in arm, in silence for a while until we find ourselves at St Stephen's Green.

'I've never asked you why,' I say, softly. 'Maybe you don't want to talk about it.'

'Actually I do,' she responds, to my surprise. We sit down together on a bench facing the lake, watching the ducks. 'I think I'd like to tell you about it, Katie.'

And here in the middle of Dublin, on the last day of my hen weekend, almost exactly halfway between my thirty-first and my thirty-second birthday, I'm hearing the story that's going to change my life.

JOYCE'S STORY

I might be auntie to these two great big grown-up 'girls', but I'm only forty-two myself. I'm not much older than Katie's friend Helen – but I feel like I'm from a different generation. I grew up as the 'afterthought' baby to a pre-existing family of three. Mum, Dad and Marge were already an established unit, and when I came along I had to fit in with their lifestyle rather than the other way round. Marge was twelve years old when I was born, and my earliest memories were of trying to be like her. It was as if I spent my whole childhood running, trying to catch up with her, never quite grasping the fact that it wasn't ever going to happen. Mum used to say I was old before my time. She used to sound quite proud of it until I got to about ten or eleven and started behaving like an eighteen-year-old.

Marge was married by then, and far more interested in having her own babies than paying any attention to her troublesome little sister. My parents, having had me so late in life, were in their fifties now and were also more excited about the grandchildren than me. It was understandable. Lisa, with her solemn dark eyes and sweet, easy temperament, and Katie with her sunny baby smiles and fierce independence, were a joy and a blessing for the whole family. Coming home from visiting their delightful grandchildren to face their sullen, moody and disobedient schoolgirl daughter was probably not a lot of fun at their age. Their way of dealing with my moods and bad behaviour was to completely ignore me. I interpreted this as abandonment by my whole family – and I slid off the rails.

First I stopped working at school. It was surprisingly difficult to do. I'd always been quite bright, and enjoyed my schoolwork. I had to make a conscious effort to stop trying: to 'forget' my homework, to fail exams, to deliberately lose assignments or write nonsense answers. I clowned around in class, talked during lessons, and cheeked the teachers. This got easier the more attention it earned me from the other naughty kids in the class. I enjoyed their approval. At last! Someone was noticing me!

Of course, the teachers could see what was going on.

'You're not really *like* this, Joyce,' my headmistress used to say when I was sent to her office time after time for various misdemeanours.

And part of me knew that I wasn't. But I pretended for so long that I was, in time it became impossible to turn back.

By the time we were thirteen or fourteen, the crowd I was hanging around with were drinking, smoking, and beginning to experiment with sex. My parents had pretty well given up on me. I know this sounds awful, but I don't really blame them. They didn't have a clue how to cope. Probably nowadays they'd have got a social worker involved, but in those days families looked after themselves, and were ashamed to tell anyone if they couldn't. When the school wrote to them about my bad work or my bad behaviour, they'd send me to my room. I'd simply get changed, walk out of the house and meet my mates. They couldn't stop me! The feeling of power was superb. And frightening.

I hid the fear by laughing and showing off with my friends, by drinking cheap cider in the park and snogging older boys with bad reputations. I'd go to school with hangovers and love bites. My life was exciting and dangerous; other kids looked up to me. At the age of fifteen I was wild, I was daring. I was one of the in crowd. And then I was something else. I was pregnant.

This was a different kind of fear. I know some very young girls who get into this situation go into denial and ignore all the signs, but my periods had been regular almost to the minute, every month since I was eleven, and I'd never in my life had anything like this awful debilitating nausea and retching, every single morning. I didn't need a pregnancy test: I knew. I sat in the bathroom for hours on end, crying, praying to God to make my period come, to make it all right again. I bargained with Him. If He'd just make me *not* pregnant, I'd never have sex again until I was old and married. I'd stop messing around; I'd work hard at school. I'd be good! I *promised*!

It was several weeks before Mum asked me if I was all right. How could she not have noticed? I'd stayed in my room for weeks; hadn't been out with the gang or got up to any trouble.

'You're looking very pale. I've heard you being sick.'

I told her it was nothing; I'd had a bug; I was tired, a bit off colour. My heart was knocking against my ribs. She mustn't find out. She'd throw me out. I'd been nothing but trouble to her – why would she want to protect me now? Why would she want to forgive me?

Of course, I know *now* that a mother will forgive her child anything.

'You haven't used any sanitary towels . . .' she said, giving me a very direct look.

'I've been using tampons!' I lied, my voice shaking. 'I've bought them myself.'

'You should have asked me to buy them for you,' she responded quite gently. 'There's nothing you can't ask me, Joycey. Nothing you can't tell me, you know.'

I felt tears coming to my eyes. If I didn't tell her now, I'd never be able to. I'd have to hide it for the whole nine months. I'd have to run away from home, have the baby somewhere in secret, give it away, maybe never come home again. I'd never felt so scared.

'I'm OK,' I said gruffly. 'Leave me alone.'

Friends are fickle at the age of fifteen. If the crowd I'd spent so many hours drinking and playing about with in the park even noticed that I wasn't part of it any more, they certainly didn't seem to care. The boy whose child I'd so carelessly conceived was having it off with another girl by now and probably didn't even remember my name. Where were my mates when I needed them? The girls I'd been friends with before I started my wild-child behaviour didn't like me any more. I'd turned my back on them and made them wary of me. At least a dozen times, I tried to tell Marge. She was too absorbed with her own small children and her unhappy marriage to notice that I was looking miserable and sickly, but I tried to bring up the subject obliquely, talking about her own pregnancies, asking leading questions about how early she'd started to get big, how long she'd gone on having morning sickness. She took this as a good sign that I was taking an interest in the family again and I even overheard her telling Mum that she was glad I seemed to have settled down. I tried to tell her, but as I'd look at my little nieces, the reality of what was happening to me making me feel weak with panic, and the words just wouldn't come.

And then, one morning when I was about three months pregnant, I went to the bathroom with the usual hopeless prayer in my heart for my period to come, and discovered I was bleeding.

At first I thought my prayers had been answered. I wasn't pregnant after all! I sat on the toilet, crying with relief. I told God *Thank you, thank you, thank you! I'll be good forever from now on! I promise! I promise!*

But at school, during the day, the bleeding got much worse. I sat at my desk, clutching my stomach, doubled over with pain. There was blood running down my legs, coming through my school skirt. I asked to be excused, tried to stand up. The kids sitting near me were staring and whispering to each other. Their voices seemed to come from a long way away.

'Please, Miss!' shouted Hazel Lomax who used to be my best friend, 'I think Joyce is going to faint ...'

They carried me to the sick room and called an ambulance. I heard the school nurse saying the word *miscarriage* and then I allowed myself, for the first time for three months, to cry out loud. I sobbed and wailed and cried for my mum as the contractions ripped through my body and I knew that, far from answering my prayers, God was actually punishing me.

They told me I'd already lost the baby by the time the ambulance had got me to hospital. In those days, fifteen-year-old pregnant girls weren't generally treated with the same degree of understanding that we're used to now, but to the kind doctor looking after me, my situation was none of his business – I was just a patient who needed his help. He said there was probably something wrong with the pregnancy and it was nature's way of dealing with it. I wanted to tell him that the only thing wrong with the pregnancy was that I shouldn't have been having it.

They took me to theatre to give me a 'D & C'. *Just cleaning everything up for you.* And when I came round from the anaesthetic, Mum was sitting by my bed. She'd been crying. I'd never seen her cry before, and this more than anything else made me feel ashamed.

'I wish you'd told me, Joycey.'

'I couldn't,' I muttered.

'I would have looked after you. These things happen.'

These things happen I thought bitterly. Not to good girls, they don't. Good girls don't go out and get drunk and have sex with sixth-form boys who don't give a shit about them. Good girls don't bring this shame on their family and make their mothers cry. Good girls don't pray for their own babies to die, and then feel relief when it happens!

I was off school for a while, and when I went back I found to my amazement that Hazel wanted to be my friend again. I never had anything more to do with my old gang; I got back to my studies and worked hard, passed all my exams and was a prefect in my last year. After I recovered physically, Mum and I never talked about my miscarriage. I know she was doing her best for me. She probably thought *least said, soonest mended.* But the memory of my dead baby festered away in my brain for years. The idea that I'd somehow caused him to die by wishing him away gradually became a conviction. By the time I met Ron and we decided to get married, I was desperate to have another child; I felt this would be the only way I'd ever get over the guilt about that first pregnancy.

Life doesn't always hand you the things you want, does it? Even though I'm so much older now, and sensible and rational about these things, it crosses my mind occasionally when I'm feeling a bit low, that I'm still being punished.

I've been lucky in other ways – so lucky, really. Ron's a lovely man. Kind, gentle, easy-going. I look around me at all the women I know who've had unhappy marriages to selfish, brutish, ignorant men and I wonder how I've got the nerve to be ungrateful. He would have made a lovely dad.

We both wanted children so much. We did exactly what Lisa described: got married because we decided the time was right to start a family. Every month I waited – with excitement at first, and then with resignation and finally with a kind of furious bereavement – for the missing period that never happened. Never again. Why did it happen so easily, so quickly and unexpectedly when I was a fifteen-year-old schoolgirl having sex for the first time? And now, when it was what we wanted more than anything in the whole world, it seemed to be the hardest thing in the world to achieve.

We ran the gauntlet of the infertility services. I'd already proved my fertility but they checked me over in case something had gone wrong since. Then they turned their attention to Ron. He performed tests. We performed tests together. We tried to joke about it, saying *so many tests – it's like being back at bloody school* – but we weren't really laughing. I took my temperature, we made love on the right days in the right positions and wore the right kind of under-wear. Nothing was wrong with us but still nothing happened.

I'm being punished, I cried to Ron when every month my period arrived, like clockwork, taunting me with its evidence. *I'm being punished for wanting to get rid of my first baby.*

He'd always been kind and sympathetic about my early pregnancy, but now I'd started flinging it back at him.

You think it's my fault, don't you. You think I'd be all right if I hadn't had that miscarriage. Go on, admit it – you think I've caused this problem; I've brought it on myself!

There's only so much a man can take, however patient, however understanding he is. The hospital tests, the temperature-taking, the regimented lovemaking by appoint-ment with only one futile aim in mind, the bitter, neurotic, self-pitying wife constantly whining and crying and provok-ing arguments ...

I've had enough, he said one day. I can still picture him as he said it, wiping his hand across his eyes as if he was too tired to even look at me. *I want us to give up, to accept that we don't have children. I want us to start enjoying life again.*

But I can't. I can't live if I can't have children.

You can. Other women do. It hurts me too, but we can do this. Together.

We could adopt! It was a theme we'd returned to many times, debated over and over until we were as exhausted talking about it as we were trying for our own baby.

No. We'd just be putting ourselves through another series of ordeals. Interviews, inspections, our lifestyles dissected, our marriage pulled apart by social workers, police poking into our backgrounds, our families, our beliefs, all under scrutiny ... No! Joyce, I've had enough.

I cried. I protested, I ranted; I called him heartless and uncaring. I knew that wasn't fair. He was right. If we'd gone on, we'd have driven ourselves apart. We'd have become more and more bitter, started blaming each other, probably ended up splitting up and then what? We'd have had no children, and not even each other.

I've got a good man. We've learnt, over the years, to cope with our disappointment. Heartache. Seeing other people having kids effortlessly and treating them carelessly. Hearing about abortions, child abandonment, child abuse. Watching our friends' children growing up. Being *Auntie* and *Uncle* but never Mum and Dad. Loving our beautiful nieces and seeing them, now, having children of their own.

Don't play games with your fertility, Katie. If you don't want children, don't have them. But if you do, for God's sake, don't leave it too late. Don't treat it lightly, as if a baby is just something you can pop down to the supermarket and buy when you decide you want it.

God doesn't play our games. Nature doesn't work by our rules. Just because we understand how to control it, don't assume you can take back that control whenever you like.

At the end of the day – you're not in charge.

ABOUT ENDINGS

'Blimey, you two! Are you going to sit there all day, yakking away like a pair of old *men*?'

'Yeah – cheer up, the pair of you! You look like you've got the troubles of the world on your shoulders!'

The rest of the gang are standing in front of us and we didn't even notice. How long have we been sitting here?

'Thank you *very* much for walking off and leaving me in the shop!' scolds Mum. 'Good job Lisa and Emily were looking for me, wasn't it?'

'Sorry,' I say humbly. 'Thought you were following us ...'

'And anyway! It's lunchtime,' says Lisa, waving her watch under my nose. 'Aren't you hungry?'

'Yes. Yes, I am, actually,' says Joyce with a last squeeze of my hand. She gets to her feet and stretches. 'Come on, then. Where are we going for lunch? Not another boxty, please. My stomach won't take it!'

'Nah. Think they were overrated – but don't tell Jude I said that,' laughs Emily. 'To be honest I *really* fancy a Kentucky Fried Chicken or a Big Mac!'

'No!' we all shout her down.

'Not on our last day in Ireland, please, Emily,' says Helen, looking pained. 'We should at least have something *vaguely* Irish.'

'Another pint of Guinness?' Karen teases.

We all groan and start muttering about never drinking again.

'How about a bowl of Irish broth, then?' suggests Lisa. 'Just the thing to get our strength back after shopping till we're dropping.'

'Excellent idea,' agrees Emily.

Within ten minutes we've found ourselves a restaurant – not a pub this time – and we're waiting for our soup to be brought to us.

'Must admit I'm starving now,' says Lisa.

But I'm too tired to be hungry. It's warm in the restaurant and I'm leaning on the table with both elbows, feeling my eyelids drooping. I can't remember when I last had so little sleep over the course of a few days.

'Are you OK, Katie?' asks Joyce, reaching across the table to tap me on the arm.

'Yes. Sure. Just knackered.'

She smiles.

'That's about right for a hen weekend.'

'I suppose so. But I haven't been sleeping, even when we *have* got to bed.'

'Not surprising, really.' She gives me a look. 'Sorry for bleating on, back there – telling you all my troubles. Don't know what got into me.'

'That's OK.'

It's not OK, actually. To be perfectly honest, it's not OK at all. If one more person tells me their deepest darkest secrets this weekend, and then says they're sorry for telling me, I think I'll scream.

'Let's play a game or something, while we're waiting,' says Emily. 'Some of us need to keep ourselves awake, by the look of it!'

She means me. I shift my elbows off the table and try to sit up straight.

'How about another game of Truth or Dare?' suggests Karen brightly.

'No!' I retort much too sharply. Suddenly I'm wide awake. 'No, I think we've all heard just about enough truths to last us a lifetime, thank you very much.'

'Katie prefers fiction, don't you, love,' says Lisa with a smile.

'Yes. Absolutely. Much safer.'

'OK, then. We'll make up our own story. *Once upon a time . . .*' begins Karen.

'*There were nine beautiful princesses*,' joins in Emily.

'Oh, do me a favour,' groans Helen. 'I don't want to be a beautiful princess. I'm not exactly right for the part.'

'And I'm too old to be a princess,' says Mum.

'God, some people do make it difficult to create a decent bit of fiction, don't they!' says Emily. 'OK, then. *There were seven beautiful princesses, a beautiful queen and a Wise Woman.*'

Helen smiles appreciatively.

'*One day,*' Lisa takes up the story. '*One day, the Queen goes to the Wise Woman and asks her advice. She wants to find handsome husbands for all the beautiful princesses ...*'

'For God's sake!' says Helen. 'Is that the best you can do? Why do the poor cows have to be sold off to handsome bloody husbands?'

'Shut up, Helen – what's it matter to you? You're the Wise Woman!' laughs Emily.

'OK, then. *So the Wise Woman says to the Queen: "Listen to me, Queenie Baby. Send the princesses out into the world to earn their living. What do you take me for? A fucking Princess Dating Agency?"*'

'*So the Queen tells the Beautiful Princesses: "Sorry, girls. The market for handsome husbands seems to have dried up,"*' I continue. '*"You've all got to set sail for Far Off Lands with one silver coin each in a velvet purse—"*'

'Why a velvet purse?' interrupts Joyce. 'Why not a leather one?'

'It's always a velvet purse. Don't spoil the story.'

'*So they spend their silver coins on a Ryanair flight to Dublin,*' says Suze.

'Must have been pretty big silver coins.'

'No, the flights were on special offer. A pound each way plus taxes.'

'Get on with it!' says Emily. 'When's the sex coming into it?'

'Emily!' I exclaim. 'This is a *fairy* story. We don't want sex coming into it!'

'Yes we do!' chorus all the others.

'All right, then,' says Joyce. '*Let's say, The Queen had given each princess a task to do. The first princess had to find the man with the softest kiss in the Kingdom.*'

'I thought these were liberated princesses who were going out to earn their own silver?' points out Helen.

'Nah. Boring. *Princess number two had to find the man with the sexiest smile,*' says Lisa, a dreamy look coming into her eyes. Guess who she's going to conjure up for *her* lucky prince.

'*And number three's got to find the one with the biggest dick!*' shouts Karen.

Everyone hoots with laughter and two ladies at the next table nearly faint into their dinners.

'*The cutest bum!*' joins in Suze.

'*The strongest tongue,*' says Emily, making a very rude gesture and grinning wickedly.

'*The longest . . . staying power,*' adds Lisa meaningfully.

'*And the luckiest princess of all,*' I say, '*Gets the richest, handsomest prince in the land. He's hung like a horse, with a tight little arse and a smile like George Clooney's. And he can keep it going for forty days and forty nights . . .*'

'Sure you've just described meself almost perfectly!' says a voice at my shoulder suddenly.

I jump almost out of my chair, knocking his arm so hard that the bowl of soup our waiter's trying to place in front of me flies out of his hands and lands upside down on the table. Irish broth seeps from beneath the bowl, spreading slowly across the tablecloth. I don't know who's more embarrassed, me or the little wiry red-haired waiter (who bears more resemblance to a fox terrier than to George Clooney, even if he *does* have all the other attributes).

'Oh my God, I'm so sorry! You startled me! I mean, I didn't see you coming . . .'

There's a sniggering around the table. Very immature.

'I mean, I didn't know you were there!'

'He took you by surprise from behind, Katie,' mutters Emily under her breath.

I can feel myself going red with the effort of not laughing. The poor lad's scraping up the worst of the mess, scooping up our place settings and glasses and everything and another waiter's come to help him change the tablecloth.

'I'm really sorry,' I tell him again.

'That's fine. No problem,' he says, giving me a grin as he brings up fresh soup and baskets of soda bread. I'm keeping my elbows by my sides this time.

'Anyway,' says Lisa, after a suitable length of silence when he's finished serving and gone back into the kitchen, 'Serves him right. I *bet* he couldn't manage forty days and forty nights.'

'Forty seconds, more like!' giggles Suze.

'No change there, then!' says Emily and we all start to laugh out loud, spluttering soup everywhere.

'I wish Jude was here,' says Lisa suddenly.

Shit. We need to phone the hospital and see if she's OK to be discharged now. Hurry up with your soup, girls. Anyone would think we were here to enjoy ourselves.

'That,' says Helen seriously, as we're wiping our soup bowls enthusiastically with the last of the soda bread, 'is the trouble with fairy stories. Totally unrealistic.'

'Duh! They're not *meant* to be realistic, Helen!' protests Lisa. 'That's the whole point of them.'

'But people tell them to children! Do *you*? Do you read them to your kids?'

'Of course I do. They're part of our heritage,' says Lisa huffily. 'Kids need to hear ...'

'What? Stories about elves and goblins and fairy princesses and magic spells?'

'Yes!'

'Good triumphing over evil? All that crap?'

'Yes! And it's not crap!'

'So you reckon you believe in happy ever afters?' persists Helen, giving Lisa a challenging look. 'Do you?'

Lisa drops her eyes.

'I'd *like* to.'

'We all would, Lisa. But you have to grow up some time, unfortunately, and leave the fairy tales behind.'

And the romantic fiction, presumably. The trouble with happy endings, I suppose, is that you never find out what happens after the last page of the book.

I call the hospital while we're having our coffee, and get put through to Jude's ward. The nurse tells me to hang on and she'll get her to the phone. It seems to take forever.

'Well, I had to walk to the phone with my crutches, Katie,' she says at last, panting with the effort.

'Is it really that difficult? It always looks like fun.'

'Yes, you would say that if you've never tried it. It's as much fun as wearing too-tight shoes. D'you remember the three-legged race we used to have at school when we were little ones? Well it's like doing that, but without the other person to hold on to. Sure I'm going to break me neck before I'm much older.'

'Ankle's bad enough, Jude. Neck's out of the question. Behave yourself.'

'Jesus, God, I'd like a chance to do anything else, so I would. The nurses in here are like the devil himself, with their fuss and their bossiness.' She drops her voice a little. 'But there are plenty of nice-looking doctors if you've half a mind to look around ...'

'I think we'd better get you out of there, love, before you start getting carried away.'

'Well now, that's the best suggestion I've heard today. But unless you've got ideas for hiring a private helicopter and landing it on the hospital roof, then I think I'm stuck in here for a bit longer, I'm sorry to say, Katie.'

'Why? What do you mean? Isn't Fergus coming to pick you up? I thought he'd have been there by now.'

'There's a bit of a problem, you see, now. Fergus is working away and I can't get hold of him. Sure he's probably in some boring meeting or other, and hasn't got his phone on. You know what they're like.'

'You can't get a message to him or anything?'

'I've tried, Kate, but so far I haven't succeeded. I was thinking maybe I could get Dad to drive up and bring me back, but he's out on a job and me Mam never learnt to drive, bless her. It's also a fierce long drive in the dark for them so I've a mind to leave it till the morning and see if they can work something out then.'

'But Jude, I'm sure they'd drop everything like a shot to come and pick you up if they knew you were stuck in hospital!'

'To be sure, they would, but it's powerful unfair to ask them, when me dad needs to keep this job so badly, Katie – you know how it is.'

I do. Jude's father was made redundant from his previous sales job last year and was out of work for months. He hasn't been in this job for very long so I suppose I can understand why Jude would be reluctant to ask him to take time off.

'I'll be fine, so I will,' she says cheerfully. 'I'm just sorry I didn't get to say me goodbyes to you all, but hopefully ...' She falls silent. I know what she's thinking, too. 'Hopefully I'll see you again very soon, Katie.'

'Yes. Sure you will. But who says you're not saying goodbye to us? Did you hear that, girls?' I demand, holding out the phone over the table. 'Jude doesn't think we're going to say goodbye to her!'

'Don't be ridiculous, Jude!' shouts Lisa.

'Of course we're coming to say goodbye!' yells Emily.

'We've got to sign your plaster, you silly girl!' laughs Mum.

'We'll be there in half an hour,' I tell her, ending the call and putting my phone away. 'Come on, you lot, drink up your coffees, we haven't got all day. Can we have our bill, please? We've got a patient to visit, and a plane to catch!'

No rest for the wicked – and we should know.

'You're doing brilliantly!'

I'm watching Jude with genuine admiration as she swings herself along the ward on her crutches for the third time since we've been here. Only two visitors are allowed in at a time, so we've been taking it in turns to wait outside. She's had to do another demonstration of her prowess each time someone different comes in.

'It's desperate hard work though, Katie, so it is,' she puffs, flinging herself back onto her bed and throwing the crutches on the floor. 'Sure I'm going to end up with arm muscles like a fecking wrestler by the time I'm finished.'

'So what's the problem? Some men find muscly women quite a turn-on, so I'm told.'

'Yeah, well, *some men* will find anything a turn-on, by all accounts. There's an old boy with no teeth and his how's-yer-father drooping out of his pyjama trousers keeps wandering around the ward pestering the poor old ladies in their beds. I've told the sister twice, and she keeps sending

175

him back to the mens' ward, but it's no good – yer man just comes back again. I had to tell him meself to piss off just now when he started bothering the deaf old one in the next bed here. Fair play to her, though – she didn't half give out to him. Told him if he didn't put it away and do up his trousers she'd pull it off with her crochet hook. He's not been back since.'

'Could you, though? Could you actually pull it off with a crochet hook?'

'Jesus, I don't know, Katie. I'm not into crochet myself.'

We laugh together for a minute. Lisa, who's just come back in to replace Karen, holds up her watch to show me the time.

'We need to get going, Katie. We'll only just make the check-in time.'

The laughter stops. Jude and I can't look at each other, for a minute.

'I'm sorry this is how it's ended up,' I say. 'It's not been much fun for you.'

'Are you kidding me? I've had the most desperate time, Katie.' She reaches out to pull me towards her, and suddenly now we're hugging each other, tight, and I'm trying not to cry.

This wasn't how it was meant to be, I don't care what she says. She wasn't supposed to wind up in hospital with a broken ankle on the last day of my hen weekend – to say nothing of suffering concussion and having an overdose scare.

'Take care, OK?' I mutter against her hair. 'And if your parents can't come and pick you up tomorrow ...'

What? Walk? Hire a bike and cycle back to County Cork with your leg in plaster and your crutches hanging over the handlebars?

'I'll be fine, so I will. Stop your worrying and be off to catch your flight, or it'll be gone before you miss it.'

Irish logic. Wonderful, isn't it? I kiss her quickly on both cheeks and hurry out of the ward before I start us both off snivelling.

'Don't worry,' says Emily as our taxi speeds off on the motorway towards Dublin airport. 'Jude's parents will come and get her tomorrow.'

'That's just the thing, though,' I say, staring out of the window. 'They might not.'

'Of course they will! They won't leave her languishing in hospital, will they ...'

'It's not as easy as that. They're not well off, and her dad's just started this new job. Her mum can't drive.'

'So they'll ask someone else to come and pick her up. Or maybe the hospital will arrange something – an ambulance. Or Fergus will get her messages, and give her a call tonight. He'll come for her.' She nudges me, making me turn away from the window. 'Come on, Katie, don't be upset about her. She'll be OK. Someone's going to get her home, whatever happens.'

'Yes,' I say. I nod slowly, looking at Emily thoughtfully. 'Yes, of course someone's going to get her home, Em.'

Why have I only just thought of this? It's obvious, isn't it. I should have said so all along.

'Someone's definitely taking her home,' I repeat, as Emily looks at me in confusion. 'Me. *I'm* going to.'

ABOUT CANCELLATIONS

It's pandemonium at the airport. There's Lisa raising her voice to me as if I'm a naughty child, telling me not to be so silly. There's Karen and Suze with their arms round me, shushing me like a crying baby (I don't think I'm crying), and Helen holding up her hand, ticking things off on her fingers:

Number one: her parents are probably already on the case;
Number two: her boyfriend needs to get his act together;
Number three: it'll cost you money to change your flight;
Number four. . . .

Then there's Mum shaking her head, holding her hand to her mouth like she's just had a really bad shock that she can't get over, and muttering about the wedding, the wedding, the wedding.

'The wedding's not until next month, Marge,' says Joyce quite crisply. 'Stop fussing.' She looks at me for a minute, hesitates as though she's considering saying more, but just repeats, louder, for everyone's benefit, 'Stop fussing.'

'Yes,' I say, shaking Karen and Suze off my shoulders as gently as I can. 'Thank you, Joyce. Stop fussing, everyone. I've made up my mind. It's what I want to do.'

'In that case,' says Emily as the wails and protests die away and I suddenly realise she's the only one who hasn't said anything – not even in the taxi when I ranted at her for the last ten minutes of the journey about why I wanted, indeed *needed*, to do this. 'In that case, Katie, then I'm coming with you.'

At this there's a fresh outburst of disapproval.

What are you both thinking of?

What's the point? She's got her boyfriend, her parents,
her friends in Ireland to look after her ...
You don't have to feel guilty about Jude. It's not your
fault ...
She's a big girl. She can sort herself out.
She won't expect ... she'll be upset ... she'll be offended
... she'll be worried ...
And what about your jobs?
And WHAT ABOUT MATT?

'What did you say?' retorts Lisa sharply, bringing me out of
the jumble of my thoughts. Thoughts about cancelling
flights, booking new ones, organising a hire car, getting a
road map of Ireland. Everyone's looking at me like I've just
stripped naked, pulled out my hair in handfuls and sworn my
soul to the devil.

'I said, *fuck Matt*,' I replied quite calmly. 'Sorry.'

'Katie, honestly, that's not very nice,' says Mum. 'Just
before your wedding.'

'You ought to phone him, Kate. Before you make any
decisions,' says Lisa.

'Lisa, he's still in fucking Prague. He will be for another
two days. What difference is it going to make to him? He
doesn't care whether I'm in Dublin, or Cork, or ...'

I tail off, aware of the silence – the hush of disapproval –
surrounding me. Emily slips her arm through mine.

'Come on. We need to see about the flights. Otherwise
they'll think we've just missed the check-in.' She turns to
the others. 'And you lot *will* miss the check-in if you don't
get in that queue in a minute. We'll meet you in the bar –
OK? The one next to the Duty Free.'

She shepherds me in the direction of the Ryanair booking
desk.

'Thanks,' I say. I can't think of anything else. I'm not
even completely sure whether this is a rational decision. My
head isn't entirely straight.

'Don't mention it. I wasn't planning on doing anything
special for the next couple of days,' she says with a grin.

'Oh, Em – I hadn't even given that a thought! What am I
like?' I drop my bag on the floor and stare at her, mortified.

'You can't come! The girls are right – what about your job?'

'What about *yours*?' she counters, picking up my bag and pulling me on through the crowds. 'I've got a few days' leave owing. I'll only have to make a quick phone call to John, my manager. It'll be fine. Will Helen sort it out for you at Bookshelf, do you think?'

'Yes. She'll be glad to. She can have Greg to herself for a few days. And then I'm handing in my notice anyway. Helen says *she* is, but I won't let her do it. Australia's ridiculous. I'll get another job instead.'

'Wow,' says Emily softly. 'We *have* got a lot to talk about on the drive down to Cork, haven't we.'

'Yes.'

More than you realise.

Of course, nothing's ever as easy as I seem to go through my life believing it to be.

'You mean to tell me we can't change from one flight to another?' I ask the girl at the booking desk. 'Even if it's the same time, same price, just a different day?'

'In other circumstances, you can, yes, of course. But not at this short notice. Anything up to three hours before the flight time, it's perfectly possible.'

Emily looks at her watch.

'Great!' she says sarcastically. 'It's just under two hours to go. I thought the check-in is supposed to be two hours before?'

'Check-in is from two hours before departure, until forty minutes before, madam. But for flight changes, I'm afraid ...'

'It's three hours. Great.' I sigh. 'So what happens if we can't fly out today?'

'That's not a problem, madam. We'll just cancel your reservations.'

'What, and we stay in Dublin forever?' laughs Emily.

'You can then, of course, book onto a new flight for whichever day you intend to fly back.'

'So we pay for two flights instead of one?'

'Well, unfortunately, if you choose to cancel your reservation, madam ...'

'Sod it,' I tell Emily wearily. 'They were dead cheap flights anyway.'

They were. Nine pounds ninety-nine pence when we booked them, ages ago.

'When are you planning to rebook for?' asks our little Ryanair friend, tapping something into her computer terminal.

I glance at Emily. We haven't even discussed this.

'Two days,' she announces cheerfully. 'We'll drive down to County Cork tomorrow morning, stay overnight, as a little extra holiday with Jude, and drive back on Wednesday. Yeah?'

'Yeah.' I start to smile. I like the sound of the extra holiday bit. And to think just a little while ago I was getting upset at the thought of my hen weekend being over. I turn to the girl again. 'Can you book us onto the same time flight on Wednesday evening?'

'Certainly.' She does a bit more tapping. 'That'll be one hundred and thirty nine euros ninety-nine, madam. Each,' she adds with a glint in her eye.

'What!' Emily and I shriek together.

'How can it be?' I demand. 'That's getting on for a hundred pounds, isn't it!'

'Tonight's flight was nine pounds ninety-nine!' agrees Emily.

'Yes, it probably was, if you booked it some time in advance. I'm afraid the prices tend to go up nearer the time, you see, especially as this is a very popular departure time. The next flight, at ten past eight, is only fifty-nine euros ninety-nine, and the one *before* ...'

'All right, all right,' I say a bit snappily, before she can show off her computer prowess and her inflated prices any more. 'So what's the cheapest flight you've got on Wednesday?'

'Er ... let me see ...' She looks up brightly from the screen. 'The last flight of the evening: nine forty-five. I can still get you onto that flight for twenty-four euros ninety-nine, madam, if there's just the two of you travelling?'

'That's about seventeen quid each,' I mutter to Emily. 'What do you think?'

'Christ, Katie, it's not really much, is it, in the scheme of things. But don't forget we've still got the hire car to pay for.'

'*I* pay for it. It's my idea. You didn't have to ...'

'I *want* to. But don't you think we'd better talk to Jude first? Just in case her Mum and Dad are on their way from Cork right this minute, to collect her from the hospital?'

'Oh. Yes. Good point.'

How typical is that of me, not to think of this? We step away from the desk, leaving the Ryanair girl staring after us in dismay. All that screen-hopping and we haven't even booked!

'Jude?' I don't want to shout, with all these tourists and holidaymakers listening to my every word. 'Jude, it's me! Katie!'

'Well, hello yourself! Are you missing me already?'

'Yes.' I'm smiling with excitement. 'In fact, Jude, Emily and I are missing you so much we've decided to stay for a couple more days.'

'Am I hearing you right, you crazy woman? Have you had too much to drink at the airport, or what?'

'Come on, Jude. You know I've given up the drink. We're not joking. We're just about to change our flights to Wednesday. We're going to hire a car, and drive you home. And if you don't mind, we'll sleep on your floor for the night.'

There's a silence. I'm suddenly worried that the other girls are right. I've offended her. She doesn't need me to nursemaid her. She's probably got a lift sorted out already and she doesn't know how to tell me.

'What about your jobs?' she says in not much more than a whisper.

'Sorted. No problem.'

'And what about your lads?'

'Fuck 'em. They're still in Prague.'

'Are you sure, Katie? Are you absolutely sure you want to do this?'

'We'd like to, yes. As long as it's all right with you, and we're not treading on anyone's toes. You know – your parents, or Fergus. What do you think?'

'I think,' says Jude, and her voice is wobbling now as if she's trying to stop herself laughing. Or maybe crying. 'I think it's the best idea in the world. And you're the best friend in the world. And I'm paying for the car hire!'

'Of course you're not. It's an extra holiday for me and Emily ...'

'Well, I'm paying half, whether you like it or not.'

'We're picking you up in the morning, then – OK? Just as soon as we've sorted out the car. See you then!'

'Great!' says Emily, beaming, as I put my phone away. 'That's sorted, then.'

'Two more days in Ireland! Yee-hah!'

'Do you want to pay cash or by debit or credit card, madam?'

The bar's crowded. Emily and I get there first and manage to find a table for four, so when the others join us we have to squeeze round the table, perching very uncomfortably on the edges of each other's chairs.

'All checked in?' I ask them brightly.

'Yes. So what have you decided? Are you going ahead with this crazy scheme?' says Lisa.

Why does everyone seem to think we're crazy, for wanting a couple more days' holiday? It was OK for Matt to book ten days, apparently.

'It's not too late,' points out Helen. 'The check-in is still open.'

'It *is* too late, actually,' says Emily. She looks as excited as I am. 'We've cancelled our flights.'

'And rebooked for Wednesday evening,' I add triumphantly. 'Look!' I wave the booking confirmation at them.

'And how much did *that* cost you?' sniffs Mum.

'Not much,' says Emily quickly. 'Now – are we having a farewell drink, or what?'

'I thought you'd all given up the booze!' laughs Auntie Joyce.

'Well, I think we *should* perhaps have just one little one this evening,' I say cautiously.

At this, everyone starts to laugh.

183

'Ha! *Knew* it wouldn't last!' says Karen.

'Yeah, trust Katie! One day on the wagon and she's desperate for a drink again,' says Lisa a bit unkindly.

'It's our last evening, all together,' points out Emily. 'And we've all had a great time, haven't we? Despite everything? So don't you think we *should* all just have a little toast – to the bride?'

Chastened, they give their orders. While Emily and Helen are at the bar getting the drinks, the next table becomes free so we're soon all settled a lot more comfortably, which is probably a good thing, considering what's coming.

'OK, then, everyone,' says Lisa, raising her glass. 'Here's to Katie! Thanks for inviting us to your hen weekend, love!'

'To Katie!'

'Cheers, Katie!'

'To the bride!'

I raise my glass, but for a moment I don't drink.

'There's just one thing,' I say shakily, hesitating with the glass still held up in the air.

The others, taking their first gulps of their beer or their wine or their vodka, look at me warily over the tops of their glasses. What nonsense is Katie going to come out with next?

'What's the one thing, Kate?' asks Emily mildly.

'Just that I'm not. I'm not really the bride.'

'Has she had a couple of drinks already, Em?' mutters Suze. 'What's she on about?'

'I'm not the bride,' I say, a bit louder. 'Not any more. I didn't want to tell you all, you see, and spoil your weekends. I'm not going to be a bride, because there isn't going to be any wedding. It's off.'

I look around at the sea of astounded faces. Their mouths are all open, their glasses all hovering, like mine, in mid-air. Mum looks like she's going to cry. Lisa's shaking her head. Emily's frowning at me, panic in her eyes. I take a large gulp of my wine, and bang the glass down, making everyone jump.

'The wedding's off,' I repeat. 'Sorry. Maybe I ought to explain.'

'Yes,' says Lisa, putting her hand on Mum's, both of them trembling visibly. 'Yes, Katie; an explanation would be a good idea, I think.'

I want to tell her not to worry about the wedding dress. She can sell it.

KATIE'S STORY

It's not that I don't feel bad for them all. Of course I do. Look at Mum – she's devastated. I knew she would be; why do you think I've put off telling her? All that planning: the church, the reception, the flowers, the photographer and the printed invitations. It's all been cancelled. We've lost deposits left, right and centre. Mum paid for some of it but I'll pay it all back to her. Bad enough losing your daughter's wedding day without losing half your life's savings on it too.

And look at Emily's face. I know what she's thinking.

No, Emily – it's nothing to do with what you told me last night. Of course not. That just made it even worse: finding out that *you* knew there was something wrong between Matt and me even before I did. If you'd told me, maybe I'd have called off the wedding sooner than I did. Maybe I'd have cancelled the hen weekend. But is that what you would have wanted? The way I looked at it was – we all deserved a good weekend away so why should I ruin it for everybody? Soon enough to come clean when it's all over.

So now they all need to know what happened. And where do I start? How far back do I go? Back to the beginning? The story of Katie and Matt. In my mind, it becomes a popular paperback romance.

Katie and Matt.

They loved each other passionately. But could their love stand the test of time?

Apparently not. No need to read to the end, really.

I've spent so much time wondering when it all started to go wrong, I've almost driven myself mad. The rows about

Prague were just the catalyst. Being so angry about Prague, if I'm honest, almost came as a relief. It finally gave me a chance to turn on Matt and shout at him. I'd wanted to do it for weeks – maybe even months! – but I hadn't had a reason. If I'd suffered from PMT it might have been better: at least I could have had a good screaming, crying session, let it all out (whatever it was), and then made my excuses. Hormones. Women have used them as an excuse for bad behaviour since the beginning of time, haven't they. What excuse have men got?

If you want to know what was wrong between me and Matt, I'll tell you: nothing. We're perfect together. Perhaps we should have bickered, like other couples do. We should have had disagreements, irritations, things that drove us mad about each other. We should have snapped at each other when we were in bad moods, or sulked and not talked to each other for days. Look around you – that's what normal people do. Normal people who get married, have kids and grandkids and live to a ripe old age together: the reason they manage it is because they've seen the very worst of each other and decided to put up with it. I don't believe those ninety-year-olds you read about in the local paper who celebrate their diamond wedding anniversaries and try to tell the world they've never had a cross word. They only say that because they've got Alzheimer's and they can't remember what they had for breakfast yesterday, never mind the fights they had when they were newlyweds sixty bloody years ago.

Emily and Lisa have always been right about me: I'm too romantic. I found someone who was so perfect for me, we couldn't even find anything to argue about. We couldn't bear to be apart. Yes, it was wonderful. It was what I'd dreamt about, all those years, reading Mills & Boons under the duvet with a torch when I was a teenager. It was romantic, it was exciting, it was ... do you know what? I think it was beginning to get on our nerves. I think it was a *good* thing we started to argue.

If I tell you that during the last few months, in the lead-up to the wedding, I've been feeling like an overinflated balloon, I'm not just talking about my waistline and the tightness of the wedding dress. It's as if all the little bubbles of happiness and excitement about Matt, about our relationship, our love for each other, our life together, had filled me up so full to the brim that I was already about to explode. Then I was pumped up with stress about the wedding, the wedding, the wedding. The church, the caterers, the flowers, the bloody dress. When Matt told me about Prague it was as if he'd found exactly the right pin to burst my balloon. Thank God! I let off steam with my anger, and suddenly, our relationship stopped being perfect. We were arguing and bickering like any other couple. I was terrified. What was happening to us? We weren't supposed to be like this. We were nearing the most important chapter in our story and I'd suddenly lost the plot!

All the time, Emily was trying to reassure me. *Don't worry, love – it's normal. Everybody gets stressed out just before their wedding day. It's only nerves. You'll be fine.* And all the time, she was hiding something from me. She'd noticed something wrong with Matt and she'd actually gone out of her way to ask him about it – without telling me. Oh, I suppose she thought she was helping, that she was going to get him to see the error of his ways; make him cancel the ten days in Prague and take his mates for a sedate weekend on the Isle of Wight instead. And we'd all live happily ever after.

I knew it was about more than that. I knew he wasn't happy; but then again, neither was I. I'd even asked him outright whether he was seeing anyone else.

'Don't be ridiculous,' he flared. 'We spend our entire lives together! What opportunity would I have?'

'So it's only the opportunity you're lacking? Not the intent?'

'Katie, for God's sake! I am *not* having an affair and I don't *intend* to have one! What are you talking about?'

'Something's wrong.'

'Yes. It is.' The look he gave me was very pointed. It was saying: *And what's wrong is that you've turned into someone who accuses me of having an affair.*

'We never used to argue like this.'

'You never used to be suspicious and distrustful.'

'I'm not! I never have been! But something's *wrong* ...'

We talked ourselves round in circles. It got us nowhere. All the air had finally come out of the balloon and I felt as flat as a bloody pancake. So maybe we did fall in love too quickly, too passionately. And maybe the ending was going to be as sudden as the beginning, after all.

Last Saturday, when he was leaving for Prague, I came home from Mum's and found him sitting in the flat in silence, a cold cup of coffee beside him, his holdall zipped up and his passport lying neatly on top of it.

'What's the matter?' I asked automatically.

He held out his arms for me.

'What's the matter?' I said again, going to sit down next to him but ignoring his outstretched arms.

He dropped them to his sides. He looked defeated, as if he'd spent the whole day searching for something and had finally given it up for lost.

'I need to tell you something,' he said, without looking at me.

'What?' A hot lump of panic was forming in my throat.

'The trip to Prague. It's not exactly a stag.'

This didn't make any sense. I shook my head and frowned.

'We've cancelled the stag. It's just me and Sean now. None of the others are coming.'

'Why?' I shook his arm, trying to make him look up at me, but when he did I regretted it, because the look in his eyes frightened me. 'What's *wrong*?'

'I just want to get away – on our own – me and Sean. I want a chance to think. To think things over, Kate. Quietly.'

'To think *what* over?'

There was a long, long pause. I didn't need him to answer, obviously. I could fill in the blanks myself. I found myself wondering whether any other men went away with their best friends for ten days before the wedding to talk over their doubts. It seemed quite bizarre. How many doubts must a person have, to talk about them for ten days? I could sum mine up in less than ten minutes.

'I've got doubts too!' I said aloud, my voice wobbling with the shock of what I was saying.

189

It had only just struck me. Why had I taken so long to admit it?

'You have?' said Matt, the surprise in his voice mixed with something else that took me a moment to recognise. Relief.

'Yes. I thought it was just nerves. Pre-wedding nerves.' I laughed – an inappropriate, unnatural laugh that sounded even to my own ears dangerously like hysteria.

'And it's not?' he asked cautiously.

'I've kept telling you something was wrong. I couldn't work out what it was. Maybe ...' I looked up at him, suddenly feeling a bright spark of hope in my heart. 'Maybe it's just that we're not ready for this, Matt. If we've both got doubts about the wedding ...'

'We ought to talk about it?' he said, sounding about as enthusiastic as if he'd suggested hopping barefoot over a bed of hot coals.

'No. I mean yes, of course we should have talked about it. But we got caught up in it all, didn't we. And now there isn't time. You're going off tonight with Sean. And I'm off on Thursday with the girls. It'll be too late when we get back.'

I looked at him expectantly, almost excitely. He was frowning, not understanding me, and who could blame him? Maybe I'd flipped.

'Too late for what? We can still talk when we get back, Kate.'

'Not too late for talking. Too late for cancelling the wedding. It's probably too late already – we'll lose our deposits on things but that's too bad. Don't worry. I'll sort it all out while you're away. I won't tell Mum, though. Let's not tell anyone. I think that's best. I don't want to upset them all yet. Wait till we both get back, then we'll have to ...'

I was babbling. The sense of relief that had washed over me as soon as I'd diagnosed that the problem wasn't *us* – it wasn't me, it wasn't Matt, it wasn't an affair and it wasn't even Prague – it was the *wedding* – was so exhilarating that all I wanted to do was wipe the slate clean of the wedding completely, as soon as possible, have a good time on the non-hen weekend and the non-stag holiday and get back to being girlfriend-and-boyfriend-in-love with the least possible fuss.

Except that Matt probably thought I was on the verge of a complete breakdown.

'You don't mean it,' he said, his face pale with shock.

'Why not? You've got doubts, I've got doubts, we shouldn't be getting married. Easy. Cancel the fucking thing.'

'Katie, you're sounding very ... *hyper*. I'm not sure ...'

'Well, *I'm* sure. We were happy before this whole wedding circus took over. Let's turn the clock back to then.'

'It's not that easy. You can't turn the clock back. Things change. Things happen ...'

'What do you mean? What things happen?'

He shook his head. He looked tired, exhausted even. I'd noticed he hadn't been sleeping very well.

'Have you had these doubts for a long time?' I asked him quietly.

He shrugged.

'And are they *just* about the wedding?' I added, almost in a whisper. 'Or what?'

No response. Not even a shrug this time.

'Or about me?' I managed to squeak like a poor little frightened, wounded mouse, just about to be squashed, just about to have all the life splattered out of it. I held my breath, closed my eyes and waited for the blow.

'No,' he said, after far too long a pause. 'Not about you.'

We looked into each other's eyes then. I found myself thinking that if this had been a romantic novel he would have kissed me. But he didn't.

'Just about the wedding,' he said, nodding to himself as if to underline it. 'You're right. That's it.'

'Then it's settled. The wedding's off.'

Matt went off to Prague looking worried and uneasy, and I immediately went into a frenzy of cancellations. I made a list and ticked it. It was almost more exciting than arranging the thing in the first place. I made the phone calls, trying to sound upset about it. Church, hall, caterers, photographer, cars, florists. They all gasped with surprise and said how sorry they were. How awful for me, so close to the date. And unfortunately, did I realise that the deposit was non-returnable? A new thought struck me. Maybe I should have kept the bookings for the hall, the caterers, the cake and the flowers after all and just had a hell of a party. A non-wedding! I laughed out loud to myself at the idea and realised I was feeling happier than I had for a long time. Or perhaps I'd just completely lost my marbles. Who laughs while they're cancelling their wedding? Only crazy women, surely.

I knew, of course, that all my friends and family would be shocked and upset, but I really didn't want the weekend in Dublin turned into a wake. So I kept it a secret – from everyone except Jude. Well, I had to tell someone or I was going to collapse with the weight of it. Jude was the obvious choice, living in a different country from everyone else, and because we'd be sharing a room over the weekend away. Anyway I knew I could trust her to keep it quiet – she's just not the blabbermouth type.

'Sure and I'll get to be your bridesmaid some other time, Katie. No need to worry at all about that on my account,' she teased me gently, having pretended to recover from her initial shock.

'Ah, shit – The Pledge! Jude, I'm so sorry ... I'll make it up to you some other way ...'

'Away with you and your nonsense, you know I'm only pulling your leg. That's the last thing in the world you have to worry about; we were only children at the time and silly enough to believe in happy endings, were we not?'

'Yes. And unfortunately, I'm still silly enough, Jude.'

By the time we left for the hen weekend, I'd done everything except for sending out the cancellation notices to all the guests. The *un*invitations, as I thought of them. *Katie and Matt regret to inform you that for personal reasons, their wedding on 21st May has been cancelled.* Maybe I should say *postponed*. It sounded kinder. But then they'd be expecting a revised date. *Katie and Matt regret to say ...* Maybe I shouldn't use the word *regret*. No time for regrets. *Katie and Matt are pleased to announce that they've dumped the wedding idea and are carrying on living in sin.* Hmm. Might upset a few aunts and uncles. In the end I settled on: *Katie and Matt are sorry to tell you that we've called the wedding off. However we are still together and we hope to see you all* *soon*. There. Sorry about the disappointment, everyone. Sorry if you've bought new frocks and special hats and wasted your money on wedding presents. But at least you know we're not crying over the champagne. I printed out the *un*invitations on the computer, addressed all the envelopes and stacked them up ready to send out when I got home. After I'd told Mum and Lisa. That was going to be the hardest part.

Or maybe it wasn't.

As it turned out, the hardest part was keeping up the façade while we were away. Acting as the bride-to-be, going along with all the dressing-up and the silly games, getting drunk with my best friends and having to remember not to spill the beans and ruin the party. Being apart from Matt for the longest time ever, and beginning to wonder. Didn't he hesitate just a little too long when I asked if his doubts were only about the wedding, not about me? Didn't he look confused and anxious, instead of relieved and happy, when I said we'd call off the wedding and go back to how we were before? Why? *Was* there something else wrong? *What* was he spending ten days talking to Sean about?

You see, Emily?

You see now why I was so upset with you? Why I wanted to hit you?

You've confronted me with my own fears. You didn't know I'd called off the wedding. But you knew before I did that my boyfriend was confused and upset about something. And you didn't even tell me!

193

ABOUT GOODBYES

If I'd made an announcement that there was an unexploded bomb in the bar and it would go off as soon as the next person spoke, I couldn't have brought about such a stunned and complete silence. Even the people on the next table are quiet. They must have been listening.

'I'm sorry,' I say again, beginning to sound like a parody of myself. If I apologise much more I'll probably cease to exist at all. Like I'm apologising for even breathing, for even living, certainly for even being here in Dublin celebrating my forthcoming non-existent nuptials with some of the closest people to me in the whole world, who didn't think I was capable of such lies and deception. I hang my head.

'You should have *told* us,' says Emily, her voice shaking with shock.

'You should have waited till we got back,' says my mother, barely containing her anger. 'It would have blown over. People have arguments. People *always* have doubts before the wedding, but ...'

'But what, Mum? They should still go ahead? Like you did?'

She flinches, and I immediately feel cruel and start to apologise again.

Lisa looks at me in surprise, and I remember she still doesn't know Mum's wedding story. I shake my head at her: *Take no notice of me. I'm upset.*

'But you still love each other!' she says, frustration loading her voice. 'You're not splitting up! What's the point?'

'You could equally ask what was the point in deciding to get married in the first place,' I tell her. 'We were happy as we were.'

194

'If you can't even stand the stress and strain of a wedding,' says Mum sniffily, 'how do you expect to cope with *life*? What about if you have children? What about if one of you gets ill, or loses your job, and you have no money, and you have to *go without things*? Eh? *Those* are the things that cause stress, Katie. *That's* when you'll really start to have arguments. If you can't hack it now, you might as well forget it.'

'Yes. Life isn't always a bowl of plums,' says Lisa.

'Cherries.'

'Whatever. It isn't always sweet. Things go wrong ...'

'I know. Things like sexual incompatibility.'

I watch her go red and start fiddling with her handbag. Well, I'm sorry, but all this self-righteous indignation is getting right up my nose. Neither Lisa nor Mum has exactly made a stunningly good example of their marriage. Not saying it's their fault, but why should I sit here and listen to them telling me I should sacrifice myself on the altar of their own disappointments?

'I think,' says a voice from the other end of the table suddenly, 'that it's a very brave decision you've made, Katie. And as your friends and family, we should all stand behind you and support you.'

At this, there's a different kind of silence; it's thick with the scent of respect. It stings my eyes and makes me swallow several times before I can answer.

'Thank you, Auntie Joyce. That means a lot to me.'

I push back my chair and get up to walk over to her, but she's quicker than me and I'm being enveloped in her arms before I have time to move. I'm a little girl again and Joyce is comforting me after some childhood disaster that Mum didn't quite have the time to listen to. I'm a teenager and she's telling me not to cry about the first boyfriend who dumped me. I bury my head against her shoulder but I *don't* cry. Not this time.

'Joyce is absolutely right,' says Helen loudly. 'Well done, Katie. I think it's a very mature choice.'

'It must have taken a lot of guts,' admits Karen. 'Cancelling everything like that, on your own, without telling anyone.'

'Shame about the reception, though,' says Suze wistfully. 'I was looking forward to a good boogie.'

I'm glad she's made us all laugh. I catch her eye and she winks but her mouth is turned down with distress for me.

'You need to get going,' I tell them all, looking at my watch and knocking back the rest of my drink. 'Your flight's boarding.'

'I don't feel like we should leave you, now,' says Lisa doubtfully. 'I wish you were coming home with us.'

'I'll look after her – don't worry,' says Emily.

'Look after me? What's the matter with you all? I'm not ill! I'm not the one with the broken ankle! I've just cancelled my wedding! OK?'

They all continue to look at me anxiously as they pick up their bags and get their passports and boarding cards ready.

'We've all had a great time, haven't we?' I add encouragingly. 'Aren't you glad I didn't cancel the hen weekend too?'

A smile or two. A snigger. A murmur of agreement. Helen strides forwards and takes hold of me by the shoulders, giving me a kiss on both cheeks.

'Well, *I'll* say it, Katie, if no one else is going to! I've had an absolutely super time. Thanks a million for asking me. And I'm *glad* you didn't tell us about the wedding till today. I think we've all told quite enough morbid stories over the weekend without this one to cap the lot, don't you, girls?'

'Yes,' agrees Lisa quickly, struggling to stop looking as distraught as she obviously feels. 'Yes, it wouldn't have been half as much fun dressing you up and playing those hen party games if we'd known it wasn't really a hen party.'

I give her a quick kiss.

'Sorry for letting you down,' I whisper, 'about the dress.'

'I'm hanging it up in the back bedroom,' she whispers back, 'in case you change your mind.'

'Come on, everyone!' says Helen urgently. 'That's the final call for our flight.'

There's much more I want to say, but time has run out. They're in such a hurry, I'm not even sure if I've kissed everyone goodbye. I've ended up kissing Emily by mistake, and she's not even going. They're rushing through to the departure gate now, looking back over their shoulders, waving until they're out of sight. I can imagine the stunned silence between them all as they're showing their boarding passes, putting their bags through the X-ray machines, running to the gate and joining the queue to board their plane. And then perhaps the sudden exclamations: *Can you believe it! How did she pull that off? Pretending all weekend ... never saying a word ... absolutely ridiculous!*

Emily and I look at each other in silence for a minute.

'Come on, you,' she says calmly, taking hold of my arm. 'We need to get out of here.'

'Yes. But where?'

'I'll call the hotel. See if we can have a room back for tonight.'

'Good idea,' I say, watching her do it.

I feel like I'm never going to be able to make another decision in my life.

I allow myself to be led, like someone rather weak who's just had a debilitating illness or a bit of a nasty shock, out of the airport and into a taxi. As the driver pulls away I sink back against the seat as if I'm exhausted.

'It must be a relief,' says Emily, squeezing my hand, 'to have it all out in the open.'

'Yes. I suppose so. I feel like such a cow, though. Upsetting everybody.'

'You can't get married just to avoid upsetting everybody, Katie.'

We sit in the hotel lounge and order hot chocolate with whipped cream and marshmallows. It feels extremely necessary to have the cream and the marshmallows.

'Are you hungry?' asks Emily as we're sipping our drinks.

We haven't eaten since lunch.

'Not really. Probably enough calories in this to keep an entire family fed for a week!'

'What do you want to do this evening?'

'Can I be honest? I'd like to snuggle up in front of the TV and watch a film. Would you mind?'

'Mind? I had my fingers crossed you weren't going to suggest going clubbing!'

I laugh.

'No, you can have too much of a good thing, can't you. I'd like to get started early in the morning anyway.'

We're giggling as we get into our pyjamas at the ridiculous hour of eight o'clock, switch the TV onto a movie channel and climb under our duvets. We've brought a big bar of chocolate with us.

'It feels like we're about fourteen and having a sleep-over,' says Emily.

'Fantastic.'

'There's *Dirty Dancing* on this channel in five minutes!' she adds, her thumb hovering over the remote control.

'Even more fantastic! I've only seen it about fifteen times.'

'Yeah, I reckon I must have clocked up about twelve myself. My all-time favourite.'

'Bring it on, then, sister! We can sing along with all the songs.'

I flop back against the pillows and pop a square of chocolate into my mouth.

'Katie?' she adds just as the film's about to begin.

'Mm?'

'I think you're doing the right thing. If that helps. About the wedding – I think it was a good idea to put it off. You can always put it back on again, once you and Matt ... once you've had time to settle down.'

'I don't think we will, though, Em. I don't want to go through all this stuff again. I think I've decided not to bother getting married, ever.'

'No. I can see where you're coming from. It's not worth the hassle, is it? Everyone else getting involved ... dresses, flowers, all that crap ...'

'Exactly. Why bother, eh?' I laugh, breaking off another piece of chocolate. I feel relaxed. Carefree, almost. How long has it been since I felt such a total lack of stress?

'We'll stay as we are, then, shall we, love? Unwedded bliss?'

'Yep. Apart from one thing.'

'What's that?'

The film's just starting and she's turning up the volume. I don't think she's really concentrating but I take a chance anyway.

'I've decided I want a baby.'

ABOUT CAR HIRE

'So you haven't mentioned this to Matt?'

We're eating toast and marmalade in the morning. I wouldn't let Emily talk about it last night. She wanted to. She even tried to turn *Dirty Dancing* off, but I grabbed the remote out of her hand and turned it back on again.

'I'll tell you in the morning,' I said. 'I'm too tired tonight.'

'Then you shouldn't have *mentioned* it!' she hissed, her eyes wide with the shock – yet another one I'd inflicted on her.

'I know. Sorry. I was just feeling nice and relaxed and chilled, and it kind of slipped out.'

'How long have you been thinking about this?'

'Since yesterday.'

'So it's not exactly a rational decision?'

I looked back at her calmly. 'Yes, it is. Now, can we watch the film?'

As it happened, we both fell asleep before the end of it. This morning she started firing questions at me again almost as soon as she opened her eyes. At first, she said, she thought she'd dreamt it.

'I was hoping I had, actually,' she says grimly now. 'Have you gone stark raving mad since we've been over here?'

'You mean have the leprechauns got to me?' I giggle, spreading marmalade thickly over my second slice of toast. My appetite seems to have come back with a vengeance. I feel great. It's amazing what getting rid of a whole load of pretence will do for you.

'Look. I don't want to be a wet blanket or anything, but don't you think you and Matt have got a few things to talk about? I mean, you've literally just cancelled your wedding, and you're telling me now that you've made a unilateral decision to get pregnant?'

'I can't do it unilaterally, Em. I will actually need some help from him.'

'Yes, but ...!' she sighs with frustration. 'He doesn't even know you're *thinking* about this. Does he *want* to start a family?'

'I've absolutely no idea. Strange, isn't it? I thought we knew each other inside out, but it's only recently occurred to me that we've never even discussed the subject.'

'You must have done. For God's sake! Everybody talks to their partner about whether they want kids or not!'

'Have *you*?' I ask her with genuine interest. 'Do you and Sean talk about it?'

'Yes, we do, from time to time. We've agreed that we do want to have children, but not for a while yet. Not until after we've ...' She tails off and looks up at me warily.

'After you've got married, you were going to say, weren't you. But last night we both agreed we wouldn't bother.'

'Well. You know. Perhaps *one* day we might ... maybe after a lot longer ... maybe not till we decide to start a family. Things change. Circumstances ...'

'Of course you'll get married,' I tell her briskly. 'And of course you'll have kids. Don't look so worried. I won't hold it against you.'

'But – Katie! Not yet! Not *yet* is what I'm saying. You and Matt need a bit of time, and space, to get over this whole wedding thing. And you've had a lot of emotional upheavals this weekend – what with your mum, and your sister, and then all this stuff about Helen and Greg ...'

'That's got nothing to do with me wanting a baby, has it?'

'Well, I don't know. I don't know *where* this is coming from. I can't help thinking it's some sort of reaction.'

'What: I've had a bit of a crappy time so I think I'll go home and get pregnant? No, Em, I'm not quite as neurotic as that. I actually think I've wanted this for a long time, without even realising it.'

'You've lost me now. Sorry. I don't do psychology. My subconscious mind is uncharted territory and that's the way I like it.'

I finish my toast, wipe my mouth on my serviette and drain my coffee cup. Emily's watching me as if I'm a dangerous breed of dog that might leap up and take a bite out of her arm at any moment.

'OK. Look. My mum and my sister weren't the only ones who poured out family secrets to me this weekend. I had a talk with Joyce as well. She'd never told me before why she hasn't got any kids. Well, it's not through choice. They've never been able to have any. It just made me think – OK?'

'Yes, but ... fair enough, I feel sorry for Joyce – I feel sorry for anyone in that situation. But that doesn't mean you have to immediately try for a baby yourself, does it? What are you going to do – give it to her?'

'Don't be silly, Emily. It just made me realise that if I *do* want a baby, I need to get on with it. Not leave it too late.'

'You're thirty-one, not forty-five!'

'Even so. It can take years.'

'In some cases, yes. In others, it can take five bloody minutes!'

'Five minutes?' I retort, grinning.

'Well, if you're lucky,' she concedes, grinning back. 'Or maybe five seconds!'

We're laughing together as we get up from the table and go back to our room to get our bags.

But even while I'm laughing, I'm thinking: yes. I hope it happens quickly. Once I've made my mind up to something, you see, I don't like messing around waiting. I want to get on with it.

According to the very helpful young guy at our reception desk, there's a car hire place just along the road from the hotel. How convenient is that. It doesn't take us long to settle the bill (again) and lug our bags down the street to the place he recommended.

'We need a car for two days,' I tell the lady at the counter. She looks nice. 'Just something small. Oh, maybe not too small. It has to have a nice big back seat for my friend to put her leg up on.'

202

She looks back at me, unsmiling. Maybe not so nice. Maybe a bit suspicious of English girls with friends whose legs need to go up on the seat.

'She's broken her ankle,' I feel obliged to explain. 'But it's OK. She won't have muddy shoes on the seat, or anything.'

'So it's just for two days?' she says, ignoring this.

'That's right. We're taking her home to County Cork, you see, and then coming back to Dublin tomorrow to fly home to London. Bit of a bummer, isn't it, breaking your ankle when you're away for the weekend ...'

'And will you be the only nominated driver?'

'Yes, I suppose so. It's cheaper that way, isn't it, and it's not as if I'll be having a drink, at all. Given it up, you know, after what happened ...'

'I could drive, if you like,' offers Emily, looking anxious. 'I don't mind. You don't have to ...'

'No, no, that's fine. I'm happy to do it.'

'But you could have a drink. Tonight, with Jude. A farewell drink. You might feel the need.'

'The need, Em?' I chuckle. 'What do you mean, *the need*? I said, I've given up. More or less. Although poor old Jude's been through so much, she might like a little drink tonight, I suppose.'

'Honestly,' says Emily, seeing me hesitate. 'Let me drive, Katie. Please.'

'Well, maybe one of you would like to complete this form when you make up your minds?' says our friendly car hire lady, with a sour expression. 'Name and address here, please, date of birth, mobile phone number if you have one, and ...'

'Sure. Yes, of course, no problem.' Emily drops her bag and picks up the pen. 'I'll do it, Kate, and you can navigate. Jude can't, from the back seat. She'll get a crick in her neck.'

'OK, then. If you're sure.'

She fills in and signs the form and passes it back across the counter.

'OK, and I need to see your driving licence, please.'

'Driving licence.' Emily looks blank for a moment, then opens her handbag, rummages around inside it without looking very confident, then snaps the bag shut again and says, quietly, 'Bugger. Sorry, Kate. I didn't bring it with me. You're going to have to drive after all.'

I'm thinking quickly to myself. Thinking about the spring-clean of my handbag I performed before we came away. The English store cards and supermarket loyalty cards I left in a neat little pile in the drawer of my bedside table because I didn't want to be bringing anything unnecessary over here. I can see them now, in my mind's eye. And lying tidily beside the neat little pile is my UK driving licence. Well, I didn't think I'd be using it, did I?

'Bugger,' I echo. 'I left mine at home too.'

We both stare at the lady behind the counter, who stares straight back at us. I don't somehow think she's going to offer to drive.

'Jude?' I mutter tentatively to Emily. 'She might have her Irish licence with her?'

'Your friend with the broken ankle?' interjects our car hire friend in a very sarcastic tone. 'I don't *think* so, do you?'

'Right. OK.' I'm blustering now, completely at a loss. 'Right, well, thank you anyway. We'll be back if ... well, when we ... if we manage to ...'

'Let's go, Kate,' says Emily flatly. 'This isn't going to happen. We'll take Jude home on the train. We'll have to carry her leg between us.'

I'm glad to get back out into the street. I can feel that woman's eyes following me out of the door.

'How did we *not* think of that?' complains Emily. 'Are we stupid, or what? Of *course* we can't hire a car without our driving licences.'

'Well, we've had one or two things on our minds. Christ, what a pain. Well, I'd better warn Jude that there's a slight change of plan. I wonder what the trains are like here.'

We lean against the wall while I take out my phone and find the number in my address book.

'Whoops!' I laugh, cutting off the dialling quickly and starting over. 'Nearly did it again!'

'Did what?'

'The wrong number. Harry's. You know, it's under *Irish*, next to Jude. How embarrassing that would have been. I'd better take it out of my contacts.' I pause, look at Emily for a minute, then add thoughtfully: 'Although, on the other hand ...'

'No. Whatever you're thinking, I don't like the look of it in your eyes. No, Katie!'

'Well ... it's worth a try, isn't it? He can only say no.'

'I don't know what you're talking about. But I still say no!'

But the number's already dialling. Like I say, I don't like shilly-shallying around if I've made my mind up to something.

'Harry?'

'Hello. Who's this?'

'It's Katie. From the hen party?'

'Katie!' His voice sounds warm and pleased. It's just the tonic I need. 'How lovely to hear from you again! Are you back home now?'

'No. Actually, Harry, a couple of us have stayed in Ireland. We've got to take our friend home to County Cork – Kinsale. She's broken her ankle, and ...'

'Poor girl! Did you say Kinsale? That's only a little way from where I'm going to stay with my cousin. How are you getting down there, Katie?'

'Well. We *were* trying to hire a car, but we've ... come up against a bit of a problem. So it looks like we'll be carrying Jude onto the train.'

'Don't be ridiculous. I'm just about to leave. Where are you? I'll pick you up.'

'Well, I don't like to put you out. I mean, it's three of us, and one's got her leg in plaster. We have to pick her up from the hospital. Are you sure you don't mind? We'll ... um ... we'll pay for the petrol. And buy you a drink, or two ...'

'I'm liking the sound of this more and more!' he laughs. 'Honestly, Katie, it'll be good to have your company. I'm in no hurry, I'd just planned to take a slow drive down there. Didn't I say to call me if you needed anything?'

Yes, although I seem to remember that was in connection with a striptease. I feel hot at the thought of this, and decide maybe I shouldn't mention it.

'It's really nice of you. Why don't we walk round to your hotel to meet you?'

Emily's giving me a very old-fashioned look when I end the call. But what the hell? I've got us a lift, haven't I? Can't say fairer than that.

Harry's driving a bright blue Corsa with a sunroof. It doesn't really go with the image I've been building up of him in my mind. It's too girly. Of course, you don't get a lot of choice with a hire car (and we got no choice at all, as it happens); then again, do I really know anything about this guy? The looks Emily's still giving me as we get into the car and head for the hospital to pick up Jude are very clearly conveying that I might just as well have asked for a lift from a serial rapist, for all the sense I've displayed and all I know about him.

'I'll go and fetch Jude,' says Emily as soon as we pull up in the hospital car park. 'You can wait here.'

She slams the door as she gets out of the car.

'I have a feeling your friend doesn't approve of this arrangement,' says Harry. 'Or is it me she doesn't approve of?'

'No, don't worry – she thinks I shouldn't have accepted a lift from you, that's all. She's probably right.'

'I'll drop you all at the station if you like,' he offers with a smile, 'If you'd rather get the train?'

'I don't mean to sound ungrateful. It's just – I suppose Emily thinks we don't really know you. We don't, do we.'

I'm trying to avoid looking at him. I'm conscious of the fact that I wasn't too bothered about knowing him when we snogged each other half senseless on Saturday night.

'Well, now,' he says, leaning back in the driver's seat and opening the window to let in some fresh air. 'Harry James Cornwell. I was born on the fourth of January 1973. I'm a Capricorn. I live in London: Tower Hamlets – I share a flat with a guy called Adam and his girlfriend Ruth. I work in the Human Resources department of an IT company in Wapping. I've got two younger brothers and I'd like a dog one day. A spaniel. I play rugby for a company team on Sunday mornings and I go to the gym twice a week. I don't smoke but I probably drink more than I should do. I like fish and chips and Chinese food but I can't eat curry – it gives me heartburn. What?'

I'm holding up my hand, laughing and shaking my head.

'OK, OK! Fair enough! I know you, now! I know more about you than I know about some of my own family!'

I suddenly stop laughing as I say this. How bloody true *that's* turned out to be, this weekend.

'Are you all right?' he asks me quietly.

'Yes. But it's been a bit of a strange weekend. Everyone's found out things about each other. I've even found out things about myself. It's all been quite shocking.'

'In the old days, it was the wedding night that was a shock to the bride,' he jokes. 'Not the hen party!'

'Yes, well. There isn't even going to be a wedding night.'

He glances at me in surprise.

'We called the wedding off last week. It's OK, it was a mutual decision. I've only just told the girls, though.'

'I see what you mean about shocks!' he says, looking concerned. 'And your friend's had a rough time, too, by the look of it,' he adds, nodding out of the window as Emily comes into view, helping Jude across the car park on her crutches.

'It's been more upsetting for everyone else than it has for me, really. I was a bit of a bitch, keeping it quiet, but I wanted us all to enjoy the weekend away. Can we keep off the subject, do you think?'

'Don't worry. I'm discretion itself. I won't mention the W-word.'

Emily opens the back door of the car, but Harry jumps out and rushes round to the back, holding the door open and helping Jude onto the seat before putting her case in the boot. She slides across and sits against the other door, with her legs stretched out. Emily squeezes in carefully next to her and lifts her plastered leg onto her lap.

'Thanks,' Jude says. 'This is very kind of you, Harry. I'd never have managed on the train. I feel such an eejit, putting everyone to all this trouble.' She leans forward and grabs my hand. 'Hello, Katie. Sure and it's good of you and Emily to stay over and take me home, so it is. I can't begin to say what great friends you are, and all.'

'It's nothing,' I tell her. 'We're glad to have an extra couple of days in Ireland, aren't we, Em?'

Emily nods, looking at Harry with slightly less hostility. I wonder if she's realised now how much difficulty we'd have had getting Jude home on the train. I know she's only little, but we'd have had a job lifting her on and off, as well as her case and her crutches and our own luggage.

'All set?' says Harry, starting up the car. 'Next stop Kinsale, then.' He puts the new U2 CD into the player and starts to hum along with it as we head out through the Dublin streets.

'Good taste in music,' acknowledges Emily slightly grudgingly. I look in the mirror and catch her studying the back of Harry's head, and smile to myself. She likes him really. How long before she admits it?

ABOUT A JOURNEY

Sorry to say it, what with Jude having a broken ankle and everything, but I'm enjoying this. Sitting in the car next to Harry, watching his hands on the steering wheel, listening to him singing along to U2: 'Sometimes You Can't Make It On Your Own'. He glances at me from time to time, gives me a little smile as if to say: think about the words. The words are all about not thinking you're tough, not having to go it alone. Now that he knows about the wedding being cancelled, I think he's trying to be extra nice to me without making it too obvious. I realise I don't know him very well but I can tell he's that kind of guy – thoughtful, caring. I suppose I'm feeling a bit vulnerable. To be quite honest I'd like nothing better than to feel someone's strong arms round me right now – someone who'll look after me and tell me not to worry, everything's going to be all right. I feel safe sitting here next to Harry in his car. Safe and surprisingly happy.

It's a beautiful day. Once we get out of Dublin and onto the motorway heading south, it's all countryside. It's easy to see why it's called the Emerald Isle. The sun's quite hot through the car windows. I struggle out of my jacket and pull up the sleeves of my jumper. Harry watches me out of the corner of his eye. I think he fancies me. I've thought that all along, actually. He fancies me, and of course, I fancy him too. But I mustn't dwell on that. It's one thing to have a drunken snog at the end of the evening in a nightclub. Quite another to fancy a snog when you're stone cold sober and sitting next to someone in his car.

'I'm sorry we can't take turns with the driving,' I say, to take my mind off wanting to snog him. 'How stupid were we, leaving our driving licences at home!'

'That's OK,' he says, laughing. 'I like driving. But if you're not used to it, driving in Ireland can be a bit of a shock to the system. For one thing, the Irish are lousy drivers ...'

'Hey!' pipes up Jude. 'That is *not* fair!'

'Well, OK. Let's put it this way, then: all the lousiest drivers in the world are Irish.'

'There's a reason for it, so there is,' says Jude defensively. 'You see, some years back there was a desperate backlog of learner drivers waiting to take their tests. There was no way they were ever going to catch up with themselves, so the government decided to give licences to everyone that was waiting, without them having to taking a test.' She stops and looks at us, triumphantly. 'See?'

'And that was a good idea?' says Harry sarcastically.

'Well, fair play to them, it got rid of the queue for the driving tests, didn't it, so?'

'And chucked a whole mob of unqualified lousy drivers out onto the roads!'

'Well, you do have a point, I suppose,' Jude agrees a bit sulkily. 'But it's not their fault, is it?'

'You're not even Irish,' I remind her, laughing, 'but you always jump to defend them!'

'Well I'm Irish by adoption, aren't I, so? I feel like England's a foreign country when I go over there now, everything's speeded up ten times faster there than when I was a kid.'

'That's true. It's manic, working in London,' says Emily.

'The pace of life at home is horrendous,' agrees Harry. 'That's one of the reasons I enjoy coming to Ireland. Dublin's much more cosmopolitan these days, of course, but outside of Dublin, everything is slower and gentler, somehow.'

'Apart from the drivers, apparently!' I laugh, as a maniac in an old Beetle swerves across the lanes in front of us, making Harry brake and curse.

'Exactly. They're complete nutters. And the other thing is, the road signs are so unreliable! I was driving along the West Cork Coastal Route last year, and the nearer I got to where I was heading, the further away the signs were telling me I was. I thought I was going mad, or driving in the wrong direction. I actually stopped the car at one point, got out and walked up to the signpost to make sure I was reading it right. I even got hold of the post and shook it, to see if the wind had turned it round the wrong way.'

'Sure there'd be some signs in miles and some in kilometres, that's all. Did you not think of that?' demands Jude.

'Well, yes, I did, eventually, but it still didn't account for all the distances getting steadily greater. I felt like I'd driven round in circles by the time I'd finished.'

'You probably had,' she retorts. 'You were maybe driving the Ring of Kerry and no one had bothered telling you!'

We're all laughing now, even Emily. I glance back at her and she smiles at me. She looks more relaxed. Maybe she's beginning to realise Harry's being a very good friend to us, doing us all a very great favour, rather than a dangerous stranger or potential rapist.

As I say, of course I do fancy him like mad. But I'm trying to put that out of my mind. I'll be going home to Matt in a couple of days' time. Home to try and sort out the rest of our lives, and to start planning our family.

It was after eleven this morning when we finally left Dublin and at about half past one Harry suggests we make a stop for lunch.

There's a rousing chorus to the effect that not only is everyone hungry, they can't remember when their last good meal was and their stomachs feel like their throats have been cut. Must be the fresh country air, even if it is only through an open inch of the window.

We stop at a place called Urlingford.

'Almost halfway,' pronounces Jude as Harry parks the car. 'Everybody always thinks of Urlingford as the halfway place between Dublin and Cork.'

'Never mind all that,' says Emily impatiently. 'Is there a toilet anywhere? I'm desperate for a wee.'

She's out of the car, hopping from foot to foot with a very anxious look in her eyes.

'There's a pub just across the car park there,' says Jude, pointing it out as she shuffles herself across the back seat. 'Where are my crutches?'

'Sorry, Jude. I'm going to have to dash for the pub,' says Emily. 'See you in a minute.'

'Well, that's nice, isn't it!' I say, staring after her. 'She should have gone before we got started.'

'Yes. Did her mother not teach her that?' laughs Jude. 'She's more concern for her bladder than she has for me crutches!'

'Here: I've got your crutches,' says Harry. 'Put your good foot on the ground and lean on me for a minute.'

I watch him helping her out of the car and feel another surge of warmth and gratitude towards him. It's true we hardly know each other; but how many other men would befriend three strange women in a crisis and be so kind and supportive? I can't help wondering whether Matt would be the same, in the circumstances. Maybe he would. Or maybe he'd be just a little bit impatient, a bit irritated about the change to his plans. Am I being unfair? I don't know. Perhaps I should ask him about it, when we both get home at the same time as I ask him about having a baby. Get everything out in the open at once.

Not only is he kind, helpful and good company – Harry also insists on paying for our lunch. I'm beginning to wonder if he's too good to be true. What with his stunning good looks and everything.

'It's fine, honestly. We've still got some euros to use up!' protests Emily.

'Save them. You can go out on the town in Kinsale tonight.'

'I don't think I'll be going far, to be honest with you,' says Jude sadly, indicating her plastered foot propped up on a chair.

'What're you going to do about your work?' asks Harry. 'Do you have far to travel?'

'I work in Cork city. But I'm hoping a colleague of mine will be able to pick me up. He lives in Kinsale too.'

'Or Fergus can give you a lift, can't he?' I point out. I'm beginning to wonder about Fergus. He never seems to be around when she needs him. I feel a flicker of annoyance at the thought that he might not be treating her properly.

'Oh. Well, yes, maybe. Depends what he's doing …
where he's working …' she says vaguely. 'Is that the time?
Should we be getting along, do you think?'

Emily and I exchange looks as Harry gallantly helps Jude
to her feet once more.

'Are you thinking what I'm thinking?' she mutters.

'That Fergus might need his arms and legs breaking off and
his torso chucked in the Irish Sea with a rock attached to it?'

'Sounds almost too good for him.' She chuckles. 'I
wouldn't like it to be said that we jumped to conclusions
about him without even meeting him. But I think he's a dickhead.'

'Obviously, there could be very good reasons for him not
rushing to help her in her hour of need. But I think you're
right. He's not only a dickhead, he's going to be a dickhead
without a dick when I get hold of him.'

'Or without a head,' adds Emily.

We've been whispering, but we both burst out laughing at
this.

'No dick, no head – what kind of a dickhead is that?' I
giggle.

'A dead one!'

'Exactly!' I'm not laughing now. 'If he's hurting her, I'll
kill him.'

'Let's hope he's not. Seriously, she seems happy enough.
And I can't stand the sight of blood.'

Jude has swung ahead of us on her crutches, with Harry
walking solicitously beside her, and at the pub doorway she
turns to call us.

'Come on, you two! Stop gossiping like a pair of old
women!'

'When are you going to tell her?' Emily asks me quietly
as we follow them out of the pub.

'About Fergus being a dickhead?'

'No, Katie. About the wedding being cancelled.'

'Oh, yes. I … um …'. Emily's going to be really hurt if
she finds out I've already told Jude. 'I'll talk to her quietly
on our own,' I prevaricate.

'Have you told *him*?' She nods in the direction of the back
of Harry's head.

'Yes.'

'And did you make it clear that you and Matt are still together? Or does he think you're fair game now?'

'Don't be silly. I . . .'

'*I'm* not being silly, Katie. I'm not the one kidding myself. The chemistry between the two of you is sending off so many sparks I'm practically getting burnt just sitting in the same car.'

'OK, yes – I do like him. But I won't do anything about it. I'm going back to Matt and I'm going to talk to him about having a baby.'

She doesn't say anything. Just shakes her head and looks away, which is irritating, but I decide to ignore it. Maybe she'd like to have a baby too, really. Sometimes people don't admit it.

Emily and Jude both fall asleep in the back seat as we head southwest towards Cork. I'm studying the map, looking at all the strange Irish place names.

'Lots of *Kills*,' I say wonderingly.

'It means church, apparently.'

'Oh! And *Raths*?'

'Fort, I think.'

'*Inis?*'

'Island.'

'I didn't think you spoke any Irish?'

'I don't,' he says with a smile. 'That's just general knowledge.'

'In that case my knowledge obviously isn't very general.'

'You must know more about books than I do, though. More than most people do.'

'Nice of you to think so. I mainly read light fiction, though. I'm sure it's not easy to write, but it doesn't exactly strain my brain cells reading it. I did study English lit. at uni. But you know how it is. All that learning, and then you go back to the real world, out to work, and you probably retain about five per cent of it. Shame, really.'

'Yeah. Still, they say uni teaches you life skills.'

I snigger.

'I think the only life skills I learnt, certainly in my first year, were how to survive alcoholic poisoning and how to get laid ...' I stop, freeze, and turn to look out of the window. You see? He's so easy to talk to, I'm finding myself saying the sort of things I'd normally only confide to my girlfriends.

'Oh, really?' he says, sounding highly amused. 'Well, that's a very interesting life skill. Would you like to share your knowledge with me, do you think?'

'I was joking,' I say shakily, still looking the other way. I'm boiling hot. I search for the button to open the window on my side but he does it for me. Fresh air gusts in but it doesn't help to cool me down at all.

'*I* wasn't,' he says, softly.

I spend most of the rest of the journey talking about Matt. I don't suppose Harry appreciates this, but it's kind of reassuring to me. I have to keep reminding myself – I have a boyfriend at home. Well, in Prague. I have a boyfriend who was almost going to be my husband. We might have decided to ditch the wedding, but I love him, and he loves me. We're going to have a baby together. He doesn't know that yet, but he'll be thrilled when he finds out. I even end up telling Harry this.

'What if he isn't thrilled? He might want to wait a while. He might not want kids at all. How come you haven't discussed it before?'

How come everyone keeps asking me that?

'We've been too busy talking about everything else. Enjoying ourselves. Planning the bloody wedding,' I add tersely.

'So you don't feel ready to go ahead with the wedding, but you think it's time to have a baby?'

'Yes! Look ...'

'It's OK. It's none of my business, after all. I'm just intrigued. I've never been with a girl who wanted a baby.'

'You haven't been with me, either!' I retort, shocked.

'No. But I'm hoping to.'

This is getting worse. It's brazen. I can't believe his nerve.

'Sorry,' he says, with an impish grin like a little boy who's been caught nicking biscuits out of the tin. My heart does a double somersault. 'I didn't mean to offend you,

Katie. I should have kept it to myself. I won't mention it again.'

'What? Kept what to yourself?'

'How much I fancy you. I have done from the moment I saw you. There – I've said it. It's totally inappropriate, I know that; you've got a boyfriend, and I'll probably never see you again anyway, and I'm totally out of order for talking to you like this. But – today, getting to know you a bit better – well, I feel like we've known each other for ages, to be honest ...'

'Me too,' I admit.

'So am I forgiven? No offence taken? I won't say another word about it. We'll talk about something safe and neutral. Dustbins. Or cleaning the oven.'

'What?'

'It's the most unsexy thing I can think of. I always have to imagine cleaning the oven when I need to try to get my mind off sex.'

'And do you ... often ... have to think about cleaning the oven?'

He glances at me, like he's checking to make sure I'm smiling. I am.

'All the fucking time,' he says with a growl.

We're both laughing when the other two wake up and ask how much further we've got to go.

And surprisingly – disappointingly in a way – Harry says we're just coming into Kinsale.

216

ABOUT FERGUS

As we turn onto the coast road I get a glimpse of the sea and catch my breath. It's beautiful.

'Look,' says Harry, stopping the car at the top of a headland. The bay is stretched out beneath us. 'Lovely sight, eh?'

'Amazing. You're so lucky, Jude.'

She's only been living here a little while. When I've visited her in the past it's always been to her old home just outside Cork.

'I know. It's a sight to stir your heart, to be sure. But where I live, Katie, it's down a back street and out of sight of the sea, I'm afraid.'

'You'll have to direct me from here, Jude,' says Harry, starting the car again.

We're outside her flat in five minutes. It might not be within sight of the sea, but it's still lovely. It's half of a converted pink-washed cottage – the bottom half, fortunately for Jude's current situation – and it's tucked away down a little side road just a stone's throw from the town's main shopping streets.

'You'll come in and have a cup of tea or something to eat with us, Harry,' says Jude in a tone that brooks no argument, 'after all you've done for us, driving us all this way.' She slides across the back seat as he's holding the door open for her. 'Could you ever get me crutches out of the boot for me, please, Katie?'

I'm already out of the car, stretching my legs. I open the boot and move our bags out of the way, looking for the crutches.

'Not in here,' I call back to her. 'You must have put them inside.'

'Don't be daft – there's no room in the back here. They're in the boot to be sure, Katie. Would you have a proper look!'

Emily joins me as I start lifting the bags out of the boot. She takes out a couple of jackets and the boot's empty. No crutches. I turn to look at Harry.

'Shit,' he says. 'I think I forgot to put them back in the boot. After we stopped for lunch.'

'So ...' Emily's looking at him like he might be having a laugh with us. 'So you're saying the crutches are still in the car park back at Urlington?'

'Urlingford,' Jude corrects her automatically.

'Urlington, Urlingford, bloody Tipperary – it all amounts to the same thing!' says Emily irritably. 'Poor Jude's stuck here with her leg in plaster and no means of transportation.'

'Sorry ...' says Harry, scratching his head.

'All right, Emily – I expect we can get her some more from the local hospital or whatever,' I try to pacify her. I don't want her to moan at Harry after he's been so kind to us. These things happen, don't they? People probably leave their crutches in car parks all the time.

'You must be joking,' says Jude. 'It's not the NHS over here, you know. They don't give out crutches willy-nilly to any old person who turns up asking for them. They'd probably charge me an arm and a leg just to borrow them.'

Very appropriate.

'Well,' says Harry with a sigh, 'there's only one thing for it.' He reaches into the back of the car and easily lifts Jude up in his arms.

'That's all very well,' says Emily churlishly, 'but you can't carry her around indefinitely.'

'I wasn't planning to,' he says with a grin. 'I'm going to phone the pub and ask someone to see if the crutches are still there. Or if they've been handed in. Then I'll drive back and pick them up.'

'Oh, no, you can't do that, Harry, for the love of God, I won't be letting you do that!' squeals Jude, twisting round in his arms in protest. I find myself wondering what it feels like to be held like that.

'Keep still, Jude, or I'll drop you in the gutter! Have you got your front door key? Or are we going to stand out here all day arguing? Of course I'm going back for your crutches. It was my fault, not putting them in the boot.'

'Well, no, it wasn't your responsibility ...' I begin, but Emily silences me with a look.

'That's very kind of you to offer, Harry,' she says primly. 'But it's an awful long way to drive there, and back again, isn't it.'

'Like I said before – I like driving.'

We've got the front door open now and we're standing in the hallway of Jude's new flat. It's gorgeous. But then, knowing Jude, it would have to be. She never could bear mess or shabbiness, even when she was a student. The walls are cream, the floor's dark varnished wood. We follow her (still being carried by Harry) through into a pastel-pink lounge with a rose-pink carpet and dark red leather upholstery. I feel like I'm stepping through the pages of an *Ideal Homes* magazine. Even the simple stone vase on the fireplace and the few tasteful ornaments look as though they've been chosen for a TV house makeover programme. How does Jude do it? OK, she's been away for a few days, but how does she keep Fergus under control? Where are the newspapers lying all over the floor? The empty beer cans? The TV remote control down the side of the cushion? How come the wastepaper bin's empty? Where are the crisps packets and the Kit-Kat wrappers? Why aren't there any curry sauce stains on the carpet? Suddenly I'm changing my mind about Fergus. This guy must be perfection personified. If the toilet's clean, that does it. She should marry him.

'Go through to the kitchen, Katie, if you wouldn't mind,' says Jude as Harry sets her down on the sofa, 'and put the kettle on. Then we'll talk about what to do.'

'There's nothing to talk about,' says Harry firmly. 'I'm going back for your crutches. I'll wait till a bit later, when the roads are quieter. I'll be there and back in no time.'

At least three hours, probably more. I wouldn't call it no time.

'I can't let you do it ...' begins Jude, but he silences her with a raised hand.

'I absolutely insist. I'll tell you what I'll do: I'm going to pick up my cousin, and we can drive down there together.

We'll have a meal at the same pub, where we had our lunch, and drive back later in the evening. Is that OK?'

'Well, if you really want to do that – it'd make me happier to think you were having an evening out, with your cousin, so it would,' says Jude doubtfully.

'Excellent. That's decided, then. Get the kettle on, girls!' he adds playfully.

'There are some chocolate biscuits in the cupboard,' Jude calls after us.

'What do you make of all this?' Emily asks me as we're standing in the neat little kitchen waiting for the kettle to boil.

'It's lovely, isn't it? I knew Jude would choose some-where nice, but I had no idea how—'

'No, Katie – not the flat. I mean Harry. What's he after, do you think?'

'After?' I ask faintly, pretending not to understand. I busy myself with the teabags and biscuits, aware that she's watch-ing me.

'Yes. What's he after? Going all that way, halfway back to Dublin, to look for Jude's crutches ...'

'He's going to phone the pub first, to make sure.'

'Yes, I know. But even so – he's certainly putting himself out, isn't he?'

'I think he's just a nice guy. And he feels bad about leaving the crutches behind, that's all.'

'Hmm.'

'Hmm, what?'

'Oh, nothing. Call me suspicious, but I think he's trying to impress us.'

'Well, fair enough, I *am* quite impressed.'

'Exactly,' she says, giving me a pointed look.

I turn away again and look in the fridge for the milk. Everything in here is tidy too. No smelly remains of vegetables going rotten in the drawer at the bottom. No mucky crusty dollops of spilt yoghurt or dried blood from dripping steaks. It's hard to believe that a man has been living here.

'That's who I'm *most* impressed with,' I say, turning back and surveying the clean worktops and empty sink. No washing-up piled up waiting to be done. No coffee grouts slopped into the sink congealing around the plughole. It's just miraculous!

'Who?'

'Fergus. The mysterious, house-trained, house-proud boyfriend. I admit I had my doubts about him, but now I can't wait to meet him!'

And this is so bizarre, I feel like I must be dreaming. Because, at the exact same minute I'm telling Emily I can't wait to meet Fergus, the doorbell rings and we hear Harry go to answer it while we're carrying the tea and biscuits through to the lounge.

'Hello young man,' says someone with a very broad Cork accent. 'I saw the car outside – would Judith be back from her trip? I'm Roisin from upstairs, and I'm very pleased to meet you, so I am. Shall I come in? Only I've brought Fergus.'

I nearly drop the tray with all the mugs of tea all over the rose pink carpet with no curry stains. Roisin appears in the lounge doorway, jumps in surprise at the sight of Jude and her plastered foot, and deposits a very small, short-haired cream-coloured cat in her lap.

'He's been a good boy while you've been away – haven't you, Fergus,' she croons. 'But for the love of God! What have you been doing to yourself with your foot?'

You could hear a pin drop; if it wasn't for the cat, who's settled down immediately and comfortably on Jude's lap and is purring louder than most of the men I've ever heard snoring.

'Fergus!' I say faintly, staring at Jude. 'You've ... you've named your cat after your *boyfriend*?'

'No,' she says, with a long, thin sigh, without looking up at us. 'No, Katie. Not at all. I should have told you. I was going to, when Harry'd gone. My boyfriend ... *is* a cat. This is Fergus, everybody.'

The silence grows deeper. We don't seem to want to look at each other. Roisin hovers, half turns towards the door, obviously uncertain whether to stay or go. Harry gets to his feet. I pick up one of the mugs, meaning to hand it to him, to tell him to sit down, don't go, stay for tea and biscuits. But he's not thinking of leaving. He walks over to the sofa where Jude's sitting, bends down, takes Fergus's delicate little paw in one hand, shakes it very solemnly and says:

'Good evening, Fergus. Very pleased to meet you.'

Everyone laughs. Jude looks up at him, gratitude mixed with the embarrassment in her eyes. Roisin sits down and stays for tea and biscuits. And I look across at my oldest friend, sitting on her perfect sofa in her perfect flat where no slobby messy man has ever set his muddy feet on the perfect pink carpet, where her *boyfriend* sits on her lap, purring and looking at her with adoration in his slitty green eyes.

And I wonder if things can possibly get any fucking stranger.

JUDE'S STORY

Fergus is a Burmese, two years old, very clean and very affectionate. I got him from Kathleen who runs the pub at the end of the road. She'd bought him as a kitten, the runt of a litter, but her other two cats didn't accept him and she was fed up with the fighting.

'He needs to be an only child, so he does, bless his heart,' she told me. 'The other two eejits won't give him a minute's peace, poor little devil.'

He had red angry claw lacerations on his little pink nose, and a badly bitten left ear. What could I do? I said I'd take him in temporarily to get him away from his tormentors while Kathleen tried to find a home for him. It took nearly three weeks for his ear to heal up properly, and by then I'd fallen in love with him. And he with me. It was so nice to come home after work and find someone waiting for me, purring with pleasure at seeing me, winding himself around my legs as I dished up his food, jumping onto my lap as soon as I sat down and gazing at me as if I was the most wonderful person in the whole world.

I sent Katie an e-mail:

I've got myself a new boyfriend! He's name's Fergus, he's sweet and funny and I love him to death!

I was planning to wait for her reaction before I told her he was really a cat, and then we'd have a laugh about it together. But her reaction was so over-the-top, so full of patronising shit about how wonderful that I'd finally found myself a man, how much she hoped he'd be good to me and that we'd be happy together, blah blah blah, that I felt humiliated and cross and didn't bother to reply. And as the months went by and she carried on e-mailing me and phoning me with this attitude of surprised excitement about the amazing news that poor old Jude had actually managed to pull, I couldn't bring myself to tell her the truth. I built up a little fictitious character for Fergus the boyfriend, not terribly far removed from Fergus the cat-friend except that I missed out things like him bringing mice in through the cat-flap. And I'm sorry – I know it was lying. I know it was silly, and deceitful, and in the end I've probably ended up making a complete arse of myself. But Katie was asking for it.

I'm her oldest friend and I shouldn't say it, but she can be so *bloody* annoying. She really doesn't have the faintest idea – how easy life is for girls like her. Even when we were still at school together in England, going through that awful stage round about puberty when I spent my entire time suffering agonies of insecurity about everything – *everything* – from the way I looked to the way I walked, the way I spoke and even the way I smelt – even at that age, Katie always appeared supremely confident. And why shouldn't she? She never had a single spot or pimple in her life. Her hair was never greasy or flyaway or just *wrong* – it always hung, sleek and glossy like a shower of dark satin. She didn't need to worry, like I did constantly, about what might happen when she opened her mouth to speak in a crowd, how her voice might wobble or squeak or dry up altogether, leaving everyone to laugh while she blushed and stammered and wanted to die. She didn't even have to give it a thought, because all she had to do was walk into a room, smile and laugh and say 'Hi!' to everyone, and they'd be falling at her feet, wanting to be her friend, wanting to be in her team, wanting to invite her to their birthday parties and their holiday outings and make up foursomes with the best-looking boys in the class.

I tried everything. I saved up for expensive clothes. I learnt how to use make-up properly. I went to the best hair-dressers in town and copied the latest styles. I got into the habit, very early on, of taking care of myself, doing my nails properly and never letting my eyebrows get out of control. I even read books about how to walk tall and talk to people confidently. They didn't help. I just felt even more of a failure than ever when I still hung around at the edge of the group, stammering with nerves when anyone asked me a question.

Because Katie was my best friend, I lived in her reflected glory. I knew people thought of me as Katie's quiet little sidekick, but I didn't mind – it meant all the popular girls and boys in the class accepted me. They were generally nice to me. They'd say kind things about my clothes or my hair and tell me I was pretty; but I knew it was only because of all the hard work with the make-up and blow-drying. It wasn't much fun because I was scared to go swimming or run around on wet and windy days the way they did, without a care in the world, unless I had my hair stuck down with about a gallon of hairspray.

And then my parents ruined my life forever, the way parents can when you're fifteen, by taking me away from Katie, away from my school and all the friends I had, not just away but *abroad*. At the time, I thought my life was over, that I might as well be dead and I'd never get over it. Of course, I did, and I made friends too, but what I never did get over was my shyness – and I didn't have Katie to help me any more.

We spent our holidays together, but the gulf between our lives seemed to grow wider every year. When Katie visited, and told me about her boyfriends, her parties and discos, her first kiss, the first time she fell in love, the first time she had sex ... I listened, I laughed with her, I was happy for her ... and I never stopped wishing it was me.

'When are you going to get yourself a boyfriend, Jude?' she used to ask cheerfully, completely oblivious to the fact that I was trying desperately, I'd have done anything to get one, but no one ever seemed to notice me. I'd spend hours getting myself ready to go out, only to sit in the corner and wonder why I'd bothered.

In the end, I got very drunk at a party at university, threw myself at a fellow who was almost as drunk as me, and kind of ordered him to have sex with me. I badly needed to get rid of my virginity. Needless to say it wasn't a pleasant experience, partly because he threw up as soon as he'd finished and partly because I passed out before *I* finished, but at least I didn't have to spend the rest of my life wondering about it. I went out with a couple of guys after that, but normally they only wanted sex and then lost interest. And I didn't enjoy the sex so what was the point? I might have tried being a lesbian, but none of the girls seemed to fancy me either.

I know Katie's always been anxious about me. But I don't like her anxiety. You know what annoys me most about it? Her continual nagging at me to *lighten up*. To stop worrying about my hair; to go out without my make-up on and *enjoy the freedom*. Freedom? The thought of it horrifies me. I'd feel even more vulnerable than I do already. What does she know about such things? She runs and hops and skips through her life, in her frayed jeans and trainers with her hair flying carelessly around her face, while I totter self-consciously beside her, in my high heels and my war paint and hairspray and my fixed smile. We must look an odd couple of friends. But I love her to bits and that's the trouble. I can't be jealous of her because she's my best friend and I love her. So what could I do? If I invented a boyfriend, at least it kept her happy and kept her off my back. And it worked a treat.

Of course, one lie always leads to another, and I found myself having to make up a whole package of excuses for Fergus. Why he couldn't come to the wedding; why he couldn't come and pick me up from hospital. No wonder Katie and Emily were beginning to get that anxious look in their eyes. Well, I know I could have told them the truth by now. To be sure I should have done, especially once I realised they were coming back to Kinsale with me. But there was a wicked little part of me that was getting a bit of a kick out of seeing the disapproving glances between them. Imagining them thinking: *Poor Jude, sounds like she's picked a right bastard – what a shame for her – after so long on her own and all!* I know it was mean of me, but I thought I'd keep up the joke just for a bit longer, till we got home and they saw Fergus for themselves. I thought we'd have a huge laugh about it all together. But looking at them now, they just look totally stunned and, to be honest, I think they're wondering whether I'm completely off me head. Poor old

226

Jude, still on the shelf, can't get a real man, has to make one up. Bloody sad, probably needs therapy.

I suppose I ought to put their minds at rest and tell them that actually, it's been the most tremendous fun inventing Fergus the Boyfriend. Shame he wasn't real – although to be honest, I'd probably have ditched him long ago if he was!

ABOUT A PHONE CALL

We drink our tea, eat our biscuits, and try to keep off the subject of Fergus. Not Fergus-the-Cat – we've done a lot of talking about *him*; about how cute he is, how sweet, fluffy, furry, purry and lovable. We're all talking nineteen to the dozen about the bloody cat because we don't want to broach the subject of Fergus-the-Fictitious-Boyfriend. Certainly not in front of Roisin-from-upstairs, who has the air of somebody who would spread the story all over town by midday tomorrow, and even more certainly not in front of Harry. However nice he is, I don't know him well enough to have a full-on discussion about Jude's mental health and her love life, or lack of it, until he's well out of the way. That's got to be girls-only stuff.

Instead, we tell Roisin all about our weekend in Dublin and how Jude came to break her ankle. She tells us about the one and only time she's been to England, in 1979 to the wedding of a niece who *emigrated* to Swansea.

'But Swansea's in Wales,' I point out.

'Yes, you could be right, I did hear tell of that once meself. These foreign places move around, do they not – England one minute, Wales the next, 'tis very confusing, so it is.'

'Do they?' says Emily, looking blank.

'Sure, 'tis only here in God's own country that the towns seem to stay put in one place,' she says smugly. 'Have you ever noticed Kinsale moving out of County Cork, Judith, or Cork becoming part of Northern Ireland, God save and preserve us all?'

'No, Roisin.'

'You see?' she nods triumphantly at Emily. 'Didn't I tell you so?'

I'm thinking privately that Roisin's barking mad and it's probably best just to humour her, but I can see Emily frowning and squaring up for an argument.

'Would you like more tea, Roisin, before you get back to Paddy's dinner?' says Jude hastily before she can start anything.

'Bless yer heart, I could sit here drinking tea and telling you me traveller's tales all day, if it wasn't for me arthritis.' Emily's frown deepens at this, and I catch her eye, shaking my head, warning her off any attempts to make head or tail of Roisin, who, if not barking mad, is probably rolling drunk. 'But you're right about Paddy's dinner, God love you. If I don't have his tatties in the pot by the time he sets foot in the door, he has a face on him to scare the devil himself out of hell, God save our poor souls from his mighty wrath.'

'Paddy's mighty wrath?' echoes Emily faintly, looking worried.

'No, the devil's, I think,' Harry whispers behind his hand. 'Just smile and nod.'

'Thanks a million again for looking after Fergus,' says Jude, as Roisin struggles with her arthritis to haul herself to her feet. 'Give Paddy my regards.'

'Goodbye. Nice to meet you,' I say, going to the front door with her.

'And likewise yerself, bless your sweet innocent heart,' she says, laying a heavy florid hand on my arm. *Innocent?* 'May all the blessings of St Anthony be with you on your holy wedding day.'

Oh, fuck. No way am I telling this fruitcake that there's no holy wedding day happening. I'll probably have her here for the rest of the day talking about the devil's wrath.

'Thanks,' I say. Smile and nod, smile and nod.

'And don't you be worrying your head about Judith, now. I'll bring her down some tatties and stew every evening till her leg's mended, bless her heart. You and your little friend can just get yerselves home to Wales.'

Harry heads off, straight after Roisin goes, to pick up his cousin. He's already phoned the pub in Urlingford, where, amazingly, someone handed in Jude's crutches almost as soon as we must have left them in the car park. When he commented to the barmaid on the surprising honesty of the crutch-finder, he was apparently treated to a lecture on the inherent integrity of the citizens of Urlingford, culminating, indignantly, with:

''Twould be a mortal sin indeed to steal the crutches off the legs of a cripple!'

'Cripple?' retorted Jude, when he told her. 'I've only broken me sodding ankle!'

'Yeah, and you're getting tatties and stew from upstairs for as long as it takes to mend it,' I said with a grin.

'Jesus. She means well, the daft old bat, but I've had her stew before, and it's enough to set your intestines in concrete, so it is.'

God save us and preserve us from Roisin's stew, then.

It's quiet now, with just Emily and Jude and me. We put the telly on and slob out in companionable silence.

'So, Jude,' I say lightly after a while. 'Are you going to tell us about it? About Fergus?'

'Sure, and isn't he the sweetest little cat that ever ...'

'Not the damn cat, Jude. You know what I'm asking you here. Why? Why the need for that dumb trick? Making up a boyfriend, making excuses for why he wasn't around whenever he should have been? What the hell was all that about?'

'Just a joke, Katie, for the love of God. No need to get upset ...'

'A joke?' I shake my head at her. 'We were worried about you – did you know that? We thought he sounded like he was messing you about. I was going to chop him up and throw him in the river.'

'And what river would that have been, Katie?' she asks, completely straight-faced. 'Only I'm not sure you know your way around here, and the river is ...'

Emily giggles. I glare at her.

'So suddenly this is really funny, is it?'

'Come off it, Katie,' says Emily mildly. 'Jude's taken the piss out of us, we fell for it, serves us right.'

'It stopped the nagging, for a while,' Jude adds quietly.

'Nagging?' I'm cross, but only because I recognise the truth of this and I don't want to admit it. 'I have so *not* nagged you, Judith Barnard!'

'You so *have*!' she returns, laughing, imitating my Essex accent. 'Every phone call, every e-mail, every time we see each other! "When are you going to get a boyfriend, Jude? When are you going to find yourself a man, Jude?"' She stops and gives me a very pointed look. 'Don't you realise it's just rubbing salt into the wound? Don't you think I'd give anything to have a nice man in my life like the rest of the population of the world? Do you think I *like* being lonely and unloved?'

She says this flippantly, as if it's a joke, but I suddenly see – years and years of *nagging* too late – that it isn't. It's hurting her, and I've been adding to that hurt. I jump to my feet as if I've been stung, run across the room and throw myself at her.

'I'm so sorry,' I tell her, through the tangle of her hair and mine as our faces bump together. 'I didn't realise ... I didn't think. I was worried about you; I just want you to be happy.'

'So do I, Katie, so we're both after the same thing, are we not?' she responds lightly. 'Now will you get off me for the love of Jesus, before you break my other leg, with the weight of you, you great lump, you!'

'Well, that's nice, isn't it!' I retort huffily.

There's a moment's silence and then Emily sniggers and before we know it, we're all killing ourselves laughing.

'All right, I suppose I asked for it,' I admit eventually.

'It *is* quite funny,' says Emily. 'We're all dying of curiosity about this guy – is he nice, is he good-looking, is he going to marry you and give you babies. And he's a bloody Burmese cat!'

'Don't you be swearing about my pussy, young lady!' Jude admonishes her, and we all start laughing again.

'Just don't ever say that again,' I tell her when we finally calm down. 'OK?'

'What? Say what?'

'That thing about being unloved. It's not true. Whether you've got a man or not, it isn't true.'

'Cos *we* love you, baby!' says Emily.

'Yes, we do. Better than any man ever can, Jude. Don't you ever forget it!'

She nods and grins at us both. She looks too choked up to reply. Probably too much laughing.

'Shall Katie and I cook us something for dinner?' asks Emily when we've finally slobbed in front of the TV for long enough.

'Or shall we send for a takeaway?' I put in quickly. I'm still on my holidays, thanks very much. Soon enough for normal cooking to be resumed when I get home. 'Do you have takeaways around here, Jude?'

'*Do we have takeaways*? Did you think Kinsale is a sleepy village in the back of beyond? It's the gourmet capital of the Irish Riviera, Katie Halliday! There's a queue a mile long for some of our restaurants, with fine good chefs from all over the world and tourists coming here specially for the seafood!'

Shit. That's telling me, isn't it.

'So do you have takeaways?'

'Yes, we do, Katie – is it Chinese or fish and chips you'd be liking?'

It's not till we've piled the sweet and sour prawns and egg fried rice onto our plates and we're just about to get stuck in, that I remember to ask Jude:

'Who's St Anthony?'

'Patron saint of weddings, amongst other things. Although if you ask me, there's a lot of confusion between these patron saints as to who's responsible for what. St Valentine is obviously supposed to be the saint for lovers, fair enough. And I've heard some folk say St Nicholas is your man when it comes to brides and weddings – but how he can find the time to attend to that as well as playing Father Christmas, I couldn't say.'

'Does seem too much of a job for one guy,' agrees Emily with a forkful of rice halfway to her mouth.

'So I think, Katie, I'd put my money on Anthony if I was thinking of a quick prayer in relation to a wedding,' says Jude quite seriously.

'And is there a patron saint for cancelled weddings?' I ask her without missing a beat.

She looks up at me, a question in her eyes. I have a sudden vision of the lilac bridesmaid dress hanging in my wardrobe, and a lump comes to my throat. Maybe I should be looking for the patron saint of broken promises and jilted bridesmaids.

'Is it all out in the open now, so, Katie? You've told Emily?'

'Yes. Emily knows. They all know, now, Jude. I told them all at the airport.'

Now it's Emily's turn to drop her fork and stop eating. We'll never get through the meal at this rate.

'Jude *knew* about this?'

'Em – I had to. I had to tell someone or I'd have gone mad.'

'Sure I only knew a few days before we went to Dublin, Emily.'

'*I* only knew a few days before, myself!' I say grimly.

'And you couldn't tell me?' Emily asks softly, looking back at her dinner.

'It wasn't like that. It wasn't that I couldn't ... didn't trust you ... don't be silly, that's ridiculous. It's just that I wasn't ready for Mum, or Lisa, or Auntie Joyce and all the family to know about it. They'd have wanted me to cancel the hen weekend, for one thing. I know everyone thinks I'm peculiar for still going ahead with it – but it was what I wanted to do. Maybe it sounds mad, but I thought, if I just carry on, keep it to myself, have the hen weekend, pretend nothing's happened, I won't have to face it all till I get back.'

'And I encouraged her,' Jude tells Emily. 'What would be the point of sitting at home, miserable, while her man still buggered off to ...'

Emily shoots her a warning glance and Jude tails off, 'To that place where he's gone to,' which makes us all smile, despite ourselves.

'It was too soon,' I try to explain to Emily. 'Too soon to talk to any of you about it. I couldn't face you with it. It was easier telling to Jude on the phone; I didn't have to see her face. See the disappointment ...'

233

'Jesus, will you listen to the nonsense of her? Disappointment? Sure I was only concerned about your own disappointment, you silly girl, and when you told me you thought it would be better for the two of you to not be married, that you'd been arguing and you wanted to go back to how you were before – well, it sounded like it was for the best, when all was said and done.'

'Well, I suppose I'm glad you weren't keeping it all entirely to yourself,' Emily tells me. 'I must admit I was stunned, when you told us, to think you'd never let it slip, not to me, not to your mum or anyone.'

'Yeah. To be honest, with me and Jude sharing a room, I'd probably have blabbed to her over the weekend if I hadn't done already.' I sigh. 'Come on, girls, the food's getting cold. No point crying over split milk. At least I haven't got to say any prayers to St Anthony, anyway.'

But just as I start to dig into my Chinese again, I realise the strange music I've been hearing from somewhere in the distance is my chosen ring tone on my mobile phone, calling to me from my bag out in the hallway. I run out to answer it, but it's only my voicemail, telling me I've already missed four calls. What's the matter with me? Have I gone deaf, or what? All the calls were from Matt. And when I return the call and he answers, I have to sit down on the floor to recover from the surprise.

He sounds absolutely furious. And his first words to me are:

'Where the fucking hell are you?'

'I've been sitting here waiting for you,' he thunders across the ocean at me. Well, the Irish Sea. Matt never normally thunders.

'Here? Where?'

'At home, Katie, where do you think? Why didn't you come home with the others?'

'Because of Jude. She broke her ankle. Emily and I ...' Hang on a minute. Why am I on the defensive? 'Why aren't you in Prague?'

'I came home early. I needed to talk to you.' His voice sounds grim. I don't recognise the tone he's taking with me.

Has he been drinking? 'I cut short my holiday because I needed to see you. I sat up all night, waiting, wondering if your flight was delayed, and then I phoned your sister and . . .'

'But didn't she tell you? About Jude's ankle?' I'm so stunned by the accusation in his voice, I can only talk in short sentences. He cut short his holiday because he needed to see me? Oh, that's rich, after all this time refusing to consider anything less than ten days!

'Yes, yes,' he says impatiently. 'Lisa told me some load of crap about you and Emily driving down to Kinsale with Jude. What the *hell* are you playing at?'

'Playing at?' I'm repeating him like a parrot. 'We're not *playing* at anything, Matt! We had to help Jude. She was stuck in hospital, and her parents couldn't come, and Fergus couldn't help because he's a cat. Burmese. Her neighbour's been looking after him but she had to go and get the tatties on for her husband.'

I've gone from gasping in short sentences to babbling like a racing commentator coming up to the finishing line.

'Are you drunk?' asks Matt when I pause for breath.

'No! I've given it up, as a matter of fact. On account of a fight I had with Emily . . .' I stop, thinking back over the events of the last few days. 'Which was your fault,' I add crossly. How dare he be annoyed with me for not being there just because he decides to come home early? And how dare he accuse me of being drunk? This is all his fault!

'My fault?'

'Yes! Emily told me all about her little meeting with you. About how you were feeling *confused* and *mixed up*.'

'Yes! Look, Kate, this is exactly why I flew home early to talk to you . . .'

'So you were able to talk to Emily about it, were you, even though you didn't manage to tell me until last Saturday that you'd called off your stag party and were only going away with Sean? To talk about your *confusion*? I suppose you told Emily, in your cosy little chat, about all your doubts over the wedding?' I'm suddenly, inexplicably, furious again with Emily for her secret meeting with Matt. Furious with both of them.

'Katie, you know we both had doubts about the wedding. We admitted it. We needed to cancel it, to put it all on hold – it was your idea, if anything. You wanted to go back to how we were . . . and I wanted time away with Sean, to think, and decide . . .'

'Sounds like you'd already decided!' I snap. 'Seems to me you decided when you had your little talk with Emily! Your cosy little —'

'Will you just shut up about my talk with Emily!' he retorts. 'Yes, I'd decided I didn't want to go ahead with the wedding. You're right, OK? I'd already decided; I was just trying to find the right time to tell you.'

'So if you'd decided, what was all the crap about the *confusion*?'

He sighs. I can hear it all the way across England, across Wales, across the Irish Sea, across Ireland. It's a sigh of irritation. Why did he have to phone, anyway, just as I was enjoying my Chinese takeaway?

'Look, Katie, I don't want to get into all this over the phone, OK?' he says more quietly. 'That's why I came back. I wanted to talk it through with you, face to face.'

'Talk what through? What are you going on about? We've already decided about the wedding. It's off. Fine. I don't think I'd fit into my dress now, anyway. I'm in the middle of sweet and sour prawns with—'

'For Christ's sake! It's about more than a fucking wedding dress! Why are you talking to me about sweet and sour fucking *prawns*, when I'm going out of my mind here?'

To say I'm astonished would be an understatement. I'm sitting on the floor, holding my phone, staring at my feet and wondering if it's possible to faint while you're sitting down. Matt never shouts like this. I'm actually, briefly, even wondering if it's really Matt on the phone. He sounds like he's about to start crying. Like he's about to have a nervous breakdown. I feel a tremor of fear.

'Are you all right?' I ask quietly.

'No.'

'Is something wrong?'

'Yes.'

'What? What is it? Tell me!'

'When you come back.'

'No! You've frightened me now. You'd better tell me, Matt. Please! What is it?'

'Oh, for God's sake! All right – I'm sorry: I didn't want to tell you like this, but ... it's over, OK? I'm finishing it, Katie. You and me – it's no good. It's over. Finished. All right?'

All right?

I feel trembly and light-headed, as if I'm going to be sick. I'm trying to say something but my voice comes out like a whisper, hoarse and tinny and echoing inside my own head.

'But I was going to talk to you,' I hear myself saying. 'I wanted us to talk, when I come back. About a baby. Having a baby!'

There's such a long silence, I'm wondering if he's hung up.

'Hello?' I whisper. 'Did you hear me?'

'A baby,' he says flatly, as if it's a statement. 'A *baby*!'

I wait, wondering. Will this change everything? Will he realise it's the one thing we haven't talked about, the one thing that could save our relationship?

'You're off your head,' he says, quite calmly. 'You know what? I think you need help.'

MATT'S STORY

I suppose I'm the villain of the story now. The pig, the nasty bastard, who dumps his girlfriend over the phone because he wants to be with another girl. I know how it sounds. Why do you think I'm going to pieces here? But I'm *not* that kind of a guy. Don't look at me like that – I'm not!

I was crazy about Katie from the day I first saw her in the pub with that prat James. I could see straight away that he wasn't any good for her. And I was. Yes, of course I nudged her elbow on purpose to make her drop the sausage. I was desperate to get her attention; who wouldn't be? As soon as she looked up at me, laughing, sparkling like a bloody diamond in a coalmine, I fell in love with her. The next couple of weeks I was walking around in a trance, desperate to see her again. It was already over, really, between Sara and me but I finished it with an almost callous haste so that I was free to go back to the pub and lurk around waiting to see Katie again. I knew instinctively that she'd come back there, looking for me. Don't feel sorry for Sara, by the way. She didn't shed any tears. She told me she'd been wondering for a while whether she preferred her friend Becky to me, anyway.

If you've met Katie, you'll understand what I'm saying. She's got something special. She's not beautiful in the perfect model-girl way. For a start, she has a constant struggle to stay in a size 14 – but it looks good on her. She's quite tall, so she carries it well. She's the most natural-looking girl I've ever been with. Sara used to drive me round the bend with her constant bleating about her skin, her hair, her bum, her hips, her cellulite; in the end I gave up trying to tell her to stop worrying, that she looked lovely and there was nothing wrong with her, because it didn't seem to make any difference. Why don't girls realise what a turn-off it is, hearing them whingeing on and on about their imperfections, their pathetic stupid worries about their looks, when half the world's dying from terrible diseases and the other half would faint with happiness if they could afford one single jar of their silly creams and potions?

After Sara, and other girls like her, Katie was like a refreshing summer shower. She's almost childlike in her enjoyment of life. It's infectious. I was addicted to her, couldn't get enough of her. What did she see in me? I don't know; you'll have to ask her. I think we liked the same things: walking in the woods, enjoying simple food, listening to music. We just loved being together. It was fantastic. I'd found out that I actually believed in love.

Looking back, I think it all happened too fast. We were greedy for love, grasping at it with both hands, guzzling it up, eating it alive. We didn't give ourselves time to breathe – we didn't want to. We moved in together, and virtually closed the door on the rest of the world. We thought we were enough for each other.

Now that I've had time to think about what went wrong, I blame Katie completely.

She's got this ridiculous, immature addiction to *romance*. If she hadn't been so obsessed with it, perhaps we would have settled down eventually to a sensible, ordinary relationship and we could have lived together like other normal couples, accepting the ups and downs, having rows and getting over them, maybe even having separations – having *lives*. Lives that didn't necessarily have to entwine around each other every fucking minute of every fucking day. Trust me: what starts out as cosy and exclusive ends up feeling like incarceration.

To Katie, *keeping the romance alive* meant more than just the occasional surprise trip to the theatre or a bunch of roses on Valentine's Day. It meant that we were still supposed to gasp with delight every time we saw each other, even after living together for a year or more. We were supposed to think about each other constantly, shiver at each other's touch, feel hoarse with excitement when we spoke on the phone. It was absolutely fucking exhausting. I would have given anything to come home after a hard day at work, collapse on the sofa with a beer and a curry and watch football all night, without being asked if I still loved her and wouldn't I rather have a candlelit dinner and look into each other's eyes while listening to a CD of hideous love songs?

Eventually, of course, it became almost impossible to keep the romance alive, at least to Katie's standards, and from my point of view, things started to become more normal and bearable. Don't get me wrong. I still loved her like crazy. If I didn't, for God's sake, I would have ditched her long ago, wouldn't I? But predictably, as our lives started to get back into gear – going out to the pub with friends like Sean and Emily, for instance, instead of spending every night cuddled up on the sofa being *romantic* – Katie started worrying that things weren't right between us any more. And her solution was a romantic wedding.

I admit, if she hadn't suggested it, I might not have thought about it for a couple more years, but I was up for it, absolutely. You love someone, you live with them, you eventually want to marry them; on the whole, I think girls still want that, and I haven't got a problem with it. I didn't want anyone else, just Katie, and I wanted her for life. So we were both excited about the wedding idea. We started off planning something very quiet and simple. It would have suited us both; we didn't have much money anyway, and Katie has never been the type to insist on lots of fuss and overindulgence. She didn't even want a wedding dress until her sister insisted on making it for her. She wasn't bothered about having bridesmaids but she felt guilty about her sister and Emily, and then she remembered promising Jude . . . and you see how these things escalate? I didn't mind. It was mostly for her benefit, so I was happy to go along with whatever she, or perhaps her mum, wanted. Anyway, all the plans seemed to be coming along fine to me – but as the months passed and we got nearer to the wedding, Katie just got more and more cross and irritable. I couldn't understand what her problem was. Was it the wedding? Or was it me? I certainly seemed to be getting all the backlash, anyway, and it was beginning to seriously piss me off. Look – she was getting the full works – big white wedding, reception with caterers and disco, champagne, cake, the lot. What did she have to be arsey with me about? Emily kept saying it was just pre-wedding nerves, but all I could see was that the lovely happy girl I'd fallen in love with was vanishing in front of my eyes and being replaced by this scowling, nagging rat-bag who picked on me, accused me of being uncaring and then expected me to be *romantic*! It was all very well thinking things would get back to normal after the wedding. But what if they didn't?

I don't care what you're thinking – I hadn't even noticed Claire, hadn't even given her a second look, although she worked in the same office as me. It's a big, open-plan office with screens dividing the various sections of the company and we worked in different sections, sitting back to back with a screen between us. Occasionally I heard her laughing, or talking on the phone, but apart from that I didn't have any contact with her. When I passed her on my way to the lifts or the water cooler or the photocopier I found myself wondering how old she was. I have this sort of mental compulsion about trying to work out people's ages. It's usually easier with blokes, and it gets harder with women the older they get. Claire, with her cropped brown hair and those kind of elfin features that only look right on small-boned people, could almost have passed for twenty-five. But I knew that was nonsense because there was something much more mature about her: something about her tone of voice, the calmness of her movements – a sort of serenity that it's hard to put a finger on, but which is very attractive and enigmatic.

I didn't take any conscious notice any of this, as I was saying, until the day I found her crying over the photocopier. Quite literally. She seemed to be having a fight with it – her hands were covered in black ink, with an endearing smudge of it on the tip of her nose and another splodge on her right cheek – and she was half leaning, half lying, over the open front of the machine, tugging at a piece of jammed paper and calling it a fucking bastard. And crying.

Not many women look attractive when they cry. Claire managed to look astounding. But it was the fighting and swearing at the photocopier that really made me smile. It was so completely at odds with her normal calm composure, which I suppose is what made me suddenly so aware of it.

'I'm only crying,' she told me, looking up and seeing me but not bothering to get up, wipe her nose or her hands or make any attempt whatsoever to be polite, 'because I'm so fucking *angry*! My whole life depends on this document, and the *fucking* machine has mangled it up!'

I've never been so pleased in my life to be a comparative expert in photocopier technology. By the time I'd extracted her document, admittedly slightly mangled, and discussed various possibilities of lifesaving strategies with her – (Take the document home and iron it? Ask the client for another copy, claiming it's been stolen during an invasion by aliens? Hack into their computer system and try to find a copy of it saved in their confidential files by guessing the password?) – while she scrubbed the ink off herself and dried her tears, we were both laughing together. I hadn't laughed much for quite a while. It felt good. Very good.

I suppose you think you can guess the rest, but you can't. We didn't fall into bed together. We wanted to. We talked about it. We also talked about Katie, and relationships, and love (not romance), and integrity. Claire's very big on integrity.

'I'm not stealing another girl's man,' she told me with her chin held very high. 'And I'm not being a bit on the side. Forget it.'

'I can't forget it – I can't forget you. I'm thinking about you while I'm with her.'

'Then you have to choose,' she said more gently. 'But I'm not going to ask you to choose me. I couldn't live with that responsibility.'

By the time she'd explained why she was so determined not to be the cause of any break-up, I'd also found out how old she was. She'd just turned forty – eight years older than me. She'd been married when she was much too young, had two sons while she was still in her early twenties, and soon afterwards her husband had walked out on her for one of her friends. When I tried to express my sympathy she quickly shook it off.

'I've moved on. It was tough while the kids were little, but they're nearly grown up now and I'm on the verge of freedom again. It's a good feeling, having the world at my feet, just as some of my friends who left it all a lot later are struggling with toddlers' tantrums or trying to balance their careers with the school run, sports days, bouts of tonsillitis and ear infections ...'

'Yeuk!' I laughed. 'You make it sound so appealing.'

'It is – at the time,' she replied seriously. 'But in retrospect ... you're dead right. Yeuk! I certainly wouldn't want to go back.'

The fact that we laughed about this together probably tells you all you need to know about my take on having kids. You might think it very weird that Katie and I hadn't really talked about it. I suppose it is; but the fact is that it's never interested me much at all. Maybe in time, if Katie had started all the stuff that women do, about her body clock ticking and needing to be fulfilled, I'd have gone along with it. A bit like I did with the wedding idea – to make her happy. I'd probably have done anything to make her happy. But not yet. Not now. And when I was with Claire, listening to her describe her vision of freedom – of waiting until her boys were finished college and then taking off to travel the world, with no responsibilities or ties and nothing to hold her back apart from the rucksack on her back – I found myself thinking: *No – no kids. Not ever.*

I don't care what you say. It *is* possible to love two people at the same time. Why shouldn't it be? Think about it logically. How many people are there in the world? How many of them will pass through your life? Is it really rational to imagine that you'll only ever love one of them at a time?

'Of course it's not rational,' Claire told me calmly. '*The One!* It's the great romantic myth.'

You see? *Romance*. It causes nothing but trouble.

While Claire and I were having conversations as serious and frightening as this, I was having almost daily arguments with Katie about my stag trip to Prague. Look, it wasn't my idea to go away for ten days. But I could understand Sean jumping at a bargain when he saw one and, to be honest, the more fuss Katie made about it, the more I was looking forward to it. I still don't understand what her problem was.

I wouldn't have cared less if she went away for a week, two weeks or a fucking month for her hen party, for Christ's sake, as long as she had a good time and came back in a better mood. In the end, I got the stag cancelled anyway; but I didn't tell her until the very last minute. And I didn't cancel it for her benefit, but so that I could go away with Sean on our own and try to get my head sorted out. It was also because I was already trying to pluck up the courage to cancel the wedding itself. I was in an complete mess – wanting Claire, but at the same time wanting Katie back the way she used to be, before the whole wedding and stag party scenario seemed to have robbed her of her sense of humour.

It wasn't as if cancelling the wedding was an easy option. For a start, it was such a waste of money. I don't want to sound mean, but when you've forked out more than you really wanted to on caterers and flowers and stuff, it's a bit of a double whammy when you don't even get what you've paid for. To be fair, Katie's mum had paid for a lot of it and that made me feel even worse. She'd hate me forever for not marrying her daughter *and* crippling her financially, all in one fell swoop. And more to the point – what about my parents? I'm an only child and my mum was looking forward to this wedding. She'd told me it was going to be the *best day of her life*. Being responsible for such a huge disappointment wasn't doing anything to make me feel any better.

'Cancelling the wedding isn't exactly the way to make Katie happy again, either,' pointed out Sean tersely. Sean thought I was having a nervous breakdown, and he probably wasn't far wrong. 'It'll destroy her.'

'So what am I supposed to do? Go through with it even though I'm not even sure if I want to be with her any more? Put the ring on her finger, smile for the photos and *then* finish it?'

'Look, mate – this thing with Claire ...'

'There isn't any *thing* with Claire! We're not having an affair. I just ... I just really like talking to her,' I said miserably. 'It feels good being with her. She doesn't nag me about being romantic, looking at her in a certain way or pretending to be perfect. We're ... kind of good friends.'

244

Sean frowned.

'Are you saying you and Katie aren't good friends?'

'No. We're lovers. We never went through the friends phase.'

'It shouldn't be a phase. Emily and I are still best friends.'

For some reason, this made my heart hurt.

Like I say, I was a mess.

In the end, the fact that it was Katie who suggested cancelling the wedding was such a surprise, I still find it hard to comprehend. When I told her the stag wasn't happening and that Sean and I were going away on our own to talk things over, I expected her to be shocked, confused, maybe even frightened and angry. Instead, she seemed so relieved – almost excited – that I'd suggested I was having doubts, it was quite bizarre. She had doubts herself, she said. Since when? It was news to me. One minute she's trying on the wedding dress, the next minute she's suggesting calling it all off. I was worried about her state of mind, to be honest. All this talk about us being too perfect together, and needing to forget about the wedding so we could go back to the way we were – the perfect couple in love – it sounded hysterical and a bit unhinged. I wanted to tell her she ought to change her job and stop reading those bloody novels, but it obviously wasn't the time.

In the end it was this last conversation with Katie that stayed in my mind the whole time I was in Prague. Talking endlessly to Sean over too many cheap beers, trying to make sense of my feelings and work out what I really wanted, I kept coming back to how easily she'd decided to ditch the wedding plans and how little regard she'd seemed to have for how this was going to affect our families and friends – what a shock and disappointment it would be for everyone – as well as how excited she'd sounded about getting back to being the *perfect couple*. Something about it made my blood run cold. I realised with a sudden certainty that I didn't want to play a part in Katie's personal romantic fiction for the rest of my life. I'm not her real-life hero. It was easy in those first couple of years of desperate passion, but when that wears off, what's left? Two cardboard cut-out characters with no real life in them. It was no good pretending. I had to finish it, the sooner the better, and if it hurt her at least she'd be feeling something genuine.

Once I'd arrived at a decision, I wanted to come straight home. Sean was all for waiting, giving it time, making sure I wasn't going to change my mind. I know he wanted me to. He's a lovely guy, Sean – very straightforward. He had a hard job following the ramblings of my mind during the week in Prague. But we came home, in the end, on the day the girls were due back from Dublin. Of course I was dreading telling Katie: do you think I'm some sort of a monster? But I wanted to get it over with as quickly as possible. A clean break. No twisting of the knife. I'd pack and move out the very next day. We could talk about the flat, the mortgage, the furniture, all that stuff, when we were both calmer.

But she didn't come home. At first I was worried. I checked the Ryanair website – no delays, no security incidents or terrible, unimaginable accidents. I tried her mobile. No reply. I tried to ring Emily and got Sean, who was equally worried but pretending not to be.

'Look, they didn't expect us yet. They've probably decided to extend their stay.'

'And turn off their phones? Aren't *any* of them back?'

'I don't know. I haven't got numbers for any of the others.'

So I tried Lisa, who turned out to be at home. She sounded irritated. Why was I back early from Prague? And whose fault was it – mine, she supposed? – that the wedding had been cancelled so inconveniently close to the date, with the dresses finished and everything? Had I got any idea how upset her mother was? Did I even care? And was I aware that Katie and Emily had now taken leave of their senses completely and gone tripping off to Kinsale with Jude? I couldn't even get a word in or I would have said of course I wasn't aware, you silly cow, why did you think I was phoning you?

Kinsale? What the *hell* was she playing at?

I shouldn't have kept trying to phone her while I was cross. I should have waited. But the more times I tried, without getting an answer, the crosser I got. What was she doing? I left four messages, and came to the conclusion she must have lost her phone. It made me even angrier. Silly cow – why couldn't she be more careful? I know it sounds bad. But I was only cross because I was shit scared of what I was going to do: hurt this girl, ruin her life, when not so very long ago I was planning to promise to love her for ever. But what could I do? There was no point going on with a lie.

When I finally got through to her I was expecting tears, hysterics, maybe anger and abuse. I couldn't have blamed her. Instead, it was the most incomprehensible thing: she started talking about having a baby! I think she must have completely flipped. A baby – *now*? When we'd already called off the wedding because we both had doubts? When I'd just told her it was all over? What the hell had been going on in her mind while she was away – while I was out in Prague tearing myself to shreds trying to stop myself from hurting her?

If anything could persuade me one hundred per cent that I'd made the right decision, this was it. Far from being the mythical perfect couple, I don't think we ever really knew each other at all.

Sean didn't realise it, but he'd said all he needed to, when he told me he and Emily were best friends.

That's what I want, you see? With *Claire*.

247

ABOUT A GHOST

If I'm honest I'm not sure who I'm crying for most: Matt, myself, or the baby that's not going to happen now. I know Emily thinks I'm being absurd, about the baby – that it's too sudden a decision to be sensible or reasonable or even fair to any child – but you see, I think the idea of starting a family has actually been lurking there in the shadows of my consciousness for quite a while now. Maybe Lisa was right all along that it was, subconsciously anyway, the reason why I wanted to get married. It probably would have stayed subconscious, too, if it hadn't been for what I've heard this weekend. Not just Auntie Joyce's story, although of course that's what's brought it so powerfully to the forefront of my mind; but also everything else that's come out. Mum covering up, for all these years, how badly my dad treated her; Lisa pretending to have a wonderful marriage when it's just a sham and she'd rather be with someone else … it's scary. It's made me realise that nobody's relationship is really safe and secure. As far as love is concerned, there's only one absolute certainty that I can see and that's the way a mum loves her children. Nobody seems to raise an eyebrow when marriages break down, families fall apart, lifelong relationships come unstuck; but if you ever read anything in the papers about a mother deserting her children, the shockwaves are terrible. You feel disgusted. It's unnatural, unforgivable. Nobody can imagine how she could do it. You see? A mum and her babies – that's one hundred per cent real solid enduring love. That's what I want: my own family. I wanted it with Matt. Why did it take me so long to realise it? Why didn't I tell him before he fell out of love with me?

I'm sitting on the hall carpet, still holding the phone, crying to myself when Emily comes looking for me. She kneels down on the floor next to me, takes the phone out of my hand and puts her arms round me without even asking me what's wrong. For a long while she just holds me, murmuring soothing noises like she's rocking me to sleep. *Ssh, ssh, it's OK baby, shush now, don't cry, don't cry.*

'He doesn't love me,' I blub, wiping my runny nose on my sleeve. 'He doesn't want me any more. He thinks I'm off my head!'

I feel Emily's arms tighten round me protectively.

'You're not. Don't listen to him. If anyone's off their head, it's him. He's a total fucking dickhead and he didn't deserve you.'

Her anger on my behalf startles me as much as it warms me. It only takes a few more minutes, a few more sobs before I put two and two together.

'You knew, didn't you!' I push her arms off me. 'When he told you he was *confused* and *mixed up* – it was because he was thinking about dumping me, wasn't it?'

I get up, shakily, staggering to my feet, holding onto the wall. Everything's spinning as if I've had too much to drink.

'Sit down, Katie. You're very pale – you've had a shock. Come and sit in the lounge and I'll make you a strong cup of . . .'

'I don't want a strong cup of anything. I want you to tell me the truth. Christ! Is there *anyone* in my life who hasn't been keeping secrets from me?'

'I'm sorry.' She hangs her head for a minute, but when she looks back up her eyes are defiant. 'No, what am I saying? I'm *not* sorry! I only arranged to meet Matt because I was worried about you, and you're my friend, and I care about you. Yes, he told me everything. What was I supposed to do? He was going away with Sean and I was hoping to God that Sean would be able to talk sense into him. At least there was a chance that everything would be fine when he came back. If I'd told you, there'd have been no chance. As soon as you'd heard about Claire you'd have finished with him, and I wouldn't have blamed you, either.'

'Claire?'

249

I'm sliding back down the wall, sitting down with a thump that actually hurts my bum.

So it was another woman, all along.

Look at Emily. She's covered her mouth with both hands, as if to stop the words escaping; too late. Too late! *Claire*. I wonder who she is? We used to joke that it wouldn't be possible for either of us to meet anyone else because we were hardly ever apart. She must have worked with him. He was working late a lot, recently. An affair with someone at work. How unoriginal, how dreary and trite and predictable. He might at least have managed to fall for someone at a bus stop, or in a supermarket, crashing into her trolley. Or in the pub, stamping on her sausage. Why am I crying? I'm obviously well rid of him. The cheating, lying, bastard!

'I thought he'd told you. On the phone: I thought he'd said ...'

Poor Emily. She looks like she's going to cry, herself. Not her fault. She couldn't have told me, could she? She was doing her best. I'd have done the same thing myself.

'No,' I manage to splutter. 'No, he didn't tell me about *Claire*. I suppose he was saving that bit for when I go home. All he told me was – it's over. Over, no good, finished. I can't believe he needed ten days in Prague to make up his mind; to choose between us. So much for Claire! She can't be so very wonderful.'

'If it helps,' says Emily quietly, 'he told me he still loved you ...'

'Bollocks he does.'

'And that he hadn't slept with Claire.'

'And bollocks to that, too.'

'I'm so sorry, Katie.'

We're both crying now. In each other's arms, sobbing properly. Thank God Emily still loves me. Why can't men ever love us the way our girlfriends do?

'Hey!' We both jump at the sound of shouting from the lounge. 'Hey, you two! What's going on! Who's crying? What's happened? Your bloody prawns have gone cold and the rice is congealed! Do I have to roll off the sofa and crawl out there to find out what's going on?'

250

'OK, Jude,' says Emily, wiping her eyes and giving me a shaky little smile. 'Sorry. We're coming.' She grabs my hand and squeezes it hard. 'You're going to be OK, darling,' she whispers fiercely. 'You're going to be fine. *Bollocks* to him.'

It doesn't take long to bring Jude up to date.

'I'll fucking kill him, so I will. I'll cut his stupid dick off and feed it to the ducks,' she says furiously, spitting wine across the lovely velvet cushions on her lovely leather sofa.

We've found a couple of bottles of wine in the fridge and we're halfway through the second one. The giving-up of alcohol forever doesn't apply in situations where you've just been dumped by the love of your life.

'I hate her,' I say morosely. It's easier than hating him. I'm still too shocked to start hating him. 'The cow. I bet she's huge and ugly and desperate and can't get a man of her own. I bet she forced him.'

'She's probably a witch,' says Jude. 'She'll have put something in his tea, sure as heaven, and he'll have fallen under her spell.'

'A wicked witch,' agrees Emily, slurring slightly.

'He'll get tired of her, Katie, so he will. You'll see, he'll be tired of her before the end of the year and he'll come back to you with his tail between his ...'

'Jude, I don't care where he puts his fucking tail. He's not coming back to me with his tail anywhere. Not after this. Not ever. I'm finished with men! All of them. They're all liars and cheats and fucking bastards.' I glance at Emily, who's looking at the floor, miserably. 'Except for Sean,' I add quickly. 'He's lovely.'

'He is, so,' agrees Jude, nodding solemnly. 'Sean's a lovely man, so he is, and it's a great sorrow to me that there aren't more Seans in the world to go round so that we could all have one of our own, Emily.'

I've had too much wine by now and this just starts me off crying again.

'Oh, Emily!' I wail. 'Why couldn't Matt have been more like Sean? You're so lucky! You're so right for each other! You're so perfect together!'

'Not perfect, Kate,' she says, shaking her head so hard that she almost falls over. I think she's had too much wine as well. 'We're not perfect. Sean's not perfect. We're didn't have that kind of grand passion thing that you and Matt had. We were always just really good friends.'

This makes me howl out loud.

'That's what I want! That's what I should have been looking for! It sounds so perfect! Why didn't I find that?'

'Come on, Katie, don't cry,' Emily says unsteadily. 'Tell you what – let's get into our jamas, shall we, and watch something old and soppy on telly? Yeah? And finish the wine off?'

I'm aware, vaguely, of turning out the contents of my holdall in Jude's spare bedroom, looking for my pyjamas. And I'm aware, even more vaguely, of collapsing back onto the sofa with a glass of something in my hand. It isn't wine. I think it's vodka but I've lost interest in anything other than pouring it down my neck.

And the next thing I'm aware of is waking up in the dark and wondering why there's a ghost outside, tapping on the window.

Strangely enough the ghost doesn't frighten me. I'm in that state of half-sleep, to say nothing of drunkenness, where anything, absolutely anything, that can happen in a dream seems completely reasonable and acceptable.

'Ghost,' I mutter to myself, stumbling to my feet, with no more surprise than if it had been an insurance salesman or a Jehovah's Witness knocking at the door. I stagger to the window. I'm not too sure where I am. Is this a dream? The window doesn't look like the window in my flat.

'Hello?' I say softly, standing at the window and staring out. Something about this definitely doesn't feel right. Should I be standing at the window of a strange room, in the dark, talking to a ghost? Am I awake?

Before I have time to decide, a face appears at the other side of the window, making me jump almost clean out of my skin and scream 'SHIT!' in such a demented squeak, I actually frighten myself. In fact I think I've frightened the ghost, or whoever the face belongs to, even more, judging by the way it leaps back away from the window, its eyes almost popping out of its head.

At least I'm now wide awake, although the alcohol hasn't done much for my sense of balance. I'm trying to hold onto the window to stop me falling on the floor. Windows aren't easy things to hold onto. The glass tends to slide under your fingers and if you're not sure which way is up, it can make you feel really giddy.

'Katie!' the ghost is whispering at me now, through the window.

That's me. Katie. I recognise the name.

'Katie, it's me! Open the door!'

Me? I recognise that, too. If I'm Katie, who is *Me*?

Fortunately, I don't have to puzzle over this for long, or I'd probably have passed out with the effort.

'It's me – Harry! Katie, can you come to the door and let me in? Isn't anyone else at home?'

Aha! Harry. Yes, I remember Harry. The good-looking one, the one I shouldn't really have kissed, shouldn't really have fancied, because I was still supposed to be with What's-His-Name. What was his name again? I let go of the window and sway slightly, frowning, worried that I can't remember.

'Katie!' comes the urgent whisper again. I can see his face through the window. Not a ghost. Harry. His face looks white and ghostlike, though, in the moonlight. 'I've got the crutches. Look, if you don't want to let me in, I'll leave them outside the front door, but I don't want them to get nicked!'

Crutches? I start to giggle at the absurdity of the word. Why is he putting his crutches outside the front door? And where *is* the front door, anyway? I look around me at the darkened room. There's a pillow and a pink-covered duvet on the sofa where I was sleeping. They're not mine. Whose are they? Where am I?

I hear the crunch of Harry's footsteps walking away from the window. Holding onto the wall now, I take a couple of steps, trying to follow in the direction that he's going. A door! I go through, out to the hall. I remember this. I remember sitting on this carpet, some time in the past, crying.

God knows why. There's the front door. There's a clunking noise outside. I grab the door handle, wrench it open, sway in the doorway, blinking in the fresh air.

'So there you are!' says Harry. 'I was just putting the crutches . . .'

There's a long silence.

'Are you all right, Katie?' I hear him say, just before I fall into his arms and pass out cold.

When I come round, I'm back on the sofa, under the pink duvet. There's a cold flannel on my forehead, a glass of water next to me, and a bowl, presumably in case I'm going to be sick.

Harry leans over me and stares into my face.

'Are you all right?' he asks again as if there hadn't been any interruption in the conversation.

I shake my head, not trusting myself to open my mouth.

'Here. Have a drink.'

I drain the glass. The room spins, lurches, settles down again. I close my eyes, realise that makes everything even more frightening, and open them again quickly.

'I'll fill it up again. Don't try to move.'

I couldn't even if I tried. I watch him walking out to the kitchen. Slowly, slowly, I remember. This is Jude's flat. Where is she? Where is Emily?

'The other two are sound asleep in the bedrooms,' says Harry as if I'd asked out loud. 'I checked.'

'We were watching a film,' I mutter thickly. I don't think I'm going to be sick. I try to sit up. Drink the second glass of water. That's better. The room's stopped spinning. 'I must have fallen asleep.'

I'm searching my memory. Give me a clue. What happened?

'I thought you'd given up the booze?' he says, smiling at me gently.

'So did I. But . . .'

But what?

Oh, yes.

Matt. The phone call. I start to cry again, silently. I want to wipe the tears away but I'm too tired. Too ill.

'Katie!' says Harry, looking alarmed. He sits down on the edge of the sofa. 'Don't cry! What is it? What's wrong?'

'It's over,' I whimper. 'He phoned me. He's finished with me. Dumped me.' I fumble around, looking for a tissue, and end up wiping my nose on the back of my hand. Very elegant. 'Her name's Claire. She's ... she's a witch.'

'Christ.' That's all he says. But he sounds shocked. 'Christ!'

'I can't believe it! He was so ... so *nasty*. He's never been like that before. He said I'm off my head and I need help.'

Why am I telling him all this? Why, come to that, am I sitting here, in my shortie pyjamas, with my boobs almost hanging out of the top and Jude's pink duvet only just about maintaining my decency, sipping water and with a sick-bowl propped up next to my pillow, crying very messily with my nose running unchecked into my mouth, while the very good-looking man I naughtily snogged on Saturday night when I should have only been thinking about my husband-to-be is squeezing my hand sympathetically and offering me tissues?

'Sorry!' I gasp, grabbing a tissue from him and blowing my nose noisily and very unsexily.

'Don't be silly. I'm just ... so shocked. Are you sure he wasn't just – I don't know – pissed, maybe? Angry that you haven't gone straight home? Being an arsehole?'

'I think' *(sniff)* 'he's probably always' *(sniff)* 'been an arsehole' *(sniff)*. 'I just didn't' *(sniff)* 'realise it until now.' I start to sob.

Probably wisely, Harry doesn't say any more. He hands me another tissue, proffers the glass of water again, tucks the duvet around my shoulders as if I'm a sick child with a fever, smoothes it down over my feet, and just sits there, perched on the edge of the sofa, looking at me with grave concern while I get the wailing and sobbing out of my system. At least for now. When I've cried myself to a stop, he asks me if I want a cup of tea.

'How did you know?'

'Just a guess. My mum always gives people cups of tea when they're upset.'

He pads quietly out to Jude's kitchen and I listen to him boiling the kettle, getting mugs and tea bags out. I wonder what I look like. My eyes are probably red and swollen and my face all blotchy. Should I risk getting up and finding a mirror, or will I feel dizzy again? Actually the alcohol seems to be wearing off.

'I must look a terrible mess,' I say as he hands me a mug of steaming tea.

'No, you don't. You look ... sad, and vulnerable. How else could you look, in the circumstances?' He shakes his head and watches me sipping my tea. 'He's a fucking idiot, if you ask me.'

I shrug, don't bother to reply. He's just trying to be nice.

'Sorry,' he adds quickly. 'That's not really for me to say, is it. I suppose you love him.'

Suppose? Of course I do, don't I! We were getting married up till a week or so ago. We were going to have a baby!

At the thought of the baby, my eyes fill up with tears again and I have to put the mug down to blow my nose.

'Come here,' says Harry softly, and holds out his arms to me. Before I know it, I'm being held tight against his chest, still snivelling into the tissue that's now scrunched up in my hand.

'It's all right,' he's muttering against my hair. 'Ssh, come on, it's all right, Katie.'

Just like Emily. Just like a friend – a nice, gentle, caring friend. What did I say about men loving us the way our girl-friends do?

I look up at him through my swollen eyelids and just for a minute, a crazy fleeting minute that has more to do with the kind and concerned look in his eyes than anything going on in my mess of a head, I consider kissing him.

I think he sees the idea forming in my eyes. Or in the way I very fractionally lift my lips towards his. Just fleetingly. I notice the barest twitch of a response pass across his face before he sits up straighter, strokes my hair as if I'm the feverish child again, and mutters, so quietly that I'm not sure if he's talking to me or to himself:

'I don't want to take advantage.' He sits me back against the sofa and looks at me carefully before continuing, more clearly: 'If you think you'll be all right now, I'd better get going, back to my cousin's place. Can I come back and see you in the morning?'

'Yes,' I say, my voice sounding small and tired in my head. 'Thank you ... for looking after me. Sorry ...'

'Don't say sorry,' he says, sounding quite stern for a minute. He hesitates by the door, looking back at me. I'm almost asleep already. 'Bye, Katie,' he says gently as he lets himself out.

Surprisingly, I sleep like a baby for the rest of the night.

ABOUT HANGOVERS

In the morning, the sun's shining and the sky's a delicate shade of pastel blue with a few puffy light grey clouds scudding along merrily. There's blossom on the trees outside Jude's window. There are seagulls shouting to each other from the grey slate rooftops down the hill, the world outside looks wonderful and I feel pretty silly for believing that my life was over.

Emily tiptoes into the lounge as I'm leaning on the windowsill, looking out.

'How are you feeling?' she whispers.

'OK. Thanks. Why are we whispering? Is Jude still asleep?'

'No. I've got a thumping headache. And Jude can't even bear the curtains open yet.'

'Blimey. I've got off lightly, then.'

'Yes. Amazing. You zonked out almost as soon as the film started. Not that I can remember what the film was. Jude covered you over and you snored all the way through it. We shared another bottle of wine ...'

'What! You pair of lushes!'

'Ouch! Keep your voice down for Christ's sake!' She sits down on the sofa and rubs her head slowly. 'Well, we eventually staggered off to bed and left you where you were, as you were so completely out of it. Looks like you've slept it off!'

'Well ... I did wake up once.' I give her a quick sideways glance. 'Harry came back with Jude's crutches. He knocked on the window to wake me up.'

'Oh yes?' says Emily meaningfully.

'I thought he was a ghost. I didn't mind, though.'

'No, I bet you didn't. Nor did he, I don't suppose, seeing you in those pyjamas.'

I tug at the pyjama top ineffectively, shaking my head.

'No. It wasn't like that. I got up to let him in, but I passed out. He looked after me, Em. He put me back on the sofa and made me tea and ... everything.' How do you describe the gentle touches, the tender looks, the feeding of tissues and glasses of water, the silent, patient waiting while I cried and blew my nose? 'He was ... like a nurse.'

'A *nurse*.'

'Yes. Don't say it like that. He was lovely. He made me feel better.'

'Hm. And what exactly does his *night-nursing* routine consist of, eh? Any snogging involved in that? Any quick groping under the duvet?'

'Emily! You are *so* distrustful. There was no snogging, no groping, and nothing of the kind whatsoever. He said he wouldn't take advantage of the situation.'

'Really?' She sounds quite taken aback. I must admit, thinking about it now in the cold, sober light of day, so am I. 'Well, I could have sworn he was waiting to make a move on you, Katie.'

So was I. Actually, if it wasn't for the fact that I've just had my heart completely broken by the love of my life and am never getting involved with any man again for as long as I live, I'd have felt quite gutted, thinking about it, that he didn't seem to want to make a move on me after all.

We get Jude up, despite her protests about the light from the windows sending her half blind and mad with pain, and make her practise using her crutches to take herself into the lounge, while we rummage around in the kitchen and find eggs and bacon in the fridge, sliced bread and cook-from-frozen sausages in the freezer, baked beans in the cupboard and all the utensils we need to cook a massive post-alcohol breakfast.

'If I could only open me eyes,' says Jude mournfully as we carry her plate through to her on a tray, 'I could tell you if it looks as good as it smells.'

'Just get it down you,' retorts Emily jokingly. 'If you could open your eyes you'd give us grief about the state of the kitchen ...'

Her eyes fly open straight away and we all start to laugh.

'Don't worry. We'll clean up afterwards. It's not that bad,' I reassure her.

I'm actually laughing. I'm shocked at myself. I stop, quickly, look down at the floor, waiting for the realisation to dawn again that my boyfriend has dumped me, that my relationship is over and everything in my life has come unravelled like a terrible old cardigan. I wait for my eyes to fill up with tears again, the way they should be doing. Nothing happens. I must have cried myself out last night. I must be in shock.

'Mind the carpet,' Emily warns me as I squirt a good dollop of tomato ketchup onto my plate. 'You're not at home now, you know. Jude wants to keep her flat looking half decent!'

'Well, I've no idea how I'm going to keep it looking half decent while I can't even stand up on me own, never mind push the hoover around,' complains Jude with her mouth full of bacon. 'The place will go to rack and ruin, so it will.'

'It won't do it any harm,' says Emily mildly. 'Ours only gets a hoover once every few weeks, normally when the crumbs on the carpets get so bad we feel like we're walking on the beach.'

Jude looks absolutely appalled.

'Sorry,' shrugs Emily cheerfully, 'but we're not bothered about that sort of thing.'

'We're all different, Jude,' I tell her gently as she continues to stare at Emily in horrified silence. 'Matt and I don't do a lot of housework either ...'

The silence becomes even more horrified. The other two look at me in alarm, waiting for me to realise my mistake and start blubbing. I take a deep breath, concentrate for a second or two on dipping a piece of toast in my egg yolk, and then start again:

'I mean *I* don't. *I* don't worry much about housework, in *my* flat. I like it to be a bit lived-in. Or maybe I'm just lazy. But now, seeing how lovely your place is because you look after it so well, I'm thinking perhaps it's me that's got it wrong.'

The other two have gone back to eating their breakfast, looking relieved. Thank God Katie isn't having a nervous breakdown. Not at the moment, anyway.

Maybe that's still to come.

Poor Jude. After a lifetime of care and attention to every detail of her personal grooming, she's now reduced to balancing on one leg in the shower, propped up against the wall, doing the best she can in the circumstances with her soaping and shampooing. By the time she comes out of the bathroom she's so knackered she actually tells us she can't be bothered putting on make-up or blow-drying her hair. I look in on her, where she's collapsed on the bed in her own room.

'Let me do it for you.'

'No, honest to God, Katie, leave it. After you and Emily have gone home I'll have to find a way of managing on my own till Mum gets here, so it's no good you nursemaiding me.'

Emily brings her a cup of tea and looks at her worriedly.

'Seriously, Jude, are you going to be OK when we've gone?'

'Sure I am. Mum phoned this morning. She's coming down for the rest of the week and after that I'm hoping to get back to work, as long as Brendan from my office can give me a lift. While Mum's here, I'll start working out how to cope with everything.'

'Did the doctor at the hospital say how long you'll have the plaster on?'

'No. I've got to go to the local hospital here next week for a check-up. They said when the swelling's gone down the plaster might be too loose. Then they'll X-ray me again after a few more weeks and decide if I can start weight-bearing.'

'Poor you. What an absolute pain.'

'It could've been worse. The doctor said they quite often have to operate on broken ankles, but mine didn't need that, at least. And I haven't got to worry, now, about missing the wedding ...' She stops, glancing at me guiltily. 'Ah, shit, Katie. I'm so sorry. I didn't mean it like that.'

'It's OK. No, really, it is.' They're both looking at me, eyes wide with distress on my behalf. I can't bear it. 'Look, please, both of you. I don't want to spend the rest of my life – or even the rest of today – being treated like an invalid with an incurable disease that no one dares to mention. I'm all right at the moment. I don't know why – maybe I've gone into shock and it's all going to hit me again when I get home. I don't particularly want to talk about it, but you don't have to tiptoe around the subject and worry that I'm going to suddenly fall apart.'

'Well, I'm glad about that anyway, Katie,' says Jude, still looking a bit uncomfortable.

'Me too,' says Emily, giving me a quick hug, 'because it's the last day of our holiday, and the sun's shining out there, and crutches or no crutches, I reckon Jude has to do one final duty as our tour guide, and show us around Kinsale before we go home. What do you reckon?'

'Absolutely,' I agree. 'Stop shaking your head and making all that fuss, Jude – what's the matter with you? We can help you along, can't we? All you have to do is lean on us and point us in the right direction!'

And we're making so much noise, laughing together about a tour guide on crutches showing able-bodied visitors around the town, that we only hear the doorbell at the second or third ring. Looks like we've got company.

I'd forgotten what Harry said about coming back this morning, and certainly didn't realise he was bringing his cousin with him.

'This is Conor,' Harry introduces him, pushing him forward through the front door.

He seems to need the push. He's a smaller, darker version of Harry. At first glance I think they have the same eyes, but it's hard to say because as soon as we're introduced, Conor goes red and looks at his shoes.

'Don't be shy, mate – they won't eat you,' says Harry, slapping him on the shoulder.

Conor laughs but still doesn't meet our eyes. I think he's frightened of us. Maybe he's frightened of girls, full stop.

'Nice to meet you, Conor.'

He smiles at me shyly and looks back at the floor. This is going to be hard work.

'We were just on our way out,' says Emily, giving me a warning look.

I ignore it. I know what her warning look's all about: her not wanting Harry and his cousin with us on our last day. It's about her still not really trusting Harry and certainly not trusting Conor who we've never met before and who doesn't seem to be able to speak.

'Well, we're only going for a little walk,' I tell them brightly. At least, I'm telling Harry, because it's kind of difficult to talk to the top of Conor's head. 'Jude's going to give us a tour of Kinsale. She might not be able to get further than the end of the road with her crutches but we're taking our chances!'

The warning look Emily's giving me is now being accompanied by kicks to my ankles. I'm pretending not to see the look or feel the kicks, although if she kicks much harder I'll be plastered up the same as Jude.

'Do you want to join us?' I manage to add to Harry while skipping away from Emily on one foot.

'That'd be great – if you're sure you don't mind,' says Harry, 'wouldn't it, Conor?'

He nudges Conor with his elbow, making him jump slightly and mutter, 'Yes, grand!'

What with Emily kicking me, and Harry elbowing Conor, we're all going to end up black and blue before we get out of the door.

'But I've got a better idea,' adds Harry before we can incur any further injuries. 'Why don't you all pile into the car, and we'll have a guided *drive* around Kinsale. Jude doesn't look too safe on those crutches yet, if you ask me. I wouldn't trust her to walk down that hill outside!'

'Well, I've been having the same thought meself, thank you very much for caring!' says Jude, sounding relieved. 'Only you can't say anything to this shower here, sure they've not an ounce of sympathy for a poor girl with an impediment, they'd have me climbing mountains with me crutches strapped to me back, so they would.'

'Never let it be said, Jude,' says Harry solemnly, 'that

Harry Cornwell doesn't have sympathy for people with impediments. Your carriage awaits you.'

'Just come in for a minute, then, while we get our coats and shoes on,' says Emily with an air of resignation.

Seeing the speed at which this has been agreed, Jude makes a little squeak of dismay and swings herself off into her bedroom, shutting the door firmly behind her. She's still in there when Emily and I are ready to go out.

'Come on, Jude!' I tap on the door. 'Are you ready?'

I peer round the door. She's sitting at her dressing table frantically tugging at her hair.

'Jesus, God, will you look at the state of me? Did I ever look such a mess? I've hardly a scrap of make-up on yet, you'll have to wait ...'

'Aw, Jude, leave it out – you look gorgeous. We're only going for a drive around the town. Come on – if we don't get going, we'll run out of time. We've got to head back to Dublin this afternoon.'

She flings her hairbrush down and sighs.

'Oh, to hell with it, then. I'll put a scarf over me face, shall I not, and if anyone looks at me ...'

'They'll think you're beautiful, like you always are. Come *on*, Jude! Stop rabbiting on about scarves on your face. I'm not going home without seeing Kinsale. Let's go!'

Hallelujah. I never thought it'd happen, but I've just got Jude Barnard out of the door without spending two hours doing her hair and make-up. Definitely a first! Whatever next?

ABOUT CONOR

'How are you this morning?' Harry asks me quietly as he holds the car door open for me.

'Numb,' I tell him flatly. 'I'm acting like nothing's happened.'

'Sorry. I don't suppose you want to talk about it.'

'No, not really. In fact . . .' I shuffle across the back seat to leave room for Jude, 'I think I'd rather hang upside down on a skewer over a barbecue than talk about it at the moment, if you don't mind. I just want to enjoy my last day in Ireland.'

Thinking about it now, I'm relieved to realise that I'm actually feeling more angry than upset already. How dare he! Over the *phone*! What a complete bastard!

'Fair enough,' says Harry as he helps Jude into the car. 'Subject closed.'

There's not enough room for us all in the car, what with Jude's leg, so Conor sets off at a jog to meet us down at the harbour. The road into the town centre from Jude's flat is all steeply downhill and I realise with a pang of guilt how impossible it would have been for Jude to manage it on her crutches. She'd have fallen headfirst down the slope.

At the bottom of the hill there's a little square flanked by pretty green, yellow and red-painted touristy shops and dotted with tubs of spring flowers. The shop windows are full of Celtic jewellery, slate paintings and hand-knitted sweaters.

'It's lovely, Jude!' exclaims Emily. 'I can't believe you live here!'

'Sure it's a pretty enough spot,' agrees Jude. 'Although most of the year you can't move for the tourists. But when I

265

first moved down here from the city I must say I thought I was in heaven.'

'I'd love to live in a seaside town,' I say enviously. 'I'd open my own little bookshop, and I'd *love* the tourists.'

'Most of the shopkeepers around here *do* love the tourists!' laughs Harry.

But I mean it. I'm thinking about it seriously. Why not? After all, what's stopping me, now?

We park near the harbour, wait for Conor to catch us up, and get out of the car, having decided we'd all benefit from a blast of fresh sea air. Jude announces that she'll make it to a bench just over the road on the seafront.

'Got to learn to use these frigging things,' she says, gritting her teeth and struggling to get her balance as we all stand round her in a circle, trying to hold her shoulders, her elbows, her hands, and clucking like a load of demented mother hens.

'Don't you be helping me,' says Jude, swinging out across the road at an alarming speed. 'I have to do it myself.'

We make slow progress along the harbourside towards the bench. The sea's the same colour as the grey slate roofs of the town, despite the sunshine. But the clusters of little boats with red, white, blue and yellow sails jostling cheerfully together in the breeze brighten up the scene, as well as our spirits. We're exposed to the wind along here, and with it the tang of salt and seaweed in the air. Jude wobbles dangerously a couple of times but she's laughing. She looks pink-cheeked from the fresh air and sunshine, to say nothing of her efforts with the crutches. It strikes me suddenly that she's always been beautiful, but today, with her hair slightly tousled and her face free of her normal layers of make-up, she's absolutely stunning.

Conor's just behind her when she nearly overbalances completely.

'Careful,' he says, a bit gruffly and, suddenly and as if he's been intending to do it all along, he puts his arm across her back, very lightly – a guiding, protective touch – and edges closer to her so that they're moving along together.

She doesn't shake him off; she doesn't say anything back, or even look at him – but he doesn't seem to mind. He doesn't take his arm away. They don't say any more, and they still don't look at each other, but they carry on like that, silently but closely together – Jude wobbling on her crutches, Conor slowing his pace to hers, steadying her with the almost imperceptible touch of his hand on her back.

'Are you thinking what I'm thinking?' Emily whispers to me, watching them.

'Mm. Perfect together. No chance of a cross word – or any word at all!' I whisper back, giggling.

Then I suddenly feel really mean for laughing, and I find myself crossing my fingers instead. Because actually they do look perfect together. And it's time Jude had more than a cat in her life.

'Conor's a nice guy,' Harry says to me quietly. We've reached the bench where Jude has parked herself with Conor still staying close to her, while we lean on the harbour wall and stare out to sea. 'Doesn't have a lot to say for himself when he doesn't know someone, but he's ... well, all those things girls are meant to like, I suppose. Genuine. Decent. Caring. Faithful.'

He counts these attributes off on his fingers, sighing slightly as he does, as if it pains him to even talk about them.

'Good,' I say firmly. 'If he's going to carry on sitting that close to Jude, he'd better stay genuine, decent, and all that stuff, or he'll have me to answer to.'

'You're very fond of her, aren't you.'

'Of course! She's my oldest friend.'

'Girls are so much nicer to each other than guys are,' he says, with another sigh.

'Well, I'm not arguing with that.'

He doesn't reply to this; just continues to stare at the sea, nodding, as if between the two of us we've discovered an incontrovertible truth.

Which, I suppose, we have done.

'I think Jude's probably had enough,' I say, watching her leaning back on the bench.

'Yes, I have so,' she admits. 'I'm done for! It's such hard work walking even a few yards with these buggers. Why don't the rest of you go for a boat trip? I don't want to spoil your day. I can sit here and enjoy the sunshine.'

'No, we're not leaving you here on your own – it's fine; we'll head back when you've had a rest,' I tell her.

'In fact I'll go back for the car, and pick you up,' insists Harry.

'Or I can sit with you, if you'd like it,' adds Conor shyly. 'I've done plenty of boat trips of Kinsale harbour in me time – sure I've no need of another one.'

I'm not sure which is the bigger surprise: the fact that Conor's spoken more than one sentence, or the fact that Jude agrees so readily. But we can hardly refuse to leave them now, can we?

So Harry, Emily and I climb aboard a small pleasure craft that looks as though it's seen better days, for a half-hour trip around the harbour. Jude and Conor have both said they've been on this boat before and it didn't sink and they didn't need to bale out, so we're trusting in their judgement.

I'm sitting next to Emily at one end of the boat. I don't know which end. I suppose if I am going to move to the seaside I'll have to find out about things like *stern, starboard* and *crow's nest*. It's not all ice creams and peppermint rock, I do realise that.

'I'd *really* like to move to the seaside,' I tell Emily wistfully. 'I mean it.'

'Where? Southend? It's not quite like Kinsale ...'

'I don't know. Anywhere. When I leave Bookshelf I might find a job somewhere completely different. Kent. Norfolk. Devon. Scotland.'

'Are you serious, then? About leaving Bookshelf?'

'Yes. I don't think I can carry on working there now, with the situation with Greg. And anyway I think I'd like a new start.'

She looks at the horizon, swallowing hard, not saying anything.

'But then again,' I add quickly, 'I wouldn't want to leave my friends or my family ...'

'As long as you don't go *too* far!' she says, laughing, and linking arms with me. 'Southend's far enough. I could come over and walk on the beach with you. We could buy candyfloss and Kiss Me Quick hats, and ...'

'You don't do things like that when you *live* at the sea-side, you daft wally!'

'Well, *we* will! And we'll buy cockles and whelks and eat them out of those little polystyrene trays, and we'll walk down the pier, and play the fruit machines and go on the dodgems, and we'll make sandcastles with cockleshells for windows and little paper flags and ...'

Her voice is wobbling a bit. I glance at her and she's swallowing fast, desperately trying to keep on talking.

'And we'll always be friends,' I finish for her, gently, squeezing her hand, 'Whatever.'

'Good!' she says fiercely. 'I should bloody well think so, too!'

Harry's leaning back in his seat at the other end of the boat, his legs stretched out in front of him, watching the seagulls circling. The sea breeze is ruffling his hair and squinting into the sun, which I'm sure always makes *me* look like a wrinkled old hag with cataracts, has the peculiar effect of making him look better than ever. I catch his eye and he gives me a smile and a wink, and I turn away again, suddenly embarrassed, not to say surprised at myself. What the hell am I doing? Looking at another man, finding him attractive – *fancying* him – when I've just had my whole life ruined by Matt? I'm obviously in shock – that must be it. I'm bound to do, and feel, a lot of strange things right now. I should keep my head down, keep my thoughts to myself, and *not* trust my instincts, for the time being. And if I know what's best for me, I should stay right away from good-looking guys like Harry.

I've got to hand it to him, though – when we get back from the boat trip he insists on running – actually *running* – back for the car so that he can drive Jude home. Emily goes with them to help with getting Jude in and out of the car. Conor and I are going to walk back. Having decided not to trust my instincts, I don't want to be sitting in the same car as Harry any more than I have to.

Conor's quite pleasant company if you like to be left alone in silence. He seems happy enough as we walk back along the harbour road but I can't help it – I feel uncomfortable around people who don't talk. I need to start him chatting, especially if he's getting friendly with Jude. Tactfully find out whether he's suitable for her, you know, without being too obvious.

'So!' I start breezily. 'Whereabouts do you live, then, Conor?'

'Oh, just a little way up the coast from here.' He nods, and goes back to his silent contemplation.

'That's nice. And you ... er ... you're single, then, are you?'

'I am, so. I live with me mam and me three sisters.' He turns to me suddenly, his eyes twinkling with amusement. 'And if you're wondering would I be thinking of messing around with Judith, well, I was contemplating asking her out at the weekend if you want to know the truth. But you've no need to worry on my account. I'm not like my cousin in any way at all, so don't you be bothering your head about her on that score.'

I'm somewhat taken aback by this, and not just because it's the longest speech I've heard from him so far.

'What do you mean,' I finally force myself to ask, ' "Not like your cousin" – in what way?'

'Ah, sure you know well what I mean,' he says with another broad grin. 'If you've known Harry for more than five minutes you'll have seen what he's like with the girls, will you not?'

'Not really, no. But I suppose – well, he's a good-looking guy ...' Whoops – there I go again. Change the subject, change the subject. 'He's free, single ... I suppose he has a bit of fun with the girls. Can't really blame him, can you?'

I think Conor's probably jealous. You can see why. Harry's tall, sexy, confident, gorgeous ... oh, God, what's *wrong* with me? I'm not *really* obsessing about him being sexy and gorgeous. It's just my traumatised mind playing tricks. But he obviously has no trouble getting girlfriends, whereas Conor's quiet and shy.

'Sure 'tis true he has his fun with the girls, and that's a fact. To be fair we both have a laugh when he comes over to Ireland.' Conor blushes and looks away, as if he's afraid I'll see pictures in his eyes of the sort of fun they have when Harry comes over. It doesn't need a lot of imagination. 'But he's not the sort of man I'd want any of me sisters to get involved with – except that I know he already has,' he adds, looking down at his feet.

'He's been out with one of your sisters?'

'Well, see, Katie, they've all had the most enormous crushes on him. Even when they were still little schoolgirls they used to giggle and go red when he walked in the room. Bernadette, the youngest, asked him for a kiss under the mistletoe one Christmas, years ago, when she was only about fifteen, and when he gave her a peck on the cheek, she had her arms round his neck snogging the living daylights out of him before I could pull her away. To be fair even Harry seemed fairly taken aback by that. "I'll have to watch that one, Conor," he said. "She's just a child. I'm not taking advantage of her – not till she's a few years older at least!"'

'It sounds like he was joking, though – wasn't he?'

'I thought so too, Katie. Then last year I found out that me middle sister, Bridget, had been sleeping with him.'

'Really? And how old was Bridget then?'

Must have been a bit older than fifteen, at least!

'Twenty-four, Katie, but sure it's a shameful thing to think of your own sister . . . in that situation . . . I'd have liked him to have shown a bit more respect, her being his cousin and all, if the truth be known.'

He tails off, looking very awkward, and I feel kind of sorry for him. Without a father, he's obviously been thrust into the position of responsibility for his younger sisters and it must have been something of a shock to discover that they'd become grown-up women with sex lives. Sex lives that involved his – rather gorgeous – older cousin.

'I hope he didn't treat Bridget badly?' I prompt him, not wanting to think it myself. Not that I should care. Why should I? I've never even met his sister, who, at twenty-four, was surely as perfectly capable of handling her own relationships as I am. Was. I think.

'Well, she walked around the house with a soppy look on her face for a few weeks, singing songs about falling in love – it was a painful time for us all, so it was,' he adds with the ghost of a smile. 'But he was going out with another girl by the next time he came over, and she cried herself to sleep

271

over it. Of course I knew he had no intention of marrying her – and she being a good Catholic girl! When I tried to talk to her about it, though, she snapped me head off and called me *old-fashioned* and *boring*.' He says these two words in a tone of great offence and incredulity. 'Can you ever believe the cheek of her?'

I can't believe we're having this conversation at all. I've only just met this guy, he's barely spoken two words to me all day, and now I'm getting the complete history, volumes I and II with annotations, of his whole family's sexual careers. Why?

'I just thought you ought to know,' he continues as if I've asked this aloud. 'He's a lovely fellow, Katie, but be aware of what you're getting into.'

'Getting into? Christ, Conor, I'm not getting into anything! I think you've got the wrong end of the stick – we hardly know each other – we just met in Dublin and he's helped us out, because of Jude, and . . .'

'Sure I know that fine, and I know my cousin too, and I know the looks he's been giving you. When I drove with him back to Urlingford yesterday to find Jude's crutches he talked about you the whole way, the whole time we ate our dinner and the whole way back again. I wouldn't normally be so rude as to mention it, Katie – sure it's none of my business and you can tell me to shut up if you like. But with you only just coming out of one relationship, with your wedding cancelled and all, well, I don't want you to get the wrong idea about Harry. He's my cousin and he's a great mate and I love him to bits, but he's not the type for a serious relationship. He's a lady's man, if you follow my meaning. He's the type that has his eye on a girl, has his way with her, and has himself out of the door before she's even got her underwear back on. Sorry,' he adds, going very red. 'Sorry for being crude.'

I'm staring at him in amazement. He's certainly found his tongue.

'You needn't worry about me,' I tell him firmly. 'As you say, I've just finished with one man – or rather, he's finished with *me* – and I can't even get my head round that yet, never mind thinking about seeing anyone else. I've got no interest in your cousin, other than hoping for a lift back to Cork later on ...'

'Sure your words are coming right at me, Katie,' he says, looking up at me and smiling again. 'But can I tell you: the look in your eyes when Harry's around is saying a different thing altogether.'

I'm laughing at this as we turn the corner and walk back up the hill to Jude's place. I suppose it's nice of him to tell me all this and do his gentlemanly thing to try and warn me off his cousin. But for God's sake – I'm not his innocent little sister. I'm thirty-one and probably know a lot more about the world than he thinks I do, and if I'm not old enough by now to know how dangerous a good-looking, charming bloke like Harry can be – well, let's face it. I never will be.

ABOUT COMING HOME

Lisa's waiting for us when we come through Arrivals at Stansted. I didn't know she was coming.

'I've been worried out of my life about you,' she says, grabbing my bag and holding onto me as if I'm about to fall over. 'Hello Emily. How are *you*?' she adds.

There's heavy emphasis on the *you*, accompanied by a shake of the head in my direction that implies I've single-handedly caused more than enough trouble to last everyone a lifetime. Well, I'm so sorry.

'How did you know?' I ask her.

'I sent Lisa a text,' says Emily quickly. 'I thought it'd be … easier for you … if you didn't have to come home and start telling everyone.'

'So now the whole of Essex knows I've been dumped. I suppose it'll be on Essex Radio in the morning.'

'Don't be silly,' says Lisa briskly, leading us out to the car park. 'Only the family. And Karen and Suze – I thought you'd want them to know. Oh, and Helen, of course, and Greg. I wasn't sure whether you'd be back at work tomorrow, or …'

Or what? Sit at home on my own, crying? Tempting though it sounds, I still need to earn a living. Even more so now, presuming Matt will want to come out of the mortgage. I don't suppose *Claire* would be too thrilled at the prospect of him supporting me in the style I'm accustomed to, for the rest of my life. Just the thought of sorting out the finances depresses me.

'Don't worry.' Lisa links her free arm through mine and holds my hand. 'It'll be hard for a while, baby, but we're all going to help you through this. It's for the best.'

'How do you work that out?'

'Things weren't right between you. If they were, you wouldn't have cancelled the wedding. You know that really, don't you?'

'Do I? I'm not sure what I know. I feel completely numb at the moment, to be honest.'

'That's only natural. It must have been such a shock. Over the phone! The bastard!' she says viciously, letting go of my hand to unlock her car and toss my bag into the boot. 'You'll get over him, Katie, I promise you.'

'Just don't tell me there are plenty more fish in the sea. OK? I'm *finished* with men. All of them.'

'Even Harry?' puts in Emily, giving me a puzzled smile.

'Especially Harry.'

Harry and Conor had hung around at Jude's until it was time for us to head back to Dublin. Conor was sitting on the sofa with Fergus on his lap, stroking him absent-mindedly and sneaking glances at Jude as she hobbled from room to room on her crutches, trying to tidy up before her mum arrived.

'Do you like cats, Conor?' she asked him shyly, watching him out of the corner of her eye.

'Yes, I do so, and I've got a little fellow at home just like this one. He's Burmese too, a Red. We call him Rudy. Do you find this one yowls like all the demons out of hell when he wants his dinner?'

'Absolutely! Jesus, you've never heard such a din – I thought it was just meself that was starving the poor little devil. And when there's a bird outside the window, the noise out of him could wake the dead in their graves!'

Jude and Conor had obviously found common ground in their own private Burmese Cat Appreciation Society. She actually appeared to be relaxing. I think she'd even forgotten she hadn't got her make-up on.

'So!' said Harry eventually, when we'd packed our bags and were looking at our watches. 'Am I going to drive you back to Dublin again?'

'Absolutely not!' said Emily, and for once I agreed:

'Don't be ridiculous – that's completely out of the question.' I smiled at him. 'We wouldn't say no to a lift back to Cork, though. Jude says it's easy enough to get the train to Dublin from there.'

We were all quiet in the car. Saying goodbye to Jude was difficult: both of us trying not to cry, clinging onto each other as if our changed circumstances – her broken ankle, my broken heart; me having a failed relationship instead of a wedding, her having a cat instead of a boyfriend – had tilted the whole axis of our friendship and thrown us closer together than ever.

'You'll see her again very soon,' Emily soothed me as I sniffed into a tissue after we'd driven away.

We'd sat together in the back of Harry's car. I wanted Emily next to me to comfort me, not Harry to confuse me with his smiles.

'I know. I'm just being silly and emotional.'

'Ssh. Of course you are. It's only natural.'

Harry, wisely, remained silent until we pulled up outside Cork station.

'Have a safe journey,' he said, leaning closer to me as he handed me my bag out of the boot.

He aimed a kiss at my cheek but I shifted slightly just in time, so that his lips merely brushed my ear. It was still enough to make me shiver.

'Thanks,' I said.

I tried to avoid looking at him; but he touched my face and turned me gently back towards him.

'Katie – I know things are difficult for you at the moment ...'

I nodded. Difficult to speak with him still touching my face.

'But I'd like to stay in touch. If you ever need a friend ... maybe we could meet up in London some time for a drink?'

'No,' I said, mustering all the strength I could find and remembering Conor's warning. What was the point? How was it going to make me feel any better to have a quick fling with someone who just wanted another notch on his bedpost? I sure as hell wasn't ready to face another rejection for a while yet. 'No, I don't think so.' He let go of me and his hands dropped to his sides.

'But thanks for everything,' I added quickly, feeling a

sudden and unreasonable pang at the look on his face. 'The lifts ... and – the other night – and everything. You've been really ... kind.'

He nodded as if this were little more than an insult. As he turned to say goodbye to Emily, I grabbed the handle of my holdall and wheeled it down towards the station. I didn't look back to see if he was still watching.

On the drive home from Stansted, Lisa fills me in with all the family news. It's weird. I've been in Ireland for less than a week but I feel like the whole world has changed since I've been gone. It's only been two days since Lisa and the others came home without us, but it's like I haven't seen them all for months.

'I've told Richard,' says Lisa quite calmly, changing gear as she pulls onto the motorway.

'What? About ... Andy?' I had to think for a few seconds to remember his name. 'God, Lisa! What did he say?'

'He wasn't too surprised. Upset, but not surprised. We're probably going to split up.'

'Probably?'

'We're trying to be civilised. Because of the kids. I didn't want to do this to the kids – you know that. But I think, over the weekend, talking to all of you about it, it made me realise I couldn't go on forever the way I was. I've had enough of lies and secrets. Pretending we had the perfect marriage when we both knew it was crap. Now it's out in the open, we can decide what to do. I think Richard needs to face up to the fact he didn't ever love me. Not really. He just wanted a wife.'

Poor old Rick the Prick. Now he won't even have one, by the looks of things.

'Are you OK?' I ask her gently.

'Me? Yeah. A bit shaky, I suppose. Funny, isn't it? I should be over the moon – I'll be free to see Andy as much as I want, move in with him, whatever ...'

'But ...?' I prompt her, but she just shakes her head and shrugs slightly.

'I think hanging onto the status quo is always an attractive option,' she says eventually, quite lightly.

I think she's right. And we're not talking about rock music, either.

Matt's not at home. I'm so relieved, I almost feel faint. The thought of seeing him, of trying to talk to him without both of us either losing our tempers or becoming hysterical, had been making me feel quite physically sick as we got nearer to home. I've made Emily and Lisa come into the flat with me for moral support.

'He's left a note in the kitchen,' says Lisa, who's gone straight in there to put the kettle on.

I go to pick it up but my hand's shaking and I can't read a word of it. What's the matter with my eyesight?

'Don't cry,' says Lisa, putting her arms round me.

Oh! I'm crying. That's OK then. I thought I'd been struck blind. I wipe my eyes roughly with the back of my hand and stare again at the couple of lines he's scrawled on the back of my shopping list. Two lines to end our life together.

Gone to stay at Rory's. Don't think it's a good idea for me to hang around here. Only make things worse. I'll get in touch about the flat and the bills. See you.

See you.

Fucking *see you*?

Not – *Sorry for seeing another girl, dumping you over the phone, treating you like shit, ruining your life*?

Not even – *Hope you had a good time in Ireland; sorry I'm not here to see the photos*?

Or even – *Enjoy the rest of your life, be happy, hope you meet someone nicer*?

After nearly four years together, being madly in love, spending every spare minute of our lives together, nearly getting married! After I planned to have a baby with him! After all that, it comes down to two lines and a *See you*? Well, fuck him!

Emily's watching me anxiously. Lisa's still got her arms round me, soothing me, trying to read the note over my shoulder.

'Are you OK?' says Emily.

'OK?' I retort, and my voice is shaking with anger. How healthy this anger feels! How deliciously it fires my veins. I can feel my muscles tightening, my back straightening, my jaw setting and every fibre of my body prickling with positive, furious new life. 'Yes, I'm OK. I'm more than OK. I'm going to be fine. I'm going to be absolutely fucking *perfect* without Matthew Davenport in my life, I'll make absolutely bloody *sure* of it!'

I attempt a triumphant smile but I think it comes out as a bit of a toothy grimace. I may look a little bit mad, but what the hell? These two girls know me. They probably know me better than anyone in the world. Who needs a man anyway? I've got my sister, and my friends, and my mum, and they all love me, and they're never going to mess up my life, or hurt me, or say goodbye to me with a phone call and a crappy little note on the back of a shopping list.

Romance?

From now on, it can stay where it belongs.

In the fucking paperbacks.

ABOUT RECOVERY

It's very strange being back at work. For a start, I can't look Greg in the eye. He started off, when I walked in this morning, by making an excruciatingly embarrassing little speech to me about how sorry he was about my *unfortunate circumstances*, how he hoped that I'd soon be feeling better (as if I was suffering from flu or had just had a tooth extracted) and back to my *old self*, and that he hoped it went without saying that he would always be (this bit with a little self-conscious cough and much studying of his feet) *there for me* if I needed anything, any kind of *support* or *financial advice* or *indeed, anything else at all*. Having got that out of the way, and being very worried now about what he meant by *anything else at all*, I got my head down over my computer and busied myself writing up my reviews for the rest of the morning.

Now, at one o'clock, Helen's trying to goad me into agreeing to a pub lunch.

'Well … I don't know if I should, really,' I say cagily. 'There's a lot of work to catch up on …'

'Katie, please,' interrupts Greg, looking up at me over his glasses, 'Go out to lunch with Helen. Take all the time you need. We can catch up with the work tomorrow. You need a break.'

'Thanks,' I respond, grabbing my handbag and making a dash for the door.

'It's very unnerving,' I complain, perching on a bar stool while we wait to be served. 'He's treating me like an invalid. Like he doesn't want to be responsible if I suddenly collapse, or throw a fit, or swallow a bottleful of paracetamol …' I stop, remembering Jude. 'Shit, that wasn't funny.'

'He can't help it, Katie,' says Helen moodily. 'I keep telling you. He's crazy about you.'

'That's rubbish. He isn't. He's probably just got a crush on me. It's making me feel uncomfortable now you've told me about it. Don't worry, Helen – I meant what I said: I'm going to look around for another job. But I'll just have to get things sorted out about the mortgage and the bills first, with Shit-face ...'

'It's OK. You don't have to. That's why I wanted to talk to you today. I've booked my flight.'

'Your flight?' I frown, trying to remember. So much has happened, it's addled my memory. 'Are you going on holiday?'

'I told you. I'm going to Australia.'

'Helen! No!' This is madness. 'You can't! You don't go flying off to the other side of the world just because ...'

'Because I'm slowly dying every day I have to spend here? Because I feel cold, and tired, and unhappy, and I want to feel the sun on my face again?'

I look at her sadly. She does look tired. She has dark circles under her eyes and her cheeks are pale and sunken. Is this what love is supposed to do to you? I feel the anger welling up inside me once more. This is Helen! She's the strongest woman I've ever met; the woman who's always told *me* not to give up my life for a man. She doesn't believe in romance! How can this have happened? How do we *allow* this to happen to ourselves?

'Please don't go!' I say again quietly. 'You can get through this, Helen. We can help each other. We'll *both* leave Bookshelf. We can look for a new job together. I need you! I need you to talk sense to me – to make me strong ...'

'Sorry, Katie.' She shakes her head. 'I'm not even strong enough for *me* any more. I've just told Greg I'm taking extended leave for the moment. I'm not completely stupid. I won't rush into anything. I'll stay with my brother, get a job, see how things go. But I don't think I'll be coming back.'

We pay for our drinks and carry them, in silence, to a table by the window where I pick up the sandwich menu and study it with a shaky hand.

'You'll be fine,' she says at length. 'You're tougher than you think you are. You're designed to bounce back – like one of those children's balls on a bit of elastic!'

She's smiling, gently, trying to make me laugh.

'Until the elastic snaps.'

'It doesn't; it stretches. Better than a tough old bit of string that hasn't got any give in it, eh? That just tears itself to shreds, in the end.'

I'm a bit slow. It's not till much later, when we're back in the office, that I realise she's referring to herself.

Emily and Sean are being lovely. They won't let me be on my own.

'I don't actually think I mind,' I tell Emily tonight when she calls. 'I'm tired. I'm going to have a bath, curl up on the sofa in my 'jamas, watch TV and pig out on chocolate.'

'I'll come and join you, then. In case you eat all the chocolate and get fat.'

'OK. As long as we can watch *EastEnders*.'

'Absolutely. If I stay at home, Sean will have the football on.'

And I suddenly realise something. If Matt was here, he'd have the football on, too. He wouldn't even have asked me what I wanted to watch. And inside, I'd have been pissed off, but I'd have pretended not to mind. And then I'd have shared the chocolate with him, but he'd have eaten most of it – and I'd still have pretended not to mind. And I wouldn't have been able to chat to him about his day, or have a giggle and a laugh with him the way I will with Emily, because he takes the football so seriously I'd have to be quiet and pretend to not mind that, either.

Suddenly, I'm not having to pretend anything to anyone any more. And I think, eventually, I could get to like it.

Everyone says it, and it's true: the night times are the worst. The double bed feels big, and Matt's side is cold and empty. I've tried moving onto the other side, or lying bang slap in the middle, but it doesn't seem natural. I like my own side. In the end I've put a pillow in his side, so that when I roll over and reach out, like I keep doing, automatically, to feel the comfort of a warm body lying next to mine, I feel the softness of the pillow instead of the heart-wrenching bare flatness of the cold sheet. It's a little thing, but it helps. I feel better, stronger, for having thought of it. Another week, another month, and I won't even be finding it strange any more. I'm going to get over this. I'm going to bloody well survive. I'm not going to pieces. Am I?

And another thing: in the night, when I reach out for someone, it isn't always Matt I've been dreaming about anyway. That's one of the reasons I'm so cross with myself. I've erased Harry's number from my phone. I've erased him, permanently, from my life, but how do you erase someone from your dreams? What's the matter with me? Haven't I got enough problems in my life without dreaming about some guy I hardly even know? Why did I ever even give him a second look? He was just a ship passing in the night, for God's sake! I must be in a really bad way if I'm so desperate for sexual excitement that my subconscious mind allows me to dream myself into bed (naked and gagging for it) with some guy we just picked up as part of a hen party game.

Of course, I can't help my dreams, but I never think about him when I'm awake. That would *really* be pathetic. The only little scenario that occasionally flits through my mind, just when I'm sitting at home quietly on my own you know, is the memory of him looking after me that night in Jude's flat – covering me up and bringing me water and a cold flannel and stroking my hair back from my face and letting me cry on his shoulder ... well, OK, it's a nice memory if you like that sort of thing. But obviously it's not something I want to waste too much time on. When you think about it, most guys would probably have been reasonably kind to someone who was crying her eyes out and hanging onto a sick-bucket, so it's no big deal. No big deal at all.

Lisa comes to see me at the weekend.

'Mum's joined a group,' she says, sitting down next to me with a steaming mug of coffee.

'A group?'

I'm thinking amateur dramatics, maybe flower arranging.

'AA.'

'Oh!'

Shock hits me somewhere mid-chest. I've talked to Lisa once or twice, since the hen weekend, about Mum's drinking and whether we should worry about it or not. I thought the consensus of our opinion had been pretty much that we shouldn't. Lisa hadn't even seemed as shocked or as upset as me, when I told her Mum's revelations about our dad.

'I've always suspected something like that,' she said fairly calmly.

'Have you?'

'Yes. I've even asked Mum once or twice whether there was more to it than she admitted – but she obviously wasn't ready to talk to us about it.'

'Why didn't *I* suspect anything? Am I thick, or what?'

'No, Katie. You're just the baby of the family. Everyone probably tried to protect you,' she said with a smile.

'Up till my hen weekend. Then they chucked it all at me at once!'

'I'm sorry,' she says now, seeing the look on my face. 'I didn't think this would come as a shock to you, Katie. It was you that brought it to my attention, in the first place.'

'Yes, but Jesus, I didn't think she was actually – well, you know, *really* ...'

'What? She drinks when she's on her own.' Lisa's counting off on her fingers. 'She drinks to stop herself from crying; from thinking her life's a mess. She hides her drinking from her family. She pretends she drinks less than she really does. She says she's stopped, but she hasn't. She makes excuses for needing just one more. You don't think she's an alcoholic?'

'I suppose. ... God, Lisa, I wish we'd known. We should have realised. We could have helped her ...'

'No, we couldn't. You know what they say. They have to want to help themselves. In the event, your hen weekend did the trick – it all came out and she had to confront it, herself. She's determined now. She seems so much stronger after just one AA meeting.'

Strong, stronger, strongest. It's all I seem to hear about, these days. I wish we didn't all have to go on and on about

284

being strong. It reminds me of cartoons of Popeye with his tins of spinach. To be quite honest I'd like nothing better than to collapse in a heap of weakness, like a melted jelly, and let someone else get on with being strong for me. And for Mum, and for Lisa too.

Where are you, Dad?

Shame you turned out to be just another bastard. A tin of spinach would actually be more use to us all than you were. No wonder I've wasted half my life searching for some non-existent perfect man. I never even had one as a father.

ABOUT HELEN'S PARTY

Where has the time gone? It's nearly the end of May already. The weather's beginning to feel like summer; the trees are wearing their new summer clothes and as I walk to the bus stop in the mornings, I've seen pink and red and lilac coloured flowers on shrubs in the suburban front gardens. I ought to learn their names. I'm going to move – somewhere with a garden. I want a patch of grass to call my own. I'll plant things, and talk about perennials and climbers and herbaceous borders with my mum and my sister. All I've ever grown, up till now, was a cactus in a flowerpot – and that's beginning to look a bit yellowy.

Matt and I are selling the flat. We've found a buyer already because flats in this area are snapped up as soon as they go on the market. He's moved in with his mate Rory – presumably until he and Bitch Claire decide where to build their love nest. I've only been round there once and it reminded me of when I was a student. At least three days' worth of washing-up piled next to the sink; an assortment of mugs, plates, socks, and beer cans scattered artistically around the living room, and the kitchen floor so sticky I had to wipe my shoes when I came *out*. I wonder if Claire will still want him when she sees him in his new habitat. She might think twice about any dreams she may have of deep-pile pale beige carpets or white leather sofas.

'Why do men revert to such disgusting habits without a woman around?' I asked Helen idly the next morning at work.

'Because, dear, that's their natural state. They're not actually civilised. They only pretend to be, to please us.'

'I'm beginning to think all relationships are built on a load of pretence.'

'You're only *beginning* to think that?'

Today's the day I was supposed to be getting married. I lie in bed until late, trying to focus my mind on the thought that I should, by now, have been getting myself into the dress that's still hanging in Lisa's spare room wardrobe under its plastic cover. I should have had my hair done and my nails French-polished and be getting jittery about walking down the aisle on Uncle Ron's arm and committing myself to one man for the rest of my life.

Now, it already seems unreal and slightly ridiculous. Why did I ever think it was a good idea? Why did I ever think I was in love with Matt? I don't miss him any more. I can hardly even remember what it was like living with him, sleeping with him, washing his socks and underpants and listening to him going on and on about Arsenal.

And instead of getting married, I'm going to a farewell party tonight – for Helen. Yes, she's off to Australia on Monday. We're all going to the pub; I've asked everyone who came on the hen weekend. Helen considers them all her friends now, and it's sad, but she hasn't really got many of her own. She said her goodbyes to Greg at the office yesterday. At least, she thinks she did – but I've invited him along tonight, too. Whether or not he turns up is a different matter. He's such an odd guy. Beats me how he hasn't noticed it's tearing her up inside to leave him.

Emily and Sean pick me up at half past seven. Emily's been round for most of the afternoon anyway. She was worried that I was going to fall apart, thinking about the wedding dress and the church and the reception and everything. At half past three – about the time that I would have been officially declared Mrs Davenport – she handed me a cup of tea and a double choc-chip muffin and told me my life was just about to start improving. Bless her. I didn't like to tell her it's improved already. It must be hard for her to imagine, when she's so happy with her man. I'm not jealous. Well, only a little bit. I'm actually quite happy now.

287

It's weird seeing Karen and Suze again, today of all days. They wave to me from across the pub, elbow their way through the crowds to reach me, hug me and look at me with concerned, wary faces, asking if I'm OK. I should be at my wedding reception by now. Cutting the cake. Being led onto the dance floor by my new husband for the first dance. 'I Will Always Love You'. That was what we'd chosen. How ironic!

'I'm fine,' I assure them. Fine, fine, absolutely fine. 'Lovely to see you all. Sorry about the hen weekend. About it not being ... you know ... a hen weekend.'

I laugh a little too hysterically. They watch me nervously. But I *am* fine. It's not the drink. I've given up – really, this time. I'm on orange juice.

Helen's arrived, looking flustered, like someone panicking in the middle of packing for a trip. Precisely.

'I can't stay too long,' she says, collapsing onto the seat opposite me. 'I've still got such a lot to do. I'll be awake all night.'

'So what? *Be* awake all night. You can sleep for twenty-three hours or whatever it is, on the flight!' I don't want her to leave before Greg turns up. If he turns up. 'Come on, I'll get you a drink. This is your last night with us. Make it memorable!'

'Too many of these,' she retorts as I plonk a double vodka and tonic in front of her, 'and it won't be memorable at all!' Her face starts to crumple. 'I'm going to miss you, Katie,' she says very quietly, into her glass.

I reach across the table and grasp her hand.

'Me too. But isn't the Internet a wonderful thing? We can be on-line simultaneously, talking to each other from different continents on different dates. Absolutely bloody amazing!'

I'm trying to keep things light. Really, I want to tell her to cancel the flight, stop being stupid, stop running away, stay and fight. Fight for Greg, or fight for a life without him. Anything's better than going to the other side of the world, away from everything she loves. London's theatres, Paris's restaurants, Florence's art galleries, Vienna's opera houses. What's she going to do? I just can't see her throwing a kangaroo steak on the barbie with a can of Foster's in her hand.

'I'll come back,' she says jerkily. 'If it doesn't work out I'll come back.'

'Good.'

'But if I stay ...' She looks up at me, and I think she's going to ask me to go out and visit her. I hope so. I'll never know, now, because as she looks up, something or rather some*one* behind me catches her eye and she turns pale, then red, and nearly drops her drink. I have to take it out of her hand and put it down on the table for her. Well, thank God for that. Greg's turned up.

'I said goodbye to him yesterday,' she mutters as he makes his way over to our table.

'Well. Now you can say it again,' I encourage her. I get up, nodding to Greg to take my chair, and move off to talk to the others at the bar.

'Get her another drink,' says Lisa, who's been watching. 'She's just polished that one off and she looks like she could do with at least another six.'

In the event, she actually has about another eight before the evening's over. I've never seen Helen quite so drunk. I like it. It's an improvement.

'You're all my *very* dear frrrriends,' she tells the whole population of the pub, very loudly, at about half past ten. 'I love you *all*. You're my *family*.' She's standing, swaying slightly, holding her glass aloft as if in a toast. 'I'm going to miss you, every one of you. Miss you like hell. Katie, my dear, dear friend!' She sways towards me, spilling vodka down her jeans. 'I'll miss you *so* much! You've been the best friend ...'

I hug her, quickly, worried that she's going to break down and cry. Greg's got to his feet. He's mumbling something about it getting on a bit, having to drive back, not wanting to make it too late. For God's sake! Boring old man. Helen hears him and turns, almost overbalancing.

'No!' she says, surprisingly distinctly. 'Not yet, you don't!' There's a hush in the bar. Everyone turns to watch her.

'It's my *party*!' she tells him, plaintively, in the silence. 'My leaving party! I'm going all the way to Australia, in the morning, Greg. And do you know why?'

I can almost hear everyone holding their breath.

'Helen,' I warn her, touching her arm gently. She shakes me off.

'I'm going to *Australia*,' she continues relentlessly, taking hold of one of Greg's arms and shaking it roughly as if she were fluffing up a pillow, 'because of *you*.'

'Helen!' I hiss. 'Come on! You've had a few drinks ... come and sit down!'

She doesn't even bother to look at me.

'You don't even know, do you? You've never even noticed!' she carries on relentlessly. Poor Greg's staring fixedly, miserably, at her hands gripping his arm. 'You have *no idea* how I feel about you!'

She stops, flops against him for a minute as if she's run out of steam. Phew, thank God for that.

And then, suddenly, with no flicker of warning whatsoever, she's grabbed him round the back of his neck and is kissing him forcefully, desperately, on the lips. His hands flail uselessly in the air for a minute as he's pinned against the wall and everyone gasps, giggles, whispers, and then a cheer goes up from the back of the room and everyone joins in, wolf-whistling, stamping, clapping, chanting: *HeLEN, HeLEN, HeLEN* as if she were a football player heading for the goal of the match. And then Greg's hands come round her waist and he pulls her closer. And he's not resisting any more. And the football chant dies down, and everyone turns away and gets back to their drink, and their own conversations.

I'm talking to Lisa about Mum. But out of the corner of my eye I can see Greg, finally, after what seems like too long to be good for his health, gently disengaging himself, holding Helen by the shoulders as if to steady her, stepping away from her backwards, mumbling something about a parking meter and stumbling awkwardly, hurriedly, out of the door.

She's watching him go, her eyes lit with love and alcoholic idiocy. She's smiling to herself. She's going to collapse into bed happy tonight, thinking that he's finally seen the light and is poised to fall in love with her. I'm glad she'll have one night of happy, drunken, sleep.

Tomorrow morning she's going to wake up with an almighty raging hangover. She'll remember tonight with horrible, cringing embarrassment and be thankful that she's putting several oceans between her and everyone else in the pub. Because, at the end of the day, he's still not asking her to stay, is he?

ABOUT DAWN

And now life has to go on. Without Helen in the office, Greg and I maintain an uneasy, uncomfortable balance. It feels unnatural, like trying to put your weight on a stool that only has two legs instead of three. We're off-centre. Wobbly.

Obviously I'm uncomfortable around Greg anyway and have been ever since Helen told me all that stuff, in Dublin. But now that she's gone, I'm really wondering again if she had it wrong. He's so obviously missing *her*! He's moody, and miserable, and he keeps looking at her desk as if by staring at it for long enough he can conjure her back up again.

By the end of the week, I can't stand it any more. He's getting on my nerves.

'What's the matter?' I ask him, trying not to snap. 'You're like a bear with a sore head.'

He sighs, shakes his head, stares out of the window.

'I shouldn't have let her go,' he says.

Jesus! Understatement of the year, or what?

'So why didn't you try to stop her? You could have done. You must have realised! Even if you didn't before, you must have realised at her leaving party that it would only have taken one word from you ...'

'I'm not a complete idiot,' he responds tersely. 'I knew she liked me.'

OK, so you don't have to love someone back, just because you're aware of their feelings. No one can make another person love them – it's what stinks, sometimes, about falling in love.

I bring him a cup of coffee and try to give him a sympathetic smile to show I understand, but as I'm turning to go back to my own desk he catches my arm.

'Katie . . .'

Shit. Please don't let him start coming on to me. Please, please, let Helen have been wrong. I couldn't bear the embarrassment.

'Katie, I've never told you about my ex-wife, have I?'

Well, that's a relief, anyway. As long as he doesn't talk about me, he can tell me his whole life history if he likes. I sit down and turn my chair to face him.

'Only that you weren't married to her for very long. And her name was . . . Dawn, wasn't it?'

He nods, looking away and sighing again.

'We were only married for three years. She was so lovely – bright and funny and popular with everyone – I couldn't believe my luck when she agreed to go out with me, let alone marry me.'

'Don't be silly. I'm sure that's not true.'

'Of course it is. Her friends all found me boring. I must have been a novelty for her. She used to say all the other men she'd been out with were football-mad and always down the pub.'

'Most of the men I know are like that.'

'Yes. I suppose so. You know, you're very much like her, Katie.'

I feel a shiver of apprehension again. I turn away, suddenly awkward, and take a mouthful of my coffee.

'*Very* much like her,' he continues, as if he's talking to himself. 'When you first came to work for me, you reminded me of Dawn instantly.'

'So what happened? With Dawn?' I prompt him, wanting to turn the conversation away from myself again as quickly as possible.

'What do you think? She got bored with me – obviously. In the beginning I think she was a little in awe of me. She used to pick up the typescripts I brought home to read, and turn them over in her hands as if they were . . . I don't know – some sort of rare specimens! When we went out for meals with my colleagues she'd sit like this –' he rests his chin on his hand, gazing across his desk at me – 'listening to our conversations, laughing at my jokes, making me feel clever. When I was with her, I didn't feel dull and socially inept,

293

like I normally did. She made me feel as bright and attractive as she was. What an illusion!'

'You're not socially inept,' I murmur. I feel sorry for him, despite myself. 'Of course you're clever, Greg.'

He ignores this.

'The trouble was that she thought she wanted to be part of my world: stuffy cocktail parties and pseudo-intellectual debates over smoked salmon and caviar. We all called each other *old chap* rather than *mate*, and called our partners our *good lady wives*. I hate myself for introducing her to it. It was like ... well, like throwing a beautiful jewel into a muddy pond. Wasted. I should have gone with her to watch West Ham or Westlife instead.'

'But that wouldn't have been right for *you*, would it. Maybe you just weren't really suited. These things happen ... people make mistakes ...'

I'm trying, desperately, to say the right thing here. How did I get myself into this? The last thing in the world I want is for Greg Armstrong to pour out his heart to me. Christ, Helen – thanks a million. Before you buggered off, he apparently used to confide in *you*! I do *not* want to become his new best buddy. However sorry I feel for him. God, he didn't have to marry someone he so obviously had nothing in common with, did he?

'What an idiot I was!' he says, rubbing his head as if the memory is hurting him. 'I'd bathed in her admiration for so long that I didn't even notice the light going out of her eyes.'

And I've known Greg for all this time without realising he could wax so lyrical. Or even speak more than a couple of sentences about anything other than physics or engineering.

'She left you?'

'I found out, eventually, that she was seeing someone else. A DJ, who went by the name of Dog, had several studs in his nose and lips, and a very large tattoo on his arm. It involved daggers and spiders' webs – apparently something to do with an obscure heavy metal band.'

I'm trying to imagine this. Dog. Poor Greg.

'So – you threw her out?'

'No. She asked me for a divorce, and went to live with Dog. She was ... the worst thing, for me, was that she was expecting his child.'

A case of a bitch having a puppy Dog.

'That was hard on you.'

'Yes. I suppose I had a kind of breakdown after she left. Nothing dramatic. I was brought up not to indulge in crying, or shouting, or anything unsavoury like that.'

I'm thinking that probably he would have been a lot better for a few bouts of crying and shouting. Maybe he should have gone for therapy.

'How did you get over it?'

He looks embarrassed.

'I stayed in bed for several days, and then ... well, I had difficulty leaving the house. When I did manage to go back to work, I found I couldn't talk to people. I couldn't answer the phone. I started to shake if anyone got too close to me.'

'Greg, you needed help! You should have seen your doctor.'

He shrugs.

'Too proud, I suppose – but you're right. I should have done. Eventually, one morning, standing on the platform waiting for my train, I came so close to throwing myself on the railway line that I had to force myself to back away from the edge of the platform. I was sweating and shaking. I staggered out of the station, got a taxi home and stayed there. I lost my job.'

'That's terrible! Your doctor should have signed you off sick. You should have been referred for therapy. Your firm should have paid you and kept your job open ...'

'Yes, yes. All those things are true, Katie, but it was my own fault – I refused help. I just stayed at home and mouldered away. Anyway, in the long run it wasn't a bad thing. I was good at the job, but I never enjoyed it. And I was fortunate: I didn't really need the money. I'd inherited my parents' house, rented it out for years and then made a killing on the sale. My investments were good, and—'

'You told me once that you started Bookshelf as a hobby,' I interrupt him, not really wanting to hear all about his personal finances any more than his broken heart.

'That's right. It was just an idea I had – something to get up for in the mornings. To begin with, I worked at home on my laptop. I knew the idea had potential because I'd been watching the phenomenon of Amazon, and the share of the book-buying market it had taken. I worked on it day and night, and gradually I realised I was enjoying myself.'

'So you never regretted leaving publishing.'

'Absolutely not. Especially not the scientists whose books I published – half of them irritated the life out of me. And I certainly didn't miss commuting into London.' He pauses and looks at me thoughtfully. 'It took very much longer, but eventually I didn't miss Dawn any more either.'

'You've never spoken to me about her before.'

'No.' Again, he hesitates. 'The thing is, Katie, by the time you joined me, it'd been about three or four years since the divorce. I was almost over it.'

'Well, that's good, then.'

'But being around *you* stirred it all up again.'

Help. Helen, come back! Where are you now when I need you?

I don't want to be part of this conversation. In fact, I'm out of here. I'm going, right now, to stand up and leave the room. And I might even get on the next plane from Heathrow and come out and join you in Australia.

'Right. I've ... er ... got to ... um ... go to the toilet now.' I grab my bag from under my desk.

'Katie, don't go ...'

'Sorry, Greg! Nature calls, as they say!'

'Listen. I'm not going to embarrass you. Please. Katie!' I'm halfway out of the door. 'I know Helen's probably given you the wrong impression.'

I stop.

'Go on,' I say flatly, without turning round.

'It isn't you. Look, I've tried to talk to Helen about all this – about Dawn, about Dog, about the baby. Helen and I ... we seemed to be able to talk to each other about almost anything. I always found her ... no disrespect to you, Katie, but I found her easier to talk to. We've got similar views. Similar personalities, I think.'

'But you couldn't talk to her about Dawn?'

'Yes – I did. I did talk to her, and she listened; but ... I know this sounds ridiculous, but ...'

I turn back to look at him. He's squirming with embarrassment.

'I think she was jealous,' he admits, going slightly red.

'Of course she was!' I laugh. 'You fool!'

'And you see, when I told her how much *you* reminded me of Dawn – look, I don't mean anything by this, Katie. But you *are*! Same height, same colouring – and you're just so much *like* her in other ways. You even laugh like her. At first, it gave me a pang every time I heard it.'

'You should have told me!'

'What, and make you stop laughing? I don't think so! I wanted you for this job – you've been perfect. It was my problem. I had to get over it.'

'But Helen thought ...'

'I think she got the wrong end of the stick. She assumed, when I told her how much you reminded me of Dawn and how difficult I found it, that I had *feelings* for you.' He's now so red, he can't look at me any more. 'Not that I'm not very fond of you, of course, Katie!' he adds quickly.

I sit back down at my desk. I've forgotten about needing the loo. I feel almost faint with relief. He isn't interested in me. Helen got it all wrong. Why the hell hasn't Greg got all this out in the open before?

But I know the answer, really. He didn't like talking to me because I reminded him of Dawn. And he never *needed* to talk to me before – because he had Helen.

'How long have you known about Helen? About her ... liking you?'

'I don't know.' He shrugs, immediately embarrassed again. 'I suppose I cottoned onto it soon after she started working here. It was a bit of a shock, to be honest – it's not exactly something I've been used to. I'm hardly a sex symbol, I don't need anyone to tell me that.'

'Oh, well ... but ... I don't know ...'

Fortunately, he laughs.

'It's all right, Katie, we don't need to pretend I'm George Clooney and you're secretly having trouble holding yourself in check! It was very odd knowing that Helen liked me, and especially that she was jealous when I told her you reminded

297

me of Dawn. But I wasn't interested in her in that way. We just got on well together. She's a good listener. I felt comfortable with her. Not that she didn't try – she made a pass at me a couple of times, but all it really did was embarrass both of us,' he added, squirming a bit again.

Ha! Good for Helen. Might have known she'd have given it a go. What a terrible thought, though!

'But of course, I was sorry when she said she was taking extended leave – and a little put out, to be honest. I told her it was really inconvenient and it'd put me in a spot.'

'Poor Helen! No wonder she went. Couldn't you see what you were doing to her?'

'No, not really. I was totally perplexed by it all, especially the fact that she was going to *Australia*. I had no idea it was anything to do with me. Look, OK, I knew she fancied me, and I admit I found it flattering, but I honestly didn't know she felt *that* strongly.'

'You'll miss her now she's gone,' I told him a bit crossly. Stupid man! How thick can you get?

'Katie,' he said quietly, looking down at his desk, 'I do. I do already. Actually, I started missing her before she'd even gone. I don't know when it hit me – gradually, I suppose, over these last couple of weeks, while she's been preparing to leave. She was a good friend, and I've let her go.'

'So why didn't you *stop* her going?' God, this is so exasperating! 'She was *begging* you to tell her not to go!'

'OK, she kissed me, at her leaving party – and some people might say that a kiss like that is another way of begging to be asked to stay.'

'Of course it was!'

'I'm not that stupid. I'm not reading anything into that. She was far too drunk to know what she was doing. She'd made up her mind; she was going to Australia. And if she decides not to come back, I'll have lost a friend and that's all there is to it.'

'Greg. Are you telling me, honestly, that you think of Helen as just a friend? Only let me tell *you* something: all you've done, all week, is mope around with a face like a long bloody wet weekend ...'

'Did you hear any of what I told you, Katie? About Dawn? Ever since she left me, I've avoided having anything to do with women except as friends, or colleagues. It's taken me a long time to recover. I'm not in a hurry to go through that kind of rejection again.'

'But Helen's *crazy* about you, Greg!'

'So you say. But so was Dawn, once.'

'Helen's not like Dawn, though, is she. You need to trust the opposite sex again sooner or later, Greg! We all have to *live* again, eventually ... don't we?'

It's not just the look on Greg's face that stops me short.

I've suddenly realised I'm not one to talk. I'm doing exactly the same thing myself: cruising along in neutral, staying safe, staying single, never wanting to risk being hurt again.

But that's different. I'm not moping around the way Greg is!

ABOUT PHONE CALLS

I'm moving next week. I've found a downstairs flat, with a garden, in an old converted house in Leigh-on-Sea. The rent's cheap because it's a bit basic but I'm excited that I'm really going to be living at the seaside! I can commute to work for now – but, to be honest, I want to look for a new job. The problem is, how can I leave Bookshelf, when Greg's already struggling without Helen? We've had a series of temps, most of them looking not quite old enough to have left school and not having much IT knowledge beyond how to play computer games and how to produce CVs giving distorted impressions of their abilities. At the moment I feel like I'll have to stay, at least until he finds someone half-decent, or until Helen comes back. If she ever does.

I've e-mailed her several times, telling her how much Greg misses her, but her replies have been a bit terse. *Don't try to humour me*, she wrote last time. *It's not helping*. Perhaps Greg's right. Perhaps she really does want to be left alone, on the other side of the world, to forget about him. But somehow I don't think so. Am I still hankering after the happy ending, after all – even if it's someone else's instead of mine?

'Seaside?' says Emily when she comes to have a look at my new flat. 'Estuary-side, more like!'

'But we can still have candyfloss, can't we? And Southend rock? And build sandcastles?'

'Mud castles,' she corrects me, laughing, but she slips an arm through mine and squeezes it. 'It's perfect, Katie. All it needs is a lick of paint. I'll help you – we'll do it together. It'll be great.'

'And you'll come and stay? I'll get a sofa bed. You and Sean? You can have weekends at the seaside ...'

'We're only going to be half an hour away! You're not going to the other side of the world, love! Thank God,' she adds quietly.

But I'm already planning it, in my mind. Breakfasts at waterfront cafés, looking out at all the little fishing boats bobbing on the tide. Beach parties on warm summer evenings. Sunsets over the sea. Oh, all right then – the estuary! It doesn't sound so romantic, does it.

Of course, I'm not the only one whose life has turned upside down since the hen weekend. Lisa and Richard have split up, too. Our poor mum must be wondering what the hell her daughters are playing at. Happy families? Well, I suppose we didn't start off with a very good example.

Richard's moving out, and Lisa's staying in the house with the children. I ask her whether she's going to move in with Andy.

'Not yet,' she says cagily. 'I want to give it some time, Katie. I'm not rushing into anything.'

'Want to make sure he's The One?' I say, smiling, nudging her. But she doesn't smile back.

'Not sure about all that stuff.'

No, I'm beginning to wonder myself, too. It's one thing to be romantic about sunsets and beaches ... but men? Finding *The One*? If I hadn't been so caught up in *all that stuff* when I met Matt, maybe I would have realised it wasn't right. I talked myself into believing it. Why do we do that? What happens to us – do we develop a kind of mind and brain bypass when we meet a new man that we *want* to be *The One*?

'Somewhere out there,' says Lisa, seeing the look on my face, 'there's someone that's right for you, little sister.'

I used to think so, too. But after those ridiculous dreams and fancies I had about Harry, I'm beginning to think my judgement is shot to pieces.

Of course, I never think about Harry now. But it's strange how many people around here remind me of him. I'd say there must be a lot of Harry lookalikes in Leigh-on-Sea – but that isn't strictly true, because every time I get one of these absurd heart-stopping moments when something about the back of a complete stranger's head, or the way they walk, makes me think for a split second that it's actually Harry, they turn round and in fact they're nothing like him whatsoever. And the sinking feeling I get then isn't anything to do with disappointment, of course. It's probably just indigestion.

The first phone call comes at the most inappropriate moment you could possibly imagine. I'm in a job interview. It's all very well hanging on at Bookshelf, but I just happened to see this advert for someone to help run the bookshop in Leigh-on-Sea, just round the corner from me. I couldn't resist it. OK, the money isn't great, but I won't have any fares, I won't be running a car and there was a hint in the advert about possible advancement for the right person. I don't quite understand how you can advance, in a bookshop, but I thought it was worth trying to find out. Yes, I feel guilty about Greg, but maybe the next school-leaver that comes from the agency will be better. I've got to start thinking about what's good for *me*, for a change.

When my phone starts singing its silly little electronic tune in my bag, I'm just being asked why I want the job.

Shit, shit, shit. Why did I forget to turn the bloody thing to silent?

I smile cheesily at Mrs Blake, the bookshop manager, and mumble something about my phone having developed a fault that makes it switch itself on when it's supposed to be off. If she believes that, she'll believe anything. I fumble in my bag, and manage to grab the phone just as it stops ringing. I'm hot and flustered with embarrassment and the knowledge that I've almost certainly blown my chance of the job. So flustered that I just shove the phone back into my bag without turning it off.

'So sorry about that,' I say, with another cheesy grin that probably makes me look slightly on the mad side. 'Technology, eh! Fine till it goes wrong!'

'Yes,' smiles Mrs Blake. 'Quite. Now, then – I think we were talking about your reasons for wanting the job?'

'Oh, yes.' I smooth my skirt and try to calm down. Maybe all is not lost. 'Well, I've worked in the book trade all my life, and I'm looking to diversify at this stage. In my current role, as you'll see from my CV, I'm single-handedly reading and reviewing . . .'

Unfortunately I don't get as far as telling her how many books I'm single-handedly reviewing, because at this point the phone starts again. This time I lose my composure completely and only just manage to stop myself shouting 'Bollocks!' at the top of my voice as I grab it out of my bag again and, in my agitation, drop the fucking thing and it slides under Mrs Blake's desk.

'Oh! Sorry! I'll just . . . sorry, let me just . . .'

I'm on the floor now, reaching under the desk, desperate to stop the ringing. The phone hits one of Mrs Blake's sturdy lace-up shoes and she inadvertently kicks it sideways out from under the desk. I reach out for it as it flies past, desperately jabbing at any old keys I can manage, instead of the only one I should be hitting – the *off* button – and for a minute I'm frozen with horror as an electronic voice informs the whole room, out loud:

'Voicemail has one new message. New message one: . . . . . .'

I'm far too disconcerted to ponder my terrible luck – that I must have not only answered the call, but turned the phone onto loudspeaker as it slid across the room. Instead, paralysed, not really believing that this is happening to me, I just sit on the floor staring at it, as the voice changes and the message is beamed out loud and clear:

'Katie. This is Harry. I'll come straight to the point. I've tried not to contact you. I've tried not to think about you – but it's no good. I need to hear your voice. I need to see you! You've got my number. Ring me . . .'

Finally, much too late, I pull myself together sufficiently to crawl after the phone, snap it off and just about find the self-control to refrain from hurling it out of the window. Mrs Blake is looking at me with a curious expression.

'Wrong number,' I tell her wretchedly.

I don't think I'll get the job.

He tries again the next day. I don't recognise his number from the caller display; it's been a while since I deleted it from my Contacts.

'Katie!' he begins, sounding relieved that I've answered.

'I was in an interview!' I say furiously. As if it was his fault. 'I won't get the bloody job now.'

'Sorry?'

'Yesterday. When you called. The phone went under the desk, and then I answered it instead of turning it off, and ...'

He's laughing!

'It's not funny,' I say petulantly.

'No. Sorry.'

But I can hear him still smothering a chuckle. The annoying thing is, it's making me want to laugh too.

'Anyway,' I continue, taking a deep breath and trying hard to stop myself from imagining him smiling. Imagining the way the smile would be reaching his eyes, the way his cheeks would be dimpling. What's the matter with me? 'What do you want?'

There. That was impressive, wasn't it?

Actually, it sounded rude and aggressive, but I can't afford to let my guard drop.

'Well,' he says, having taken a sharp breath at my rudeness and aggression. 'I *was* going to suggest we meet up for a drink.'

'No. I don't think it's a good idea.'

Short of just hanging up on him, I couldn't be a lot more discouraging, could I?

'That's what I wanted to talk to you about,' he persists. 'Why is it not a good idea? I thought we got on well in Ireland – didn't we? I know you've just broken up with your boyfriend. I just thought maybe we could stay friends, Katie. I'm not talking about ...' he laughs, 'having a *relationship* or anything!'

His laugh sends shivers down my spine. My resolve is weakening. Of course it'd be lovely to see him. Have a drink with him. Have him looking into my eyes with that warm, gentle, concerned smile that turned my knees to jelly ...

Shit! What am I *thinking*?

'I know you didn't want me to contact you so I've left it a while, Katie,' he's saying. 'As long as I could bear to.'

'So leave it a bit longer, Harry. In fact – please don't phone me again.'

There's a silence. He's not laughing any more. Part of me, ridiculously, wants to say I didn't mean it. But instead I keep thinking about how I need to be strong, and how seeing Harry is going to weaken me.

'I just wanted to ask how you were,' he says eventually.

'Thanks. I'm fine. I've moved, and I'm looking for a new job.' So you'll never find me, mister. 'And I might change my phone number,' I add for good measure.

'OK.' He sounds resigned. 'I get the message. If that's really what you want . . .'

'I'm sorry if you got the wrong impression, Harry.'

'I don't think I did,' he replies, so softly that I only just catch it.

I feel quite proud of myself when I hang up.

At least, I think that's what I'm feeling.

Jude phones me a few days later. She sounds happy.

'Still seeing Conor?' I ask her pointedly.

Of course she is. I'm pleased for her. How ironic that the cousin of someone I really want to avoid could turn out to be so perfect for my friend.

'He's been saying that maybe, God willing, we could make a trip over to England together next month after I get the plaster off,' she says, a bit tentatively, as if she's worried it's taking far too much for granted to even mention it.

'Oh!' I squeal. 'That'd be *so cool*, Jude! You can come and stay with me. I've got a sofa bed, and we can go for walks on the beach, and—'

'Well,' she interrupts me, sounding even more tentative, really quite cagey. 'To be honest, Katie, Conor has the idea for us to stay in London.'

For a minute, I don't grasp the significance. Stay in London? Maybe he wants to do the tourist bit – you know, visit the Tower, see the Crown Jewels. Take pictures of Big Ben.

'OK,' I say, trying not to feel hurt. 'That's fine, I can come up to London and meet you both, and we can go out together, do some clubs and stuff . . .'. And then I suddenly get it. 'Oh. You mean you're going to stay with his cousin.'

'With Harry, yes, we are so. He invited us, and Conor says 'twould be rude an' all, to turn it down, but sure Leigh-on-Sea is only just down the road, Katie. Sure we can see you every day, or every evening, and go out together, and . . .'

'With Harry.'

There's a silence. Then:

'Katie, Conor's told me that Harry's phoned you. I know he's after going out with you – any fool could see that, even when you were over in Ireland, he had the hots for you – and if it wasn't for the whole thing with Matt, I'd have said you had the hots for him too . . .'

'No, I *didn't*. I *haven't*! I don't want anything to do with anyone at the moment. I . . .'

'I know. Sure I understand that, of course I do, and so does Harry. Don't worry, Katie. I've told him he's not allowed to pester you or even so much as look at you when we meet up together.'

'And what did he say to that?' I ask, smiling despite myself.

'That he'd still rather have the opportunity to be with you for so much as five minutes, even if he's not allowed to look at you.'

I'm so taken aback by this, I can't even answer for a moment.

'I think he's got it pretty bad!' laughs Jude.

'Yeah, right,' I mutter, trying not to smile. 'Like he gets it bad for every bit of skirt on the planet, I suppose!'

I really don't want to see Harry. The thought of seeing him is making me feel quite shaky. But this isn't about what I want. It's about Jude, and her new, very lovely, very important relationship. I'm going to have to sacrifice my feelings for my friend's sake. It's out of my control. I can't do a thing about it.

ABOUT E-MAILS

To: <u>helen.fuller1965@aol.com</u>
From: <u>katieHalliday@hotmail.com</u>
Date: 22nd June 2005

Dear Helen

I can't tell you how excited I was to get your e-mail. Not as excited as Greg was, of course! He was practically dancing around the office when I got to work this morning. Not a pretty sight, as you can imagine. I pretended I didn't know what was up with him – just so that I could hear him say it out loud.

She's coming back. I took your advice and wrote to her, Katie. She's coming back in a couple of weeks' time! Thank you! Thank you for your very sensible advice. If only I'd listened to you sooner!

Yes, it does make a change for somebody to listen to my advice, I must say. All my efforts with you, nagging you by e-mail, was just water off a duck's back – but one letter from Himself, begging you to come back, has done the trick. Thank God! I felt like knocking your two heads together, if only you weren't too far away to do it. It wasn't till I told him I was leaving Bookshelf that he was shocked into getting in touch with you – and before you say it, no it *wasn't* just because he needs you back in the office now that I'm going! I think, though, that this kind of gave him the excuse he needed, to write to you. He wanted to, all along, but he just kept saying that you should be left alone to get on with your life.

Well, it's great to see Greg so happy, even if he does have a rather strange, stilted way of showing it. Like making me a cup of tea 'to celebrate' – anyone else would have suggested nipping down the pub. But it's just as well, really, as I'm off the booze these days.

So the plan is to have another couple of weeks in Australia to see a few of the sights, and then come back – yes? Great. Can't wait to hear all about it. Hope your brother isn't too upset that you're not staying permanently. Come on, Helen. Be honest. Reading between the lines of your e-mails, I get the impression you haven't really been enjoying living with him, his wife and their four 'horrible' kids. Yes, I think it's OK to be critical about your own niece and nephews – after all, you've never even met them before, it's not as though you're close, and having your handbag thrown out of the window and your mobile phone buried in the garden *isn't* just normal childhood mischief, whatever your sister-in-law says. And I know you're not that keen on dogs, so the Alsatian and the three puppies must be a bit of a trial. You'd have had to move out pretty soon and find a place of your own – and that would make it all too permanent.

Greg says I'm not to meet you at Heathrow, because he wants to. He wants you all to himself, I think! Hopefully he's planning a celebratory night out. Take my advice – for what it's worth. Don't let him take you for a nice cup of tea and a scone. Insist on nothing less than a slap-up four-course meal in a good restaurant. He can afford it. He needs to get out more. I bet he used to be more sociable in his old days in publishing. He's turned into a recluse since his divorce. You're going to make each other happy, my love – that's the thing. I'm so pleased for you!

You asked about my new job. Well, it's strange really. I was totally gobsmacked when Mrs Blake offered me the post. I think she must have felt sorry for me. Honestly, I couldn't have ballsed up the interview more if I tried. I told you what happened with the phone, didn't I. After that I just gave up – I reckoned there was no way she was going to give me the job so I relaxed and, bizarrely, we went into this kind of cosy chat about ourselves and I ended up sitting there for ages, with her telling me all about her ex-husband who left her for her *niece* of all things – totally gross – and how she bought the book-shop out of the money she got from the divorce settlement. She owns the shop outright. Then the niece left him (served him right!) and he got made redundant, couldn't pay the mortgage on the house they'd bought together and ended up in a squat with two drug addicts. Meanwhile she's doing very nicely, thank you, and every now and then she sends him a cheque – not very much, just enough to buy himself a few basic groceries. I asked her how she can bear to do it – I thought *how noble*. But no, she laughed and said she was doing it to humiliate him. To look at her, you wouldn't think she had it in her. Tough old cookie. And then she started asking about me, and before you knew it, we were actually laughing together about the phone call, and she was asking if Harry was my boyfriend and I told her ... well, I think I pretty well told her my whole life history. I felt really embarrassed afterwards – I mean, you just don't do that, do you – go to an interview and end up chatting to the employer about cancelling your wedding and being ditched over the phone by your boyfriend and all that stuff! So can you imagine how I felt when I got the letter offering me the job? Don't get me wrong – I'm really chuffed about it. She's offering me good money because she wants me to learn the business and gradually take over managing the shop while she looks after her other interests (she owns a couple of flats in Leigh and rents them out to people like me!), and then, eventually, she wants to retire altogether and have someone – hopefully me – manage the shop full-time. So yes, I'm very, very excited about it. Of course I'm sorry to be leaving Bookshelf – I finish there at the end of the month – but now you're coming back, Greg will manage fine. The latest temp has at least got a grasp of IT, can type and is a voracious reader so he's considering taking her on permanently. And you can both come and see me – my little flat is looking much nicer now that Emily and Sean have helped me paint all the walls in pastel colours. The dark green and brown were beginning to depress me. I love living at Leigh. I walk along the beach at weekends and dream of ... oh, well, I won't go on now about my dreams. I'll tell you about them when you come back!

Lots to catch up with, then. Looking forward to it!
Take care; watch out for those snakes and spiders!

Lots of love, Katie xx

To: HJCornwell@Goldsmith-Adams.co.uk
From: katieHalliday@hotmail.com
Date: 24th June 2005

Harry

I don't know how you got my e-mail address. Thank you for your good wishes about my new job.

I'm sorry you haven't been able to sleep. I don't agree that it's my fault. Maybe you should see your GP.

I suppose we will meet up when Jude and Conor come over.

Best
Katie

To: judith.barnard@ntl.ie
From: katieHalliday@hotmail.com
Date: 24th June 2005

Hi Jude

Thank you *very* much – *not* – for giving Harry my e-mail address. I thought I said no? You know very well I said no! I don't care how much he's been texting you, getting on your nerves going on about wanting to get in touch with me. Why do you think I changed my mobile number? Change yours, then, if he's annoying you that much!

It's bad enough that we'll be making a cosy little foursome when you come over to London. I don't want him e-mailing me telling me all about his sleepless nights. Like I give a shit! I have enough trouble sleeping myself, thank you very much.

Next time he asks you, tell him I've gone out to Australia with Helen. Or joined a Silent Order of nuns. That'll do it.

Talk soon.

L.O.L. Katie xx

PS: Sorry. I know he's Conor's cousin and everything but I keep telling you: I do *not* want to get involved.

To: judith.barnard@ntl.ie
From: katieHalliday@hotmail.com
Date: 24th June 2005

What do you mean, why not? How about – because I've just been dumped by one man and I'm not up for another bout of pain. If I was into self-flagellation I could just go out and buy myself a barbed-wire vest or a bed of nails. Or how about – because I just don't like him very much. Will that do?

x

To: judith.barnard@ntl.ie
From: katieHalliday@hotmail.com
Date: 24th June 2005

No, I didn't seem to like him well enough when we were in Kinsale! You're getting romantic notions all over the place, young lady, just because you're in LURVE yourself! Just because he's good-looking and charming and all that crap, doesn't mean I have to like him. And I don't.

Now, can we change the subject? How's Conor? xx

311

To: judith.barnard@ntl.ie
From: katieHalliday@hotmail.com
Date: 24th June 2005

Can't you leave it alone, Jude? Yes, sure, I'm sure Conor *has* told you what he told me – that Harry's always been *a bit of a one* with the girls, as you put it. And I'm very sure Harry has also said that he's had enough of all that and wants to settle down now. That's what they all say! Sorry – look, I'm just not interested – OK?

K xx

To: emily.furlong@virgin.net
From: katieHalliday@hotmail.com
Date: 29th June 2005

Help, Emily! I think I've upset Jude, and now she's not talking to me. I wish I'd never said anything, but I was getting irritated with all the stuff about Harry – why didn't I like him, he's desperate to see me again, why didn't I want to go out with him – Christ! I know he's Conor's cousin but that doesn't mean I have to shag him just to please Conor, does it? Anyway I've gone a bit over the top now and I think I've offended her, and she'll tell Conor and he'll be even more offended because I'm slagging off his cousin. You know what the Irish are like about their families. I suppose now neither of them will ever talk to me again.

It's been nearly a week and I keep e-mailing her and texting her and trying to phone her and she's not replying. They're coming over to London next week and now I suppose they won't want to see me. That's it; I've blown our friendship, over some stupid man. I'll never forgive myself. I want to die.

Katie

To: emily.furlong@virgin.net
From: katieHalliday@hotmail.com
Date: 29th June 2005

What do you mean, I'm acting like a drama queen? This is serious, Emily! Jude never ignores me like this. Can't you offer anything more helpful than Are you more worried about Jude or Harry? For God's sake! I couldn't give a shit about Harry. There are hundreds of good-looking, charming, sexy, funny men around just like him – in fact almost every bloke I see round the shops in Leigh reminds me of him so he's obviously not so very special. And, the whole point is – he's not a very nice person. Even Conor told me that! If Jude can't cope with me saying it, well, what can I do? Yes, OK, Jude's right – when we were in Ireland I actually thought he was really, really lovely – the way he looked after me that night, when I was ill, and crying, and everything. I nearly kissed him that night, Em – obviously under the influence of the alcohol and all the distress I was in, you know – but he seemed to be too much of a gentleman to take advantage of me. I admit it, I did like him. And I did really think he liked me. But I am *not* ready to start seeing someone again. And especially not a dangerous sexual predator with a reputation for humping and dumping. Who needs that just after being cast off by her fiancé in favour of some middle-aged adventuress?

So what do I do about Jude?

To: emily.furlong@virgin.net
From: katieHalliday@hotmail.com
Date: 29th June 2005

Well, thanks so much for your help. Yes, very funny. I am not in denial about anything, especially not about him.

Talk to you soon.

PS: What's all this about a barbecue at your place on Saturday? Special occasion, is it? What are we celebrating?

To: emily.furlong@virgin.net
From: katieHalliday@hotmail.com
Date: 29th June 2005

OH MY GOD!

You're getting *married?!!!!!*

ABOUT THE TRUTH

They look so happy. She's staring into his eyes as he stabs a chicken drumstick and drops it onto the barbecue. She's got this kind of radiant glow. I'm bloody sure, looking back now, that I didn't have it when I was planning to marry Matt. I think I had the hump most of the time.

'You OK?' Sean asks me, as he turns, fork in hand, to pick up his beer. 'Don't you want any wine?'

'No. I'm fine, thanks.' I force a grin. 'I'm just feeling a bit ...'

'What?' Emily comes over and links her arm through mine. 'What's up, honey?'

It's not what you think. I'm not jealous. God, no! I'm so glad, now, that I didn't get married. It would have been a disaster. Look at these two: they're so right for each other. I'm thrilled for them, I really am.

'Sure you're all right? You look a bit pale.'

'Yeah. It's nothing, probably just the sight of all that chicken and steak. Sorry, no offence intended about Sean's cooking, but I think I might become a vegetarian.'

'Sean!' shouts Emily. 'Stick another veggie-burger on!'

'Bloody hell!' he complains mildly. 'Half a dozen chickens and a cow have died in vain for you lot!'

Emily walks me into a shaded area round the side of the house, away from the heat of the barbecue, where we sit down in silence for a few minutes.

'That's better,' I admit. 'It was getting hot over there.'

It's a beautiful July evening, seven o'clock and still a perfect blue sky, only broken up by a few little cotton-wool-ball clouds like infant-school children draw in their pictures. When I left Leigh-on-Sea today to come over here, after finishing work in the bookshop, there were still families playing on the beach, children paddling in the sea (all right then, the estuary), and queues forming beside the ice-cream vans. This is how English summers should be, as I remember them from my childhood, looking back through those rosy-coloured lenses that we all develop.

'I'm glad it hasn't put you off getting married, Em, you know – my disaster.'

'No. If anything, it made me and Sean talk about the whole marriage thing, and decide we were definitely up for it. You and Matt had doubts. Sean and I realised we haven't. Not a single one. We're positive this is right for us.' She laughs suddenly and adds, 'I don't think I'll have the hen party in Dublin, though. Might be jinxed!'

'You're right there!' I give her a hug. 'I'm so happy for you!'

'I know. Thank you, love. And you *will* be my bridesmaid, won't you? Of course?'

'Of course! Try and stop me! When's the big day going to be, anyway?'

'At the end of the year. We don't want to wait, now we've made up our minds. It's going to be a bit frantic, getting it all organised, but we're thinking a Christmas or New Year wedding might be nice. What do you think?'

'Oh! That soon!' I glance back over at the barbecue. 'Whoops! Better get a bucket of water, Em – Sean's just set fire to the kebabs!'

We both make a dash for the kitchen, laughing, and it's not till halfway through eating the burnt kebabs and veggie-burgers that she asks me again.

'So – promise you'll be my bridesmaid? You haven't got anything else more important planned around Christmas time?' she adds, teasing.

'Of course not. What could I possibly have planned that's more important than your wedding?' I say with a smile. 'Sean – you've cooked these veggie-burgers in the fat from the sausages and they're absolutely gross!'

The new job's going well. I've been there a week now, and I'm surprised at how busy it is; especially on Saturdays, of course. People pass the shop on their way to the supermarket or the post office and come in to browse. I've been helping with the window display today as there's a new local history book that's just been published, and we're giving it prominence to attract passing residents and visitors. Of course, this time of year people are looking for holiday reading – paperback romances to take with them in their suitcases and read while they're lying on the beach. Lucky devils; my holiday – *honeymoon* – to the Caribbean was cancelled along with the wedding, and I don't think I'll be able to afford anything else this year. I've been able to give these customers quite a bit of advice about the latest paperback releases of course, and Mrs Blake's been smiling a lot and telling me how glad she is that I've joined her. Poor thing, I think she's had a hard time of it, running the shop on her own.

'It's nice to have some young company, dear,' she says. 'You remind me of my daughter.'

Her daughter, tragically, died about ten years ago in an accident, and I think she's pretty lonely, what with the business of the husband and the niece and all. She's quite a sweetie, really, and when the shop's quiet and we have time to chat over a cup of tea, I find myself confiding stuff to her, too, like she's my surrogate mum. Stuff that might make my own mum freak out a bit too much. Mrs Blake, who keeps saying *Call me Felicity, dear*, though I feel a bit awkward about it really since she doesn't look anything like a Felicity and I'm worried I might giggle when I say it – *Felicity* doesn't seem to turn a hair, no matter what I tell her, and it's somehow kind of restful, sitting in the little shop surrounded by all the books and the silence of their closed covers. Like telling things to your priest, I suppose, in the confessional. I've only known her for five minutes but I feel better already for talking to her.

Jude finally phones me, two days before she's due to arrive in London. I'd given up hope.

'I thought you were never going to speak to me again.'

'Don't be so bloody silly. Sure I just had a lot on me plate, for God's sake.'

I'm not going to argue. But whatever was on her plate in the past, she never ignored my texts and e-mails – did she?

I'm meeting her, with Conor and *Harry*, at a pub near his flat. I've travelled up on the train after work; it's been a hot day again and I'm feeling tense and a bit irritable. Someone steps on my toe accidentally as I'm at the bar, getting myself a drink, and I nearly smack him one.

'Sorry!' he says. 'Oh – watch out!' I've nearly spilt my orange-and-lemonade on him, too. And then: 'Katie!'

Just to put the lid on it – it's *him*.

We sit at a table on the crowded little patio outside the pub, to wait for the others. He's wearing office clothes: a light grey suit and blue shirt. He throws the jacket over the back of his chair, loosens his collar and takes a long gulp of his beer. He looks even better than I remember. I have to bury my face in my orange-and-lemonade and fight hard to stay in control. To remember Conor's warnings about him, and forget the night he nursed me on the sofa.

'You off the booze again?' he asks, smiling lazily into my eyes.

'Yes.'

There's a silence. He doesn't look at all awkward, but I certainly feel it.

'Anyway, it's nice to see you again. I know you didn't *want* to see me, but ...'

'This is only because of Jude,' I retort, a bit too sharply. 'I'm here for her, and Conor. That's all.'

'OK. If that's how you feel. But let's not make it un-comfortable for them, eh?'

'Of course not. I do know how to be polite!'

'Good. All right, then, Miss Politeness. How's the new job going?'

He's laughing at me. I wish he wouldn't, the bastard. It's making me want to smile.

'It's going well, thank you. I didn't like commuting back to Romford after I moved. The shop's just round the corner from where I live now and my boss is very nice.' God, this is purgatory. I'm talking like someone being interviewed on the radio. I'll never be able to relax in his company. I wish he wouldn't keep looking at me as if he's going to burst out laughing any minute. 'Where are Jude and Conor?' I add desperately.

'On their way. I picked them up from the airport and dropped them at my flat while I went back to the office to finish a few things off. They've only got to walk five minutes down the road. They should be here any time now ...'

'Good.'

'Katie ...'

'Please. Let's just keep it ... polite.'

'But I need to tell you something.'

'I don't think I want to hear it.'

'You don't know what it is yet!' He's smiling at me again. 'Listen. What Conor told you, in Kinsale—'

'Was none of my business.'

'But look – I never pretended to be an angel, exactly.' He's not smiling now. He's leaning forward across the table, looking at me earnestly. I don't like that earnest look. I don't trust it. 'OK, so perhaps I haven't always treated my girl-friends fantastically well. I'm not an Irish Catholic like my cousin, brought up to ... to treat women like you treat your mother, and if you don't you have to marry them. I've played around a bit. But I've had enough of it. I don't want to do that any more.'

'Just like that? Suddenly you're different?'

'Yes.' He looks straight into my eyes. 'Suddenly.'

'Yeah, right.'

'I just wanted you to understand, Katie ...'

'What? Like I said, it's none of my business what you do, and there's nothing for me to understand ...'

And thank God. Here are Jude and Conor.

It's amazing. The transformation of Judith Barnard is absolutely incredible. She's like a completely different person – confident, happy, laughing, full of life and enthusiasm. Any fool can see she's in love.

There seems to be a lot of it about.

'Katie!' she cries, grabbing me and hugging me hard. 'Sure it's great to see you looking so ...'

Yes, you might well tail off a bit there. So pale, sick and tired-looking? Don't beat about the bush.

'Lovely to see you, too, looking so loved-up and happy!' I tease her. 'How's it going?'

'It's going great, thanks! Brilliant!' She sits down next to me and pulls her chair closer. 'Look, Katie, first off I'm sorry I took a while to get back to you. About himself over there,' she adds in a whisper.

'What about him?'

'It was difficult to explain over the phone, or in an e-mail. But Harry ...' she glances over at the two guys, who are chatting together about the comparative price of a pint of Guinness in London and in Cork. 'Look, I know what Conor told you about him. But Harry's been back over to Kinsale for a weekend since you were there, and even Conor admits he's never seen such a change in anyone. He spent the whole time talking about you. Never looked at another girl – didn't even want to go out for a jar or two with Conor. Just moped around, asking me all kind of questions about you.'

'Questions?' I can hardly talk for the hammering of my heart. 'What kind of questions?'

She sighs.

'You know. What you were like when you were a little girl. What your favourite colour is. Whether you like rock music, or horror films, or holidays in the sun. Katie – he's totally crazy about you. I don't think he'd mess you around. But how are you ever going to know, if you don't give him a chance?'

'I don't *want* to give him a chance, Jude. I've had enough of men, at the moment, and I just need to be on my own for a while. I've ... got my reasons.'

She looks at me for a moment with her head on one side.

'OK, Katie. So, do you want to tell me?'

Of course I do. This is Jude, after all: my oldest, dearest friend in the whole wide world. The only person I dared to tell about my wedding being cancelled. I've always told her everything – and she's always supported me.

This time isn't going to be any different.

ABOUT THE FUTURE

How does it happen? How do we move from a point of complete resolution, to beginning to have doubts, to caving in catastrophically? I suppose, looking back, perhaps I always knew I would change my mind eventually and give in. I was always going to go out with Harry in the end; I just needed time.

We see a lot of each other over the weekend that Jude and Conor are over. To be fair to him, he couldn't be nicer. He's kind, friendly, polite, charming; but he keeps his distance. He doesn't put any pressure on me – other than the smiles he gives me, the way he catches my eye and holds my gaze, the way he touches my hand briefly without making a big deal of it. I begin to feel a bit like an iceberg – on the surface I'm gradually thawing but there's a huge frozen mass of me hidden from sight. It's going to take a bit more than friendly smiles to get this shifted.

After Jude and Conor go back to Ireland, he stays in contact with me. Again, it's light, friendly, bantering stuff but there's an underlying message all the time: *So – you still don't fancy going out for a drink one evening? Just as friends? As we seem to be getting on so well?*

It's another month before I finally agree to a date, and then only on condition that it's strictly platonic. I tell myself that it's to stop him keeping on at me, but I know I'm kidding myself. I can't wait to see him again – but just as a friend, you understand.

He comes over to Leigh-on-Sea on a Sunday and we go out for a pub lunch. He's not drinking.

'I want to stay completely sober,' he says so solemnly that

321

it makes me laugh, 'So that I can remember every moment – every single detail, every word you say.'

'Don't be daft!'

Nice, though, isn't it? It's flattery, of course, and I'm not getting taken in by it. But it's been ages since I've been taken out, treated like I'm somebody special, or had someone looking at me as if they'd found what they'd spent their whole life searching for.

'If I promise not to kiss you,' he says when he takes me home afterwards, 'can I come in for coffee? I don't want to leave you yet. I'm greedy. I want another half an hour.'

'If you promise not to kiss me,' I say, going back on all my resolves, 'then I'll be very disappointed and it will have been a complete waste of time coming in for a coffee. Won't it?'

What am I saying? Have I completely lost the plot? This is not turning out to be the platonic date I insisted on. But after the cup of coffee, that's actually all we do – kiss. A lovely, slow, stomach-weakening, head-spinning, mind-blowing kiss. Then he stops, holds me for a while and we smile at each other as if we both know a secret but we're not going to talk about it. He's behaving like an old-fashioned gentleman: not at all what I was expecting. It's strange – a relief, but frustrating, all at the same time. I'm beginning to think he's trying to prove something to me.

We agree to go out again a few days later, to the cinema. The next weekend we go to a Chinese restaurant on the Saturday night, and on the Sunday he comes over to my place and I cook him a meal. By the end of the third week we're phoning each other on the days we don't see each other, and I know I haven't got a chance in hell of turning back. It's all too late. I've got all the symptoms. I've stopped trying to deny it. He's gorgeous; I've always thought he was gorgeous, and now I'm walking around grinning from ear to ear, just thinking about the fact that we're finally going out together. But I need to tell him something quickly – because he's probably going to finish with me when I do. And the longer I leave it, the more it's going to hurt.

I nearly tell him during the next week.

Then I *very* nearly tell him during the week after that.

322

Then a couple of times during the following week, I get really close to telling him but I change my mind at the last minute.

On the Sunday of the week after that, we're snuggled on my sofa together, watching a DVD, and I know I have to say something now. I can't leave it any longer. He's going to be upset that I haven't told him sooner. I don't want that.

'Harry.' It comes out in a whisper. A trembly, frightened whisper. 'I need to tell you ...'

'Ssh. It's all right,' he whispers back. 'I know.'

Tenderly, ever so tenderly, he places both hands over my stomach, where I'm just beginning, very slightly, to show a gentle little bulge.

'When's it due?'

My eyes suddenly fill up with tears. 'January. When did you realise?'

'Katie – I might not be an expert on these things, but did you really think I wouldn't notice? First you were feeling sick and giving up alcohol. Then you started having cravings for strange things ...'

'Peppermint seaside rock,' I admit. 'I've kept the sweet-shop in Leigh from going out of business.'

'And you're emotional, and you get tired easily, and ...'

'But I'm always like that!' I try to smile through my tears.

'And Emily told me.'

'Oh!!' I sit up and push him off the sofa, throwing a cushion after him. 'She said she wouldn't! I thought you were being *observant* and loving, and caring ...'

Whoops. That wasn't really what I meant to say.

'I am being,' he says, quietly, sitting next to me again and putting both arms round me. 'I always will be.'

I pretend I haven't heard him. I don't think I dare to believe him. *Always?* That's a scary word.

'I had to tell Emily first. She wanted me to be a brides-maid when I was about eight months pregnant. She'd have had to buy a bridesmaid dress to fit an elephant and have the midwife standing by at the reception.'

He laughs.

'I know. She told me that's why they've put the wedding

323

back by a month. Now we'll have to push the pram down the aisle behind the bride.'

'*We*?'

He looks at me very, very seriously.

'Unless he . . . Matt . . . ?'

The question hangs in the air between us, unfinished. I need to tell him the whole story. It's only fair.

I didn't see Matt until about a week after we got back from Ireland. We'd had conversations on the phone – if you can call them conversations – terse, angry exchanges, normally finishing with me banging down the receiver. We were getting nowhere. He was trying to apologise, I wasn't having any of it. He was trying to explain, I was refusing to listen. He was attempting to broach the subject of the flat, the mortgage, the bills, the furniture, and I would just start crying. In the end, he sent me a text message:

We need to sort this out. Whatever; it has to be done. When shall I come round?

Perhaps it was the brusqueness of the simple stated fact, unadulterated by apologies, arguments, or emotion, that helped me to accept it better. It was a Saturday. I sent a message back:

OK. Come round now.

I behaved with surprisingly civility. I think he was as surprised at this as I was. I made him coffee. We sat at the kitchen table and went through paperwork together. I became an automaton. This wasn't anything to do with splitting up from the love of my life, breaking up our home, breaking my heart: it was closing a business transaction. I tried not to look at Matt as we discussed putting the flat on the market and he made lists of the things he was taking. I was calm, I was sensible, I was in control. I was going to get through this without it killing me.

He broke first.

'Katie . . .' he said, suddenly and with a terrible crack in his voice. 'Katie, please don't do this.'

'Do? I'm not doing anything. I just want to get through this and . . .'

And get you out of my life. The quicker the better.

'I know I've hurt you ...'

'Oh! Oh, you don't say! Well done!' I was shuffling papers, still not looking up at him. 'I don't want to have this conversation. Let's just get on, *please*.'

'Can we not get over this? Try? Finish as friends?'

Now I looked up. *Friends?* The anger that I'd been trying to keep the lid on bubbled up to the surface again.

'How can you *say* that to me?' I spat across the table at him. 'You ... you've done this to me, you're ruining my life, and you dare to say ...'

'I don't think I am,' he said very softly.

'What?'

'I don't think I'm ruining your life. I know I've handled it badly. It wasn't easy for me either ...'

'Well, poor you!' I was shouting now. Fuck! I was crying too. I so did *not* want to cry.

'But I think what we're doing is the right thing, Katie – for both of us. I think we both knew it already. You knew it, or you wouldn't have called off the wedding. Be honest with yourself.'

With myself.

That was the whole point, wasn't it. It didn't matter about anyone else. I'd been playing the heartbroken deserted bride, eaten up with misery and pain – but how honest was I being, really? Yes, it had been a shock. It had hurt to be dumped like that; as he said, Matt had handled it badly. But would I have been eyeing up another man, even while I was still in Ireland, if I was really so devastated? Would I have been cheerfully trotting off on my non-hen-weekend if cancelling the wedding had been as upsetting as it should have been? Come to that, would I have had the sort of doubts I was already having, long before the wedding ... the doubts about our relationship that actually prompted me to imagine that getting married might make everything right again?

Jesus! How long had I been lying to myself? This relationship should have finished long before now. If I hadn't been so determined to hang onto it, we'd both have been saved a lot of grief.

'Don't cry, Katie,' said Matt, but I couldn't stop, now. His voice sounded like it was coming from a long way away. I could hear him, through the waterfall of my tears, pleading with me not to be upset, everything was going to be OK, he'd sort it all out, he was sorry, he was sorry, he was *sorry* ...

He was crying too. He was holding me now, wiping away my tears, brushing my cheeks with his lips. Making it all feel better. There was a moment, just a fraction of a second, when he held me slightly apart from him, looked into my eyes and I saw the question in them – *Is this sensible?* – when I could have stopped. And then he was kissing me and it felt so right, so comforting and nice and *familiar*. And I thought: *One last time. Why not?*

Afterwards, I remembered why not. He wasn't my boyfriend any more. He was with someone else. And I'd stopped taking the Pill.

'I hope that wasn't a mistake,' he said gently as I was getting dressed.

'I hope so, too.' Surely I couldn't be that unlucky? There was the morning-after pill, of course, but ...

Was I already thinking that perhaps a mistake wouldn't be such a bad thing?

'I'll always love you, Katie. You know? In my way. Just because it hasn't worked out ...'

'Ssh. You don't need to say that. You were right. It's over, and we're moving on.'

I left it to chance. And two weeks later, I knew I was pregnant. And I knew that, for me, it was the best thing that could have happened.

'Matt's not going to be involved,' I'm telling Harry now. 'Of course, he's going to contribute financially. But he never wanted children, and obviously this wasn't planned. Look, I know I said I'd decided I wanted a baby, but getting pregnant – like this – it was the last thing on my mind. It's kind of ... like it was meant to be.' I look up at him and shrug. 'Matt and Claire want to travel the world. Her children are nearly grown up and babies aren't exactly going to fit into the lifestyle they've got in mind – backpacking down the Amazon and trekking in the foothills of the Andes.

She's been terribly upset with Matt about this baby – can you imagine?'

He shrugs. 'I wouldn't have expected you to care about her being upset.'

'I don't know. To be fair, I don't think he lied to me: I don't think they actually slept together until after he ... finished with me. She didn't exactly steal him from me.'

'And now she won't trust him again. She'll be wondering if he's going to keep on coming back to you.'

'Harry.' I look at him seriously. I know he doesn't care what some unknown Claire thinks about that possibility. He's feeling insecure himself! 'Harry, there is *no* chance of Matt coming back to me. Not ever again. Believe me!'

'Well, then – you believe *this*, Katie: I'm going to be around for you now. You and the baby.'

'Don't. Don't make any promises, Harry, please. I couldn't bear it. I'm looking forward to having this baby and I'm happy to bring it up on my own. Mum and Lisa are both so excited – I've got ready-made babysitters there, whenever I want them. And Mrs Blake, Felicity, is going to help me. She's offered to have the baby while I run the shop. It's all going to be fine. I ... I don't need anyone else.'

'Maybe you don't,' he agrees, giving me another kiss. 'But if it's OK with you, I think I'll stick around and see if you change your mind. If you don't want me to make any promises, Katie, I won't. I understand what you've been through this year. I'm not rushing you. But I just need to know one thing.'

One thing?

I don't like the sound of this. It sounds too serious. I don't want to make the same mistakes all over again. I think I'm falling in love with Harry – but look what a complete idiot I've been about love, all my life. I've got it wrong. I've confused it with romance. I'm still not sure I understand the difference. I need to take this slowly, see how it goes, see how we get on as friends, lovers, hopefully both. But this time I've got something else, or rather *someone* else, to consider. My baby will have to come first. I can't promise anything, to anyone, until after he's born. Maybe not till he's started school. Or not till he's at college. Maybe when he's fulfilled his potential, become an airline pilot, or a brain surgeon, or a university lecturer. Maybe not ever.

'What? What's the one thing you need to know?' I ask warily.

'That wedding dress. The one your sister made you. Is it still hanging in the wardrobe in her spare room?'

He's grinning.

'Piss off!' I shout. We both burst out laughing at the same time. 'No! I am *not* wearing that dress! Not ever! Not for anybody! She can sell it! It's unlucky! I hate it! I never wanted to wear it in the first place! In fact, if I ever decide to get married again – if I *ever* get that brave, or that stupid, or that ...'

'Certain?' he suggests, smiling.

'Whatever ...' I agree, grudgingly, thinking briefly of Emily and Sean. 'If that day arrives, I'm sticking to my guns this time, and wearing my jeans.'

'If they ever fit you again,' he teases, patting my tummy gently.

And I have to admit, at the moment, it's as unlikely a possibility as me getting married.

ABOUT HAPPINESS

There's something stirring and exciting about this music, I don't care what anyone says. As soon as it starts up, I feel the flicker of electricity in the air. I can imagine the anticipation inside the church. Rows of friends, sitting straighter in their seats, looking over their shoulders, grinning to each other. Mothers, aunties and grandparents swallowing back lumps in their throats, getting their hankies ready for the emotional moment of that first sight of the bride stepping down the aisle.

'Come on then, sweet'eart,' says Emily's dad. He's a big man with a deep gruff voice. I used to be a bit nervous of him many years ago when I first met him, because he looks like he beats people up for a living. But I catch a wobble in his voice as he adds, 'Let's get this show on the road,' and leads his only child into the church for her wedding.

I'm walking behind them with Emily's cousin Laura who's the other bridesmaid. It's a cold, bright afternoon in early February and we're wearing warm, dark red dresses with just a few flowers in our hair. It's enough. It's fine. I did worry about whether I'd get into the dress after Thomas was born, but I needn't have done: breastfeeding a hungry baby every three or four hours seems to have acted like an automatic crash diet and Harry keeps telling me that motherhood must suit me because I look better than ever. Of course, he's biased. He loves me.

There he is, on his feet near the front of the church, turning round – supposedly to look at the bride like everyone else – but his eyes seek out mine instead and I find myself smiling straight back at him. At Harry, and at my baby son, cradled fast asleep in his arms. My man, with my child.

When I think about how my life has turned around, it almost makes my head spin. Was I really planning to marry Matt such a short time ago? I'm watching him now. He's the best man, standing at the front of the church with the bridegroom. He steps to one side as the bride approaches, and I see him give an encouraging squeeze to Sean's arm and a smile of approval to Emily. He's a good guy. I'm glad we're going to stay in touch – for Thomas's sake. Despite everything he said, he has been round to see him since he was born a month ago – only the once, mind you, and he didn't want to hold him – but I noticed something flicker across his face when I referred to him as *Daddy*. It may just have been irritation, of course. We'll see. I realise the fact of the baby has put a strain on his relationship with Claire, and, strangely enough, I do want them to be happy. I think it comes from being so happy myself.

Laura and I go to our own seats while the vicar starts the wedding service.

Dearly beloved ... we are gathered here together ...

Yes, we are. All *my* dearly beloved are gathered here today. Jude and Conor are over from Ireland. There's a lot of speculation amongst Emily, Sean, Harry and myself that they're going to be the next couple planning a trip down the aisle. They've even been making very clucky noises over Thomas's cot.

I sneak a glance a couple of rows back, where Mum's sitting between Auntie Joyce and Lisa. Lisa's got her arm tucked through the arm of the man sitting next to her and looks as though she's melting into him. Andy. She might still be dithering over whether he's *The One*, but from where I'm sitting, he's certainly doing a good impression of it. The children apparently like him, he's talking about marrying her as soon as the divorce is through, and she's obviously crazy about him. Why's she still hesitating?

But then, I'm a good one to talk, aren't I?

My gaze shifts to Mum. She looks radiant in a new cream dress and navy blue jacket. I thought this wedding might upset her by bringing back memories of the one I cancelled but she's smiling and serene and I suddenly realise: she looks happy. She *is* happy. This thought makes me smile too, as I turn back to concentrate on the wedding service.

I found out about Mum at Emily's hen party. Emily wanted it as close as possible to the wedding date so that Jude could be here for both. That suited me fine, as it gave me a bit of time to recover from the birth. I'd spent Christmas at Mum's, with the whole family fussing round me because I was so hugely pregnant and apparently incapable of doing anything, and since Thomas had arrived, two weeks early on the second of January, I'd been floating around at home in a haze of hormones and confusion, being waited on and helped by a constant stream of visitors: Mum, Joyce, Lisa and the children, Emily and Sean, Helen and Greg, Felicity Blake, various neighbours from my street, and of course Harry. It was a good thing I'd had so much help, as I barely knew which end of the baby was up to begin with, but by now I was feeling calmer, rested and in control.

Of course, despite my pregnancy dopiness, I'd noticed something about Mum over Christmas. She wasn't drinking at all: not the customary pre-Christmas-dinner sherry, not a single glass of wine with dinner, not a brandy or a port afterwards. Because I wasn't drinking myself, it took a while to sink in that nobody was. There was water on the dinner table, and a fruit juice punch in the evening. There was a lot of laughter and merriment – but no booze.

'She's doing very well,' agreed Lisa when I mentioned it to her. 'Her AA group really seems to be helping.'

'You're looking great!' I told Mum. 'Younger than ever.'

'Thank you, dear. I do feel better these days.' She looked away, and then added, quietly, 'I've got my self-respect back.'

I gave her a hug.

'Well done. We're all very proud of you.'

'Oh, but I haven't achieved anything. It isn't over. It's an ongoing battle, you see. You know what they say: One day at a time.'

'And you're achieving *that*. No wonder you feel better.'

The hen evening was at a pub near Emily's place, two days before the wedding. I drove over during the day and left

Thomas with Mum. It seemed strange, getting dressed up to go out, putting on make-up and high heels and pretending I was still the same young, free, single girl I was before the second of January, when in fact I was now the mother of this tiny boy who depended on me completely. Gone were the days when I could roll home drunk in the early hours of the morning and spend the next day in bed with a hangover. I smiled as I bent to kiss my sleeping baby son goodbye. I wouldn't change a thing!

There was only a small group of us in the pub: Emily; her mum and cousin; Karen and Suze; three or four of Emily's friends from work; Jude, Lisa and myself. Emily had been determined that this would be a quiet, low-key evening.

'Katie's weekend in Dublin was more than enough for anyone,' she said jokingly.

'This is more like Mum's famous hen night at Southend!' commented Lisa, which was greeted by a chorus of groans.

'Not funny,' I pointed out. 'Not now we know how it ended up.'

'That's true. Your poor mum,' said Emily sadly.

'Not so poor, now, actually,' smiled Lisa.

'No,' I agreed. 'She looks so much better – happier – she says she's got back her self respect now that she's not drinking ...'

For a moment everyone looked down warily at the wine glasses in their hands. I chuckled and took another gulp of my orange juice.

'It doesn't do you any good, you know, girls!' I teased.

'Will you listen to the cheek of her, sanctimonious madam, just because she can't have a glass or two herself!' exclaimed Jude.

'Maybe we *should* all cut down a bit?' pondered Lisa.

'Nah!' retorted Emily, knocking back the contents of her glass and slamming it down on the table. 'Not tonight! Tonight's my hen night and we're all getting sozzled. Apart from Katie, of course. Can't have my godchild being breast-fed second-hand white wine, can we, now?'

'And anyway,' added Lisa after everyone had followed suit and emptied their glasses, 'there's more to the new perky, happy Mum than meets the eye.'

'How d'you mean?'

'You really haven't noticed, have you! For God's sake – I know you're all caught up in the throes of new mother-hood ...'

'And new *lurve*-hood,' added Emily with a glint in her eye.

'But you must be going in and out of Mum's house with your eyes and your ears closed!'

'Why? What's going on?'

'She dresses up to the nines to go out to her AA meet-ings.'

'So? I'm pleased for her. It's good that she's taking an interest in her appearance again. Now that she's not drink-ing ...'

'And she's on the phone all the time, giggling and going all pink and excited like a teenager.'

'Yes. I *had* noticed that. I'm glad she's in touch with her friends again ...'

'*Katie*! She's got a *boyfriend*.'

My mum – a boyfriend?

'Close your mouth, Katie! You'll start dribbling in a minute,' laughed Karen.

'But – I can't believe it!' I gulped. 'I mean – she hates men! She never wants anything to do with them.'

'Well, she seems to have changed her mind since she met Bob,' said Lisa meaningfully.

'Who the bloody hell's Bob?'

And what are his intentions towards my mother?

'He's a member of her group. A widower. He seems really nice ...'

'You've met him?' I stared at Lisa accusingly. 'You never said!'

'Look, I've only just met him the other day – and only because he happened to call round when I was there. She hasn't said anything to you yet because she thinks you've got enough on your plate with the baby. Didn't want to worry you.'

'Well, it *has* worried me. I mean, what do we know about him? How old is he? Where does he live? What did his wife die of? He could have bumped her off for all we know ...'

'Katie!' exclaimed Lisa, laughing out loud. 'Give it a rest! She's dating this guy – not marrying him. Let her be happy!'

'Lisa's right, Katie,' Jude soothed me. 'Sure we all have to take a chance on being happy, do we not, so?'

I looked around at them all: my lovely bride-to-be, Emily, who was taking her chance in getting married, despite my experience, despite all the statistics about break-ups and separations, divorces and misery; my oldest friend Jude, who seemed like a different person since she'd fallen for Conor; my sister Lisa, who'd taken the plunge and got out of her loveless marriage; they were all making a bid for happiness in one way or another. Why shouldn't Mum do the same?

'Here's to happiness,' I said, raising my orange-juice glass. I smiled around the table at them all. 'Here's to friends, and families ... and lovers!'

'Especially the lovers!' muttered Jude with a growl, making us all laugh again.

'And for God's sake, somebody, get another round in – how can we drink a toast with empty glasses!' said Suze irritably. 'Is this a hen party or a fucking wake?'

We've got to the part where the vicar tells the groom he can kiss the bride. They're smiling at each other in a way that somehow makes me ache inside. Will that ever be me? Will I ever actually do it one day – walk up that aisle, make those promises, walk back out of the church arm in arm with my own new husband the way Emily is now, grinning at the congregation, happy and secure and *married*?

I don't know. I think it's still what I want – eventually. It's the ultimate dream – one man, one love, for the rest of my life. I catch Harry's eye again as I follow the bride past the end of his pew. He's smiling at me and I feel a rush of love for him. Maybe, after all, it'll come true for me. It happens in the books I read; it can happen in real life – and perhaps, you know, I'm still a romantic at heart. And what a bizarre tale it would be to tell my grandchildren one day: how I met my future husband on my own hen weekend.

A Dangerous Dress
Julia Holden

Every woman deserves a dangerous dress…

Among the clothes that Jane Stuart inherited from her late grandmother is a gorgeous – and dangerously sexy – Parisian flapper dress. It's a dress so beautiful that it makes Jane wonder if her grandmother had a secret life before settling down in the small town where Jane now lives.

But unbeknown to Jane, the dress has come to the attention of a movie director looking for the perfect outfit for his leading lady to wear in the finale of his 1920s-set movie. Stuck in a dead-end job since college, Jane's been waiting for her life to start. Now she's been given the opportunity to follow in her grandmother's footsteps all the way to Paris, where love and excitement await her if she's brave enough…

'Julia Holden is addictive…' Meg Cabot

Wedding Belles
Zoë Barnes

Nothing is going to go wrong with Belle Craine's dream wedding to Kieran. Her mum won't let it. Unfortunately, nobody's told an Australian girl called Mona Starr, who turns up on the Craines' doorstep without warning and announces that she's Belle's long-lost half-sister. It's bad enough, but Belle also has to face the fact that her fiancé, Kieran, is spending an awful lot of time with ex-model Mona – a fact which her teenage sister, Jax, delights in pointing out.

Is Belle being paranoid, or has she got a fight on her hands if she wants to keep her man? And more to the point: is he worth fighting for?

'Funky fun chick lit' *OK Magazine*

Second Sight
Amanda Quick

It isn't as though attractive widow Venetia Jones doesn't have enough problems. She's worked hard to become a fashionable photographer catering to Victorian Society's elite. Her career has enabled her to provide a comfortable living for her brother, sister and elderly aunt.

Disaster looms, however. Venetia has some closely held secrets, not the least of which is her uncanny psychic ability. Now her life is in danger because she has viewed the unique aura of a killer fleeing the scene of his crime. But the really unsettling news is that her conveniently dead husband has just returned from the grave…

'A fun read…' *Bella*

Lord Perfect
Loretta Chase

Tall, dark, and handsome, the heir to the Earl of Hargate, Benedict Carsington, is known for his impeccable manners and good breeding. In the eyes of the Ton, he's practically perfect...

Bathsheba Wingate belongs to the rotten branch of the DeLucey family: a notorious bunch of liars, frauds and swindlers. Small wonder her husband's high-born family disowned him. Now widowed, Bathsheba is determined to give her young daughter a proper upbringing.

Only Bathsheba's hoyden daughter has other ideas: luring Benedict's precocious nephew into a quest for a legendary treasure. To recover the would-be knights errant, Benedict and Bathsheba must embark on a rescue mission that puts them in dangerous, intimate proximity. Fortunately, Benedict is in perfect control – despite his sudden mad desire to break all of the rules of polite society...

Lord Perfect **is part of a witty and romantic quartet of Regency adventures concerning the Carsington family.**

The Dream Hunter
Sherrilyn Kenyon

In the ethereal world of dreams there are champions who fight to protect the dreamer and there are demons who prey on them ...

Arik is such a predator. Condemned by the gods to live for eternity without emotions, Arik can only feel when he's in the dreams of others. Now, after thousands of years, he's finally found a dreamer whose vivid mind can fill his emptiness.

Dr. Megeara Kafieri made a reluctant promise to her dying father that she would salvage his reputation by proving his life-long belief that Atlantis is real. But frustration and bad luck dog her every step. Especially the day they find a stranger floating in the sea. His is a face she's seen many times ... in her dreams.

What she doesn't know is that Arik has made a pact with the god Hades: in exchange for two weeks as a mortal man, he must return to Olympus with a human soul. Megeara's soul.

Jewels of the Sun
Nora Roberts

Determined to re-evaluate her life, Jude Murray flees her complicated life in Chicago to take refuge in a beautiful cottage in the picturesque village of Ardmore in Ireland. Surrounded by the beautiful scenery and refreshed by the more relaxed lifestyle, Jude finds herself fascinated by the local folklore. Even her cottage seems to have a resident ghost and Jude decides to embark on a personal research project to find out more.

Finally back home in Ireland after years of travelling, Aidan Gallagher is also something of a expert when it comes to his country's haunting myths. He's returned to devote himself to managing the family business. But in Jude Murray he sees a woman who can soothe his heart and stir his blood. And he begins to share the legends of the land with her – while they create a passionate history of their own...

Jewels of the Sun **is part of the enchanting Irish trilogy; other titles in this series are** *Tears of the Moon* **and** *Heart of the Sea.*

Cover of Night
Linda Howard

Cate Nightingale owns and operates a struggling guest house in a small community; occasionally enlisting the help of Cal Harris, the shy, enigmatic local handyman.

To Cate's shock, Cal proves much bolder than expected when a trio of thugs invades her home, demanding the possessions of a guest who vanished some days before. Though Cal manages to run off the intruders, the men soon regroup and shut down phone access in the village, holding its citizens hostage.

In a desperate bid for survival, Cate and Cal strike out on their own, determined to solicit help from a neighboring town. But as Cate witnesses Cal's astonishing evolution from reticent carpenter to fearless protector, she begins to wonder if there is more to Cal than meets the eye ...

The Adultery Diet
Eva Cassady

Like many women her age, Eva Cassady has tried – and failed – every diet under the sun – but nothing has concentrated her efforts more than the possibility of an affair with an old flame.

The weight begins to fall off, and Eva realises that her email flirtation with Michael has given her a new sense of herself. She resolves to make the most of her sudden burst of motivation and reclaim the body – and hope – she'd believed were gone forever. Meanwhile, she's finding excuses to avoid any meeting with Michael, refusing to allow him to see her – or to surrender this fantasy to the reality of an affair – until she has lost enough weight to recover the body she'd been so proud of in her early twenties.

Can a woman ever be thin enough for adultery? And no matter how hard she diets will Eva's conscience still weigh her down…?

A sharp and wonderful witty debut for every woman who's ever been tempted to cheat…on her diet.

A SELECTION OF NOVELS
AVAILABLE FROM PIATKUS BOOKS

THE PRICES BELOW WERE CORRECT AT THE TIME OF GOING TO PRESS. HOWEVER PIATKUS BOOKS RESERVE THE RIGHT TO SHOW NEW RETAIL PRICES ON COVERS WHICH MAY DIFFER FROM THOSE PREVIOUSLY ADVERTISED IN THE TEXT OR ELSEWHERE.

0 7499 3763 7	A Dangerous Dress	Julia Holden	£6.99
0 7499 3788 2	Wedding Belles	Zoë Barnes	£6.99
0 7499 3728 9	Lord Perfect	Loretta Chase	£6.99
0 7499 3797 1	The Dream Hunter	Sherrilyn Kenyon	£6.99
0 7499 3733 5	Jewels of the Sun	Nora Roberts	£6.99
0 7499 3791 2	Second Sight	Amanda Quick	£6.99
0 7499 3771 8	Cover of Night	Linda Howard	£6.99

ALL PIATKUS TITLES ARE
AVAILABLE FROM:

PIATKUS BOOKS C/O BOOKPOST
PO Box 29, Douglas, Isle Of Man, IM99 1BQ
Telephone (+44) 01624 677237
Fax (+44) 01624 670923
Email; bookshop@enterprise.net
Free Postage and Packing in the United Kingdom.
Credit Cards accepted. All Cheques payable to Bookpost.
(Prices and availability subject to change without prior notice. Allow 14 days for delivery. When placing orders please state if you do not wish to receive any additional information.)

OR ORDER ONLINE FROM:

www.piatkus.co.uk
Free postage and packing in the UK (on orders of two books or more)